THE
LIGHT
OF THE
MIDNIGHT
STARS

BY RENA ROSSNER

The Sisters of the Winter Wood
The Light of the Midnight Stars

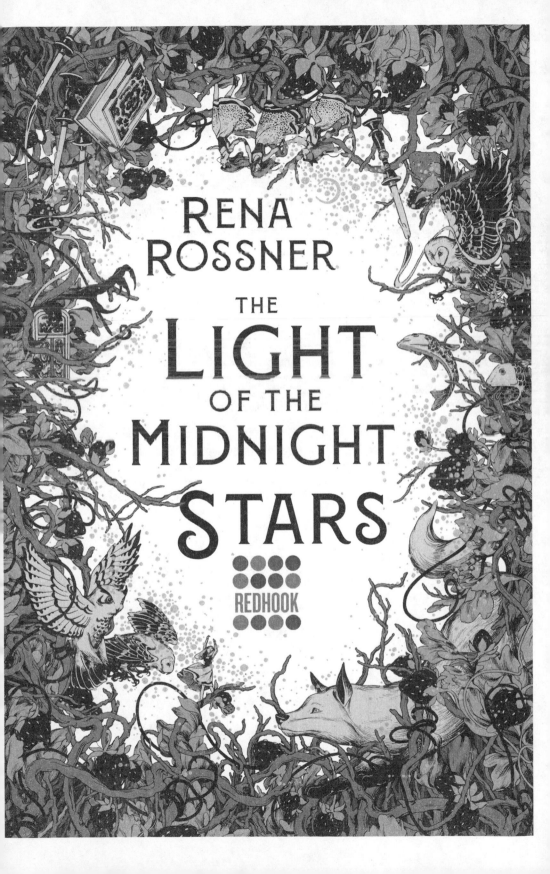

RENA ROSSNER

THE LIGHT OF THE MIDNIGHT STARS

REDHOOK

Redhook Books/Orbit
Hachette Book Group
1290 Avenue of the Americas
New York, NY 10104
hachettebookgroup.com

First Edition: April 2021
Simultaneously published in Great Britain by Orbit

Redhook is an imprint of Orbit, a division of Hachette Book Group.
The Redhook name and logo are trademarks of Hachette Book Group, Inc.

The publisher is not responsible for websites (or their content)
that are not owned by the publisher.

The Hachette Speakers Bureau provides a wide range of authors for speaking events. To find out more, go to www.hachettespeakersbureau.com or call (866) 376-6591.

Quote on p. ix excerpted from *Dancing at the Edge of the World*, copyright © 1989 by Ursula K. Le Guin, used by permission of Grove/Atlantic, Inc.

Library of Congress Control Number: 2020947784

ISBNs: 978-0-316-48346-9 (hardcover), 978-0-316-48363-6 (ebook)

Printed in the United States of America

LSC-C

Printing 1, 2021

For my father, Miles Bunder, who remembers the candles, and in memory of my grandmother, Nettie Bunder ז"ל, who lit them

A note

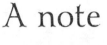

While this is a fantasy novel, it is set against the backdrop of real historical figures and events. Because the book is set in the mid- to late fourteenth century, I had to base any prayers and terms that were used on pre-existing texts—all of which, at that time, would have been in Hebrew. There is no way to know what accent my characters may have had and therefore if their pronunciation was close to Yiddish in intonation, or the modern Hebrew of today. What we do know is that this was a time period in Jewish history that was pre-Yiddish, which is why, though there is a "shtetl" feel to this book, there was no Yiddish language at the time. The epigraphs at the beginning of each section are from an invented *Book of the Solomonars*, but every word is based on contemporaneous Hebrew religious texts, among them, Rabbi Isaac Tyrnau's *Book of Customs*, written in the early fifteenth century. I did the best I could to accurately reflect the knowledge, texts and customs that the characters would have been aware of at the time. There is a glossary at the end of the book with definitions of all the foreign words used (most of them Hebrew). Note that the sound represented by "ch" in Hebrew is pronounced as a throaty "h," such as that found in "loch."

*"To find a world, maybe you have to have
lost one. Maybe you have to be lost."*

—Ursula K. Le Guin

*"Once upon a time what happened did
happen, and if it had not happened, you
would never have heard this story."*

—"Boys With Golden Stars",
The Violet Fairy Book

There was a time when everyone knew about Trnava. Once, it was a bustling market town that sat at the crossroads between the kingdom of Poland and the rest of Bohemia. Once, the king of Hungary, Charles the First, visited the town and conducted important negotiations there. But there are stories you don't know. Stories the residents of the town like to keep secret.

If you listen closely, sometimes you can still hear the old stories whispered. Legends about Trnava and the people who lived there, about the great forests that once surrounded the town. There are tales of red-haired mountain men and women who could work miracles, of a people who could trace their lineage all the way back to the great King Solomon himself. Tales of a people who kept to themselves, who lived in a tiny quarter of the city of Trnava where they built their own house of worship. They say that on the ceiling of their synagogue there were a thousand tiny stars.

There are stories told that the congregants who worshiped in the synagogue could work miracles; that the oldest among them could fly cloud dragons in the sky. It is said that when the Black Mist spread over the kingdom of Hungary, these people were the only ones who fought and didn't flee.

But the real story is much more complicated than that. It is the story of a people who forever lived at the edge of others' kindness and yet still found a way to thrive. It is the story of a family that survived, and of three girls who, when faced with unimaginable tragedy and impossible odds, did what they had to do even though it wasn't what was expected of them.

Some say they were just an ordinary family who lived in an extraordinary time.

But I know the truth.

This is the story of the Black Mist which swept through the Carpathian Mountains on the wings of a black dragon. Some say they can still feel it when they touch the trees, in the rich black sap that runs down to the roots to the rot that's buried under the ground. Despite the beauty of the trees and the crystal-clear waters of the lakes and the incessant babble of the rivers and streams, the mist still carries its echo. The animals feel it in their bones.

It could return at any moment.

Once, Trnava was a village like any other village. It was made up of brick houses, a town square, large wooden churches, a small synagogue, a fortified wall that surrounded the town, and a river, named the Trnávka for all the thorny bushes that lined its banks. Once, there were three different forests around the town of Trnava: the Šenkvický wood, the Kráľovský wood, and the ancient Satu Mare which once stretched all the way through the Kingdom of Hungary until it reached the Şinca Veche forest, right on the border of Wallachia. Strange things happened in these forests, things that nobody liked to talk about, but everyone did. There was a saying that was popular in the region once, and some still whisper it, even today. "Do not speak of the forest, for it will remember your name."

But that is another story, for a different day.

Sarah

It's just after sunset. I can still see the bare oak branches, black against the deepening blue of sky, that make up the forest beyond Trnava's wall. Eema takes a coin out from her pocket and clears her throat. "Girls, candle lighting," she says. I look away from the window and my heart skips a beat. *It's time.*

Eema kisses the coin and says the word "*esh*," and to me, it seems like the word crackles and hisses like flame. She puts the coin in the box that sits on the windowsill. Then she transfers fire from her lips to her fingertips, then to the wick of the candle that sits atop her silver candlesticks. "The soul of man is a lamp in the darkness," she says as I watch the flames she sets on the windowsill—a sign in our window for all those who are lost and weary, and I hear the echo of my father's voice in my head, the benediction he says over each of our heads on Friday nights—"Only light can hold back darkness. We are the children of Solomon, children of the light."

Every week, I stare in awe at how my mother does it. She weaves a prayer of words in the air and turns the strands she weaves into fire in the same way my father manipulates air. Eema lights a candle and suddenly everything is brighter. Abba raises his hands to the sky and the clouds lift and clear. "This is the law of Solomon," Eema chants. "Man and woman, *ish* and *isha*:

without the *yud* and the *heh*, they are *esh*—fire." She places a coin in my hand. "Here," she says. "Now it's your turn." The coin is warm—like her hand, like the fire.

It's my turn. I've waited a long time for this moment. I am twelve now, a *bat mitzvah*, a daughter of Solomon, blessed by his commandments. I am a part of it now. A part of everything. A wielder of the flame of Solomon—like my father and mother and grandmother and all those before me leading back all the way to the great King Solomon himself. I hold the coin in one hand and twist a dark red curl around one of the fingers of my other hand.

Eema opens a small prayer book and hands it to me. She doesn't need it—she knows the prayers by heart. I've been mouthing the words along with my mother and Nagmama and older sister Hannah as they said them together each week. This is the first step. The beginning of my journey into the world of my ancestors. There is so much I have yet to learn.

After today, I'll be able to start studying with Abba. I know that once the light of the *ner tamid* burns within me, I'll start to follow the ways and read all the books and practice all the exercises so that one day I'll be as powerful as my father. So that one day I'll be able to lead a community myself—not as a wildflower tamed back, but like a fireweed that lights up everything around her. I want to be someone—or something, that cannot be put out.

Fire-singe tingles at my fingers and mixes with the heady scent of chicken soup and *challah* bread. Everything feels right about this moment.

Eema points at the words and with a trembling hand I place my finger on the page. "*Esh tamid tukad al ha-mizbeyach, lo tichbeh*—an eternal fire shall be kept burning upon the altar; it shall not go out." I close my eyes and feel the heat within me. I imagine the lighting of a spark which will now grow each day. I write the stroke of each letter of the word—*esh*—in my mind, strokes of white fire in the darkness. I imagine the wilderness of

Sinai, like Eema taught me, the place where Abraham and Sarah met *Hashem* for the first time. I see the fire of the white letters they saw painted across a dark desert sky.

I kiss the coin and whisper the word *"esh,"* imagining the word composed of letters, the letters composed of strokes, the strokes twining around each other, the flame burning inside me, now shoved out of my chest by my breath, up through my throat and out past my lips into air. My lips are warm. The coin feels hot. Even though my eyes are closed, I see it happen. There is a crackling, like lightning running up and down my arms and legs and to the ends of each strand of my hair. I quickly open my eyes and place the coin in the *tzedakah* box on the windowsill.

"Power demands sacrifice and the holiest form of sacrifice is giving alms to the poor. What we take from the universe, we must give back." My mother's lessons buzz in my head like the hiss of flame. Her words twin with my father's words, *"children of the light,"* and I touch the candle-wick quickly. The spark transfers from my fingers. Lightning fast, the candle bursts into flame. I feel wild and a little bit dangerous. Pure power and potential. I want to see what else I can light. I know in that moment I could burn our house down in a flash.

But then I hear Eema's voice.

"Baruch," she prompts.

The prayer. I almost forgot. I close my eyes and concentrate on forming the strokes of the letters in my mind again. This isn't two letters that form a word—this is a whole blessing. *"Blessed are You, Lord, our God, King of the universe, who has sanctified us with His commandments and commanded us to light the Shabbat flame,"* I say, loud and clear and true. This time I weave the letters into words and place the words into a white void—the words reassemble themselves into burning white fire made up of three holy letters—שבת—Shabbat. An emptiness which is full of heavenly light. I usher it in. The fire dissipates and shrinks to the size of a spark. It's still burning inside me, but now it's just a spark and nothing more—a smoldering ember. I feel a different kind of energy now—something cool and soothing. Relief. *I did it!* My chest heaves and I smile, tears prickling in my eyes.

I look up. There are tears in my mother's eyes too. I've waited years for this moment, for her approval. There are so many things I've done wrong over the past years, so many mistakes I've made. Not listening to my parents, fighting them at every turn. *Sziporka*, they always call me, little spark. But this time, I did something right. My face glows. Gold and bright, like the light of a thousand flames.

"Amen," Eema says and leans down to kiss my forehead. Her hands smell like smoke and the nettle tea she prepared for Nagmama's joints right before we lit candles. I wonder if I will always remember this moment. If I will always associate lighting candles with the scent of nettle tea.

I am a bit like a nettle—stinging others in all the wrong places—but I know: something that can sting can also heal. Something that can burn and destroy can also light up the night and keep the darkness at bay. I am a spark of light now, no longer bursting with flame and words I can't contain. I close my eyes again to make sure that for once I did everything right.

There is only white space inside me.

I take a deep breath and open my eyes.

"Welcome, Sarahleh," Eema says. "You are a daughter of Solomon now. I'm so proud of you." She embraces me and I smell dough and lavender, nettle and flame, and everything is crisp and clean and bright.

"*Brucha haba'ah!*" Hannah says. "Welcome, sister!" She's waiting next to Eema. When she embraces me, I close my eyes to savor the feeling. Her thick auburn hair smells like grass, like fresh air and rosemary. Maybe now I can be more like her. Maybe

Eema and Abba and Nagmama will look at me the way they look at her—with pride and respect, not frustration and anger, doubt and regret.

"Nagmama!" Her arms are waiting to enfold me. But when she touches me I see only darkness, and smell something burnt and rotten, like smoke. My heart skips a beat. I quickly kiss her cheek and turn away. I don't want to ruin this moment. I have to keep the light shining bright.

I remember how jealous I felt when I watched Hannah enter into the covenant. I remember how I felt like my turn would never come. I look over at Levana to see if she feels the same now, but she is staring out the window, looking at the stars. One year from now seems like an eternity, but I know her turn will come sooner than we expect, and someday I will pass the light on to my daughters.

Levana turns her head and grins at me—her pale copper hair surrounds her head like a halo. I lift her in my arms and twirl her around. "*Shabbat shalom!*" I say, and she giggles. I put her down and Hannah picks her up. I watch and laugh as they spin themselves dizzy. Then Levana holds a hand out to me and we spin until we fall down, over and over again. It's easy to feel safe here, with a thick thatch of roof over our heads, a fire burning in the hearth, and holy candles lit on the windowsill for all to see. Easy to forget what I saw when I hugged Nagmama.

For the next spin, Hannah doesn't join us. I see her stand taller, holding herself differently. Now that I'm a *bat mitzvah*, she is a woman. We are both wielders of the flame of Solomon, but soon she will marry and join her fire with another's. It's a burden I'm happy not to have to bear yet, but Hannah wears it like a crown on her head.

There is a knock at the door. Abba bursts in, home from syn-agogue. He dusts the snow from his big red beard and stomps his boots on the mat by the door. Eema takes his coat and whispers into his ear and his big green eyes find mine. "*Mazal tov*, Sarahleh!"

I cross the room and leap into his strong arms. I see the pride in his eyes and his face lights up with a glow that comes from the same source as the flame inside me.

Later that night, I lie in bed and even though it's Shabbat I reach out to the fire that now burns freely within me. I play with it on the inside—not daring to light up the room I share with my sisters, and arguing in my head that I'm not really breaking Shabbat if I'm only playing with a fire I already lit. I stare out the window above Levana's bed and I wonder what she saw. If she felt the layer of wrongness like I did when I hugged Nagmama—something infected and rotten curling at the edges of everything bright.

I must fall asleep at some point because the next thing I know, I'm dreaming of darkness. There is a black mist winding its way through the trees, creeping along the earth. Everything it touches turns black as tar and then withers, shrinking in upon itself. The mist creeps its way from the edge of the forest, down the stone-strewn muddy streets of town, up the street that runs through the Jewish quarter of Trnava, and through the cracks in the wall of our house. It feels like the darkness is coming for me.

As it starts to drift its way through the window, I sit up in bed and conjure a flame. I'm awake now and fully conscious of the fact that it's Shabbat and I've set fire to my bed. I frantically try to put it out, but before I manage to smother it with a blanket, it rises up and takes the thin shape of a serpent, then slithers up from my bed and out the window. It chases the mist, which shrinks back into itself and goes away. I get up and look out the window—but there's nothing there. I rub my eyes and keep staring, looking for the light snake and wondering if it was only a dream.

Levana

While my sisters are in the kitchen with Eema and Nagmama, I connect the stars. It's a game I like to play. My eyes trace the shapes the stars make as they emerge.

Halfway through the meal, I pretend to fall asleep on the bench under the window. Now that everyone's cleared out of the room, I'm free to open my eyes and stare up at the sky.

Nothing gets in the way of the stars—not the Šenkvický wood, nor the long wall around Trnava—not even the four church spires in our town. The stars shine as brightly in the *Judengasse*—the Jewish quarter, as they do anywhere else in our town.

Even if I could light candles the way my sisters do, I prefer the fire that shines in the stars. Inside our home, Shabbat is a day of rest, but outside, the stars don't sleep. I feel them, shining bright like pinpricks on my skin. They want to be seen—like me. They want me to see them—I do. They have things to tell me.

I listen.

Today is an auspicious day. Sarah is *bat mitzvah*, and the skies are more restless than usual. She conjured flame and transferred it, but there are flames in the sky she doesn't see.

I trace them now again—the arcs they make. One star leads

to another, and another. Left, then right, and around in a curve that splits in three.

Three stars. Three sisters. Three paths light the sky.

The stars don't lie. They change with the seasons, but they tell the truth.

Eema sits down next to me. She runs her hand softly through my hair. "What do you see out there, little one?" she says.

I am not little, I want to say. "Just stars," I say instead.

"We are a nation of twinkling stars. Have you ever tried to count them?" Eema says.

I shake my head no.

"*Hashem* told Abraham to count the stars. He made him a promise that his children would number as many as the stars. Do you know the story?"

I shake my head.

"Come." Eema gets comfortable.

I curl up on the bench and place my head in her lap.

$$\star \quad {}^{\star} \quad {}^{\star} \quad {}^{\star} \quad {}^{\star} \quad {}^{\star}$$
$$\star \qquad {}_{\star} \qquad {}_{\star} \quad {}_{\star} \quad {}_{\star} \quad {}_{\star}$$

The night that Abraham was born, a star fell from the sky. "It's an omen," everyone said. "Look how it swallowed all the stars in its path—this child will devour nations."

Abraham's father, Terach, said it was nonsense, that stars fall every night. But one of his guests went to tell King Nimrod how a star rose in the east, darted across the heavens, and swallowed all the stars in its path.

"What does it mean?" Nimrod asked.

"It means this star will conquer time. It will destroy your empire. You must kill the child so the prophecy will not come true," his advisors told him.

Nimrod gave Terach three days to bring the child to him.

Terach told his wife, whose name was Amsalai, for she too was born of the heavens.

"I will not allow the king to kill our son," she said. "Take another child and offer it to the king in his place. He will not know the difference, and I will take our son into a cave and go into hiding until there is a new king who knows not of this prophecy."

So Terach took an ill child from the village and brought it to Nimrod, and the king killed the baby with his bare hands.

Amsalai took Abraham to a cave in a forest.

Terach visited his wife and son often, and when Abraham was ten years old, they let him out of the cave.

But Abraham had not been raised among the other children of the village, so he did not believe in their gods.

"It is clear to me," Abraham said, "that the only things worth worshiping are the bodies that bring light into our world—the sun, the moon, and the stars. But who put the light into the sky? Perhaps that is who we should worship."

Abraham asked his father this, and Terach told Abraham to ask the idols.

But when Abraham asked them, they had no answer, for they did not speak.

When Abraham asked his mother the same question, she told him everything he needed was already in his grasp—there was no need to look to the stars for answers.

But Abraham spent all his time looking at the sky, trying to read what was written on the face of the moon and the stars.

*   .   *   *   *   .
*   .   *   *   .   *   .
       *   *

"Like me," I say to Eema.

"Yes, just like you, my love," she says, and kisses the top of my head.

*   .   *   *   *   .
*   .   *   *   .   *   .
       *   *

But one day Abraham broke all the idols in his father's shop, she continues. *When he was blamed, Abraham said, "The largest idol devoured all the smaller ones."*

The news that he'd broken all the idols reached the king, and Abraham was summoned. The king demanded to know who broke the idols.

"I did," Abraham admitted. "Because they have no sense."

Nimrod said, "Then you should worship fire."

"Water can put out fire," Abraham said.

"Then you should worship water," the king replied.

"Water disappears into the clouds," Abraham said. "And wind can blow clouds away, but when the wind blows, the stars stay fixed in the sky."

The court magician realized what had happened.

"You are the star-child!" he said.

"Is it true?" King Nimrod asked. "If so, cast him into the fire."

And so they put Abraham into a fiery furnace.

But Abraham was not consumed.

King Nimrod was scared. He said he would bow down to Abraham, for clearly his god was stronger.

But Abraham said, "Do not bow down to me: worship the god who created the sun and the moon and the stars. For it is His glory that lights the heavens."

*   *   *   *   *   *
  *   *   *   *   *
            *   *   *

"You are my star-child," Eema says, kissing the top of my head again. "But never forget who it was that made the stars. Come, it's time for bed."

She reaches her hand out for mine. Reluctantly, I follow her. She tucks me into my small feather bed under the window in the room I share with my sisters.

I want to tell her what I see in the stars. All is not well. All will not be well. There are stars falling every night and I know something is coming, something is about to happen that will split the shining star that is our family.

I'm scared, but it doesn't stop me from looking at the stars. I keep hoping they will tell me more, that I will look at them and see something different. But I don't.

Eema starts to sing the *Sh'ma*—"*Hear O Israel, the Lord our God, the Lord is One,*" I repeat after her.

May the angel who redeems me from harm bless the children and call them by My name and by the names of My forefathers, Abraham and Isaac, and may they multiply like fish in the midst of the earth.

I think about Abraham and the stars as I drift off. I am not a *bat mitzvah* like Sarah is, not yet a woman like Hannah. I am only me, Levana, Reb Isaac's youngest daughter—still a child, or so they say, and so I stay silent. No one else sees what's coming. No one wants to hear the story I have to tell.

Hannah

7 Nisan 5119

I went outside as soon as Shabbat was over and counted three
stars in the sky. I said the right prayer—*Blessed is He who separates light from darkness*—even though I know Abba prefers
we say Havdallah with him, when he comes home from synagogue. But the garden had waited untended since sundown on
Friday, and it called to me like a dog might bark for attention
from its owner. It's Eema's garden, and it was Nagmama's
before that, but now it feels like it's mine in a way that was
never theirs.

I am connected to this land, to the earth. There is restless-
ness here—the soil shifts uneasily. It grows darker each day.
Lately, I can't drown out the sounds of the garden—the pops
plants make when they burst through soil, the sound of leaves
unfurling to light and freedom. I'm only able to silence the hum
when I'm outside—my toes curled in the soil and my hands
touching the red shoots of the dogwood and the green shoots
of horehound, when purple flowers curl around my fingers at
my command.

I hear Abba's sonorous voice in my head: "Lest you should

say in your heart—my power and the might of my hand did this wondrous thing." I know it is not me who controls what grows— it is God, the *Borei Olam*—father of all living things. My hands channel His will. That's what Abba would say. Still. Out in the garden, where every green thing responds to my touch, it is hard to think that it's all divine energy.

I need to start documenting what I see. Eema writes down the recipes for her poultices and remedies, she writes down the stories she tells. Abba writes down everything lately as well—and I've become his scribe. It's time for me to write down my own observations, but there is no room in a spellbook or a holy book for a young woman's thoughts.

These are the things I know:

Our house sits at the edge of town in the Jewish section of Trnava.

Four gates and thirty-six towers make up the brick wall that surrounds the city—the Malženická gate is not far from our house and it leads to a road that takes you to the Šenkvický forest and the mountains, and eventually all the way to the kingdom of Poland.

I was a baby when we came here, to Trnava, and I've never left our town.

Though it's large, and the brick wall and her guardians keep us safe, sometimes I want nothing more than to walk beyond the gate, to keep walking and never stop.

That's also a fact, but perhaps it doesn't belong in this list.

Still, lately I can't help but think—*There must be more to see out in the world than this village.* Maybe these things are happening elsewhere too. I don't know if it's my own mind speaking, or the whisper of a trail I should follow.

Abba has been traveling more often lately to consult with the other Solomonar families in neighboring towns, Reb David Ben Zakkai in Nitra, Reb Daniel Bezalel in Bratislava. My father himself was born and raised in Vienna—a place I only dream of seeing one day.

The last few times he traveled, I wondered if he'd come back with a name—a son of one of these illustrious families who he'd hand-picked to be my groom, someone steeped in the Solomonar tradition. But he never did, and he's never offered to take me with him. Perhaps my future is not the purpose of his visits. But that makes me want to know what is.

I know everything happens for a reason, every blade of grass has an angel that tells it to grow. But can't he take me with him just once?

I also know that as quickly as King Béla granted free market privileges to our town, which he calls Nagyszombat—named for the very market that gives us so much freedom—those rights could be taken away again. Maybe that's the reason Abba doesn't take me with him. It's not safe. Our town's charter and protection could be revoked in an instant, and we, the Jews, could be cast out and set to wander again.

"*The Jew is always a wandering star*," my mother always says, but her stories don't offer me comfort anymore. They make me nervous. Because as much as I'd like to travel, I don't want to be a wandering Jew.

Every green thing in my garden has taught me that laying down roots is the most important thing we can do—it is only when we have roots that we can grow.

It's only when I'm out here in the garden that I feel a modicum of control.

Out here, there are rules.

Out here, if anything winds beyond the confines of the garden, I tame it back. Nothing wanders unless I tell it to.

But lately, the wild strawberry vines follow me. They reach tendrils laden with plump red fruit in the direction of my bedroom window. This is also contributing to the wrongness I feel.

I could tame it back, but some things need to be allowed to grow free.

Back to my list:

Trnava is a big town—our market is one of the largest in the kingdom of Hungary, but the Jewish section of the town is small. *"Man cannot live on bread alone,"* Abba always says, but that doesn't stop Dina and her husband Samuel from having the most popular bakery stall in the market. They light the ovens on Fridays and keep them burning all through Shabbat, so they can employ non-Jews to sell their wares on Saturdays.

I wonder if Abba will suggest a match with one of their sons. Their family is large and strong, their sons study at the yeshiva. But most of their boys are too busy helping at the bakery to take their studies seriously. So perhaps not.

My mind spins in circles all the time. What type of man do I want to marry? What type of life do I want to lead? A choice in one direction or another will set the course for the rest of my life. Like the Trnávka river, I want to know beyond a shadow of a doubt which way my life will flow.

What if I married someone who has the power to choose which way a river flowed (like Abba)? What if together we could chart our own course?

But these thoughts feel too big for the small life I lead, and I've digressed from my list again.

Maybe it's better this way. Flowers don't get to choose when they bloom—they depend on so many factors—the sun, the water, the soil they root themselves in.

Melech and Chaim Ben Yanai grin at me in the market like they'd smile at anyone. Even a flower. How much of what I feel is in my imagination?

Now that Sarah is a *bat mitzvah*, my future feels like an untamed vine.

Despite the fact that we believe that everything has a

purpose and an order to it, as Jews we still dig our toes into the soil cautiously, silently, waiting and watching for the next storm to come and uproot us. A weed can be pulled out on a whim.

But all these thoughts are too heavy for a bright moonlit Saturday night, so perhaps I will stop here. Maybe if I read tomorrow what I wrote today, something will make sense.

It's always after Shabbat that I feel the heaviest.

I'll finish my list with some observations:

The anise flowers fanned their white bouquets at my touch tonight and seemed to glow more brightly, but their roots are tinged with gray. I gently pressed my fingers to the soil and watched the gray drift away.

The purple puffs of angelica felt like they leaned into me—but something is growing on the underside of their leaves. I stroked the leaves softly and the black spots disappeared.

The borage trembled. I reached my fingers to reassure their slightly fuzzy stalks and sent them warmth.

Sage leaves pressed their soft skin against my ankles.

Leaves of rue twined themselves around my fingers.

And strangest of all, the dill, lovage and hyssop were tangled. Everything vying for my attention.

It's not much to go on, I know. Perhaps these are all just the musings of a young girl. Perhaps it means nothing. But something's definitely wrong.

* * * * *

I heard something and got up to investigate. I stared out the window at the road that leads to the Dolna gate and eventually to Bohemia.

First, I saw a dot of movement on the horizon. I held my breath and made a wish. I continued to watch, and as the figure in the distance made its way in my direction I saw it was only Abba, walking home from synagogue.

I'll draw the black spots I saw on the rose stems and the angelica leaves. That way, if they're not back tomorrow, I'll have proof.

It is unlike any blight I've ever seen.

Blessed is Hashem who hasn't departed from his righteous and just ways and has placed me on the true path to present and correct and make order of the yearly customs of the Solomonars and list them here. To enable and make it easy for every man, in simple words, so that it might be accessible to all—even to those who are not scholars—I have therefore refrained from listing the most complicated and serious of customs. Similarly, I have expounded upon certain laws and customs when appropriate because in this generation there are fewer and fewer true scholars. Every day we hear of the loss of great men, true men of good deeds.

From Osterreich to Trnava, I have traveled and found many communities where there are not even two or three men or women who know our ways and customs, so I have had to rely on neighboring communities for assistance. I am but a young man, but I have learned from my father and teachers, men like Rabbi Moshe HaLevi, may his lamp shine, and Reb Abraham Klausner, may his memory be for a blessing. One moment he was guiding his community with light, and the next moment he was gone, and they knew not how to behave. So I must record what we must say on the night of Simchat Torah, what holidays may fall during the seven days of wedding celebrations, and what to read on weeks where there are double chapters of Torah verse to read. Customs are uprooting laws everywhere, even in some cases when dealing with law mandated from the Torah itself.

I begin in the month of Nisan, for it is in that month that the world was created. I have done all of this not for my own honor, only for mankind so that they might know our ways and I might be a lamp that shines for them—a holy guide. May God bless this endeavor and may we see an end to suffering speedily in our days. Amen.

—The Book of the Solomonars, preface

The night the Black Mist first came to the Satu Mare forest, no one saw the small flame that slipped outside a bedroom window and roared at it like a dragon, chasing it all the way back to the tree line, keeping the darkness at bay.

The next day, when the sun set on the town of Trnava and the stars came out, unusual things began to happen. The stars shone brighter in the portion of the sky above the town. They seemed to dance until they shone with unearthly light and then blinked out. Weeds grew stronger along the banks of the Trnávka river, winding their way out of the confines of gardens, restless and seeking, taking over small patches of forest. Here and there, little flames of fire burst in strange and random places, but then were quickly put out. Sweaters unraveled when no one was looking, and wool sometimes wove itself into garments at night. A fox appeared in the forest and did very un-foxlike things—and owls swooped and dove upwards at the moon instead of down towards the fields.

People always said that the weather in Trnávka was temperamental, not something that could be trusted. Every once in a while, especially around harvest time, when the Solomonars built huts and raised strange branches up at the sky, there was a cloud-shaped mass over the town that looked very much like a dragon. But that was the way of clouds, the residents assumed, and most were content to leave it at that.

A curiosity. Nothing more.

Months went by, then years. It took a long time for the first spots of black to begin to appear on the trees.

And by then, it was too late to stem the tide of what was coming.

Sarah

It happened slowly and then all at once. The darkness was determined to creep in and there was nothing we could do to stop it.

Now, no night goes by without my dreams tormenting me with darkness. I am defenseless against it. The serpent doesn't come to me again.

I'm outside watching Abba trying to push back the Black Mist out of our garden by spreading dew that turns into a white mist over the field. I watch him weave letters into words as he mouths, "*Bestow dew and rain as a blessing*," and I follow every motion he makes. I see little wisps of cloudlike smoke swirl out from my hands and join his. Neither of us notice until it's too late. I created smoke, which sparked, and before we know it, our garden and the field behind our house are on fire. I watch in horror as everything burns. And I can't shake the look I see in Abba's eyes when he turns around and sees me there.

"Go back inside the house where you belong! Look what you've done! You are not ready."

"I was trying to help!" I yell back. "Maybe if someone taught me, I could actually help."

"'Those that churn out nothing but sparks are driven by rage.

When fire blazes from anger, it devours the earth and all its produce,'" he quotes from *The Book of Devarim*. "Go study the passage and do not come back out here until you understand."

"But I wasn't angry!" I rage at him. "I was calm! I did everything you did!"

He turns his back to me and calls down rain to put out the fire.

I go inside, trying and failing to hold back the tears that mix with the rain that falls.

"What happened?" Eema says when I come in.

"Nothing." I shrug.

"She set the field on fire," Levana says from her perch at the window.

I lunge for her, arms outstretched. "You little tattletale!"

Hannah takes two large strides and stands between us, her green eyes like hard gems. "Don't you touch her. She's not to blame for your mistakes."

"It wasn't a mistake," I say, looking around her to see if I can still get a grip on Levana.

Eema wraps her arms around me from behind. She intends it as an embrace, but instead I feel trapped—caged by her arms. "Enough of this. Come, let's sit and you can tell me what happened."

"Nothing happened," I grumble.

"That's what you always say," Hannah replies. "I hope it didn't get anywhere near my plants."

"I didn't touch your precious garden," I spit out at her, even though I did. I destroyed it.

"Shhhhhh . . . " Eema glares at both of us, while Levana sits by the window watching everything, a smile playing at her lips.

I'm so angry it feels as if smoke will come out of my ears.

"Hannah, Levana, go outside and see if your father needs help."

Hannah puts on a shawl and opens the door, and a second later I hear her scream. Levana gets up from her window perch and scowls at me as she follows Hannah out the door. Before it closes, she pokes her head back in and sticks her tongue out at me.

I try to lunge for her again, but Eema's strong arms hold me back.

"Tell me what happened." Her voice is gentle but firm.

I shrug my shoulders again.

"Sarahleh . . ."

"What? Why can't he teach me? Why can't I help?"

She raises her brows as if to say, *You're really asking that question now when you just set a field of wheat on fire?*

"I know I can do it. But when I follow everything he does, it turns to fire and ash in my hands. He says I need more discipline, more control. But how can I learn any of that if he doesn't give me a chance to practice?"

"It takes years to learn to do these things. One does not pick up an instrument and play it immediately. There are steps, chords, finger work, breaths that must be taken. Skills that must be developed."

I scowl. "I can still conjure fire faster than any of his *talmidim*."

"That may be the case, but that doesn't mean you can control it. Control is more than half the battle."

"But King Solomon himself says in wisdom there is anger! Fire and anger are important. Fire can heal, fire keeps us warm, fire cooks the food we eat."

The door opens and Abba walks in. "And fire can bring death and destruction."

"I'm sorry," I say, trying to look contrite. But I'm not. Not really. "I didn't mean to burn all of the grain."

"There will be no more going out of this house until you can fill a cup with water." His face gleams with sweat and his clothes smell like ash. "From the air," he adds.

I'm ashamed, but I can't help the fact that when I follow all of his instructions, I only conjure smoke. Maybe that's all I can do.

He walks over to the kitchen and comes back with a tin cup. "Close your eyes and concentrate. Pull water from the air. When this cup is full, then we can discuss you leaving this house again."

I don't say a word for the rest of the night. I refuse to meet my sisters' eyes, refuse to eat. I leave dinner early and climb into bed and stare at the ceiling. Abba doesn't make Levana do tricks. He doesn't forbid Hannah from leaving the house. I refuse to fill the cup with anything but anger. All he wants is to control me, and I won't play his games.

When my sisters fall asleep, I sit up in bed. My parents are speaking in the other room. I get up and tiptoe to the door.

" . . . she's just so stubborn."

"Where do you think she gets it from?"

"She's more powerful than any of my students, but everything she does uses raw power. She must learn control or I don't know what will be. Each time she does something like this, she risks exposing the entire community."

"I know the two of you lock horns, but you must find a way to put aside your anger and help her channel hers."

My father grunts. "She is unteachable."

Tears fill my eyes. I turn back to my bed and pull the covers up over my head. I cry until there are no tears left and there is only darkness.

★ ⋆ ⋆ ★ ★ ⋆
⋆ ⋆ ⋆ ★ ⋆
⋆ ★

The cup remains empty. Abba checks it every morning. Eema makes me sit beside her every night by the hearth and weave instead. Hannah and Levana both have looms, but she doesn't make them sit and work at theirs. Levana always has her nose buried in a book of prayer—her lips move like fish lips opening and closing, over and over again. I can't stand how smug she looks. I think she only pretends to pray so she doesn't have to do chores. Often, I catch her staring up at the sky. And Hannah can be wherever she wants to be—inside, outside, in the kitchen, or the garden, or out in father's lean-to study with him, writing down his thoughts in her perfect flowing script. Nobody makes her fill cups of water unless it's to water the garden. It's not fair.

Ecma says I'm talented, that the strands of wool in my hands look like they weave themselves. I think, if that's the case then I shouldn't have to sit here at all. It's not like she's teaching me anything. If my hands want to weave, I say, let them weave, but leave me out of it. My fingers yearn to feel the heat of fire again, but not the kind that burns in the hearth—they want to channel the fire that burns inside me. The fire I know has the power to make a difference.

* * * * * * * * * * *

One night, Abba sits down next to me after dinner. He stares at the fire, then at the loom in my hands, then back at the fire. "The *avodah* of the heart is fire," he says. "It is not your task to learn how to light fires now, but how to put them out. You must channel the burning you feel inside you into prayer—not rage." He hands me a small book of prayers. His *siddur*. I stare at it in my lap.

I still think he's wrong. In dark times, you need all the light you can get.

When I don't respond, he continues. "When Betzalel designed the *mishkan*, he used the same holy letters—the same holy fire you contain once created the world. But *Hashem* filled Betzalel with the wisdom to know when and how to use his abilities, something you still need to learn, my Sarahleh. You must weave curtains for your house before you can weave anything for the holy sanctuary."

"That's ridiculous," I finally say, breaking my week-long silence. "There is no *mishkan* anymore. No curtains I make will ever adorn the front of the holy ark or the entrance to the holy of holies."

I stare into the flames of the fire in the hearth and my fingers move on their own—up down, up down, up down and through. It's boring and repetitive and easy.

"Only you can make that choice," he says. "We choose what it is we call holy."

I place the prayer book under my pillow that night, but I don't open it.

I decide I will practice what I want to learn at night when no one is awake. I light a tiny fire—hot white letters of flame suspended in the air above my bed like a flare that says *here, I am here, see me burning*, and then I put it out. I do it again. Then again. I try to move the flame elsewhere, out the window—and back. To the forest—and back. All the way to the center of the town square where it dances, free like I wish I could be.

I practice weaving too—but not at the loom. First, I unravel the blankets on my bed and weave the threads into a nicer pattern. Then I try with one of my sweaters. Then I work on the living room rug. Once I've woven and rewoven everything in the house, I close my eyes and travel elsewhere. To the neighbors' house. To the smith's cottage where he and his wife sleep soundly under a blanket full of holes. I repair the holes. See? I can do good too.

In the morning, I'm tired and Eema doesn't understand why. Some things I have to keep secret. One day I will surprise them all. But not yet. And not by filling a cup with water.

I'm getting stronger and soon I'll set out and fight the Black Mist myself.

Eema calls my name and I snap out of my thoughts. "Sarah, pay attention to what you're doing."

I look down at my loom and see a faint wisp of smoke. "Sorry, Eema." I take a deep breath and stretch my arms over my head. Then I stare at the hearth wistfully.

"You must resist." Abba stands behind my chair. His voice takes me by surprise and I startle and stare up at him, though I don't mean to. I'm still angry at him, but now that his eyes lock with mine, I can't look away. I see the two tiny flames—blue with a little bit of orange, dancing in his eyes. "Your soul is a candle of God," he says. "Just as the smallest of flames reaches for a larger flame, so too you must yearn for unity with God. In unity there is strength. The prayer of one man is amplified by joining his voice with the voices of others. You want to break away from the wick that binds you, such is the nature of fire, but you must resist. The burning bush was not consumed. Do not allow yourself to be consumed." He bends down, kisses my forehead, then walks away.

I don't want to resist. But I hear his voice in my head, over and over again.

Resist. Resist. Resist.

I sit sullenly, weaving strands into fabric. Sweat breaks out on my forehead. I feel stifled. It's hard to breathe. I look down at the loom. The light wisp of smoke is there again—a hint of sulfur in the air. I'm nearly done with the section I was working on, and the loom itself is hot. I take a deep breath and close my eyes. I untangle the white letters that have woven themselves into a flame inside my head. I weave them instead into a curtain, like the one I hold in my hands, and neatly fold it and put it away. I am getting better and better at what I can do.

A little bit of time goes by and Eema takes up her loom and sits next to me.

Levana is lazily twirling one of her curls and pretending to embroider stars onto a pillow. Hannah is shucking peas for tomorrow's supper from the part of the garden I didn't destroy.

"Did I ever tell you the story of how four Jewish princes served in King Nebuchadnezzar's court in Babylon?" Eema says.

"Tell us the story, Eema, please!" Levana perks up. I keep concentrating on the motions of my hands. *Resist. Resist. Resist.*

Eema looks in my direction like she's waiting for me
to respond.

I'm not really in the mood to hear a story, but I nod.

Hannah keeps shucking peas. Nobody asks her. Lately she acts
like she's an old woman. Like she's above stories. I want to snap
at her, point out that she didn't answer, that maybe she's the one
who should tell the story, but I don't. *Resist. Resist. Resist.*

"Oh good," Eema says. "Then I'll tell you their story.

*Daniel, Chananya, Mishael and Azarya were royalty themselves—
Jewish royalty! Imagine that! Daniel was only fifteen years old when
he was taken captive from his home in Jerusalem and brought to
Nebuchadnezzar's palace—*your age, Sarahleh.

*Soon they became the king's most trusted advisors. But one day
Nebuchadnezzar decided that all of his subjects should worship his god.
He set up a golden statue made from the gold he'd plundered from the
Jews in Jerusalem in a place called the Vale of Duro—the same valley
where he'd slaughtered the Jews that he'd brought from Jerusalem to
Babylon. He also set up an enormous furnace.*

*The king sent Daniel to Alexandria so he wouldn't bear witness to
what he was about to do, but Chananya, Mishael and Azarya were
there. The king announced that anyone who did not bow down to his
golden idol would be burned alive in the furnace. He gave a signal,
music started up, and everyone but Chananya, Mishael and Azarya,
bowed down.*

"How dare you disobey my orders!" the king said.

"We only have one God," they answered. "He will protect us."

"Burn them alive!" Nebuchadnezzar said.

*The three boys were thrown into the furnace, but Guvriel, the angel,
came down from heaven to protect them. They were not consumed.*

Nebuchadnezzar told Chananya, Mishael and Azarya to come out of the fire. Then he chastised all the other Jews: "This is the strength of your God, and yet you bowed down to my idol?"

Chananya, Mishael and Azarya said, "In Egypt, when Hashem commanded the frogs to plague the land, they never hesitated: they jumped into the ovens of the Egyptians. If the frogs did so for no reward from heaven, how could we not be willing to do the same when we know that there is a reward for those who die to sanctify God's name?"

After that, the Jews of Babylon were moved to keep the tenets of their faith, even in exile, and God took mercy on them and returned them to the Land of Israel where they rebuilt the Holy Temple.

"It was their faith that kept them from being consumed," Eema says.

Levana sighs wistfully. "I love your stories, Eema. I could see everything, as if it were painted across the sky."

"Did you like the story, Sarah *Sziporka?*"

Hannah snorts and I shoot her a glare.

"I don't understand," I say. "If they couldn't be consumed, why didn't *Bnei Yisrael* worship them instead? They emerged from fire unscathed. Clearly, they were powerful. More powerful than anyone else in their generation."

"Because they had the wisdom to know that their power came from the Holy One, Blessed Be He," Eema says.

And now I see where she's going with this.

"In the *selichot* prayers we say, '*May the God who answered Chananya, Mishael and Azarya in the furnace, also answer us!*'" she continues. "Maybe one day there will be a prayer that says, '*May the God who helped Sarah* Sziporka *Solomonar also answer us.*'" She winks at me.

I fight the urge to scowl. *Resist. Resist. Resist.* My body is a candle. My hair like a flaming wick. But I am not a flame, I am a daughter of Solomon. I understand what my mother is trying to tell me. Like Chananya, Mishael and Azarya, I will not be consumed if I have faith in a higher power.

I only wish I knew what He has planned for me, because it's clear that if I stay in this house, by this fire, weaving silently at my mother's side I will burst into a blazing inferno.

Levana

I go to synagogue with Abba at the end of Shabbat. There's a twinkle in his eye, and I take his hand as we walk.

Lately, it always feels stifling inside, with Sarah moaning about how she has to stay indoors, and Hannah pouting about how she can't go out to her garden because it's Shabbat, and Eema and Nagmama looking at me with worry in their eyes every time I stare at the sky. But sometimes outside is no better. The air is thick tonight. Cold and menacing. The sky was dark long before the sun actually set.

In synagogue, I watch the men light the Havdallah candle as soon as there are three stars in the sky. I see Abba transfer flame through the curtain of the women's section. The men sing the prayer that separates light from darkness, the holy from the mundane, the Jewish people from the rest of the nations, and I hum along, mouthing the words under my breath.

Soon they file out of the synagogue and stare up at the moon in the sky, prayer books in hand. I follow them.

Eema and Nagmama don't go to the *beit knesset* except when they have to—on holidays like Rosh Hashana and Yom Kippur. But Abba knows I have a special connection to the stars—to everything that lights up the sky. He says there is much he needs to teach me and I wonder if this is the week we begin.

I walk over and stand beside him as he leads the men in prayer.

"To bless the moon at the proper time is like greeting the *Shechina* ... " Abba's baritone voice intones, sing-song in its timbre. "Like running outside to greet a king! The king of all kings." He closes his eyes and raises his hands to the sky. "But on *kiddush levana* nights, the moon comes out to greet us."

The men are all still filing out of synagogue, waiting for the dark clouds to pass so the moon can be at its brightest.

He turns to me—me! In front of all his congregants.

"You are the brightest moon in our sky, Levana," he says to me. "You were born on a night like this one. I heard your cry right after I'd finished reciting *kiddush levana*. It was like you picked the name yourself." His eyes glint with moonlight as he turns back to the men.

"Every month, as we near the seventh day, when the moon is brightest, that's when we bless it. Joseph the dreamer saw his brothers bowing down to him in the heavens. He dreamed of a ladder of angels, but even Joseph jumped to conclusions about what he saw, and that got him into trouble."

Abba winks at me.

"But our *mitzvot* are not in the skies. Our work is down here, on earth. We bathe in the light of the moon to let its intentions enter our actions."

I hear a chorus of amens answering him.

"Tonight, we sanctify the moon—tomorrow, we begin the real work." We look up. It's still dark. The moon is covered by cloud. Abba claps his hands and it sounds like a clap of thunder. The black clouds clear.

I hold the white orb of the moon in my eyes—a lamp lighting up the heavens.

The men begin singing: "*Halleluyah, praise God from the skies, praise Him in the heavens . . .*"

The sun, the moon, and the stars all join to praise God. "*Blessed be our God, ruler of space and time, who created galaxies . . .*" My heart beats in time with the words Abba says.

"*And God said to the moon—the Levana—*" He looks at me. "*—renew yourself!*" The stars and the moon are reflected in his eyes and in all that majesty, I see myself.

Soon the men around him are jumping and singing, dancing and clapping, looking up at the moon and saying, "*David, king of Israel, lives and endures!*"

David—the father of Solomon.

"All who bless the new moon in its time, it's as if they received the presence of the *Shechina*—the divine light," Abba says and the men repeat it after him.

I repeat it after him too, and I feel it—the presence of the *Shechina* is bright within me like the light of the moon and the stars.

Everyone is still looking up at the moon. My father's sonorous voice is singing beside me, and for the first time I am a part of something larger than myself—larger perhaps than the sky.

I think about Eema's story and wonder if I am destined for something greater than myself too—like Abraham. I close my eyes and let the light of the moon wash over me.

When I open my eyes, there is one star I see. It shines a little brighter, and then blinks out as the dark clouds return.

Hannah

1 Cheshvan 5120

Tonight was truly one of the strangest (and most exciting!) nights of my life. I'm not writing this from my room or even from our home—but I'm getting ahead of myself and I must put things down here as they happened.

Two candles were lit at the window as I sat next to Abba earlier, a quill and parchment before me. We were sitting in his study, a room only large enough for a desk and two chairs.

"Write this down," he said.

"I am, Abba," I replied. It frustrates me when he doesn't trust me, when he doesn't think I know exactly what to do. I'm not irresponsible like Sarah, or easily distracted like Levana. The thought of either of them in here, helping Abba the way I do, is laughable.

"This is composed by the keeper of *The Book of the Solomonars*." He turned to me and said, "There can be ten Solomonars active and alive at the same time. Just like it is said that there are only thirty-six righteous men in the world at one time. Together, we hold up the pillars of the earth. If at any moment there are less than ten Solomonars, or less than thirty-six *tzaddikim*—the very foundation upon which the world rests will collapse."

"Should I write that down too, Abba?" I asked him. It felt important in a way that other things he's taught me didn't—like these words carried more weight than other things he'd said.

"No, no." He twisted a strand of his red bushy beard between his fingertips, and stared at the door to the room as though he could see something on the other side of it. So now I add that to my ever-running list of *strange things that keep happening*.

"The secrets of Solomon are entrusted to a Solomonar and to his family—his direct descendants. The candles we light at the window are a sign—a symbol that we are a sanctuary of Solomon—a home where Jews the world over are welcome. We publicize the miracle of God's light all year long, like all Jews do on Hanukkah. And now, our light is more important than ever. We are beacons of light in the darkness, Hannah—never forget that."

"Yes, Abba." I wondered what this light meant in the face of the Black Mist, if he felt it like I do—the strange sense of foreboding in the air, the dark taint in the soil that keeps getting worse.

"Let's get back to the book," he said.

I've decided to write down all his words here as I remember them. Who knows if I may have need of them again someday?

"With Rabbi Gottlieb murdered in his bed so recently—may his memory protect us—we must preserve our precious customs. I will not cower in the forest or hide in a cave. The fire of Solomon runs in our veins. I must write down the customs of our people in a book—*The Book of the Solomonars*—into a bound volume for all future generations."

"Yes, Abba," I said again, and committed his words to memory. He paused and looked at me.

"Do you remember the story of Honi HaMeagel?"

I shook my head no, because even though I did remember the story, it's rare that Abba tells it. I also know when he gets into this kind of mood, he's going to tell the story whether I like it or not. I settled in to listen carefully.

It was a time of drought for the Jewish people in the Land of Israel, so Honi drew a circle in the dust and stood inside it. He dug his toes into the ground and told God he wouldn't move from the circle until He sent rain.

When it began to rain, Honi told God it wasn't enough—he wanted rain that would fill wells and pools and caves. It began to pour so hard that each drop of rain filled a barrel. Honi told God it was too much, that the rain He was sending would destroy the world, the earth needed something in between—a rain of blessing. But it rained for so long that everyone had to evacuate the holy temple because of flooding and Honi was asked to make the rain stop completely.

Honi said one should never pray for the removal of a blessing, but nevertheless he asked God. He said, "Our nation cannot survive with too much suffering or too much blessing. May it be your will that you should ease their suffering now and stop the rain." He nearly got put into cherem *by Shimon Ben Shetach for the way in which he spoke to God. But it worked. God listened. And after that he was always known as Honi the circle-drawer . . .*

Abba continued staring at the door. A few minutes went by. Then he turned his attention back to me. "With your steady hand, I need you to write. That's the first step towards acquiring wisdom—writing, then learning, and only then, turning words into action." His words made me question why he doesn't make Sarah write things down, why he doesn't force Levana.

"We all strive to leave a memory of our presence in this world," he continued. "What we remember of the world and what the world remembers of us is often the same. But I don't worry about you, my eldest. In *Pirkei Avot*, it says there are four types of students in this world: the sponge, the funnel, the strainer and the sieve. You are like a sponge, my daughter: you absorb everything." I wondered what my sisters were—which one the funnel, which one the sieve?

As the candles by the window burned low, there was a knock at the door.

I lifted my head from the page. All night it seemed as though Abba had been expecting company. I could hear the wind rustling through the trees and it sounded like the forest was breathing. I also heard branches crack and the sounds of small animals creeping through the underbrush. The knock was loud and bold against the soft drama of the forest that I knew, even now, was shrouded in Black Mist.

Abba nudged his nose in the direction of the door and I got up to open it. There was a young man there, dressed in heavy furs that clearly marked him as part of some kind of nobility. His eyes were a piercing blue—the color of frost.

"Your grace." Abba stood up immediately. "How may we be of service?"

The Black Mist crept in and he closed the door quickly. I saw how the light in the window repelled whatever had entered, and felt safe by Abba's side. Protected.

I bowed my head in a show of respect, then looked back at my father. "Should I go?"

The young man put his hand on my shoulder.

I startled and looked up into his ice-blue eyes. I'd truly never seen eyes so striking before.

"And your name is?" he asked me.

"Hannah," I whispered, still feeling the weight and warmth of his hand through my dress and shawl.

"Stay," he said. "I'll only be a minute."

I couldn't help but think he was the handsomest man I'd ever seen.

But then he became short of breath and started to cough. I looked over at Abba with worry in my eyes.

"Forgive me," he said. "I'm not ill, I swear it." He glanced at Abba, then back at me, as though he was hoping we'd believe him.

More and more people in town are falling sick. They say the Black Mist is a plague. We hear stories from other cities, other towns. It starts in the sky—a dark cloud cover, which then drifts into the forest, leaches into the soil, and from there, it slowly creeps up the walls of houses and in through chimneys.

Abba says it's a spiritual sickness. That the lungs inside us are like angel wings—connected to the heavens, and if every breath we take and every word we speak is connected to holiness, our lungs stay white and blemish-free. It's why we check the lungs of animals before we eat them. Diseased lungs can be a sign of a diseased soul.

Abba gestured for him to sit.

"Can I get you something hot to drink?" I offered, thinking I could brew him something for his cough.

"My daughter brews the best healing teas in town," Abba said with pride, and I smiled. His praise means so much to me.

"Some horehound perhaps, for your cough?" I said.

"No, thank you," he said. "I am Jakob, son of the dowager duchess, as I'm sure you know." He cleared his throat and coughed again. "And heir apparent to the throne," he said more softly, with a rasp. "What I have to say will only take a moment."

"It's no trouble," Abba said. "We insist."

"I'll be right back." I bowed, and left the room to tell Eema, though I couldn't help but pause to listen at the door.

"I'm here to ask for assistance. I know I can count on your discretion. My mother is ill. It is the croup—not the plague." He coughed again. "She cannot be rid of it; the cough wracks her body day and night. She is older now, and frail. We need a healer. My mother told me I was delivered by a Jewess who was skilled in the healing arts."

"Yes," Abba said. "I believe that was my wife."

"I've come to ask for your help—a charm, a prayer, a poultice, anything you think might ease her suffering. I was not aware you had a daughter . . . "

"Three daughters," Abba says.

I raced into the house. When I told Eema, her eyes went wide. Thank God she had water already heated on the stove. I didn't have time to speak to her, but I could tell she was worried, scared even, because as I took a tray back with me, laden with mugs and a teapot filled with herbs, rushing through the Black Mist as fast as I could, I saw her take out her prayer book and start to pray. My mother reads her prayer book as others might read fortunes. I wish I knew what she saw in its pages in that moment.

Jakob looked at me as I entered and his eyes lit up.

"I brought tea," I said.

"I don't suppose your daughter is as skilled in the healing arts as your wife?" he said to Abba.

"I am," I answered without thinking as I set the tray down and poured tea. I looked up as I handed Abba a mug, and he scowled at me.

"My apologies," I said, chastened. "I spoke out of turn."

"No, you spoke well. Clearly God has sent you to me, an angel for my mother in her time of distress. Rabbi Isaac, we will pay you handsomely. Will you help us?"

But Abba was shaking his head. He was most certainly going to say no.

In that moment, I didn't care. Something was twisting and turning inside me, an ache I'd never felt before. It urged me forward. I knew then, with certainty I'd never felt before, this was a path I needed to follow—a task I needed to see through.

Abba and Eema have always taught me that we never turn away someone in need.

"Some things cannot be healed . . . " Abba said, and I knew he was thinking of the Black Mist. "I will need to consult my wife—"

Jakob interrupted him. "Please, rabbi, there isn't time."

I could tell Abba saw something else in his eyes, because I saw it too—fear.

It's against the code of everything Abba is as a Solomonar to deny life, to deny healing in situations where there might be hope, this much I know—a truth at the root of my bones. As a community leader, he had no choice. Rabbi Gottlieb was found stabbed to death in his bed just one month ago with a note beside him blaming the Black Mist on the Jews. God forbid something like that should happen again—that something like that should happen here.

The potential for retaliation against us is too great.

"Hannah, go get your mother, she can—" I could tell he regretted his words the moment he saw Jakob's face fall.

He closed his eyes, then opened them and looked at me. I'm only fifteen, but I'm ready in every way and right to take on my birthright. I've been transferring flame since my *bat mitzvah*, and my ability to heal and make things grow has far surpassed Eema's abilities. I've never been given a chance to do something this important.

"Go see if your mother can pack you a bag of everything you'll need."

My heart leapt in my chest. "Yes, Abba!"

I rushed out of the small room again, afraid he'd change his mind. But then I stopped again and paused outside the door. I knew my life was about to change forever. Despite the mist, I didn't want to miss a word.

"Is Hannah of marriageable age?"

I gasped, hand over my mouth. Of all the boys and men in town I kept waiting for and thinking of—this, I never expected.

"My daughter is not for you," Abba said. It sounded like a growl.

"She's promised to another?" Jakob asked.

Abba grunted, and I couldn't hear anything else.

Then I heard Jakob say, "You haven't answered me."

"She will marry a Jew, an outstanding scholar," Abba replied.

"I see," Jakob said. "Someone you've already chosen for her?"

My heart thumped in my chest so loud I was certain they could hear me.

"No," Abba said. "You see nothing. Our ways are not your ways. I am entrusting my most precious possession into your care—please see that I do not regret it."

"No harm will come to your daughter. I swear it."

"Good," Abba replied. "I'm glad we have an understanding."

I quickly ran inside to tell Eema what happened, but I didn't tell her everything I overheard. She helped me fill her healing satchel with some things—remedies both physical and spiritual—then she pressed a kiss to my forehead and gave it to me.

"Remember that sometimes the shortest prayer can be the most effective. Focus on what is right, and don't be distracted by finery. Remember it could be a demon, or the evil eye, and if that's what it is—there's not much you can do. Remember to tie knots in the madder root in the right order, rub oil and salt on her hands and feet, and I've placed several preservation stones in there." She paused. Then she said, "And remember the story of Jacob."

I furrowed my brow. I didn't remember telling her his name.

"Jacob struggled with the angel and won," she said.

I nodded, my eyes held steady in her gaze.

"The stories say it was Esau's angel he wrestled with. Beware of false angels—don't wrestle with ones we don't know. Remember the words of Jeremiah—God has created something new on this earth, *nekevah tesovev gever*—and woman will encircle man." She pulled me into a fierce embrace.

Her words were so cryptic, I still don't understand them now. She didn't have time to tell me more, and I didn't have time to listen. Perhaps their meaning will become clear to me in time.

"I promise I won't disappoint you," I said. I went back out to the small study, excited and out of breath. "I'm ready."

Jakob grinned, his eyes impossibly bright. "My horse awaits."

Abba followed us outside. He hugged me goodbye as he whispered in my ear, "Protect your soul, my daughter."

I replied in one of the phrases of the Solomonars, something that's painted on the wall of our synagogue. I'd never had cause to use the words before. "When the bows of mighty men are broken, those that stumble are girded with strength."

Abba nodded, and I saw there were tears in his eyes. These were the words our ancestors would say when they went off to war. It felt fitting because I'm going off to battle an unknown illness, without knowing if I will succeed. But it was more than that: their customs are not our customs, their faith not our faith. I've never even been inside the home of a non-Jew—and now, I sit and write these words inside a royal residence! I will describe everything soon in great detail, but for now, I must finish recording what happened earlier.

"Don't worry, Abba. I won't let you down." I pecked a kiss on his cheek and turned to Jakob. He lifted me up onto his horse and swung himself up behind me. He grabbed the reins and tugged on them, giving the horse a quick kick, and we set off at a gallop.

I tried to turn my head and look back at the house. I saw the candles lit, burning in the window. Two beacons of light in the darkness.

I will return, I promised the house and my family in it. Then I turned to face the road ahead.

I'm about to sleep in the largest and most comfortable bed I've ever seen. May the God of Solomon protect us all.

Our great sages compiled a prayer to be said in urgent times—a blessing, and this is it:

"May it be your will, Lord our God, to help us understand your ways and circumcise our hearts so that we may fear you. Forgive our sins that we might be redeemed, and distance us from pain and suffering. Satisfy us with your abundance and gather all our scattered brethren from the four corners of the earth to bring us together in our own land. May those who err be judged, may you punish the evil with your wrath, and may the righteous rejoice in the rebuilding of your sacred city and the redemption of your holy sanctuary and the restoration of the house of Solomon and may the light of his son, our messiah, blaze bright. May you answer us before we call upon you, and may you listen to us before we speak, for you are the one who answers us at every moment of despair and distress. Blessed are you, Lord our God, who hears our prayers. Amen."

–The Book of the Solomonars,
page 2, introduction

Most of the town's inhabitants were blissfully unaware of the strange things that were happening. At first, it was only those who tilled the forest for lumber who saw the spots on the trees. Then the farmers began to notice that a thin black mist had settled on their crops like dew early in the morning—but it would be gone by midday and so would their thoughts about it. But the mist clung to their shoes. Some loggers found it on their clothes. And when families began to notice black rot at the corners of their homes and spots that appeared on their walls, then in their lungs, they began to wonder: if the red-haired Solomonars that lived among them could control the weather, then perhaps they were the ones causing the blackness to spread? Perhaps, they thought, there was only one way to cure the trees without uprooting them—they had to uproot the source of the disease.

It started as a whisper, but it soon turned into a thought borne on wind that began to infect the air.

A feeling just under the surface, as though the skin the town wore had begun to itch.

The Black Mist swept into the townspeople's homes through their chimneys. It spoke nasty thoughts in their ears.

Reb Isaac's family was about to be cast off the path they once thought they knew. And by the time they understood what was happening, it was too late.

The Black Dragon had reared its ugly head:

Find them, it said, *for their laws and not our laws, their rules not our rules. They do not obey the laws of the king.*

Find them and uproot them.

Sarah

Everyone is asleep except me, which is why I hear it—the heavy tread of Abba's boots as he leaves the house. I've never been brave enough to follow him, but I'm tired of sitting around and waiting for something to happen. Tired of waiting for his approval. What is the use of doing things the way they've always been done if the Black Mist keeps creeping in and no one can do anything to stop it?

Every day, we hear mourning bells ringing from atop the four churches in town. The Christians believe the sound will drive out the demons and send the Black Mist away, but the bells do nothing—they only increase the sense of foreboding in the air.

I wait and watch to make sure no one stirs, then get up out of bed, tug a coat on over my nightgown, shove my feet into my boots and creep out of the house to follow him. I'm done waiting for the right time to come.

I let the door close behind me and look down the road in both directions. I can barely make out his shape on the road—the mist is so thick. I see the imprint of his large boots in what's left of the snow. The mist swirls around his ankles but refuses to touch him—it parts in his wake like a trail for me to follow.

He stops when he gets to the Malženická gate. He looks

around, takes something out of his coat pocket, opens a door in the wall and steps through. I rush to the place where he stood—an urgent pulse in my chest says *please, please be open, please.* I touch the wall and it gives under my hand. *Joy!* I open the space just enough to slip through.

I see the shape of my father disappearing into the Šenkvický wood. I follow him to a clearing. There are at least ten men already there—a *minyan*. But they are not praying. Each of them is off in the trees alone. They don't speak to one another, and their lips mouth words that only the air can hear.

I recognize them from our community—men and boys. All of them Solomonars. Some as old as I am—boys on the cusp of something more. I've heard about *tikkun chatzot*—when King David, the father of Solomon, would wake at midnight to praise God. Abba always says that King David only took sixty breaths of sleep a night. The fire of curiosity inside me is kindled. I want to take sixty breaths too.

If I were a boy, I would be out here with him. Every night.

I watch them for a while as they pray. Some of them bow to a higher force—like trees bend their branches to the wind. Others reach their arms up to the sky. Abba is suffused with a kind of glow, as though he saps energy from the stars themselves. He looks serene, at peace with himself and his place in the forest. They all look like they belong there.

It's only because I'm watching so closely that I see it. One of the men disappears. I widen my eyes, then blink rapidly a few times. At first it looks like he's melted into the tree behind him, but it's an illusion—he's gone, well and truly gone. Then the mist swirls through the clearing and I rub my arms at the sudden chill. I'm so focused on him that I don't see the mist start to coalesce and rise until I look back to where my father was standing and see in his place a pillar of cloud that jets up to the sky. There is no explanation other that what my eyes see. The mist and rain and swirling wisps of clouds have formed a giant winged creature in the sky—like a serpent with wings. It has a long tail which swings up towards the heavens, the head of a horse and the mane of a lion. Its breath is so cold it freezes water in the clouds. I've seen things my father can do before, but never this. The shape shifts and merges, as clouds do in the sky, but all its forms are magical, all of them white and dragon-like and clear.

The creature sends out a roar that sounds like thunder and bends its head down in the direction of the clearing. I see my father now sits on its back, a set of silver reins in his hands. I don't understand how he shifted from man to cloud-beast and back again to man riding a cloud-beast, but then it takes off into the sky, dropping white mist from its great claws and rain from its great jaws and the wind rises each time it flaps its wings. I watch until I can't see it anymore. When I look back down, nobody seems to have paid the dragon any attention. It's as though what just happened is no different to them than having seen a bird flit through the sky.

My shock turns to rage. *I'll never be allowed to be a part of this.*

The men are all still focused on their prayers, *shuckling* with the rising wind, faster than before, but with no less concentration. I know my mouth gapes open; my breath is hitched and fast. It's a miracle none of them have noticed me yet. The sound of my heart is like the beat of a drum. I see one of the men bend his knees, like he's bowing to God in one of the blessings of the silent *Amidah*. When he straightens up, he reaches his arms to the sky and in a rush of wind and feathers he turns into an owl that takes to the sky, leaving his clothes behind him.

It's impossible. Yet I can't deny what my eyes see.

I notice one of the younger men. His long red sidelocks start to grow and twist around him. Guvriel, I think, Reb Amram's son. He crouches down. It looks like he's about to prostrate himself before God, but instead, he turns into a glowing furry orange mass that floats in the air for an instant, no faster than a breath, then reforms itself into something new. A fox. It looks around the clearing and I duck and hide, worried it will see me, smell me, but then it streaks off into the woods. I pick my head up and watch it dart and dance between the large oak trees, circling maples, then leaping into a brush of hawthorn where I can see it no more.

I feel a tug in my gut, and curiosity gets the better of me. If one man can disappear, another can melt into a cloud dragon and ride it, and another can become an owl, or a fox—what might I be capable of?

I follow the fox all the way down to the river, where he stops to drink from its banks. I'm so mesmerized by the sight of him that I don't notice until it's too late that I've wandered straight into a buckthorn bush on the riverbank. The skirt under my coat is stuck. I try to untangle myself and prick my finger on one of the thorns.

Immediately, the fox lifts its snout and turns its head. Its eyes lock with mine. I've never felt so stupid. I watch as it makes its way over to me. It sniffs my skirt and my shoes, then looks up at me.

"It's okay," I say. I have no idea if the fox can understand me. My voice sounds so loud I'm sure everyone and everything in the forest heard me. "I know who you are," I say. I'm certain the fox can hear the thrum of my heart. "I don't even know if you can understand me, but I was following you, and now I'm stuck." My face burns red.

The fox turns around and disappears into the forest and my chest spikes with panic. *What if he leaves me here? What if he doesn't come back?* I'm not sure what would be worse—seeing him come back with one of the men from our village, or with Abba. I will burn up in an inferno of mortification either way, but my father will certainly sentence me to spend the rest of my life weaving by a hearth. I turn my eyes up to the sky and blink back tears. I will not be ashamed of my curiosity. I focus on the anger I feel. When I leave this forest, I will demand that Abba starts to teach me all these things. It is my right—my birthright. But for now I say a silent prayer that the fox comes back alone.

I hear the snap of a twig and my head turns in the direction of the sound. I expect to see my father, to feel the weight of his disapproval and the fire of his rage, but it's only the fox, back in human form (and fully clothed, thank God).

He leans down and starts to work at my skirt. I can't believe I got myself into this situation. Me—the one who ravels and unravels all of our neighbors' rugs at night while they sleep—got my skirt so caught up in the thorns that even I can't untangle it. I feel something warm at the hem of my skirt and jump a bit—was that his hand? My face blooms with a new flush of red. I look down and my skirt is glowing, but there's no smoke or flame. Guvriel's lips move as his hands glow, and I watch the thorns and brambles untangle themselves and recede. *Is his magic plant-based like Hannah's?* I want to ask, but before I can control what comes out of my mouth, I say, "Teach me."

"Come," he says, and walks away. He doesn't look back to see if I'm following him.

I feel stupid. *Teach me? That was all I could think to say?* I'm sure he's going to return me to Abba, and I'll be humiliated and punished. I should run. Maybe I can find a way back on my own, slip back into bed before anyone notices I'm gone, pretend none of this ever happened. I could follow the river, but I'm so turned around that I don't know which way to go. If I was Levana, I would look up at the stars and let them guide me—but I'm not. I'm the same silly girl who always gets into trouble.

I look up and don't see Guvriel anymore. If I don't start walking, I'll lose him completely.

He stops at a small outcropping of rocks, like a cave. I expect him to wait for me to catch up, but he sits down and gestures to the rock beside him.

Does he think I need to rest before we keep walking?

"I'm fine," I say.

"I'm Guvriel," he says. "Guvriel Ben Amram."

"I know who you are." I scowl. "I'm—"

"Sarah." He dips his chin in my direction. "And you're not fine. What are you doing out here? It's dangerous."

"I didn't mean to follow you," I say, but then I stop my mouth. *Resist.* I take a deep breath. "I was following my father. I wanted to know where he goes every night, and then I saw ... well, everything. I've never seen anyone turn into a fox before. I'm sorry I watched. And then I got stuck. And you know the rest. But if you're just going to ... "

"You don't need to apologize for your curiosity."

"I'm sure my father would say otherwise," I snort. "But thank you for untangling me."

"I'm sure you've seen stranger things than I have in your time, Sarah."

"I wish," I reply.

He looks up at the sky. "There's something I need to say before this watch is over." His lips start to move, silently at first, then he says the words out loud. It's a prayer—a passage of *tehillim* and something else combined.

"What are you saying?" I ask.

He finishes murmuring the words and looks at me quizzically. "I forget that women don't study the same things we do. I only thought, as Reb Isaac's daughter—"

"Stop. He doesn't teach me anything," I cut him off. "We barely study at all."

He furrows his brow.

It doesn't make sense to me either, I want to say, but this time I have the wisdom to keep my mouth shut.

"The night is separated into three watches," he explains. "Three *ashmurot* of angels. Each watch—each group, waits with bated breath for their turn to sing *shirah*. It says God roars like a lion at the changing of the watch, and that each watch has its own sound. The first is like the braying of a donkey, the second like a pack of dogs barking, and the third is the sound of a woman whispering to her husband."

"That's beautiful," I whisper, then realize my cheeks are warm. I clear my throat and say, louder, "I've never heard that before."

"I was reciting part of *Perek Shirah*. We say it every night. Don't you?"

I shake my head.

"It's something you *should* know, Sarah," he says, surprising me with his words. I look up and see his face is twisted into a frown. "The passage I was reciting is from the Talmud, tractate *Tamid*—about the *ner tamid*, the eternal flame. Tell me you know what that is . . . " He looks troubled.

I roll my eyes. "Of course I do."

He laughs. "And you know how to use it too . . . huh?"

I look down at my boots. My face is on fire. The entire town knows what I did. I don't like being reminded of it.

"I didn't mean to upset you," he says.

I don't respond.

"Sarah, I don't know one boy your age who could have done what you did," he says. "It was impressive."

I look up at him and narrow my eyes, trying to figure out if he's making fun of me. But his eyes are green and clear and true.

Me? Impressive? Nobody has ever called me that before. Impulsive, yes. Disrespectful—all the time. Never impressive.

"I don't think my father thought it was impressive," I say softly, running my fingers over the moss on a rock beside me.

"Of course he did! The whole community did. We all knew to expect great things from you after that. It was all anyone talked about in the yeshiva. That one of Rabbi Isaac's daughters did in an instant what it would take us years upon years to learn."

I stare at him, part skeptical, part incredulous. I feel confused and a little bit angry. *Maybe he's mocking me?* "If none of the boys my age in the yeshiva can light a fire, then how are you able to turn into a fox? Something you're saying doesn't make sense."

He nods his head like he takes what I say very seriously. Nobody ever takes me seriously. I'm more confused by this interaction than ever.

"That's a good question," he says. "There are a few answers. But mainly two: one, every Solomonar in our community has different innate abilities. Some of us are born with them; others manifest them later in life. But certain things come more naturally to some of us. At least, that's what my father says. We don't understand why. And two, the ability to manipulate the elements—like what your father and you can do, is rarer still. From what I understand, you started a fire far away from where you were, without speaking a word."

"It wasn't like that—I mean, it was far away, but I was repeating the words my father said."

"Interesting. He didn't tell us that."

"That's because he didn't ask. He just sent me to my room and sentenced me to weaving by the hearth for the rest of my life."

Guvriel looks like he tries to fight the grin that spreads across his face. "Ah yes. I too have idled many hours by the fire."

"Weaving?" I gape at him.

He blushes. "Knitting, actually."

I laugh out loud, and he claps a hand over my mouth. Then he quickly removes it, as if my skin has burned him.

"Sorry." His face is as red as his sidelocks. "I didn't mean to . . ."

"It's okay, I should have been quieter. My father makes you knit?"

He chuckles and scratches the back of his neck, "No. My mother makes me darn my own socks."

"Okay, I admit that does make me feel a tiny bit better about my punishment, but still. There's only so much weaving one can take."

"The ability to manipulate the elements is something we spend years learning, and many of us never master it in our lifetimes."

"I saw you turn into a fox! Surely you can light a fire." I'm still trying to take in everything he said. *My father spoke about me in the yeshiva? Why?* I feel like there are two truths being told and reality might be somewhere in the middle. I'm only ever on the receiving end of my father's disapproval. What Guvriel says contradicts everything I've ever known.

"I can make fire," he says, "but not the way you can. It doesn't come naturally to me. All your father's disciples who've attained a certain level of proficiency in the Solomonic arts come out here every night to say the *tikkun* with him. Some say when you're having trouble controlling the flame within you, the best thing to do is recite the words from tractate *Tamid*. You of all people should know this. You should be saying it every night.

"Turning into a fox is easy. It's a manipulation of the self into another form, another being. If you meditate on the words of the *Perek Shirah*, it's not that hard. The next level is actually the nullification of the self—did you see Rafael disappear?"

I nod.

"It's one thing to transform yourself into another being—it's something else entire to nullify your very existence. But your father? He can bend the elements to his will. He can form a being, animate it, remove himself from it, and then reform himself and ride it. Do you understand how incredible that is? If you can already manipulate the elements with ease—earth, water, air and fire—you are on your way to becoming one of the greatest Solomonars that ever lived." He looks at me with wonder, with reverence.

Tears fill my eyes and I look away.

"What's wrong?"

"I'm not. I never will be." I dust off my skirt and stand up. "Show me the way back. There's no use in delaying the inevitable."

"What? Why? Where are you going?" he says.

"Aren't you going to bring me back to my father right now?"

"Not unless you want me to," Guvriel says.

I stare at him. "Then what?"

"Why did you come out here tonight, Sarah?"

I sit down and pick up a twig and twirl it between my fingers. "I want to help fight the darkness," I say, "to help push back the Black Mist. I know I can because—I only wanted to watch . . . to learn, to see where my father goes every night. I must find ways to teach myself because he won't teach me."

"What if there's another way?"

"What other way could there possibly be? My sisters are useless. They do everything they're told. My mother uses her strength to heal people in town. And according to my father, I destroy everything I touch."

He looks down at his feet and kicks a stone and I hear him say under his breath, "I could teach you." He says it so fast I barely make out the words.

Now I've made him pity me. I can't even get this right. "I should head back," I whisper and stand up, but as I do, he reaches out and grabs my sleeve, then quickly lets go. "Sorry," he says. He looks at his hand, my sleeve, then back up at me. "I'm sorry. I didn't mean to . . ."

"It doesn't matter." I rub my arm where he touched it. "I shouldn't be here." I'm angry that everything I thought I knew now feels twisted—like maybe I'm not the disappointment I thought I was all this time. *Resist. Resist. Resist. But what if I don't want to resist anymore?*

"Sarah, what's wrong?"

"It's not right." I stop myself from saying more.

"What?"

"That he's taught . . . " I stop myself again. "That you know all these things and I don't."

"Why don't you ask him to teach you?"

"He won't."

"I find that hard to believe," he says.

He won't teach me because I refuse to fill a cup with water is what I want to say, but it sounds ridiculous even to my ears.

"Sarah . . . wait!" He reaches out and touches my shoulder.

I stop. This time, it's deliberate, his hand on my shoulder.

He doesn't move his hand. My stomach flips.

I turn around to face him and study his face in the darkness for the first time. I see shadows on his cheeks, sharp angles softened by red fuzz just starting to dust his chin, and sharp green eyes that shine with the promise of a world of wisdom and a little bit of daring.

"Let me teach you," he says.

I wipe my eyes on my sleeve. "It's not right. I don't want you to disobey your rabbi."

"Come back again tomorrow night. Wait here, under the outcropping. I'll bring some books; I'll hide them here."

"My father will never approve."

"I wasn't planning on telling him," he says.

My thoughts chase one another. *I could learn all the things I've been wanting to learn. I'd be an idiot not to take him up on his offer . . . but if Abba ever found out . . .*

I narrow my eyes at him, but all I see are true intentions.

"Why?" I ask, challenging him. "What do you get out of it?"

He swallows and I see the strained motion of it in the muscles of his neck. "Maybe you can teach me a thing or two about fire?"

"What if I disappoint you?"

He meets my eyes. "You won't."

My stomach flips again.

"I don't need books," I say. "We have a house full of books. I want to be able to do what you can do."

"All wisdom comes from books."

"That's not true. Some wisdom is innate—you said that. If I was a boy, I'd be out here with you. I'd have mastered animals and I'd already be weaving clouds in the sky. I will never be like you because I will always be a girl. It doesn't matter how much wisdom I have."

"Wisdom always matters. In *The Book of the Solomonars*, there are four attributes of wisdom: humility, understanding, integrity, and courage." His eyes meet mine. "Do you trust me?"

"What if my father finds out?"

"He won't, I promise, and if he does, I'll take the blame. It was my idea, after all."

"Why?"

"Because I see the thirst for knowledge in your eyes and that's something that should never be denied."

My heart beats even faster. I take a deep breath. "Okay," I say. "I trust you." The tiny flame inside me roars to life.

His mouth twists into a grin. "Even if I force you to read books first?"

I laugh, then put my hand to my lips. I can't remember the last time I smiled like this—so wide it feels as if my lips will crack.

"Yes," I say.

"It's settled then," he says. "I'll see you here tomorrow night, Sarah Bat Isaac."

He starts to walk away.

"Wait!" I say.

He turns around. "The third watch is about to begin; I have to go."

"Oh," I say. "Okay . . ."

"You know how to get back from here, don't you?"

"No . . . " I say, feeling sheepish and silly.

"Follow me." He leaps up into the air and, in an instant, he's a fox again. He starts bounding through the trees. I dash into a sprint to keep up. I swear to myself in that moment that one day I will outrun him—in fox form.

Levana

Abba takes me with him to synagogue each week now, even when there is no *kiddush levana*. He starts to teach me everything he knows about the heavens.

"The great ones say every blade of grass has a star assigned to it that tells it to grow. If every blade of grass has a star, certainly every human being has a star too. The stars give us life, and they have stars assigned to them which give them light and life, and those stars have stars assigned to them, and so forth, until you get to the Holy One, Blessed Be He, Himself, who gives light and life to everything. Some say each star is an angel; they form God's heavenly army. We strive to be part of that army here on earth. Each star has its own power. Every soul has power too.

"Together, clusters of stars form constellations—*mazalot*—from the word '*mazal*' which can be interpreted as luck, but also comes from the world '*nozel*'—something that's fluid, like liquid, ever-changing, flowing down from the sky, subject to our interpretation."

I watch the sky as Abba speaks. I understand the words he's saying, but I don't know how to take his words and apply them. There are always shapes, and things that glow, and light that leaps from one star to another and my eyes try to follow the path of that light, but sometimes I lose my way.

"Are you listening, Levanaleh?"

"Yes. I'm trying to understand."

"I will give you an example. See those stars—the six there that make up a curve, the five there that lead up from it, and the sixth, that bursts into three?"

I follow the point of his finger and it is as if there is light that shines from his hand straight to the sky.

"That is the scorpion of the sky. Do you see how its tail sits on what looks like a river? That's the *nahar di nur*—the river of fire. It is said that if its tail did not sit in that river, then no one who is bitten by a scorpion would ever recover.

"Each star has its own power; every soul has power too, and every star has a direct influence on what happens here on earth. Groups of stars have even more power—like groups of men. And every group of stars can have an effect on every other group.

"Individually each of us has power, but together, like ten men in a *minyan*, we have even more power, and each group has the potential to influence every other group, for good or for bad. Imagine the power of hundreds, then thousands of groups of ten. It is infinite power. So it is above, and so it is below."

I continue to stare up at the sky. I don't tell him the stars he points to are the same stars I saw on my own—the same star I saw burst into three.

Three sisters. Three paths. Three stars venturing out, away from the cluster they belong to.

Hannah

2 Cheshvan 5120

When we arrived at Jakob's house, he jumped off the horse, then reached up to help me down. "You'll have your own room beside my mother's," he said.

There were no servants there to greet us, which made me understand how clandestine Jakob's trip must have been. God forbid, with the Black Mist spreading, that he be seen consorting with Jews . . .

I know this, and yet, it still hurts. Like a bruise you can barely see. But I must focus on why I'm here and put aside any feelings of hurt. I'm here to help his mother heal. That is all that matters.

I followed him to the stables where there was a young boy waiting to take the horse from him. Jakob took a coin out of his pocket and gave it to the boy as he handed over the reins.

"Follow me," he said without glancing back to see if I was there. I remember thinking, *This is what it's like to live a life of privilege: never looking back to see if anyone is following you.* But I did follow him because I was alone with a strange nobleman for the first time in my life, and completely at his mercy. I felt the weight of Eema and Abba's eyes on my back, and the eyes of the entire community. I represented them. I couldn't let them down.

Jakob took me through the kitchen, where there was a low fire burning, but no one tending to it. It was the largest kitchen I'd ever seen in my life—herbs hanging overhead to ward off demons and flies, two hearths, shelves filled with massive pots and pans and bakers' tables larger than those at the Ben Yanai's bakery. We went up a round staircase that felt like it went on and on. I felt more awake and alert than I'd ever been, even though my legs ached from the climb and my heart was heavy—a permanent lump in my chest I couldn't dislodge. I remember thinking, *What if she really is sick with the Black Mist? Will I catch it? Will it mean my end? Is that why they brought me here? Because I'm expendable?*

Jakob opened a door into a chamber well-lit with candles, a fire already burning bright. The bed at the center of the room was intricately carved, and the two chairs and a table at the foot of the bed by the fire were carved in the same style. I thought how much Sarah would love it here—a large room warm with the reflection of what felt like a dozen dancing flames.

"This will be your room," Jakob said. "I hope you find it satisfactory."

I almost laughed. As if anyone could possibly see a room like this and not find it satisfactory!

"Mother's room is right through here." He led me back to the stairwell, opened a door to a passage that led to another wooden door, which opened onto an anteroom. The room was not well-lit. There was no fire burning in the hearth. But even in the darkness, with only the light of the moon through the window to guide us, I could see the floor was covered in an enormous carpet, with soft-looking furniture in various shades of velvet and brocades arranged around the room. Hanging tapestries and drapes covered the walls, though I couldn't see the patterns upon them.

"Mother's room is right here," he whispered when we got to another set of doors. "I would be most grateful if you'd be willing to spend at least part of the night with her. Her maids have spent the last two weeks in a vigil by her bedside. We've had the best doctors visit. All to no avail. I would not have come to get you if I did not fear for her life."

"I will need to change and gather some things from my satchel," I said, and turned to go back to the first room he took me to.

"Will you be needing any assistance?" I heard him at my back, following me.

That tiny bit of power made me feel brave. It reminded me that I was the one he needed in this moment, and not the other way around.

"No, thank you," I said. "I need time to wash myself and pre-pare some remedies and poultices."

"I will wait for you outside."

"I won't be long," I said.

He closed the door and I turned to face the room. There were more blankets than I'd ever seen piled high on the bed and all I wanted to do was sink into its softness. I knew I should be open-ing the satchel and taking out the herbs and remedies, shedding my traveling cloak and taking out the overdress that Eema and I always wore when we made house calls, but I couldn't help it—I walked over to the bed and touched the sheets and felt the pillows. My boots sank into plush carpeting. I wanted to feel the fibers of the rug on my bare feet, but there wasn't time. The sheets were cream-colored and smooth, their edges trimmed with delicately embroidered flowers. I smelled lavender and balsam wood.

People live like this! It's wealth I've only ever read about in books. The walls were covered with paintings of animals and people (graven images, forbidden by our religion)—some of the paintings were so large they nearly reached the ceiling. I wondered what the purpose was of such a high ceiling. It made sense in synagogue, where there needed to be space for air and light and prayer—but here it felt decadent, frivolous.

I walked to the window and pulled the dark blue curtains aside. My hand left a mark on the window, my breath a fog. It was too dark to see outside, but the moon and stars shone bright. They comforted me at that moment. I thought of Levana and wondered if she was watching the same stars.

There was a knock at the door and I startled. I'd spent too much time exploring the room and not enough time getting ready to treat an ill woman. I was mortified by my behavior, and crossed the room quickly. "Just a moment."

"Anything you want or need is available to you," I heard Jakob say through the door. "If there's an herb you need, a servant will be sent out to fetch it for you."

"Thank you, I think I have everything. I'll be another minute," I said.

I quickly shrugged off my cloak and placed Eema's satchel on the table. I pulled the overdress from the bag and slipped my arms into it, quickly tying the ribbons at the back into bows. I took a linen cloth and laid it on the table, then removed all of the remedies I'd brought. I picked up the jar with the paste for chest infections and tore some strips of the linen cloth, and took a bottle of horehound syrup. I also took parchment and a quill. I placed everything in the pockets of the overdress, wet my hands with the water at the washbasin beside the bed, lathered my hands with Eema's lavender and lye soap, and poured more water over each hand and into the basin. Three times on my right hand, then three times on my left to remove all spiritual impurities. I dried my hands on a clean cloth next to the washbasin and went to open the door.

Jakob's face brightened when he saw me.

"I'm ready," I said, and then I was following him again.

I spent all night by the duchess's bedside, rubbing a poultice onto her chest, diluting the medicine into a cup of tea and trying to get her to drink small sips throughout the night. I massaged her chest, like Eema taught me, and as I did, the words came. "*El na refah na lah ... Please God, please heal her ...*" The potent combination of herbs from the earth and words from the air came together to make a kind of fire. I felt Eema guiding me, her hands giving strength to my hands. *The body needs clean air and water like the soil does. Our skin must breathe along with our lungs, and if there is rot in the undergrowth, we must find a way to weed it out.* My hands were warm and aching with exertion as I laid them on her chest again. I closed my eyes and murmured all the healing charms I knew. I rubbed oil and salt into the palms of her hands, the soles of her feet.

I sang all the songs Eema used to sing as I tied knots into the roots of madder stems by her bedside. Seven strands protect even against demons, though five are enough to ward off illness. I knotted seven.

If this is the Black Mist, there may be nothing I can do. And I fear if that happens, the whole community could be blamed.

I thought about the cryptic words Eema said to me when we parted. *Jacob* was a dreamer—*Joseph* was the one who lived in the king's palace. So why did she mention Jacob to me? Jacob took his twin brother's birthright. Joseph was Rachel's firstborn. I've spent my life putting stock in my mother's stories, and she always seems to have the right one for each moment. I still don't understand why she chose these words for me.

There's a knock at the door.

I'm back in my room now. One of the chambermaids came to replace me. I probably should have asked her name. I am like her now—a servant in a palace—but I was so tired it took everything in me not to fall asleep where I stood.

"This water needs to be changed and her chamber pot emptied," I told her. "The air in the room must be fresh. Do not wake her. Keep the poultice on her chest and if she's thirsty, give her this to drink," I showed her the pitcher of tea by the bedside.

I must go to sleep, but I wanted to finish writing down everything, in case I need to consult my notes tomorrow. I can finally climb into what I know will be the softest bed I've ever slept in. This has been by far one of the most wonderful days of my life.

3 Cheshvan 5120–a few hours later

When I woke up, there was sunlight streaming into the room and a smell of fresh pastry. (Sarah would want to know exactly what pastry—with vivid descriptions of everything I was served, but she'll have to forgive me for I don't have the time for it now.) I sat up in bed, wondering what time it was and how long I'd slept. On the table where I left Eema's satchel, there was a tray laden with food and steam rising from a pitcher which smelled strong and inviting. My mouth watered—but I knew I couldn't eat. The food wasn't kosher.

I spent the rest of the day by the duchess's bedside. Her color was better, her breath more steady, so I continued the treatment as before. Supper was brought to her room, though she still hadn't woken up. I placed some fruit and nuts in my pockets for later. At dusk, I was relieved by a chambermaid again—her name is Soria.

Back in my room, as I counted three stars and prepared to break my fast, there was a knock at the door.

"May I come in?"

It was Jakob, his arms laden with bread and meat and cheese.

"What's all this?" I said.

"I went to the yeshiva. They explained why you won't eat. I brought you some things to break your fast . . . They're kosher." He blushed.

I relieved him of some of the things he carried, and as I did, my hand brushed up against his. There was a spark in the space where I touched him. I pulled away.

"Sorry," I said.

"Hannah, you don't need to be afraid," he said softly, placing his hand on mine. I felt the same spark again. I looked at him and when my eyes met his I felt warm and cold all over. I can't deny I'm attracted to him. He's wrong for me in every way possible, but when he's near me, my body sings the way plants drink up sunshine. I want to feel his arms around me, I want to touch my lips to his. And it's all forbidden, which makes it that much more tantalizing and sweet. I know I'm not supposed to look at any man unless he is to be my husband. But my heart was beating so hard in that moment that I didn't know what to think and couldn't look away.

"I'm not afraid," I said back to him, defiant.

"Then what?"

I opened my mouth to say something about our people, our traditions, but nothing came.

"You feel it too?" He moved his hand to cup my cheek. "There's something between us."

Is he courting me? Or are these words he says to every pretty girl?

Less than a day ago, I thought the future had finally found

me. But now I'm not so sure. *He's not Jewish, Hannah!* I heard my sister Sarah's disapproving voice in my head.

Everything and everyone here is so foreign—so unlike my family. Many roads diverge from every space—how do we know which road to take?

4 Cheshvan 5120

The duchess is improving. She now spends much of the day awake. I suspect it is the Black Mist she suffers from, because when I lay my hands on her chest it feels the way it did when I removed the black spots from under all the leaves in the garden—like something cold and calculating. I think most of the lesions on her lungs are now gone. I saw the shape of them dissolving in air—in what looked very much like a mist—at night when she exhaled.

But what's really been taking up my time, besides being by her bedside, is that every evening, Jakob has knocked on my bedroom door.

The first two days we sat and talked. He asked many questions about Judaism and the "Order of the Solomonars"—as he calls it. I never thought of us as an order, but in his eyes, I suppose that's what we are.

Today we went out for a walk in the garden. Jakob told me that he's recently become a member of the Order of the Dragon. He wears a crest with the words "O how merciful is God, faithful and just" on it. The dragon is circular, like it's eating its own tail, and it carries a red cross on its back.

"I hope you're not offended if I say that looking at it makes me uncomfortable," I told him.

"I don't mind your saying so, but I want to know why," Jakob replied.

"Crosses have never meant anything good for the Jews."

"But you're not just a Jew," he said. "You're a Solomonar! From an esteemed family."

I wanted to tell him that every Jew is equal in God's eyes, but I didn't.

"My family might be esteemed today," I said instead, "but we are only here at the grace of King Béla. Tomorrow, he might change his mind and that would be the end of our freedom."

"I don't think you know how highly your father is respected."

His words made me feel both better and worse. The responsibility to represent my family and heal the duchess felt even heavier. *I still know how everything could be taken away in an instant*, I wanted to say.

All these thoughts were swirling in my head, but then Jakob stopped walking, his face a combination of pain and shock and fear. He fell down, grasping his leg. He screamed. It took a moment to realize what had happened, but then I saw the snake as it slithered away. I had to stay calm. I could call for help—and maybe help was already on its way, but I had to act quickly. I sat down on the ground, folded up his pants leg, rolled down his stockings, and placed my hands over the bite.

He was shaking and pale. "What are you doing?" he stammered.

"Shhh . . . " I said. "I must work quickly."

I closed my eyes "*Yimchatz ve'yadav yirpena—He wounds and His hands make whole.*" I felt the words draw upon the calming waters within me, traveling up my arms and down through my hands. Eema always warned us to use real herbs and remedies so that we're not accused of witchcraft, but there's no time now. It's a risk, but I've been taught to save a life above all.

My fingers grew warm, my palms white-hot with heat. My head hurt from the concentration and pressure I applied, but I felt the venom rising up to meet my hands, draining out of his wound. I wiped it away with the hem of my skirt, again and again, until there was nothing left but two clean puncture wounds, seeping blood.

I sat back, sweating and bone-tired. But it was done. "We'll need to bind that now." I looked up at him.

He looked at me in reverence, in awe. His color had returned but his mouth gaped open. For a moment, I worried he was frozen in shock, but then he moved, placing his hand on my arm. He winced in pain as he moved his leg an inch closer to me. "You're an angel," he said.

"What?" I laughed. "No." I crossed my arms over my chest.

"You saved me. How?"

"My mother taught me. It's a way we have of laying our hands to draw out illness."

"Is that how you've been healing Mother?" he asked.

"That and other things," I said. "Herbs and poultices, other remedies are important too. The body can only do so much— there are natural elements that help the healing process along. Like your leg—I will need to dress it and bind it. But the venom is gone."

"God has sent you to me. An angel to save me and my family." His eyes filled with tears. "I will not forget this." His eyes on me were worshipful, but I didn't feel worthy of his praise. God forbid anyone should think me an angel or a saint.

"Please don't speak of what happened here. My ancestors . . . my people have been persecuted for less," I told him.

"No harm will ever come to you. You can be my angel in disguise," he laughed. "I swear it."

He leaned his head closer. I wanted to pull back, but I felt a spark again—warm and alive and stronger than before. He pressed his lips to mine and the sensation traveled through every inch of me—like liquid fire. My lips moved against his, and it was like whispering a prayer. I closed my eyes and wished for God to show me if this indeed was the path he meant for me to follow.

15 Kislev 5120

The duchess finally feels better. I wouldn't say we have a relation-ship, but she sits up in bed and doesn't question my ministrations. She's asked me to call her Eliszabetta.

I continue to rub oil and salt into her palms and soles. I make her horehound tea and mix it with lavender, rosemary, mint, sage, and garlic. She drinks this tea as often as possible.

I apply Eema's ointments and poultices, but mainly at night.

Only when she's asleep do I mouth the words to Eema's heal-ing prayers, *Heal me God, for my bones tremble in fear.* And others. Over and over again as my hands fill with warmth and I spread that warmth deep into her bones with my touch.

The day following the snake incident, I found two dresses waiting for me when I got back to my room. They are finer than anything I've ever worn. When Jakob and I go for walks, I feel like a proper lady now, dressed in silks. We have many conversa-tions about faith. I never hide what I believe. He holds my hand as we walk and each time, I feel the same spark. It's undeniable. And I know it is not a spark of danger warning me away. A fire burns bright inside me whenever he's near—a torch ignited by the same flame. He asks me questions about the Torah, questions about the plants and flowers we pass. Each day is more wonderful than the next.

Today I noticed little white *Gyöngyi* flowers blooming in the steps our feet made. "Do you see those flowers?" I asked him.

"The little white ones?"

"Yes, isn't it strange how they're blooming?"

"Perhaps, but I don't pay much attention to the garden when I'm with you."

"Well, you're supposed to," I said, swatting his hand playfully. "I thought I was giving you lessons."

"So teach me!" He grinned and stopped to peck a kiss on my lips.

"*Gyöngyi* flowers can stimulate the heart."

"I like the sound of that." He leaned down to pick one, but I stilled his hand with mine.

"If ingested in quantity, they can poison the blood. They're also called Pearl's Blood."

"Well then, I'll have to find some other flower to pick for you," he said.

When I got back to my room, there was a vase of beautiful white flowers waiting for me.

But I wonder if the *Gyöngyi* flowers are an omen. They've unsettled me.

20 Tevet 5120

It's been more than a month since I last wrote, and the duchess is finally well. I haven't had much time to write, except for my daily treatment log. Eema would be so proud of me, but there are parts of this log that I can never show her—too many emotions written here which I would never want her to see.

I can't believe I'm about to embark on a short journey back home. So much has happened to me this past month. I've learned from Jakob—that non-Jews can be as good and kind as any Jew I know. That I can love and give of myself in a way I'd never quite tested. That I have feelings and sensations I never knew my body could contain. I've grown as a healer and as a woman. Being here has challenged me in so many ways. I wonder if my family will even recognize me. I look at myself in the gilded mirror in my bedroom and I barely recognize myself.

I think I've fallen in love with Jakob. Maybe that's what the spark is—like fire, it is both the most wonderful and most terrible thing. There is no future for us. Abba will never allow me to marry him. But the truth is worse. I'm no lady—I'm a Jew. I know that Jakob will never ask.

20 Tevet 5120–a few hours later

I'm home and my family's asleep. I missed my sisters and parents like an ache in my chest that refused to go away, but now I miss my room and my bed and my desk in the palace. Will I ever see Jakob again?

We were silent as we rode back up the road that led to the small outcropping of homes in the Jewish quarter. There wasn't much to say. It was clear this was goodbye.

I knocked on the door and Eema opened it, and in an instant I was in her arms. "We missed you so much," she said. I could only reply with my tears.

I turned to Abba, glad I'd caught him before he'd gone off to *maariv* prayers. He gathered me in his arms and kissed the top of my head. *"Blessed is God who revives the dead!"*

I smiled. It's what we say when we see someone after not having seen them for a very long time. Within seconds, I'd been catapulted back into my home and community. Our way of life. It felt doubly important today—the duchess is well again, completely healed. I did that. Me. I revived her from the dead.

"Your grace," Abba said to Jakob.

Jakob bowed to Abba. "May we speak?"

"Follow me," he said, but I saw Abba's eyes flit first to me.

My eyes must have been wide with panic because Eema said, "Your garden has missed you . . ."

I understood her meaning immediately. "Yes, I will go check on it."

Abba's lean-to office is on the way to the garden. I walked past the door and around the corner, then inclined my head, just under the window.

I could barely make out their voices, but I heard some of what they said.

"What will you take for a dowry?" Jakob asked. I gasped and had to place my hand over my mouth to keep silent.

"My daughter is not for sale. There is no sum—"

"What do I need to do?"

"There is nothing—"

"Whatever it is. I will do it. Tell me your conditions. You said she must marry a Jew and a scholar. How do I become a Jew? What must I study? Please."

"It's impossible," Abba said.

"Nothing is impossible," Jakob replied. "Tell me what to do and give me your oath that if I fulfill your conditions, you will allow me to marry her."

My heart beat fast. I couldn't believe his words. It was more than I ever dreamed possible. There was no way Abba would approve . . . no way he'd agree. I heard Eema's words in my head, the ones she said when I left, they were finally making sense—*behold the days will come when woman will encircle man.*

Jakob wrestled with an angel—that angel was me. But did he win? Do I want him to?

I knew I should leave in case they came bursting out the front door and saw me, but I couldn't tear myself away.

"I shall let you marry my daughter if you fulfill the following conditions," Abba said. "Two years of Talmud study, at which point, you must distinguish yourself as a light unto others. You must prove diligent in your studies, wise beyond your years, pious in the path of our Lord, fluent in Hebrew and Aramaic, with broad knowledge of our holy texts and sharp understanding. It is an impossible feat to accomplish in such a short amount of time, but if you succeed, I will make sure she is still here, unmarried, and waiting for you. But if you do not return within two years, with all those conditions fulfilled, she will marry another more befitting of her."

"I accept your conditions," Jakob said.

As I write this now, I know Jakob will be unable to fulfill Abba's terms. He will never come back. My hands shake. If God can bring people back from the dead, certainly he can bring two souls back together. *"Blessed are you God, King of the universe, who brings people back from the dead,"* I say.

Bring him back to me, I pray. *Please, just bring him back.*

It is important to move one's body during prayer—the word nah'anuah is the same motion we apply to the lulav on the holiday of Sukkot, the etrog is the heart, the aravot are the lips, the hadassim are the eyes, and the lulav is the spine. They all remind us that every limb of our bodies must praise God. Like a flame trying to free itself from its wick, so our souls desire to reunite with God. It is a way of coupling with the Shechinah.

—The Book of the Solomonars,
page 3, verses 8–12

The wind that whistled through the trees of the Satu Mare forest that night sang a low and mournful melody. Something in the tone had changed. Something had been set in motion. The voices in the trees echoed poisoned thoughts that reached the ears of the duchess.

Where has your son gone? The wind said. *Where has she taken him?* it whispered. *He is bewitched.* The wind roared. *Remember,* it said, *how the mist first appeared in the forest where the Solomonars pray?*

And indeed, as the mist moved in from the fields and the forest to cover the town, the holy Reb Isaac spent every night fighting back the fog. But something sinister was spreading over the town, something dark and black and old, and eventually there would be nothing Reb Isaac or his followers could do to tame it back.

Sarah

It was easy to sneak out when Hannah was away. I only had to wait to hear Levana's soft snores and then I could go. I'm worried Hannah will find a way to keep me from meeting Guvriel, that she'll find out about our nighttime trysts. Once, Hannah and I used to whisper to each other. We used to share secrets. But now she stares at the ceiling for so long I don't think she will ever close her eyes. I can tell she's keeping something close to her heart. Some kind of secret. She's changed, but I've changed too. I feel more distant from her than ever, and I have no desire to bridge that gap. Even though we still share a bed, I have my own secrets now.

Meeting Guvriel every night has become a balm for my wounded soul. I no longer have trouble controlling my impulses. I stop setting fires and putting them out, raveling and unraveling the neighbors' rugs. I go through each day doing everything exactly as I should because I know that at night, as soon as everyone is asleep, as soon as Abba creeps out of the house to go say the *tikkun*, within a few minutes I'll be sneaking out too—to go wait for Guvriel by the rocks. I've started to say the *tikkun* too and I'm studying *Perek Shirah* and it calms me in a way that weaving never did. Every night, after the first watch is over, Guvriel sits with me and teaches me everything he knows.

"There are songs that every living thing sings," he tells me. "The wild trees, pomegranates and figs, the rain, the dew, the stars, the night. When we attune ourselves to them in the right way, we can hear their song, and if we focus, and sing their songs with the right intentions—when we have the right mindset, we can enter into a state of being that enables us to take on that thing's properties. But it requires full and complete concentration, along with a very focused goal or reason why you want to become that thing."

To me, his voice is the song I've been waiting to hear. I let everything he says soak into my skin. If there was an animal or a form I could choose, it would take the shape of Guvriel Ben Amram, because then I could be the son my father could teach.

Something begins to shift inside me. I am not fighting myself anymore. I have made room inside myself for something else. For someone else. Because it is clear to me that Guvriel has found a way into my heart. In the clearing by the outcropping of rocks where we practice and pray and study together, he has helped me to finally feel free.

"How will I know what animal I should become?" I ask.

"You'll know. For some it is a tree; for others, a star in the sky; for most, it starts with an animal. You will hear it in your heart like an echo."

We go through the songs of the birds first: the rooster, the hen, the crane, the laughing dove, the raven, the wild goose. Then the insects: the spider, the grasshopper, the fly. Then the fish, the leviathan, the sea monsters. The sheep, the cow, the pig, the horse, the wolf, the ox, the gazelle, the elephant, the bear, the mouse; we stop at the fox.

I read, "The fox says, 'Woe is the man who builds a house without justice, and its rooms without lawfulness; who uses his friend's services for free and does not pay his employees.' I don't understand. How is that the fox's song? It doesn't make any sense."

Guvriel grins. "Clearly you're not meant to be a fox."

I smack his arm.

"Hey. No touching," he teases me.

Somehow one of us always manages to "accidentally" touch the other each time we meet, but we've never gone further than that. When everything we're doing is forbidden, it's hard to know where the rules begin and end.

"Why did you choose a fox?"

"The fox chose me."

"That makes even less sense."

"You'll know, Sarah. When it's time, you'll feel it. For now . . . let's keep on reading."

We go through the creeping creatures, the scorpion, the snail, the ant . . . the snake . . . *A fiery golden snake that tamed back the darkness.* But who wants to be a snake? I don't share my thoughts with Guvriel. Why would a fox ever want to spend time with a snake?

"What if I'm a creature that hasn't been discovered yet?" I ask instead.

"Everything has been discovered in God's eyes, for He created every living thing."

"But *Perek Shirah* doesn't list every song. Maybe I'm a song that no one has heard yet."

Guvriel looks at me like he's really listening. "Maybe you are."

The silence between us feels like a song of its own.

"But you still have to start with something *galuy*—something that is already revealed to us," he says.

"I want to be a fox like you," I say.

He laughs. "Then you need to meditate on the fox's song until you understand it deep in your bones."

"Help me." It comes out as a whisper, but it contains all the longing I feel in my heart. It hurts to say it, I've wanted this for so long. "I want to know what you know." My eyes search his in the darkness, as if, if I looked hard enough, I'd find the secrets of the universe there.

"You must feel it in your heart—you must internalize the words and understand why they are the fox's words. Think on it until we meet again. The watch is changing and I must go."

He reaches for my hand and I take it.

I can't help the way I feel out here with him—a little bit daring, and a little bit scared, but excited in a way I've never felt before.

It takes control not to tell Abba everything I know now, not to share with him everything I can do. It takes control not to scream from every rooftop that I think I'm falling in love with this fox-boy who listens to me and sees into the very heart of me, who is not afraid of me. Someone who is kind and patient and who thinks I'm special. That I'm worthy of his time.

*   *   *   *   *

I hear Eema and Abba whispering to each other at night.

Eema thinks it would be good for me to learn a trade—to channel my weaving into something more professional—something to help me earn a living. If I were a man, the only material I'd be studying would be the Talmud in my father's yeshiva, and the ways of the Solomonars at night in the forest under the sky. But I don't let her words hurt me anymore. If learning a trade gets me out of the house and out from under my parents' watchful eyes, so be it.

*   *   *   *   *

The next morning, I walk along the road that leads to town from the small quarter of the city where we live. I'm on my way to an apprenticeship at Mária Novak's home and textile mill. I'm apprehensive. It's not a long walk, but something definitely changes

when I get to the place where the road I'm on meets another. I
rub my arms and pull my cloak tighter around my shoulders.
It's colder here. Darker. It's early in the morning, the sun barely
visible above me in the gloom. I look right and left. A low black
fog obscures the road in both directions—both ways lead away
from everything I've ever known.

I've walked this road many times with Hannah and Eema,
past Miroslav Sklenár's glassblowing workshop in one direction
all the way to the Benedictine abbey and the river beyond it, past
Štefan Kováč's smithy and Tomáš and Helena Pekár's bakery to
the market in the town square. I know there will be people out
and about, starting the ovens, the smell of bread wafting from
shops and the sound of horses' hooves against paving stones.
But right now all is quiet and still and a dark mist coats the
road. I'm used to walking these roads in my dreams—at night
from the comfort of my bed—but only in my mind. Never like
this, alone.

We can't help but hear the things they say about us in town.
Everyone knows that Hannah healed the duchess from what ailed
her, and now there are more rumors than ever about Abba and
our community. Some blame the Black Mist on us. Eema wanted
to walk with me—she was scared to send me out on my own—
but I told her I was old enough, that I didn't need her. Now I'm
starting to worry that maybe I was wrong. I see a figure appear
in the mist, hurrying along the road, and my heart picks up its
pace. I look down at my feet, clench my fingers into fists, and
walk with purpose in the direction of town.

"Shalom, Sarah Bat Isaac, how are you on this fine morning?"

I startle, then let out a breath. It's Guvriel.

"Good morning," I say.

"Where are you headed all alone so early in the morning?"

"To town—to Mária Novak the weaver."

"Ah. More weaving? I am told it's your favorite thing to do."

I glare at him, but can't help the twist of my lips into a tiny smile. "Wherever did you hear that?"

"Oh, you know. Here and there. People talk."

"I'm sure they do," I say, wondering if he means that people are talking about me again.

"I'm, um … headed that way, would you like me to accompany you?"

I look at him sideways. "I'm perfectly capable of taking care of myself, thank you very much."

He makes a kind of funny face, like he's trying to decide what he should say, and I can't help but laugh. No matter how hard I try, I can't stay angry at him. Nobody else makes me laugh like he does. I feel like we've been aware of each other all our lives. But up until I encountered him in the forest, he was just another one of Rabbi Amram's boys—known for their flaming red sidelocks as much as for their mischievous ways. I knew so little then. He is so much more than that. One thing I have definitely learned—you can't judge someone by what they look like, or even how they act. We are all hiding infinite possibilities inside. Woman, man, fox, snake, dragon, and so much more.

"I don't bite," he says, not really answering my question. "Well … maybe only sometimes, but don't tell your father that."

"Don't worry, I won't."

"Oh good. That would be horribly embarrassing. After you." He gestures at the road ahead.

"You don't need to walk me." I wouldn't dream of telling my father anything about Guvriel and the time we spend together. But his presence here makes me wonder what my father knows. "Where exactly were you coming from?"

"It's not important."

"Actually, I think it is. Why would you, Guvriel Ben

Amram, happen to be out for a stroll so early in the morning, before *shacharit* prayers, walking away from the yeshiva and *beit knesset*?"

"I have a question for you," he says, twisting one of his sidelocks between his fingers.

"You didn't answer my question."

"Why does it matter to you where I was or wasn't coming from?"

"Hmph." I don't answer him.

"Can't a boy happen upon a girl on his way to somewhere?" He scratches the red whiskers on his chin. "I mean, how else is one supposed to meet a girl? In the woods? God forbid!" He puts a hand over his heart in mock horror.

I giggle.

"Good fortune seems to have smiled upon me," he continues. "I will have to tell my brothers and study partners—apparently the best way to meet a girl is to happen upon her on the road to town early in the morning." He winks at me. "And to think that my mother thought I should go speak to Tzipporah Benhaim. Who needs a matchmaker when you have a road?"

I roll my eyes at him.

"It's an age-old dilemma actually. Who was walking where first? There's actually something about it in the Talmud."

"Is there?" I say skeptically.

"Oh yes, lots of stories in the Talmud about maidens getting lost on their way to town and strapping young yeshiva students helping them find their way. It makes a great story to tell the grandchildren."

"I'm sure . . . "

"Rabbi Yossi Haglili says . . . " he starts to chant in a sing-song voice, "if you should come across a lost maiden at a crossroads on her way to town, you should most certainly greet her and ask her if she knows the way to Lud."

"So which way is Lud?"

He scratches his head, twirls one of his sidelocks, leans into me a bit, and whispers, "I think it's the other way."

There's a little bird in my chest, ruffling its feathers—something happy and free. Despite the gloom of morning and the mist swirling around our feet, he finds a way to brighten my day. I'm starting to find it hard to imagine what my life was like before I happened upon Guvriel in the forest—or he happened upon me. Depends on how you look at it.

As we walk, his long red sidelocks sway in the wind. He's a good head taller than I am. It's strange to see him in the light: I've gotten so used to only seeing the shape of him at night. He reminds me so much of my father in some ways, but he is open and honest in a way Abba will never be—at least not to me, and of course, much more handsome. It takes everything in me not to tug on one of his sidelocks.

"I really don't need anyone to walk me," I say finally.

"Sometimes it's okay to not walk alone."

That's when I realize he's talking about more than the road. My stomach does a flip—a long low swoop as if the ground slipped out from under me. *He's saying I can be with him. He's walking with me so he can say he encountered me by chance. So he can tell his father and mine that he met me, that we spoke.*

"I know I don't need to walk you," he says, "but I want to be by your side."

I stop in the middle of the road and turn to him. I don't say anything.

"Is it okay if we walk the rest of the way together?" he asks. I know he's asking something else. "I see so many thoughts racing through your mind," he says softly. "Care to share what that sharp head of yours is thinking?" He looks nervous.

I'm nervous too. "You can walk with me," I say, and start moving again, forcing him to follow.

"What will you be doing at the weaver's house?" he asks, in step with me.

"Weaving." I raise one eyebrow.

It's his turn to laugh.

"Actually, at first, probably not weaving. My mother says Mária's training can help me learn everything I need to someday open my own shop, but that's not really what I want to do. I don't mind the weaving so much anymore, but I have no patience for the endless drudgery of carding and spinning wool."

"Sounds like something else I know . . . something that takes a lot of practice and preparation."

I snort.

"It will come," he says, "and when it does, you'll be the finest weaver in Trnava . . ."

My cheeks flush and the little bird in my chest flutters its wings again. "It's nice to hear someone say it like that."

"What, Trnava? It does have a certain charm when it rolls off the tongue, don't you think?"

I bump my shoulder into his arm. "You know what I meant."

He rubs his arm as though I've hurt him. "Mmm, yes, weaver, it does have a certain flair to it."

"Shush," I say, trying to figure out where he's going with this.

"Then I guess I won't ask you what it is you most want to weave. Never mind. You didn't hear that," he teases.

My cheeks hurt from smiling.

"I'd like to weave holy things, not curtains for the house. Things like a *parochet* for an *aron kodesh*, or a *me'il* or a *mitpahat* for a Torah."

His eyes catch mine and I see the light that dances there. "What about a *tallit*?"

"Maybe . . . someday," I say hesitantly. *I know what he's asking. It is customary for a bride to give a groom a* tallit *on the eve of their wedding.*

"Well, if you ever do weave a *tallit*, Sarah Bat Isaac, I'm sure it will be unlike anything that anyone has ever seen before. Like you."

I don't reply. He found me in a thorn bush, following him, snooping where I shouldn't be—not exactly the qualities one looks for in a wife. My only reputation is as a troublemaker—a firestarter. People say Guvriel is destined to lead his own *kehilla* one day. Why would he want to marry me? Surely his father would want him to pick Hannah instead?

"Will you be needing an escort home?" he says.

"I think I'll remember the way now, thank you."

"I don't mind . . . " His words trail a path on the wind.

My mind races faster than a galloping horse. What does this mean? Are we no longer keeping our meetings a secret? I see he's watching me, waiting for my reaction.

"Work hard and well, Sarah. Perhaps I'll be waiting here at the end of the day when you finish," he says. I can hear a bit of dejection in his voice and my heart clenches. None of this was ever my intention. I didn't go into the forest to find a husband.

"Well," I say, playfully tossing my hair in his direction the way I see the other girls in town do when they think the boys are looking. "I guess that depends on if you can get your nose out of the Talmud in time."

"It's not really that big, is it?" He laughs and points to his nose.

I shake my head.

"Then perhaps we will meet again," he says. "It's not every day that someone compliments your nose." He waggles his eyebrows and turns back the way he came, humming a *niggun* to himself and dancing a bit, then stopping to spin in the center of the road, his hands outstretched to the sky. The dark fog lifts for an instant—the sky growing just a little bit brighter.

He is silly and funny in a way I never noticed before, and I have to take a few deep breaths to calm my heart before I turn to walk the rest of the way to Mária's shop. *There is no lesson in any book I've read that tells you how to manage this.* And with all these swirling thoughts in my head I open the door to the shop, grateful for the distraction he provided because I didn't even have a minute to be apprehensive about my first day of work.

Levana

"The stars in the sky and the moon up above mark every aspect of our days and nights," Abba says as we walk home from synagogue.

I know he's right, because they mark mine.

"Before Rav Hillel fixed the Jewish calendar, it was up to us to look to the sky for the moon. Until two witnesses saw the slightest sliver of moon, the new month could not be decreed. The moon reminds us that every month we need to search for the spark of light within us. When the sky is darkest, when we think there is no light, that's when we look to the sky for the moon. It reminds us that no matter how dark the sky gets, it is only temporary. Light is on its way."

But we haven't seen the sky in weeks now. A thick black fog coats Trnava like a blanket. We are anything but warm. I want to ask him what it means when we can't see the moon and stars at all, but I don't because I'm scared to hear his answer.

I know the stars are there even though we can't see them. The moon is the same even if it hides its face from us. It is always a ten-day-old moon that shines on Yom Kippur night as we disavow our oaths, a full moon blazing like a lantern on Tu B'Av when girls dressed in white go out to the fields to dance by the light of the moon. There is an order to the sky—the moon is not fickle, even if this mist is.

Still, everything feels diminished without the light from the skies to guide us.

Abba says, "If you help someone find the path to righteousness you can be like a star in the sky that shines forever."

Maybe that's the only kind of light we need right now.

I want so badly to be a shining star.

Hannah

21 Tevet 5120

There was a hero's feast to welcome me home. Neighbors delivered barley bread and orange cakes and nut and raisin studded pastries. Eema made spicy fish soup with caraway seed and pepper, and Abba took out *pálinka* to toast my return. It's all delicious, and kosher, and it brings tears to my eyes to be home and surrounded by family. These are nearly the same words I wrote over a month ago when I first left home. But now I miss Jakob. Caring for his mother gave me a purpose, a routine. How will I fill my days now that I'm home? I miss their large comfortable home, a kitchen and cellar filled with anything I could possibly be tempted to eat, my room, the gardens and long walks with Jakob—our conversations.

I laid awake last night in my old bed. Levana was in her small bed by the window and Sarah slept beside me. This house once felt palatial—I used to think how lucky we were that father had built us our own room—separate from the kitchen and living space, separate from where Eema and Abba sleep.

Now I felt as though the walls were closing in on me. My room in Jakob's home had stone walls and a large hearth where a fire was always lit. I had an impossibly large bed all to myself, and the ceiling was so high it felt like it contained the sky.

It says in *Pirkei Avot*, *"Who is rich? He who is happy with his lot."* I'm not sure I am happy anymore, which is the strangest thing I've ever felt. My stomach feels empty, even though I know it's full.

"Sarah." I tapped her shoulder after I tried for hours to fall asleep last night. "Sarah, are you awake?"

"What's wrong?"

"Nothing's wrong; I wanted to talk."

"Okay, so talk," she said, and it made me wonder what had happened while I was away. *What could she possibly be upset about?*

I stared at the ceiling above our head. I wanted to tell her that I felt so alone, as though I was a different person than I was when I left. But I didn't.

"Hannah?" Sarah said.

"Yes?" I replied.

"What did you want to talk about?"

I fished around for something to say. "What was it like here while I was gone?"

"Quiet, I guess. Quieter." I felt her shrug. "Nothing much happened."

"Did Abba ask you to join him in the study at all, to help with his work?"

"No. I spent most of my time by the hearth, weaving." But the edge I used to hear in her voice is gone. "What was it like there?"

I wanted to ask her more, because clearly something did happen while I was gone, but I hoped she'd tell me on her own. "It was ... really different," I said. "The house was made of stone. The dining room could seat thirty. And the Duchess Eliszabetta's room was twice the size of our house. There were arched brick cellars under the kitchen, full of wine and mead and spirits, dried herbs and stores of honey and grain, smoked meats and salted fish. You've never seen such plenty." The words spilled out of me.

"Wow," she said. "What was your room like? It must have been palatial."

I'm pleased by her interest, realizing how badly I needed to speak of what I'd been through. "The first night, I didn't think I'd be able to sleep all alone in such a large bed. There were strange noises and scents. But I was exhausted, and I slept on a feather-filled mattress, with pillows and endless warm blankets. I fell asleep almost instantly. I've never been so comfortable."

"That sounds like a dream . . ." she sighed. "What was the duchess like? Was she nice?"

"Not at first. She was quite ill when I got there and I didn't know if I'd be able to help her. But slowly I got her to drink broths and sip teas. I worked with tinctures like Eema taught me and laid my hands on her body to ease the inflammation and stimulate blood flow. Eventually, it worked. At first, she was suspicious of me, I think. But Jakob was always kind. He went to the yeshiva to understand what I could eat and brought me food from town. One day I came back to my room and there were two new dresses made for me."

"Did you wear them?" she asked, and I turned to her in the darkness.

"Of course I wore them." I laughed and elbowed her. She giggled. It was so nice to chat with her like that. Lately things have felt strained between us.

"What color were they?"

"One was green and gold, and the other was pink, with froths of lace."

"I wish I could see them," she said. Then she asked, "What's he like?"

I was surprised by her question. It wasn't the type of thing Sarah would have asked before, and I realized then that she'd grown up a lot while I was gone. "Jakob's the sweetest ..." I stopped, picturing his warm smile, his thick blond hair, his startling eyes, the taste of his lips ... "But he's gone now," I said, shaking my head to rid it of the images. "Who knows if he'll ever come back." My eyes filled with tears and I turned my face to the wall so that Sarah wouldn't see.

"You love him," she said. It wasn't a question. And I wondered how she knew.

I didn't answer because I felt like if I did, the small flower of hope that was blooming inside me might die from lack of air.

"It was like being a princess," I said instead. "A real princess."

"A Jewish princess," Sarah replied. "Can you imagine that?"

I shook my head. I couldn't—I can't. And that's exactly the problem.

It is said that Elijah the prophet himself enters the garden of Eden and sits under the tree of life and writes down the names of those who celebrated the holy Shabbat in his book. It is for this reason that we speak of Elijah during the Havdallah ceremony. We smell spices so that the rotten scents of the light of Gehennom will not return, for there is no scent to the light of Gehennom on Shabbat. But on the holy day of Yom Kippur the scent does not return, so then, there is no need to make the blessing over spices. It is customary to wash one's eyes with wine after the blessing, so that one might get a glimpse of the world to come.

–The Book of the Solomonars,
page 13, verses 3–8

The first person the mist took was Tomáš, the baker's son. He wandered too close to the beech trees of the Satu Mare and into the dense fog. But trouble didn't start until Jozef Kováč went missing. He set off into the forest to cut down lumber for the house he was working on in town, and was never seen again. The next day his daughter, Katarina, wandered off and never returned. Then people began to fall ill. The black spots moved from the trees, to the walls of homes and from there onto clothes and skin and tongues, into lungs and hearts.

The mist infected dreams and nightmares. It rose into a storm and the storm rose into a blizzard and soon the town was covered in black frost. It was not an ordinary kind of frost. It was the kind that stings your lips and nose, that pinches at your fingers and toes like an itch you can't scratch but drives you wild nonetheless. Neighbors turned on neighbors, blaming each other for failed crops, and chickens and children died in the night from the cold.

The Duchess of Trnava woke in the middle of the night and spoke a name. *Sssssssolomonar*, she hissed, the "S" crackling on her tongue like lightning. The word spread like smoke.

The community turned to Reb Isaac. "Is there nothing you can do?" But the holy Reb Isaac knew he couldn't control a storm that had taken root in the hearts of men. It attacked their souls and turned into hatred—and that kind of climate is beyond even the ability of a Solomonar to dispel.

Sarah

onths go by. I turn thirteen. I meet Guvriel every day on my way to Mária's. He's always rushing in my direction, disheveled, with a silly grin on his face, and he's waiting for me each day when I finish. It has become too dangerous for any Jew in town to wander the streets alone. Every day, we fear someone will accuse Abba of dabbling in the dark arts, or Eema and Hannah of spreading the mist. But that won't stop them from trying to ease the pain of those who are suffering, from going out on house calls under the cover of night. Even the non-Jews have taken to walking in pairs. Everyone looks at each other with distrust. But I refuse to stop working at Mária's. Now that I've gained a measure of freedom, I won't give it back.

We don't understand why the mist seems to pick and choose the homes it enters. Sometimes, all the wisdom in the world cannot explain the workings of the world. And it has affected our community as much as any other one. There is no street in town that is untouched by its darkness.

"Sarah, I have something to ask you," Guvriel says as he walks me home one day—our hands are by our sides, so close that sometimes they brush against each other—a ghost of a caress that gives me chills, like having a fever. He has become the center of my life—a light and wisdom I am drawn to, like a moth that can do nothing else but try to get close to the flame. I never understood how the light of God glowed in my father's veins until I met Guvriel. It is he who has set the light in my veins aglow with wisdom and a thirst for knowledge, but more than anything, with understanding.

My thoughts drift on the wind, distracting me.

"In times like these, we can't afford to wait," he says.

"I agree completely."

He stops and looks at me, his eyes wide, searching mine as if he seeks truth in them. "Does that mean you say yes?"

"Wait . . . to what?" I wrinkle my brow in confusion.

"I asked you to marry me . . . well, to give me permission to ask your father for your hand, which is really the same . . . "

"What?" I splutter. My heart leaps in my chest and my eyes go wide. He is everything good that has happened to me. My hands find each other and they are ice. I rub them together nervously. I want this, don't I?

"If it's too early, I understand and I will wait. I will be patient. But it is you I want to spend my days with, Sarah. Only you. I've been trying to gather up the courage to ask you for weeks."

I swallow hard. Am I ready for this? But this is the way of things. I look down at my hands.

"You can think on it. I don't want to . . . "

"Yes," I blurt out. "Yes, you may ask my father."

My emotions change as quickly as the weather. I try to stifle the grin that spreads across my face. A wind picks up. My chest fills with a surge of flame. It's a strange feeling—one I've never felt before. I press my hand to my heart and let out a breath.

"You feel it too?" He puts a hand to his chest, over his heart. "The Talmud in *Moed Kattan* says that every day a *bat kol* issues forth in a heavenly voice that says, 'The daughter of so-and-so is destined to be the wife of so-and-so.' I think that's what I'm feeling. The echo of that voice."

"I . . . I don't know? Maybe?"

"You have made me so happy, Sarah. I can't wait to go tell my father, and to speak to yours. I never understood what it meant, when Ben Azzai says in the Mishna that we should run to perform even a minor *mitzvah*—I've never wanted to run to do a *mitzvah* before in my life. But right now, all I want to do is run. I mean, I won't," he says. "I'll stay right here by your side and walk you home, but I want to run."

"So run!" I say. "I'm not stopping you."

"Later, I will run through the forest to proclaim how happy I am. I will sing *shirah*, but not now. Now I'm walking with you. My . . . soon-to-be betrothed."

Girls my age are already married. He's right to ask me. But Hannah isn't married yet. My chest feels tight with a sadness that says I am not deserving of this happiness. I'm not good at heart like Guvriel. I'm not obedient and devout. Something's going to ruin this for me. It can't be this easy. Not for me, Sarah Solomonar, town firestarter.

*   *   *   *   *
*   *   *   *   *

Later that night, I follow Guvriel into the forest. He comes to fetch me in fox form. He waits until Abba leaves the house, then I follow the lead of his bushy red tail back into the woods. It is a dark night, the coldest I remember, even though it's already spring. He runs ahead and circles back, again and again, full of nervous energy and excitement.

But I can't shake the feeling that something's very wrong in the Šenkvický wood. When Guvriel shifts back and comes to sit beside me, I can tell from his face that he doesn't have good news.

"Your father refused," he says.

"What?" I'm outraged, even though something inside me knew this was coming. "Who does he want me to marry?"

"No, no. He approves of the match. He won't allow us to marry until Hannah does."

Father's verdict knocks the breath from my lungs. I knew this was coming, so why am I upset? Tears freeze two trails down my cheeks and I shiver and wrap my arms around my chest.

"Sarah, don't be sad. Please. Seeing you cry . . . I feel as though a knife is slicing through me. I'm so sorry." I see that tears brim in his eyes too. "I never wanted to make you sad. I would never have asked you if I thought it would cause you pain. He didn't say no forever, just no for now." There's a hopeful lilt at the tail end of what he says, and I want so badly to hang onto that, like the curve at the end of a letter. I want to reach for it—for him, but I can't help but feel it like the blow it is. My father slamming yet another door in my face.

"What proof does he have?" I rage. "What *pasuk*? Please tell me! In what verse does it say that she gets to marry first?" I scream at Guvriel, though I know that none of this is his fault.

I'm angry at my sister and my father. Burning with rage. All the feelings I'd worked so hard to suppress ignite within me. I hear a sound, and Guvriel grabs my shoulders and moves me aside as branches crack off the tree above us and fall to the ground at our feet, smoldering.

"Sarah . . . " Guvriel cautions. His arms are around me and now I'm full of fire of a different kind. I'm still so angry, but his arms make me go still. This is forbidden.

"My whole life . . . " I say, my voice strained, my hands clenched into fists.

"Sarah, you need to breathe." Guvriel's gentle voice urges me.

I let out a breath in a huff. "She's always . . . I've always felt like she gets the first pick—the first of my parents' love and atten-tion—the first choice when it came to chores—maybe even the

first of the talents our parents gave us. I always get her leftovers.
She gets life and the ability to make things grow, and she leaves
me with fire—with death and destruction."

"No," Guvriel says. "You don't see yourself like I see you.
You're a hundred times stronger than she is. You're smarter, and
funnier, and so talented you haven't even scratched the surface of
what you can do. When Nimrod threw Abraham into the *kivshan
ha'esh*, what happened? There's a *midrash* in *Psachim* that says
that the angel Guvriel told God that he wanted to go save him.
And do you know what God said?"

I shake my head.

"God said, 'I am unique in my world and he is unique in
his world . . . It is only appropriate for a unique one to go and
save a unique one.' But in reward for making that offer, God
told Guvriel that he could save Abraham's descendants—
Chananya, Mishael and Azarya, when they would be thrown
into the fiery furnace. You are unique in this world, Sarah.
I wouldn't want it any other way. It is not for nothing that
I am named Guvriel and you are named Sarah. Sarah was
Abraham's wife. Our souls come into this world with their
own destiny; they choose when they come to earth and whose
bodies they inhabit. None of the things that happen to us are
by chance. I promise, Sarah—I promise that I am your angel,
your Guvriel and no one else's. I will go into the fiery furnace if
I have to so that we can be together. What is time in the grand
scheme of the universe? Nothing. I would wait for you until
the end of time."

His face is so close to mine that the tears that fill his eyes spill
over and wet my cheeks, and there is no force in the universe that
can keep our lips apart.

Maybe we are but a link in a chain of tradition that stretches all
the way back to the great King Solomon himself, but the blood
that runs in our veins feels connected—like we are part of some

giant body—something larger than ourselves. Our lips touch and fire transfers—from my lips to his.

He moves away and I'm frozen still in shock. *He kissed me.*

"I'm still mad," I say, but my voice is steadier, "because I know that if I was in her situation, I would never stand in the way of her happiness." We hear the crack of another branch, and I smell smoke.

He looks up, then back at me. "I kiss you and the first thing you have to say is, 'I'm still mad?'" he laughs.

I scowl. But then his laughter wins me over.

"That's more like it," he says tenderly. "You know, that's what I love about you. You always do the unexpected." He tucks a curl behind my ear. "But we need to get out of here before you set the woods on fire."

Everything hits me in one full swoop, like a gust of razor-sharp wind. *Love. He said the word "love".* He smiles wider as he watches my face, like he can see what's going on in my head.

"I love you too," I say, and all the anger in me drains away. "I'll wait. I don't want to, but as long as you never leave me, I'll wait for as long as it takes."

The sky grows brighter above us, as if with a rush of flame, and he leans in to kiss me again. He spins us out of the way just in time, as another smoking branch falls from the canopy above.

Levana

My eyes wander the night sky as though I'm lost in a labyrinth. When I'm awake, my eyes dart across the horizon, and when I'm sleeping, I pace the corridors of the sky in my mind. I'm searching for my star. I know I will recognize it when I find it.

At night, my lessons continue, but when I go to bed, I can't stop looking at the stars. Weeks go by, then months, then a year, and still I don't find it.

I learn that each star has an angel which is like the soul of the star.

I learn that every star in the universe has a name.

Abba tells me that the time and day on which a person is born is directly related to the stars, which map out a person's destiny. The alignment of these stars at the moment a person is born is called his *mazal*. It is why we say "*mazal tov*" when good things happen.

It means that the stars have aligned in our favor.

I wonder which angel watches over me, which ones were brought into the world when I was.

"The sky is a scroll," Abba says, "and the things written there are constantly changing. No two stars are the same. The roots of human souls are found in the stars. Every soul is a tree, whose roots are in the sky but whose branches touch the earth. Though most of us don't know that our souls beat in harmony with the stars in the sky. We are all connected, Levanaleh," my father says.

I know we are, I want to say, but I don't. I want to know which star is his.

✦ · ✦ · ✦ · ✦ · ✦ · ✦ · ✦ · ✦ · ✦ · ✦ · ✦

But Eema tells a different story. She braids my hair at night before bed—her weave sure and strong, my hair like the *challah* dough she plaits in the kitchen.

"Every star is a soul who died here on earth," she says, "planted firmly in the sky to shine down on us. My mother is up there, and my father, and my father's father, and one day Nagmama too. Every star has memories. Every star burns with the story it has to tell. It is our job to listen to the stories," she says. "The stars never forget; they see everything, and they remember, even when it feels like we are in a time of darkness."

✦ · ✦ · ✦ · ✦ · ✦ · ✦ · ✦ · ✦ · ✦ · ✦ · ✦

I'm not sure my mother and father's visions of the stars are the same, but I feel as though I can hold both things in my head, that these different versions of the sky can dance together.

I only wish I knew which part of the story I belong to. I know I will have to forge my own path, someplace between my father's words and my mother's thoughts to find my spot in the sky.

The place where I can shine brightest.

Hannah

27 Kislev 5122

Today I helped Eema as she made her rounds through the community. We visited the sick—there are so many now—and brought them food and medicine. We spent most of our time visiting Rivka Levin. Her husband Avraham, bless him, has his hands so full with their six children, he doesn't have the time to sit by her bedside. We brought them *challot* for Shabbat and chicken soup. He's worried about what will be with his vineyards, and this year's wine—the mist has afflicted the vines. The weight of Rivka's illness is heavy upon him. I don't know how he'll manage if she doesn't pull through. He can barely look at her, and when he does, I only see fear. What will be if he takes ill as well? Who will care for their children? Sometimes it's too much to bear.

I can't believe it's been two years since I last saw Jakob—two years since I moved into his home to help heal the duchess. Two years since the Black Mist first spread tendrils of rot into our community. Now, there is no house that is not affected.

The notes from my time at the duchess's home proved invaluable for Eema, and we have implemented much of the same treatment as standard for all those who suffer. Our services are in high demand since word spread about how I cured her—a miracle, they called it—though we still don't know if it was the mist. I suppose it's a good thing we've been so busy: I've had less time to dwell on the fact that we've heard nothing from Jakob. Of course I'm aware that Abba will soon suggest a match for me. There is a limit to how long I can wait—and worse, my waiting prevents Sarah from marrying Guvriel.

I think it's silly that Abba is intent on making her wait—though if you ask me, she is nowhere near ready to run a home of her own, which makes me think (and hope) that I am not the only reason Abba insists that she waits. It's definitely put a strain on our relationship. Sarah has become insufferable.

I know Abba and the others go out to the forest and do everything they can to stave off the infection, but the Black Mist is relentless in its pursuit of all living things.

It's almost time to light the Shabbat candles, and tonight we must light the Hanukkah candles too, so I must go. It was nice to find a pocket of time alone to sit and write down my thoughts. I've never stopped praying for Jakob's safe return. But perhaps the time has come for me to move on. Today, when I light candles, it will be the last time I say a prayer for him. It is time to let go.

28 Kislev 5122

My life has been forever changed by the events that transpired this Shabbat. God has been gracious to me.

We lit the Shabbat candles Friday night and Abba also lit the lights of the Hanukkah *menorah*, then he went off to synagogue.

Eema, Sarah and I sat by the fire. First we prayed, then we read. My eyes drifted to the door a few times. Usually someone in the community comes knocking—someone who needs our help. But this week everything was silent, and I almost fell asleep in my chair.

An hour or so later, Abba came home from synagogue with Guvriel who was telling him about a new student at the yeshiva—a real prodigy, with strange ways and a strange accent.

"Abba, did you . . . ?" I stopped myself, and said, "Shabbat shalom," instead.

"Shabbat shalom," they both replied.

"Has there been any word?" The same words I've repeated so many times upon his return from prayers, from the yeshiva, from town, from other cities he's visited. But there is always the same response. Nothing. No word. A new student is likely just that—someone new from somewhere else, part of yet another family trying to flee the mist as it pursues them.

"Shabbat shalom, Sarahleh, Levanaleh," Abba said, looking around the room, "and my Esther," he said to my mother.

"Shabbat shalom," Guvriel said, but he only had eyes for Sarah.

"Hannah." Eema put a hand on my shoulder. "We've talked about this . . . Even the duchess has given up hope." Her eyes flitted between my face and Abba's and I knew then that they'd already begun to discuss my future. "He disappeared like a wisp of smoke. We're only lucky that he left before the mist set in, that she hasn't yet blamed us for his disappearance."

Abba and Guvriel continued their conversation as Eema spoke to me. "His mind is extraordinary," Guvriel said. "I've never met someone so versed in the intricacies of the laws. The details he picks up on, the things he asks, it's as if he's come from a different place and time. There's passion in his eyes and deep intelligence—something that only comes from years of diligent study. And strangest of all—nobody knows who he is."

"You should have invited him to join us for supper," Abba said.

"Oh!" Guvriel twirled one of his long red sidelocks. "How could I have been so blind? Oh, rabbi, I was so eager to walk with you, and to see my betrothed, can you forgive me for the oversight? Of course *hachnassat orchim* comes first. It was only my desire to exchange words of Torah with you on the way that blinded me, which is of course, a form of vanity and—"

"Hush, now," Abba said. I rolled my eyes. I would never have the patience for that boy. My sister can have him.

"Why don't you run along and see if he can still come?" Eema said.

"And if not, there will be other meals and opportunities," Abba added. "You've done no wrong, Guvriel, don't worry. Go, see if you can still catch him."

"Yes, rabbi." He nodded, "Yes, absolutely." He looked at Sarah and said, "I'll be right back."

I realized that I'd been nervously tugging at my hair. Levana took my hand away and laced my fingers with hers. "It's going to be okay," she said.

I stepped over to the window where Sarah watched Guvriel walking back towards town. He slid a bit, kicking up the snow as he walked, his sidelocks bouncing in the wintry air.

"Could it be?" I whispered to her.

"I don't want you to get your hopes up," Sarah said.

"Esther, set for one more, just in case," Abba called from his seat as he warmed his hands by the fire.

"Levana, come here and help," Eema said.

"It sounds like he's been learning for years, Hannahleh," Abba said, trying to make me feel better, but only managing to make me feel worse. I knew that everyone had given up hope that Jakob would return. Even me.

A few minutes later, I turned from the window and went to the kitchen to help Eema.

There was a knock at the door and Sarah called my name. "Hannah! They're back!"

"Rabbi Isaac!" Guvriel said as he burst in. I was drying my hands on a kitchen cloth, and walking towards the door. "Sarah, my intended," I heard Guvriel say.

"Shabbat shalom, my name is Jakob."

My face drained of color. It was as though everything in the universe paused in that moment. My heart stopped beating. Every eye in the room went to the face of the man who entered through the front door. *Could it be?*

"Jakob?" I said, my fingers pressed to my lips. I couldn't believe I'd said the word—his name—out loud.

"Yes, it's me." Tears studded his eyes like the clearest of diamonds.

I crossed the room and leapt into his arms. I didn't care in that moment what Abba would think, what Eema or my sisters might see. It was him, my Jakob—older and dressed like a Jew—with a small golden beard and sidelocks! But it was him. There was no denying it. He came for me! I let go and stood apart from him, both our faces flushed with embarrassment, our eyes wet with tears.

He looked over at Abba. "Shabbat shalom," he said. "Thank you for inviting me. I have fulfilled my vow. I know it is not customary to speak of these things on Shabbat, but I have come back to ask for your daughter's hand in marriage. I hope you can make an exception."

"Yes!" I breathed for what felt like the first time in two years. "Abba, please say yes." I took Jakob's hand in mine. I had to touch him to believe he was actually real.

Abba closed his eyes and took a deep breath. He looked at Jakob, taking in his dress—like any other yeshiva student—and the light of Torah in his eyes. "You have taken on the laws of Moses and Israel?" Abba asked.

"I am Jakob the son of Abraham now."

"Welcome, Jakob, son of Abraham. Welcome back and welcome home. I am a man who keeps his promises."

"Oh, Abba! Thank you!" I looked at Eema, tears brimming in her eyes too. "How soon can we get married?"

Jakob and I took a walk after dinner. It was frigid outside but we didn't care. There was so much to discuss, so much to tell. I couldn't believe that he gave up everything he had to be with me—that he devoted two years of his life to study and a religion not his own, just to come back and ask for my hand. I can't write down all the things we spoke about—it was everything and nothing at the same time.

My cheeks felt like they would split, I was smiling so hard, and his hand in mine felt so right—like it filled an empty space inside me. Everything has changed—we are both two years older than when we'd last seen one another—not a boy and a girl anymore, but a woman and man, and yet, it was as though no time had passed. Only that now he is a Jew! Our children will be blessed with my family's abilities through me, and Jakob will now study at Abba's yeshiva, I'm sure of it. My life has changed in an instant. What Abba says is true—the salvation of God can come in the blink of an eye.

I must go, as it is late. Eema says we can marry as early as two weeks from now. How I wish it were tomorrow!

On Shabbat eve it is customary for women to light two candles—one for remembrance and one for protection, because I have put out the candle of the world. Before the world was created, it arose in God's thought to create a light to illuminate it. So He created an intense light over which no created thing could have authority. The Blessed Holy One saw, however, that the world could not endure this light. So he took away a seventh of it. When you study Torah for its own sake, and when you light candles, you bring back the hidden light, for wisdom is the light of the stars in the night season.

–The Book of the Solomonars,
page 28, verses 12–17

As the beast reared its terrible black head and the Black
Mist grew and grew, the holy Reb Isaac and his disciples
began to pray day and night for deliverance. There were
moments of light in the darkness. Moments when Reb
Isaac raised his cloud dragon, balancing precariously on the
air of prayer, and dispelled the mist for long enough that
the town got a peek at the moon through the clouds—
stars like freckles across the face of sky. There were days
of sunshine here and there, some hours of light. But for
the most part, everyone knew that things would get worse
before they got better.

While the people of the town panicked, the Solomonars
did the only things they could—they followed the traditions
and laws set down in writing by the holy Reb Isaac. They
prayed for deliverance, gave more charity, were kinder to
each other. And they got ready to celebrate a wedding.

Sarah

I put aside the *tallit* I've been weaving for Guvriel to work on a veil for Hannah. The *tallit* is the first thing I've ever woven with intent. Guvriel taught me about *shehiyah*—being fully present before doing something, calling upon the spirit of God, harnessing the light within me, to infuse what I do with divine intent. This is what he does before he turns into a fox. And now, when I weave, I try to work on channeling those things too.

"Every one of us has our own kind of magic," I hear him say. "I have mine and you have yours, and our preparations are going to be different because of that. It's not something I can teach you. I only know that when I read about Rabbi Akiva and the foxes on the Temple Mount in *Megillat Eichah* on Tisha B'Av, my heart leapt inside my chest, and that was how I knew what I needed to be. But you have the power to be anything you want to be."

I try to keep his belief in me at the forefront of my concentration as I sit beside Eema and we work on getting everything ready for the wedding. *A snake*, my mind says. *You're a snake.* Levana sits quietly and works beside me, reminding me that even families who bicker can find ways to come together for a common goal. She doesn't look off into the distance dreamily, or murmur words out of prayer books the way she usually does. *If I can be anything I want to be, then I can weave anything I want to weave*, I tell myself. *I can achieve whatever it is I set my mind to as long as I believe that I can.*

I've been repeating these things to myself. Now that my abilities are growing, I have to draw courage to make use of them. No more *resist resist resist*. It's certainly easier to weave when my mind is elsewhere, thinking of loftier, more important things than warp and weft. Guvriel has taught me more in the past two years than my father ever did. When I'm with him, I don't have to resist anymore. Instead of feeling anger and betrayal, I try to channel everything into weaving a future with Guvriel—one without secrets—one full of power and prayer, of fire and ice, devotion and sacrifice.

We are like opposites that go hand in hand, Guvriel and I, and I pray that the *tallit* I weave for him will protect him from all harm—even the fiery words of my wrath. I add charms into the silver and gold thread I adorn it with, incantations that will infuse the garment with protection. If he's willing to walk into the *kivshan ha'esh* for me, the least I can do is weave him some kind of protection.

It's different when I weave a veil for Hannah. I hide it from her, though she knows I'm making it, only because I want the design to be a surprise. I fold strawberry leaves and berries with small white flowers bursting off their vines into the lace. I imagine the Hebrew word for "health" and weave those letters into the word "strawberry". I weave lilacs for love and integrity, and add daisies for fertility and new beginnings. Running down the center of the train, I weave a tree—the *etz chaim*—the tree at the heart of everything we hold most sacred. The tree whose roots are in the sky but whose branches reach down to touch every one of us. I speak the words *"ner tamid"* for the eternal flame of passion and *"ohr eyn sof"* for the infinite light of God, and I pray its light will suffuse their life together.

I don't resent Hannah anymore, not like I used to. She's had a hard time too—waiting as long as she did. Every day is another step in the direction of finally being with him. Every day is a test I must pass. Guvriel has helped me understand this. That God has His reasons for everything in the world, including keeping us apart for now. He says that our joining, the thought of which never fails to warm me up inside, is going to be something so special, so otherworldly, that God needs to prepare the world for it, and that he and I must prepare ourselves too.

While Hannah and Eema prepare food for the feast and fuss over every detail, I sit in the bedroom I share with my sisters and weave. At Mária's shop, I work on Hannah's dress. But I cannot be seen mouthing words there, so I don't add any flourishes. The dress is simple and elegant—and Mária gave my parents a very big discount on it because of me. But the veil . . . it's something more. It's the first time I'll be able to show Abba what I can do—not only with my hands, but with my heart and soul, with my intentions and abilities. I can't wait for the day of Hannah's wedding, for Abba to see my hard work, but also because it means that I'm next.

Levana

While Sarah weaves a veil and Eema and Hannah fret with all the preparations for the wedding, a sense of dread grows in my belly.

I try to find a way to tell Abba what I see. I can't imagine that he doesn't see it too. But as the day of the wedding grows closer and closer, nobody seems to notice.

The day they've chosen is not an auspicious day. I see only a constellation that looks like a dragon in the sky—a serpent. I see the letters of its name lighting up the heavens—*teli*, it calls itself, and no matter how many times I look at the sky, I see it looming over us.

It glitters, black and menacing, arching across the sky.

Hannah

29 Kislev 5122

Jakob and I sat with Eema and Abba tonight to discuss wedding plans. "I don't want my mother to know I'm back," Jakob said. His voice was strong and steady, but my heart broke.

"I'm not the same person I was," he said. "I have a new family now." His eyes were clear and untroubled. But I wanted to tell him that he is the same to me. That if it were up to me, we would marry tonight. Something small. My family, two witnesses, and the sky. God forbid that the Black Mist should ruin the ceremony—or further infect others.

But Abba says that it is only right to do things as they should be. He said that if we really wanted our union to have a powerful effect on nullifying the heavenly decree that's brought on this mist, we might consider getting married in the Jewish cemetery, outside the gates of the city. The power of such a ceremony could help push back the mist, but the thought of doing such a thing chills me to the bone. I don't want that kind of omen hanging over my marriage.

What if it doesn't work? What if the Black Mist comes anyway?

9 Tevet 5122

Levana dusts the lids of my face with silver. My heart leaps inside my chest. I only want to go outside and greet my groom, but I must wait until they finish signing the *ketubah*, until they call me to lead the procession of guests that will accompany me to the *huppah*. This trapping of lace is the only thing holding me back from being with him. I yearn to be in his presence. To hold his hand in mine and know that nobody can take him away from me again.

There's a knock at the door! I must go.

10 Tevet 5122–sometime in the middle of night

It's nearly morning, today is a fast day, and we don't know what the day will bring. I can't sleep, so I might as well put these words down. I may not get another chance.

Sarah knocked on the door to tell me it was time for me to make my way through town to the *huppah*. The ceremony was held in the central square of the Jewish quarter. I held Eema's hand tight as she stepped beside me, carrying a candle encased in glass. Normally, the groom's mother would have held my other hand, but Nagmama held it, steady and true as a rock.

"Ready?" Eema said.

"Of course she's ready," Nagmama answered, and I smiled at that. I took the first step forward to meet my destiny.

The door opened and it felt like half the town was waiting outside to walk me to my wedding canopy. I took a deep breath and we walked out the door. Sarah and Levana followed close behind, making sure my dress and veil didn't snag on anything. All the women in the town accompanied me. They hummed a soft and mournful melody as we walked and a breeze blew through town for the first time in what felt like months. It rustled my veil and I remember thinking that it felt like the wind approved—like maybe Abba had even rustled it up for me. Like it carried within it all the souls of my ancestors guiding me to my groom. Despite the Black Mist and the things our community was facing—for a moment in time, everything felt right with the world.

When we reached the town square, the men of our community were already there surrounding Jakob like an army of guards. They parted to make room for me. He wore all white, as per the custom of the Solomonars, wrapped in Abba's own prayer shawl, and the sight of him was more beautiful to me than any blooming flower.

Looking back, that was the last moment that things felt right. Instead of the music and song that I knew I should be hearing, the men dancing me down the aisle to meet my groom, I heard a gasp in the crowd. Then another. At first, I didn't pay attention. My eyes were shining only for Jakob, but then his eyes departed from mine and I watched as they darted through the crowd. I was filled with panic—why wasn't he looking at me? What could possibly spoil the perfection of this day? I heard whispers but I kept walking.

"Eema!" I whispered. "What's happening?"

"The duchess is here." She gripped my hand so hard it hurt. "She fainted."

I knew at once that it was a bad omen. Abba leaned over and whispered something in Jakob's ear, but Jakob shook his head. Abba looked at Eema, and he gestured for her to keep walking even though no music played.

We'd only told the closest members of our family about Jakob's true identity. It is forbidden to tell others the identity of a convert. We kept his secret as close to our hearts as our own. But someone must have told her. Someone must have known.

I reached the *huppah* and before I started circling Jakob seven times, I was close enough to hear Abba ask Jakob again, "Are you sure we shouldn't delay the ceremony?"

I took Jakob's hand in mine, even though we hadn't said our vows yet, and pleaded with both of them, tears in my eyes. "Please, no. We've waited long enough."

Jakob looked at me with resolve and said, "*Libavtani, achoti kallah*—you have ravished my heart, my darling bride." He turned to Abba. "Marry us now, Rabbi Isaac—I won't make my bride wait any longer."

Jakob slid a ring on my finger and said the words that would bind us together: "*Harei at mekudeshet li kadat Moshe ve'Yisrael.*"

The wind blew colder and clouds rolled across the sky. Clinging to my happiness, I dismissed it as a blessing. Jakob wrapped his prayer shawl around me and drew me close to him as Abba recited the seven blessings. When Jakob broke the glass to mark our mourning for Jerusalem, it felt even more meaningful than ever, standing as we were, on the eve of the tenth of Tevet.

Then there was a cheer, a raucous cry—*mazal tov!*—that broke the silence with a kind of light that cut through the grey mist above us. That was when the music began in earnest and I started to think that maybe everything would be okay.

We spent a few moments alone together in the Ben Amram's home—they live closest to the town center. Guvriel and his brother Aharon stood watch. Jakob held me in his arms and my eyes filled with tears, I wanted to say something, to ask him about his mother, but when I opened my mouth to speak he silenced me with a kiss. We didn't stop kissing until they started to knock at the door and sing, beckoning us out of the house and back to the party and celebration.

We danced until I thought I would faint, and though I felt the absence of his mother on the dance floor like a dark sinkhole in the ground, I tried not to dwell on it. Tried to dance around it. *I've married Jakob* kept racing through my mind. *We can finally be together, and no one can tear us apart.* Not his mother, not my father.

The night felt like it dragged on and on. I only wanted to be alone with him again. As the band played one of my favorite melodies, *"El Givat Ha'Levonah,"* and I was spun from arm to arm, Sarah passed me to Nagmama, who passed me to Eema, who pulled me close and told me that the duchess was still here—a sullen, silent guest. I tried to put it out of my mind. In that moment, I was blind to anything but my own happiness. I reached my arm out to spin the next person who reached for me. I was sweaty and my face was flushed, and our dance echoed the raucous notes of the song. I was spinning. Our town was full of life and spirit in a way we hadn't experienced for so long.

But soon the dances ended and everyone began to disperse. Jakob and I stumbled hand in hand from the town square to the small house he'd rented for us, close to the Malženická gate. Abba's students and some of the rabbis from the yeshiva jumped and sang the whole way there. I worried they sang too loudly, but everyone in town knew there was a wedding happening, and nobody complained. We made it to the front door without incident.

When we stepped inside and closed the door, we could still hear them singing. We laughed a little at their antics, and the sounds of their voices soon faded.

"Hannah," Jakob said in a hoarse whisper. "My bride." My heart took off at a gallop. I couldn't believe he was finally holding me in his arms for good.

"I'm so sorry about my mother," he said. This time I pressed my lips to his. I didn't want to hear any more.

"I have something to give you," he said into my hair. He turned to the table, then slid a wooden box in my direction. I reached for the latch. Inside were two shining silver candlesticks, intricately carved with all manner of tree and woodland creature.

"They're so beautiful," I said, and I knew what I had to do. I placed the candlesticks on the windowsill, then went to the kitchen and rummaged around until I found candles. I lit the wicks like Eema taught me. "This is the law of Solomon," I said. "Man and woman, *ish* and *isha*: without the *yud* and the *heh*, they are *esh*—fire." It felt so fitting that this was the first thing I did as a married woman in my own home.

In retrospect, it was a big mistake.

I'd never felt the power and meaning of the words the way I did then—fire like a tangible thing between us. I felt as though I'd been granted a new life—a chance to make a mark in the world, with Jakob finally by my side. His hands touched my shoulders and we watched the dance of the flames. He kissed my neck softly and my body burned bright as the fire. I wanted to feel the heat of his skin against mine. He undressed me— anticipation making both of us tremble, his fingers fumbling with the stays of my dress. I couldn't believe that I, the daughter of Reb Isaac Solomonar, had married a duke! And he'd given up everything to be with me—like in *The Book of Ruth*: "Your people are my people, your God my God." We made love, quickly, hungrily. We spent a few blissful hours together, then melted into sleep.

As dawn broke there was a knock at the door that set my heart racing. We looked at each other in fear. Jakob got out of bed and pulled on his shirt and pants and I pulled up the blankets to cover me.

He opened the door.

Standing on the threshold was his mother, the duchess. "My son! My Jakob! Why have you forsaken me?"

"It's early in the morning, my lady, why are you out like this? You must watch your health," he said quietly.

"You're not even going to invite your mother in?" She raised her voice.

"I am a son of Abraham now, the son of his wife, Sarah. I ask that you leave me be. I am with my new bride."

The duchess let out a wail and she sagged against the door of our house, just below where Jakob had affixed the *mezuzah* earlier that week.

"She has bewitched you!" she cried out, loud enough for all the neighbors to hear. "I see the lights she lit in the window—they are the mark of the devil."

"I must ask you to leave," Jakob said.

I was terrified—I'm still frightened now. It feels like nothing good will come of this.

"Repent, my son," she continued. "Come back to claim your birthright please! I beg of you. You are my heir, and an heir to the throne of the kingdom of Hungary!"

"My birthright is here."

"Admit the truth! That you are my son! We will welcome you back with open arms. You will no longer be accused of being a traitor to the throne. Be reasonable, my son."

"A traitor? Since when is marrying the woman I love a traitorous act? I must ask that you leave."

"You have foresworn your birthright. If you don't repent, the king will have no choice but to sentence you to death. I will not be able to protect you."

People gathered in the street; I could see them through the open door.

"Jakob . . . " I said from the bed. "It's okay, we'll find a way to be together. Go with her."

He turned to look at me. "No. I'm never leaving you again."

"No son of mine will stay married to a Jewess," the duchess spit.

"Then you leave me no choice," Jakob said. "Good day to you." He shut the door in her face.

Jakob took me in his arms. She pounded on the door for a

while, begging and crying for him to listen to reason. I cried as Jakob held me. "What will become of us? What will she do to you?" I said.

"Hush, my love," he whispered into my hair. "We have each other now, and that is all that matters."

After he left for the synagogue, to tell Abba what had happened and seek his counsel, I sat down to write these words.

There's another knock at the door . . . I must go.

★ . ˙★˙ ★ ★ ˙★
★ . ˙ . ★. ★ . ★. ★

What happens next is written only on my skin—recorded in the very marrow of my bones. It is too much for anyone to write and not a story I want to tell.

Sarah knocked at the door. Guvriel was beside her.

"They came to the synagogue." Guvriel was breathless. "They took him away. I'm so sorry. There was nothing we could do."

"What do you mean they took him?" I screamed.

Sarah reached for me, but I turned away from her and threw my coat over my nightdress as we ran in the direction of the synagogue. And then I saw him. Strung up on a cross. His beautiful body that I'd just been naked against was tethered to a pole. The king's men were laying kindling at his feet.

"No!" I shrieked. "No, Jakob! *No!*"

Sarah held me back, and I struggled against her. "Go get Abba. Tell Abba. There must be something we can do!" I kept screaming. I couldn't stop.

"Guvriel, run," Sarah said. "Tell my father, and don't let them catch you."

"Hannah, go! Leave! Run away!" Jakob said, tears streaming down his face. "I love you . . . " His voice cracked. The king's executioner lit the fire at his feet. "I am a son of Abraham," Jakob shouted at the sky. "I die by the grace of the true God, *Adonai. Sh'ma Yisrael, Adonai Eloheinu, Adonai Echad.*

"Sarah, take her away from here," he shouted. He closed his eyes and all I could see were the tears that wet his perfect cheeks.

"No, I won't leave you!" I yelled back.

"Sarah, please ..." he begged as he cried. "Take her away. Save yourselves! Run."

"Come on. Hannah—we need to go tell Eema and Abba. Maybe Abba can still do something, come." Sarah tugged at my arm.

But I was sobbing too hard to see reason. All I wanted to do was reach for him. "Please ... No, don't leave me."

Sarah kept trying to drag me away, but I wouldn't move. I thought about the ten martyrs whose stories we read on Tisha B'Av. *I must bear witness. I want him to know I never left him.*

But when his screams started, something broke inside me and I collapsed. Sarah half carried, half dragged me away. My muscles wouldn't work anymore.

Nothing works. Nothing matters. All is ash.

I tried to turn and run back. "Hannah, no." Sarah latched on to me. "Come. We must go. Now. There's no time."

All is fire-singe and flame.

I stumbled after her. She was pulling on my arm with all her might, her grip so tight I felt the bruise of it. When we reached home, the door was wide open. "Eema!" Sarah screeched. "Abba!"

The worst kind of fear settled in my belly.

But then we heard Eema's voice and I choked out a sob of both relief and pain.

"Sarah? Hannah? Thank God you're safe. What's happ—?" She saw me and her face fell, and it was more than I could handle.

"Oh Hannahleh," she said. I sobbed against her shoulder.

She cried with me, and I didn't know where her sobs began and mine ended.

Mine didn't end. They will never end. I still cry now.

"Eema, we have to leave." Sarah started packing.

But I can't leave him. I don't want to.

"My candlesticks." I tried to stand up. "And my books. My journals. I need my candlesticks. We have to go back and get them!"

"Hannah . . . we can't," Sarah said. "Eema, they've tied him up in the center of town . . . they lit the kindling . . . " Her voice cracked. "They're calling for more blood. She can't go back."

I moaned and swayed again.

My beloved is in pain. He burns . . .

I started shivering and couldn't stop.

"They will come for us next," Sarah said. "We have to leave now!"

"Jakob . . . " My hands shook. My body trembled. The world was one big earthquake and I was falling into it again and again—an endless tumble into an abyss of flames and ash.

"Quickly," Eema said. Sarah helped Eema bring me to the bed. "Keep her here. I have to pack," she said. Sarah sat beside me and stroked my head.

An instant later, there was a pounding on the door.

Levana peeked through the window. "It's Abba and Guvriel!"

Eema unbolted the door and let them in.

"Esther . . . " Abba said, breathless.

"We're already packing."

"Where's my mother?" he said.

"Not here. Was she at *shul*?"

Fresh chills washed over me.

"I will go find her." Abba opened the door.

"No, rebbe, I'll go," Guvriel said.

"Can you pick up Hannah's candlesticks and her journal on the way back?" Sarah said to him.

I understood in that moment what my sister was willing to sacrifice for me. My stomach rolled. "No," I said as I tried to get up. "No, no. Don't send him. It's not important. I'll go."

"You're not in a state to go anywhere," Sarah said.

"Please don't let him go!" I grabbed her dress. "Don't you see what will happen?"

I can't let her do this. I won't have Guvriel's death on my head too.

"It's okay. I have to go," Guvriel said. "My father's waiting for me at the synagogue."

"Be careful ..." Sarah rushed over to Guvriel. She put her arms around him and they kissed. She took his face in her hands and looked into his eyes and said, "Come straight back here. You hear me? No heroics."

He blinked, stunned by her display of emotion. "I promise." He pecked a kiss on her lips again, blushed, then went out the front door.

I feel helpless. Empty. I want to die by his side. I don't want to live in a world without Jakob.

Eema packed up whatever she could take from the kitchen while Sarah and Levana folded blankets and clothes.

I am hollow. There is nothing left for me in this world.

"Isaac, what about your *sefarim*?" Eema asked.

"We don't worship books or objects," Abba said.

I saw Sarah pack the *tallit* she'd been weaving for Guvriel. Eema slipped her prayer book and her remedy logs into a bag, and gave *The Book of the Solomonars* to Levana, who put it in her pack. "I'll keep it safe," she whispered.

We heard another knock. It was Guvriel, safe and back with the candlesticks and my journal. But not with Nagmama.

"You didn't find her?" Abba asked him.

He shook his head. His eyes looked haunted.

Sarah went to embrace him, the look on her face a mixture of relief and fear. It hurt me like a punch to my gut.

"There's no sign of her. They've barricaded up the synagogue. They're going to set it on fire. There are people trapped inside. I can't stay," Guvriel said. "I have to help. They're trying to get the Torahs out. They want me to take one through the window, then run and hide it in the woods. I'm the swiftest . . . "

"I'll come with you," Abba said.

"No," Eema and Sarah said together.

"Isaac, you will do no such thing," Eema said.

"But my mother . . . " he said. "The Torahs! I must."

"If she's trapped inside the synagogue, there's nothing you can do. You'll get yourself killed. You yourself said we don't worship objects."

"A Sefer Torah is different," he said.

"I said no heroics," Sarah said to Guvriel. "You're here and you're safe. Please stay with us. Don't leave me."

"We need you here," Eema said to Abba. "And I won't lose more than one groom in a night," she said, looking at Guvriel. "You are already like family to us."

My heart stopped. I closed my eyes.

My groom. My Jakob. I could still hear his screams. Why was no one trying to save him?

"My community needs me," Abba said. "What if I could save everyone? How can I not even try?"

"Sometimes you need to save yourself first. Get your family to safety . . . " Eema replied.

"Rebbe," Guvriel said. "My rebbe, with all due respect—" He bowed his head before my father. "—please, go. Find a safe space in the forest. Your wife is right. You may be the only one who can save us, but first you have to save yourself. Get out. Get your family safe. We will join you as soon as we can. You may be our only hope."

Abba's eyes met Guvriel's and I didn't understand what passed between them, but I saw steel resolve in my father's eyes.

Guvriel gripped Sarah's hand and squeezed it. He kissed her again. "Many waters cannot quench love; rivers cannot sweep it away. I promise—" He looked at her with purpose. "—I will come for you. I will go save one Torah if I can, and then I will follow you into the woods. I swear it." And then he bolted out the door.

My parents' eyes met across the room.

"Okay," Abba said. "Let's go. We will walk through the forest until we reach the closest clearing and then I will see what I can do. It's the best chance we have."

Abba held Eema's hand, and Eema held Levana's hand, and we set off. I could barely feel the ground beneath my feet.

Everything I have is gone. Jakob is dead. My Jakob.

Each step took me further away from him. There is a Jakob-shaped hole inside me which grows larger every minute. I fall into it, over and over and over again with each breath I take. I couldn't write any of these words down if I tried—they are scalded into my soul, his loss written across my face like a searing brand.

All I am, all I used to be, is no more.

I am a scroll of ash.

There are three dreams for which you must fast even on Shabbat: he who sees a burnt Torah scroll, he who dreams of the last moments of Yom Kippur, or if one dreams of the walls of his home falling down.

–The Book of the Solomonars, page 19, verse 2

★ . ★ . ★ . ★ . ★ . ★
. ★ . ★ . ★ . ★ . ★

The thing about the Satu Mare forest, which was also once called the Royal Wood, was that it was the kind of forest that had a way of changing those that walked through it. Long before the mist made people disappear, there were tales told of a shepherd who walked into the forest with three hundred sheep and never returned. There were tales of a place at the heart of the forest where nothing grew. There were stories of lights that popped up in strange places—sparks of fire and faces that appeared in the barks of trees. It was whispered that if you weren't careful, strange black roots would curl around unsuspecting ankles.

Rabbi Isaac understood two things: he had to find a way to fight the center of the darkness, and he had to keep his family safe. And so they fled, out the Lovčická gate, and into the belly of the Satu Mare forest—right into the depths of the Black Mist itself. They knew they might never return. But the holy Reb Isaac hoped against all hope that he would somehow find a way to change their fate. Because if he didn't, all would be lost. The forest would change him. Their way of life would be gone forever.

As they tumbled through the trees as fast as their legs could carry them, bony branches tore at their clothes while dark black roots which seeped smoke grabbed at their ankles. Rabbi Isaac and his family kept running. They ran until they could run no more. And then they stopped. And Rabbi Isaac turned into a beast of fog and set off to confront the Black Dragon.

Some might say that the forest demanded a kind of sacrifice that night. An exchange of power. A transfer of flame. That Rabbi Isaac knew very well what he was doing and why. Others think that theirs is just another tale of a family whose faith went up in flames in the face of unspeakable horror. A family that would never be the same again because the Black Mist that afflicted the forest would change them forever.

Levana

I hold Eema's hand as we walk through dense forest. We have to stop every few minutes so she can catch her breath, step over a root, duck under a branch. We can barely see a foot in front of us. The mist is everywhere.

Abba said we would walk until we came to a clearing, but there doesn't seem to be one in sight. Eema's hand is clammy and when she doesn't grip mine so hard it hurts, she's shivering.

I don't say anything. I'm scared to speak, scared to do anything that might reveal our presence in the woods. We may never see Nagmama or Guvriel or Jakob ever again and yet I know there are still stars in the sky. Even though we can't see them, I can feel them. They are still with us—just in a different form.

How can the stars still shine so bright when everything down here is darkness?

How dare the stars still burn when everything down here is ash?

Sarah stumbles and falls. I turn to her, but Eema pulls me back. She gets up, looks behind her again, and keeps walking.

Hannah doesn't look back at all—she walks as if she's lost in a nightmare.

Light starts to bleed from the trees, leaching us of color. With every step that Hannah takes, the trees lose more of their leaves. They fall like ash around us. Everything is darkness, and every sound could mean our doom.

I don't feel safe. I may never feel safe again.

* * *

Eventually, we stop to rest. Abba looks around. He puts his hands on his hips and sighs, but his shoulders tremble.

Abba looks at Eema and she nods; he walks into the depths of the forest.

"Come, girls," Eema says. "We'll set up camp here for the night."

We sit in a small clearing where the leaves and branches form a canopy above us. When Hannah sits, hunched over, the branches reach for her. The forest grows darker and the Black Mist settles on the ground. The branches look sinister.

Hannah looks as brittle and dry as the dead trees around us.

Sarah stares over her shoulder—back the way we came. Then she looks in the direction that Abba went. Her neck turning back and forth in each direction. It looks as though she wants to follow him, but she also wants to stay put.

Then she gets up and follows Abba, leaving scorch-marks like a trail that anyone could follow.

Eema goes after her, places her hand on her arm in a way that brooks no argument. Sarah comes back and sits down.

Hannah stares at nothing. Every few minutes, I see her shiver. I want to reach out, but Eema sits beside me and holds my hand. I don't let go. She needs the comfort. Her eyes close tight, clenched against a fear she won't put into words. I see the slightest tremor of her lips moving.

Maybe I should pray too.

The mist rises around us.

★   ·   ★   ·   ★   ·   ★   ·   ★   ·   ·   ★   ·   ·   ·   ★   ·   ·   ★

Abba comes back hours later with a rabbit. I can see it still twitching in his hands. It isn't kosher, but nobody says anything. Not Eema nor Hannah nor Sarah.

He skins and guts it and gathers twigs and branches. But the second he lights a spark, Hannah stands up, one hand on her stomach, and lurches into the bushes, retching into the underbrush.

Eema releases my hand and gets up. She puts her arms around Hannah as she sobs, her body heaving in Eema's arms.

Abba stuffs his fist in his mouth as if he wants to scream, then he stomps out the sparks of the fire with his boot and walks away.

★   ·   ★   ·   ★   ·   ★   ·   ★   ·   ·   ★   ·   ·   ·   ★   ·   ·   ★

When he comes back, the rabbit is gone, but I can still smell the rust of blood on his hands. He sits down in the clearing and doesn't say a word.

The mist grows thicker.

I sit next to Sarah, but she barely reacts to my presence. She keeps searching the forest, eyes on alert.

I lay my head in her lap and her hands smooth my hair. I don't think she knows she's doing it. It's a reflex, something left over from the life we left behind.

Faint smoke rises from the earth around her, ethereal and

strange. Like something about to combust. The pressure is rising, but she doesn't notice.

*

Eema gets Hannah cleaned up and coaxes her back over to where we sit. She smooths her hands over Hannah's hair, humming soft sounds to her.

I'm hungry but I don't want to break the silence, so I curl up and try to snuggle my head further into Sarah's lap. I turn my head and try to see the stars through the mist and the trees.

At some point, I see Sarah's eyes close. I move out of her lap, slowly so as not to wake her, then go sit next to Abba. He opens his eyes.

"Why did this happen?" I whisper.

A tear falls and hangs, suspended like a crystal off his beard. He stares out into the dark, his eyes like the dying embers of a fire.

"I don't know, Levanaleh," he says. "I don't have any answers."

Hannah stirs and starts to sob again. I move to get up, but Abba stops me.

"There is nothing you can do," he says.

It takes a long time for her to stop shaking.

*

I move closer, trying to soak in some of Abba's warmth. But tonight he feels like the dry husk of a giant tree.

I'm trying so hard to keep my eyes open that I don't even notice when they close against my will. I open my eyes when Abba gets up. I lie silent and still so he thinks I'm sleeping. I count to twenty, then I follow him.

I see him stop in a nearby clearing. He puts his arms up to the sky. Light streams down into his palms. He shouts out something like a bellow, but no sound comes out of his mouth. Light pours from him like an echo of sky. I have to shield my eyes it's so bright; I'm nearly blinded by it. I don't understand what he's doing, or why. Only that this moment feels important. There's a weight to it that settles in my chest like a stone.

Abba's face is clenched in concentration. He's there one minute, then gone the next. I look up at the sky and there's a dragon of light in the darkness burning, my father on its back. He flies away and I watch the trail of his tail like a comet streaking across the night sky.

Only minutes go by, but it could be hours. I can't stop staring at the sky. And then as quickly as he left, he comes back.

The dragon's light is dimmer, and his head hangs low.

Light pours back into the clearing and my father with it.

"Abba?" I say. "What happened?"

He doesn't reply. I don't think he sees or hears me. He looks older now, sad and empty.

"All is ash," he whispers, then he wails at the sky, fists punching air. "Why? Why did you take them from me?"

My father is a great rabbi, a man who loves God with all of his heart. But the man I'm watching curses God; he turns his face away from the sky and doesn't look back.

My heart is a dark black coal—burning up inside but covered in ash. I swallow hard and wince against the pain. I won't let the fire go out.

I vow in that moment that I will never fall in love—not with God, or a man, not with any living thing. Love brings pain, only pain: this is what I've seen.

I return to where my mother and sisters sleep. I lie on my back and stare at the patches of sky I can see through the trees. The world has profoundly shifted, yet the sky doesn't look any different.

I pray silently to the God I still believe in, the one who made the sky and all the stars in it, for deliverance. *"Ani maamin,"* I say, "I believe with my whole heart in the coming of the Messiah. *Ani maamin*—I believe." I chant it silently, over and over again, hoping that maybe one of the stars I can see is an angel in disguise.

Sarah

I stumble through the trees, but these are not the same trees I've come to know and love at night, with Guvriel beside me. These trees are different—darker and more sinister. I tell myself that he promised, that he said he would always come for me. But all I can see in my mind is a fiery furnace with black-tipped flames that don't care who they touch or burn. *Some fires cannot be put out,* my heart tells me. *Some fires are unquenchable*—and as badly as I want it to apply to the love I feel for Guvriel, my mind completes the thought for me—*in their thirst for revenge and destruction.*

He doesn't have the tallit, I keep thinking. *How can I protect him from the furnace if he doesn't have a shield?*

I search the brush for sparks of red-orange, for any sign of a bushy tail. I search the branches of the trees above for the whisper of a wing or the dark hoot of an owl—a sentinel in the form of one of Abba's disciples. I see ripples of fog and mist between the trees and hope there is a face there, mid-transformation, but there is nothing but the beating of our hearts and the harsh thumps our boots make on the forest floor.

I want to leave something in my wake—a trail of crumbs for him to follow—but we have nothing except for the clothes on our backs and whatever we were able to pack before we fled. I can't bring myself to waste food. I have to trust that Guvriel is okay, that he got away, that he will follow because he must, because I can't imagine my life without him. I put my hand out as we walk and lightly touch a leaf, a twig, some bark, hoping to mark a way for him. But instead I leave broken pieces of myself as a trail for him to follow.

The anger rises in me again—my curse that I'd been trying so hard to see as a blessing. What good did it do to wait for Hannah? Everything good in my life is snatched away. Every time I close my eyes, I see him—hair blazing like a halo of flame around his head, and he's marching into the synagogue—our holy of holies, our community's sanctuary, its ceiling like a starlit sky, its walls covered in the seals of Solomon—and everything is on fire. The flames lick the precious parchment skin of our Torahs. And I see Nagmama screaming—is she there? Did he find her? Or did they disappear in the fiery furnace together with the scrolls we hold so dear.

I cough and it feels like ash coats my lungs. My breath is black as tar. The smell of burning flesh is an odor I will never forget. It fills my nostrils and haunts my dreams. He said he'd come for me. He promised. He said that not even a fiery furnace would keep him from me. Or was he just a vessel for a prophecy destined to come true? My curse will consume us all.

We walk for endless miles, feet blistered by the ice that crunches under our boots. We hear packs of wolves howling in the night and I stay awake, huddled under my cloak, hoping he will find me. Maybe if I'd been honest—if I'd told Guvriel my true nature, things would be different now. But I am a fiery serpent, a slithering thing that no one wants to hold. He could have married someone else. Someone warm and full of spirit—someone more like him. But I wanted him for myself and now he's gone.

The forest changes and we change with it. The Black Mist

lifts until it only curls around our wrists. The branches at first claw at us; they try to trip us, to trap us, but after a while we stop running, our hearts stop thrumming heavy panicked beats with every step we take. The branches go from black with sickly rot, to brown with only spots of death. The short stabbing branches, sharp as knives, get smooth and green until healthy moss-covered limbs part for us. There is a canopy of green above us at night. The linden trees shed heart-shaped leaves and their pale yellow blossoms spread sweet perfume. The sky is brighter. We see the stars again. Our pace becomes slower. Our breaths become steady, the air no longer tainted. Our hearts freeze and crack and melt and then reform again against our will. The trees turn pale and the sky fills with clouds so white they blind us with their brightness. The ground is dusted with the first frost of spring. We are entering a new world. One without Nagmama, without Jakob, without our community.

We don't know what landscape the next clearing will bring, and we know nothing of the path of our lives after this. Where do we emerge from the forest, and how? It is clear that we are not the same family that walked into these woods—but neither is it the same forest. The blood of grief chills us from the inside, running through our veins. What if we can't be replanted? I don't think that I can bloom anymore. Everything that was once alive in me feels severed. I never want to light another fire as long as I live.

I will be chaste, I promise the pale green leaves that sprout from the white branches of the birch trees. *I will fill endless cups with the water of my tears*, I tell the fresh clean rivers we pass. *I will be kind*, I tell the finches that flit from tree to tree—just please bring him back to me. Find him. He's a bright little fox with a red bushy tail who knows all the secrets of my heart except one. *Bring him back to me*, I beg the rabbits that we see, bring him back and I'll tell him everything. That I'm here, that I will wait forever and a day if that's what it takes.

"Sarah," Eema says. "Please drink something. You look pale."

And I do. I take a cup of river water from her and I drink. All the fight has gone out of me. All the fire. I am a husk of a girl now, fiercely alone in her sorrow.

Angels don't walk into fiery furnaces. They walk among us only briefly before they return their souls to heaven. Angels shine their light down on us from the stars above. They blaze too bright for this world.

Eema knows she tends to the corpses of our souls. Hannah won't eat or drink. Father still sits *shiva* for his mother, for his students, for his community—alone. With no men to answer amen to his *Kaddish*. Only Levana shines bright. She blazes like a star here in the forest, her soul still filled with the hope of thousands of stars. I hope that she will never live to see everything she ever loved going up in smoke and flame. I hope she wishes on a star and it stays constant for her. It is not a prayer I offer the sky. I don't have words inside me to praise God right now. It is more like a wish I send, buoyed only by my own despair.

My eyes still flit from tree to tree. Searching for fur and fire. I can still hear his voice in my head. I can still feel the touch of his lips against mine.

I promise, Sarah—I promise that I am your angel, your Guvriel and no one else's. I will go into the fiery furnace if I have to so that we can be together. What is time in the grand scheme of the universe? Nothing. I would wait for you until the end of time.

Hannah

Everything is ash.

The tree of life is the heart of the world. The I Ioly One,
Blessed Be He has a single tree and it has twelve diagonal
boundaries. They continually spread forever and ever—they are
the arms of the world and wherever we are in the world, we
are held in their embrace.

—The Book of the Solomonars,
page 47, verses 12 14

Once upon a time, a man and his family emerged from a
forest and came upon a town. In the forest there was a tree
that had been there longer than anyone could remember,
and a cave under the tree that was said to contain the
heart of the world. That is how the man knew he should
stop and make a new home. Because where a linden tree
grows there is peace, truth, justice—and protection against
dark magic. The man's name was Ivan and his wife's name
was Elena, and they had three daughters, Anna, Stanna,
and Laptitza.

This is their story.

Stanna

Papa goes out early one morning and comes back with light in his eyes. Funny. It reminds me how we used to say "May his lamp shine" when someone looked like that, or when we wanted to bless him with long life. But now it feels like that comes from some kind of folktale.

I saw Papa sneak away every night from the camp we made in the forest, every few days another camp, to hunt, and to scout— at least, that's what Mama said he was doing when I asked about it in the morning. I wondered where he went and what he did, but to go after him would be to disobey my parents, and I would never do anything like that. Still, it's been cold at night, especially now that we don't light fires. Anna is afraid of them, and though I don't like to admit it—I think I am too.

We stopped here last night, not far from a line of forest that looked as though it promised a river. Papa went out and when he came back, there was light in his eyes.

"We've reached the borders of Wallachia," he says to Mama. "I've found us a home and a job. I'll be tending to the fields on a large farm near a town not far from here. Curtea, they call it—Curtea de Argeș. The owner of the cabin passed away. The house is vacant. We'll need to clean it up, but it's ours. They say there's a new ruler here, the Voivode Basarab, that he's fair and just. They say he welcomes people of all faiths. It's a place to start again. What say you?"

Mama holds back tears. "Come, girls, help me pack up."

As we make our way through the edge of the forest and emerge out into a field that abuts a large river, we squint at the bright sun that lights everything before us like a picture. Perfect and pastoral. We can see the town of Curtea beyond it.

"*Blessed is He who has delivered us to this day,*" Papa says in Hungarian, arms outstretched to the sky. It's been a long time since I've heard my father pray—the words sound foreign on his lips.

There's a key under a window eave that opens the pad-locked door.

The house is large, with two big rooms—one with a grand hearth, and the other with a stone oven. There is a barn out back and a silo for grain, and even the remains of a small garden. Though we are bone-tired, Mama finds a birch broom and begins to sweep away the cobwebs. She orders us to beat the mattresses and take all the bed linen down to the river. Even Anna helps, and of course, sweet Laptitza—what would we do without her helpful ways? Anna is, of course, still convalescing, but she does her best. She is weak, but Mama says a new start will make her strong.

Hours later, having cleaned and scrubbed, swept and scoured, Papa comes back with a load of firewood and lights the hearth for warmth, though I see how Anna cowers from its scent. My stomach turns, but I squelch it down. It's the warmest we've been in weeks. We must find a way to begin again.

Soon, we collapse onto the pine-stuffed mattresses, grateful for a place to rest our heads that isn't the forest floor. It's been three weeks since I've felt a mattress beneath me and, despite the emptiness I feel, my body can't help but relax, my eyelids can't help but drift closed.

I dream of foxes frolicking in a nearby meadow and there is no Black Mist to taint the sky. I wake up, my heart beating fast in my chest, but I see only my sisters beside me.

The next day, the first thing I want to do is go back into the woods that border our property. I want to find that meadow. I want to wait and see if the fox will come. I will go there every day if that's what it takes. Anna is the only one of us who is still despondent, and Laptitza is eager to join me but Mama fears to let her go, even though we trekked through endless kilometers of forests on our way here. I somehow manage to convince them both—Anna to come, and Mama to trust me. It feels good to finally have her approval.

"Watch the sun, girls. Be back while there is still light in the sky. We don't want to tempt the spirits of the dead." I see Anna flinch.

I take her hand in mine and squeeze it.

Mama is not yet convinced the house is free of the spirits that once inhabited it. But that feels like an old superstition. Something from a religion we no longer follow.

I don't understand why mother keeps speaking of it. Anna is just starting to come back to us—there is a tiny bit of light dancing tenuously on her face, as though it isn't sure it belongs there, and in an instant it's extinguished.

"Oh, Mama," Anna says, squeezing my hand back. "Those are superstitions." She tilts her chin up to the light that shines from the window and I'm so proud of how hard she's trying I could cry. But I don't. I must be strong. For her. For Papa. For Mama and Laptitza.

"Listen to your mother, girls" is all that Papa has to say as he looks up from the wood he's whittling. It hurts me to see him like this—diminished—doing something with his hands rather than poring over tomes like he used to.

"Yes, Papa," I say as I usher my sisters out the door.

I know that Anna's blistered feet match her blistered heart. I've heard her nightmares and her dreams—I've been by her side when she wakes up screaming, choking at imaginary smoke and clawing at her cloak as though it is burning her alive. I curl up beside her on those nights and hold her, soothe her, try with all my might to drain the pain she feels. But I know I can't. Some pain runs too deep. The forest changed us all, but I'm not sure there was enough of Anna left to change.

As we stroll through this new forest, I think about all the endless kilometers of branches we walked through. They say that there are many kinds of forests, with different types of trees and foliage, magical forests, haunted forests, forests with secrets, and we saw them—so many of them—but when you're trudging through the snow with only a shattered heart to guide you, and you don't know where you're going, and the only hope you have is that the place you reach will be better than the place you're fleeing from—all forests look the same. Even enchanted ones. I'm sure that Anna never even noticed the change.

Laptitza straggles behind us, then quickly catches up and takes Anna's other hand. How have we come to this? Three sisters who used to bicker about every little thing—formed and reformed by the flames that took away everything we once held dear.

For a while, it felt as if Laptitza was the log in the pile upon which everything was balanced. If something were to have removed her from the bottom of the woodpile, everyone and everything around her would have come tumbling down. It was a lot of weight for a thirteen-year-old to bear. I'm trying to ease that burden. Trying to look forward to the future. Yet here I am taking them back into the forest with me, because all I want is to look back.

I remember the moment we passed into the borders of Wallachia. It wasn't a line per se, or a border, just a sense in the air that something had changed. It feels the same now—like we're crossing some kind of invisible line. The air is different—like a threat has been removed. Like the forest's taken a breath. I wondered if it was part of the forest's song—the *shirah*. I wanted to turn to and tell Guvriel . . . but he wasn't there.

If you believe in something hard enough, you can make it come true. That's what I keep telling myself. No one will chase us here, no one is after us. There is nothing left for us to hide anymore.

Only that . . . I desperately wanted to be found. Perhaps a fox will appear to me if I will it. I know I'll never stop watching and waiting, hoping to hear the one sound that means he's found me.

*   ⋆   ⋆   *

We're lost in our own thoughts and the soft sounds of the forest, but when we get to the largest birch we've ever seen, Anna pauses. "Here," she says, confirming the sensation I'd felt in my gut, but couldn't name, "this is the perfect spot."

She bends down and starts digging by the roots of the large tree. When she's finished, she gets up and dusts off her hands. She places the silver candlesticks that Jakob gave her on their wedding night in the hole and then covers it with loose earth. "I will plant strawberry seeds," she says, sprinkling them on top of the silver, "together with Jakob's candlesticks. Perhaps they will grow here, and we can come harvest them. And when we eat them I will remember him."

Her eyes are shining and wet.

I'm in shock, because I brought Guvriel's *tallit* out here with me, planning on finding a place to hide it, but I hadn't said a word about it. I start to think that maybe my sisters are closer to me than I ever thought before. That maybe I was always looking to pick a fight and find the things that separated us, while staying blind to all the things that bound us together.

"Anna!" I say. "I didn't . . . You don't have to . . . "

"It's better this way. A fresh start. Papa has forbidden us to light candles in windows anymore."

I look down at my feet and take out the package I brought. Anna nods, almost as if she anticipated this.

I place the *tallit* I was making for Guvriel in a hole beside the one she dug.

Anna puts a hand on my shoulder. "You don't have to."

"I think this is where it belongs. I brought it with me today to find a place for it here. It felt like the right thing to do." I look up at her. "Papa says we will no longer have to cower like a sheep here. We have left these parts of ourselves far behind."

My tears wet the white wool as I whisper a prayer—"*Protect me, God, for I put my faith in thee*" and cover it with loose earth.

I look to Laptitza. Her face looks white as milk in the moonlight, her soft copper hair falling around her face. She bends down and takes *The Book of the Solomonars* out of her pocket.

Anna gasps. "Does Papa know you have it?" she asks.

"No—Mama stuffed it in my bag before we fled, but maybe it's better this way."

"I don't think Papa would want it in the house if he knew," I say.

"Go ahead," Anna says.

Laptitza digs a shallow rectangular hole that looks like a small grave, then gently rests the book inside. I think I see three tears drop onto the book—they look like little glinting stars—but I can't be sure. It's dark and getting darker. She covers the hole she made with earth, kisses her fingers, then presses her palm down to the earth—the way we used to kiss every holy book we opened, or closed.

Anna waves her hands three times over all the little mounds of earth, the same way Mama always used to do before she lit candles. "*With this we leave our past behind us. Dust to dust, ashes to ashes, may the earth consume the past. May these items strengthen the roots of this tree as we put down roots in this new land.*"

"Amen," I say.

"Amen," Laptitza echoes.

"*Blessed is the true judge*," Anna says, because that is what we would have said, once upon a time, had we gone to a funeral in our old town. And I know that Anna's words are not for the candlesticks she put in the ground, but for the funeral she never got to attend.

I take my sisters' hands in mine and we make our way out of the forest.

Suddenly, a fox streaks out of the trees. I take a sharp breath and stop; my heart beats fast. *Maybe . . . maybe . . . maybe . . .*

But it winds its way through the tombstones and disappears into the forest, and of course my sisters have no idea that it means anything to me at all—only that I appeared to have been startled. All three of us exhale, hands held tighter, and keep walking.

Every few steps, I see Laptitza look back, but I squeeze my younger sister's hand in reassurance. "There's nothing to see there," I whisper. "Just three mounds of earth beneath the boughs of a lonely tree. Nothing more."

We are safe here. For now.

We arrive home and get ready for bed. I see Laptitza looking out the window at the forest, then at the sky. I watch her until she falls asleep. When I hear Anna's light snoring, I get out of bed and go to the window, wondering what Laptitza was looking at. And then I see it too, and it strikes fear into my heart. There is a trail of golden stars, shimmering in the moonlight, running all the way from the forest to our front door.

We ran so far and yet the light still follows us.

Anna

10 Shevat 5122

I've started a new log. A new book, for this new life.

The rawness inside me is still there, behind a thin veil, but today I can breathe for the first time in weeks, and so today seems as good a day as any to start. I am not the person I was. None of us are. We were born again in the forest. Made into a new kind of creature—one that survived.

My name is Anna Simion and I am ready to leave my past behind me.

11 Shevat 5122

When I woke this morning in my new bed, in our new home, I felt a tug on my ankle. I woke in a panic, thinking my ankles were bound, I was trapped, I smelled smoke . . . but it was only a strawberry plant that had sent out a runner and curled itself around my ankle as if to keep me there in bed, or here in Curtea. A plump ripe berry sat below my ankle bone. I reached down to touch it and everything crumbled to ash in my hand.

My fingers touched my lips, and I tasted ash on them too—fine and gray and powdery.

Everything is strange and different. I can't separate dream from reality. Did I ever get married? Was I once able to heal with a touch?

I followed Papa out to the fields today. I was afraid to touch anything in fear that it too would turn to ash, but I longed to feel the softness of the earth and the cushion of green beneath my feet. I hoped the scent of growing things might mask the acrid smoke that still fills my nostrils.

We walked side by side along the road that skirts our field, and saw a man driving a horse and cart approaching us.

"Good morning," the man said. "And welcome."

Papa put his hat in his hands, and I saw his bare head for the first time.

"You are a Jew?" the man asked.

"No," Papa said, "just a poor humble farmer. You must be mistaking me for someone else. Good day, sir." Papa kept on walking and I followed him.

This is all my fault. No matter how many times I go over the events of the past, I come to the same conclusion. I have brought about my family's destruction. If I hadn't fallen in love with Jakob, if I hadn't insisted on waiting for him, on marrying him . . . our life would still be as it was. My sister would be married to her beloved. I might have found happiness with one of the baker's sons, or with someone else entirely. But I chose love, and it destroyed my family. It destroyed an entire community. Let no one say that love is not the most powerful force in the world. It is stronger than hate. Love is fire. Raw and devastating in its power.

We continued to walk past the place where the forest meets our field. The strawberries I planted with my sisters earlier have begun to bloom. They are thriving. I don't remark on how fast they have grown. There is no point to the lists I used to make. I only have observations now. There are no answers. I have brought misfortune upon us all. That is all there is to say.

"A blessing," Papa says of the strawberries. "This new land is already rewarding us."

I wish he was right. He doesn't know that I planted the seeds. That I can make anything grow—anything but my heart.

We heard the sounds of hooves in the distance, the ground thundering beneath our feet. My eyes met his and I saw that the father I once knew wasn't there. There was no light in his eyes, no spark of resistance. He took my hand and we ran to the darkest part of the forest to hide.

"Do you think they've come for us?" I whispered.

"There is nothing we can do but wait until they pass," he whispered back.

My father who never cowered a day in his life is broken, crouched and hiding in a forest.

"I will creep to the edge and try to see who they are and where they're going."

"No, Anna," he said.

I'd never betrayed my father before, but for a while I'd been feeling like all the rules we ever had were gone. This was yet another one I was breaking.

I walked forward. My heart matched the sound of the horses' hooves. I don't know what we'll do if trouble truly comes to our door again. I can't bear to lose anyone else.

We didn't flee all the way to Wallachia, didn't discard everything we believed in as though it were a cloak that no longer fit, only to face the same kind of persecution.

Stanna is the bravest of us all. She has the most to live for . . . so I decided to be brave today, like her. I would give my life to be in her situation . . . to still have hope.

Tears smart at the corners of my eyes but I wipe them away.

I crept silently through the trees and made it to the edge of the forest. Papa didn't follow me—he crouched and hid like an animal in the brush.

The sound of hooves got louder and louder and then I saw them. A hunting party. An entire entourage of men who look well dressed—royal. There was a young man in the lead, surrounded by men who looked like guards. They were headed into the forest. To hunt.

My heart beat faster. I had to get my father out of the woods.

The young man at the center of the party called out to everyone around him and they ground to a halt.

His eyes scanned the trees and then stopped. He was staring straight at me. I felt like a deer, caught in dense thickets, unable to move, unable to run. Fear tasted like ash on my tongue. If I ran, he might see the rustle of leaves and open fire. If I stayed, he might come closer and find me. There were no good choices. I decided to creep back, step by step, inch by inch, until he could no longer see me and I could fade into the trees.

I called on the power that was once inside me. It's still there, a tiny glowing spark like a forgotten ember. It stings. I ask the trees to hide me, to protect my father, to make it impossible for him to track me. For them to show us a way out, a way forward.

I'm out of practice. I never thought I'd call on my powers again. But I would do anything to protect my family. Even this. It felt as if it took a long moment—then I heard the slow awakening of the trees around me. As I took small noiseless steps back in the direction of my father, I felt the leaves begin to cover my trail.

Laptitza

L ate that night, after my sisters have gone to sleep, I go back to the forest. I enter the woods near where the strawberries grow. I can still see the path that my feet made. I walk from golden star to golden star—they light my way. There is no fog. The mist doesn't coat the air here—greasy and slick. The moon shines brighter. The stones in my path are bathed in light and I'm able to make my way more quickly—the moon and stars hurrying me along—follow us, this way, you must bear witness.

In the woods where the moonlight is dimmer, the stars glow brighter.

First, I stop in the dark shadows of the forest by the roots of the big tree where we buried the relics of our past. I dig, shoving earth aside until I grip the book with my hands.

I clutch it to my chest and look up at the sky.

I open the book and start to hum a melody—

"Adon Olam—Master of the universe, who reigned before every being was created . . . "

The words are coming from my lips being borne along on the wind. My heart is tight in my chest. I've missed the words of these prayers, the time I used to spend hidden under my father's *tallit* as his followers danced circles around him under the moon.

The words provide comfort to me now, wrapping themselves around me like a prayer shawl. I lie down on the ground. I feel roots, branches, wet leaves beneath me. The earth looks silver-gray in the moonlight and the trees are bent at odd angles around me. The air here isn't thick, dead, wrong, devoid of life. Here, I am moonlit.

I lift my hand. My pale skin is almost blue. I press my hand up to the sky. I need for something to press back. I can't wait any longer. If I am to save my family, the time is now.

I must find a star. My star. My guardian angel.

And that's when I see it. A falling star grows bright and golden as it falls.

Close.

    Then closer.

            As though it is about to fall and injure me.

I know I should jump up, scream, move out of harm's way, but as the light falls, burning its way through the sky, growing bigger and brighter, I am not afraid.

Maybe this is the light my father lost. The light he let go.

I must not be afraid to receive it.

At the center of the fiery mass there is a pulse, a bright spot that glows, reaching for me in the same way that I reach for it. I cup my palm as though I'm waiting for it to be filled. The light envelops my body, wrapping itself around me until I glow. I am starlit.

None of this is possible. And yet, I know I am awake and breathing. It's the moment I've been waiting for. It was written in the stars—a prophecy I'd missed somehow because of all the mist. I see it now, splayed out against the sky. A trail of light for me to follow.

I'm too afraid to move, to say or do anything that will break the magic of this moment. I should be burning up, or frozen solid, but I am neither. Exhilaration courses through my body like a river of light. The *nahar di nur* that father always speaks of runs through me.

As the light starts to recede, only my head is surrounded by starlight. The light pools into one slowly churning spiral that brands my forehead. I can't see it, but I can feel the weight of it, and for the first time, it burns. The light shimmers and shifts and, with one last painful sear of light, it shoots off my head and back up into the night sky.

It is only a trail of stardust now. My forehead burns.

An instant later, I see the blue flame of a star in the sky, slightly brighter than everything around it. This is the star that branches off from the clear path.

My star.

I touch my hand to my forehead. There is a raised mark there. I look at my fingers and see that they shine with what looks like stardust.

I walk back through the forest. Golden stars follow in my wake—brighter than they were before. I slip back into the house, slide into bed and touch my forehead again—my fingers come back shimmering with light.

I stare up through the window above my bed up at the sky. Have I been touched by an angel? Has he come to save us all?

*The night of Passover is a night of vigil, a night when the mazikim
come down to this world. One is not to lock the doors on Seder night
for it is a night when God himself protects us. A night when we cover
ourselves with light like a garment. Though it is said: a wise king is
the upholding of the people, on Passover night there is only one king.*

–The Book of the Solomonars, page 52, verse 9

In a neighboring land, a man named Basarab the First
came over the Caucasus Mountains. Some say he was a
Turkic man; others say he was a Vlach. The circumstances
of his ascension are completely unknown. We only know
that one day, he seized the Banate of Severin from King
Béla and raided the southern regions of the kingdom
of Hungary, then formed the independent province of
Wallachia, which granted freedom of religion for all.

After Basarab the First lost his first wife, who left him
childless, he married Marghita, a widow like himself,
who had been the wife of Radu Negru the Great. She
brought a daughter with her in her belly to the castle, and
Basarab raised the girl as his own. Soon after, Basarab and
Marghita had a boy named Nikolas, and together, they
ruled all of Wallachia.

Anna

4 Iyar 5122

Mama keeps encouraging me to go out to the garden, but I don't know what she expects me to do there. The plants don't speak to me like they used to. Only the strawberries try, each night, to wrap their vines around my ankles.

Stanna likes to go to the forest every day. I know what (or who) she's looking for, but I don't think she will find it (him). Still, it's something to do, so I don't mind. I want to accompany my sisters now. Life can change in the blink of an eye. One spark can mean total destruction. I will do everything I can to protect what I have left in this strange new world.

Today, we went looking for wild mushrooms. Mama makes the best mushroom soup. Where we used to live, the forests were flooded with mushrooms, and this forest is no different, but you need to know which ones to pick. Out in the fresh air, I had a moment today where I thought I could taste the thyme and honey that Mama used to use to flavor the soup. As I put the mushrooms in my basket, the memory of the taste turned to ash in my mouth, the mushrooms to ash in my hands. I dropped the basket. They all spilled out.

I called Laptitza over to me. "Here, you pick these." I didn't explain more. Mama says that here we have nothing to fear. Maybe she's right. But nothing will ever be the same again.

Still, being in the forest nourishes me. I can draw courage from the things which grow in the most unlikely places—seeds that fall and are buried in the darkness but still find a way to sprout. I gather strength from the air around me, from the roots beneath my feet and the sap inside them. In the forest, there is room for new beginnings.

It was perhaps because Laptitza and I were deeper into the woods than Stanna was that we didn't hear the sound of hooves until it was too late.

Laptitza stopped humming a song. Stanna dropped her basket and stared off into the distance.

"What's wrong?" I whispered.

Stanna only pointed, and then I saw them, the same group of men—the hunting party. They'd stopped in a field nearby. Their horses were grazing so close that I could see them breathing and hear their teeth clacking as they nibbled the grass.

How did I miss it? How did I not hear them come? How did the trees not warn me?

"Shhhh . . ." Laptitza whispered.

Then Stanna surprised me. "I'm sick of hiding," she said. "I will emerge from the trees and one of them will raise his head and see me—a forest maiden, raised only on berries, rising up from the darkness of the woods."

Laptitza giggled.

"Stanna . . . " I warned.

"What?" she whispered. "Maybe they're handsome. You could find someone. Marry again."

I brushed off a chill. "Don't."

"Come on." She elbowed Laptitza. "Let's play a game. Who would you pick?"

"What?" Laptitza said, still watching the men.

"Who would you pick?" Stanna repeated.

"What did Anna say?" Laptitza answered absently.

"Ahh . . . we caught you," Stanna laughed.

"Caught me what?" Laptitza responded, still staring at the men in the clearing.

"Anna didn't say anything yet. She was still thinking. You are clearly distracted. Tell us which one you'd pick."

I am not the person I used to be.

I found myself opening my mouth. "If I were ever to marry again, I would bake my husband strawberry bread every day from the berries here in the forest to keep his lips and cheeks pink and his heart red and full so he could stay young and brave and mine forever." I felt the earth and everything around me responding to my words in a kind of hushed chorus: "Amen."

Yet another thing to add to the strange things that keep happening.

Stanna looked at me, eyes wide, as if she couldn't believe I'd spoken. That I agreed to play her silly game. "That's so ridiculous." She laughed. "Okay. I will make something up that matches how wild this conversation really is." She whispered a sound like a call to battle. "If I were to be chosen by one of those fine strapping young lads, which I won't be, but in case I was . . . I would weave him a sha—" I knew she meant to say shawl, but she stopped and swallowed hard and said instead, "—a shirt . . . out of the branches of this tree and it would wrap itself around him and fit him perfectly, and keep him from drowning and protect him from fire . . . " She paused and cleared her throat and we didn't say anything; we just listened to the wind.

Then she continued: "It will leave him unscathed when he fights dragons and other kinds of beasts and he will live forever. There."

"Amen," Laptitza said, and I rolled my eyes, but then the wind picked up and tossed Stanna's hair. I shivered and wrapped my arms around me.

"I wasn't finished." Stanna lowered her voice and the wind seemed to change its tone too, swirling around her and carrying what she said on its wings. "When he puts the shirt on his body, it will turn into the finest armor anyone has ever seen—it will shine silver in the moonlight and gold during the day and it will be intricately carved with branches and trees and all the creatures of the forest. They will protect him too; he will be invincible." A gust of wind sent all the leaves around us up into a frenzy.

I watched the sky. "We should go," I said.

"I thought that was a good one." Stanna grinned. "Because baking bread that will keep someone brave and young is far more realistic, right, Anna . . . ?" She rolled her eyes at me. "Laptitza, your turn," she said.

I can't remember the last time the three of us were laughing and joking like this. It feels like we inhabit another life. Another lifetime.

Laptitza looked like she was holding the most delicious secret between her lips. "I will not marry a man . . . " she said softly, then her voice rose. "I will give myself to the stars!" She laughed and then looked at me and Stanna. "If we're being ridiculous: I will give birth to two boys—twins. And each of them will be born with a golden star on his forehead. Bright as the stars in the sky. I will name one for the star of morning and the other for the star of light. And everyone will think that golden stars are the mark of a king. Not something to be ashamed of anymore."

We didn't say anything after that. There was nothing to say. Our faith is like a stain we can't wash off, no matter how hard we try.

I sighed and it felt like the forest sighed with me, stirring the leaves again. The men turned their heads in our direction. Even the horses looked up from their grazing. One of the men stood. He walked towards us. Suddenly, I felt like the forest maiden Stanna mentioned, brave and bold in a way I hadn't felt in a very long time.

I am not the person I used to be.

It felt like we were standing at the edge of a cliff. At the beginning of a tale. I remember thinking—*maybe I'm the one who should emerge, not my sister. Maybe this is how my life begins again.*

I heard a voice in my head and realized it was Laptitza, saying, "*Once upon a time, three girls stepped out of a forest . . .*"

I took a step . . .

Stanna

I step out from behind a tree. I must be brave. I must protect my sisters. I won't let Anna or Laptitza go out there alone. This is something I can do—for her, for all of us. I am a red-haired forest creature, shy and timid, but brave nonetheless.

The man in the center of the guards gets off his horse and starts to walk towards me. Four guards dismount and follow him. He comes closer, still closer. He moves with the assurance of some-one who has never had to fear anything in his life. I don't know what possesses me to be so brave. But I can't let Anna be the one to sacrifice herself. She has sacrificed enough.

My hands are shaking. Maybe this is a bad choice, the wrong choice. I have a moment when I want to retreat, slowly losing my courage—but before I can take a step back, his hand is reach-ing for me.

"Stop," he says. "Don't go. Who are you?"

He takes off his helmet and his hair cascades down around his shoulders. It's the shade of a fox's tail and I gasp.

"Don't be afraid—I mean you no harm," he says, taking my response for fear. "Where do you live?" he asks.

This is too much. Is it a coincidence that he reminds me so much of Guvriel? Am I seeing my beloved in every reddish hue?

Or is it a sign—an omen? What if Guvriel couldn't come and so he sent a messenger—an angel. We once used to believe in such things.

"I am Theodor, and you are . . . ?" he prompts, now clearly trying to gauge if I even speak his language. My heart patters in my chest like the pulse of a frightened rabbit.

"I am . . . " My throat catches. *What do I say?* He is young, perhaps my age. His eyes are green like the leaves that surround us. But the more I look, the more I see he doesn't look like Guvriel at all. His face is elegant, softer, more refined, with no whisper of hair on his cheeks or chin. I shouldn't be afraid, except he's finely dressed and clearly the commander of the guard he travels with. Yet . . . it is something unnamable I feel. I think of the way Guvriel's orange sidelocks swayed as he walked, the sound of his voice when he laughed, how the hairs on his arm would sometimes brush my hand when he leaned close to whisper to me.

Theodor takes a step, breaking me out of the cage of my thoughts. "Don't be afraid. I just . . . I saw something rustle in the trees—I thought it was a deer! But now I've found you, I must know your name. Please. You are new to these parts?"

"Stanna," bursts out of my mouth.

"A beautiful name for a beautiful girl."

The words feel false on his lips. Only one person ever thought me beautiful.

"Will you join me on the hunt? I can have a horse prepared," he asks.

"I cannot," I say.

He looks taken aback.

My chest clenches. Once upon a time, a girl named Hannah was made an offer she couldn't refuse . . . and look where that led us.

Sometimes it's okay to say no, I think, *or at least, it should be.*

"It is likely not often that you are refused," I say. "I apologize for my rudeness."

He tilts his head. "You intrigue me. If you do not want to join us, I accept that. It is not right of me to impose my will on others."

"I am not from here," I say. "Forgive me if I don't understand the customs of your land." In my head, I berate myself for giving that much away.

"Where do you hail from?" he says.

I pause, racking my brain for a safe answer.

"I must go," I say instead. "I left my basket in the woods. I must find it."

He cocks an eyebrow at me and tilts his head again. "So be it. You have your secrets; I have mine. I wish for you to hunt with me for I would like to learn more about you so I will return to see if I might change your mind. Good day to you, Stanna of the Woods."

He turns and motions to his guards to follow him, and I turn back towards my sisters. Why does he want to learn about me? My sisters pepper me with questions, but I only tell them that the men went away.

We finish picking berries in silence. We have all been shaken by their presence. What it could have meant. But everything will be okay. I know it will. It has to be. I will do whatever it takes to keep my family safe.

Laptitza

I sneak away at night again through the window and out to the fields. I can think of nothing but the light—the way it filled me up. I only want to feel that again.

I get to the clearing and press my hand up to the sky. I wait. And wait.

I wait so long my arm begins to hurt.

Just when I'm about to give up, I see it—a falling star that grows brighter as it falls.

This is it. My heart beats fast.

Close.

Then closer.

I remember how I wanted to run away, but I don't want that anymore.

I don't move—I don't even flinch.

The light continues to fall.

I see a form at the center of it, a pulse, a bright spot that takes shape into a hand of light, reaching for me. I open my palm to the sky.

There's a sensation of frost that touches the center of my palm, then spreads the icy sensation through me.

I gasp for breath. Is this pain? Will I die?

No. I breathe in and out, then in again. It's frosty in my veins, but it generates warmth, like hundreds of sparks igniting within me.

My mouth opens in a gasp—it's an intense sensation I've never felt before.

The light spreads from my palm to my forearm, then my shoulder, it engulfs my chest. My entire body is suffused in its glow. I am bright, but the world around me is brighter.

A laugh bubbles up inside me. I'm happy for what feels like the first time in forever. Like I'm floating on air. I haven't felt this light since we left Trnava. Since the nights I used to follow my father to synagogue and watch his Hassidim dance while they blessed the new moon.

The light takes shape, and that's when I see him for the first time. A man lit up. Naked, clothed only in light.

His hand reaches for mine and the light wraps itself around us.

I turn to face him and hold out my hand.

We are palm to palm and there is something tangible between us.

I stare into his eyes. They are bright blue, crystal clear like a river, with a bright spark of flame at their center.

I can't stop staring at them. Like lamps in the darkness.

Then his palms leave mine and I gasp, missing his warmth, missing the burning.

His hand touches my face, his other hand is on my shoulder and it slowly moves down to my chest. Everywhere he touches me I feel the same glow—burning fierce in its intensity while a chill runs through me that thrills me to the bone.

He traces my face, my hair, my brow, my forehead, my cheek down to my neck, and then lower still. His hands leave sparkling marks everywhere they go. My body drinks in these strange sensations.

Cold and hot then cold again, and everything burning in a way that makes me buoyant. There is warmth between my legs that has never been there before and tingling everywhere that churns and rises through me. I feel I will burst from all the sensation.

I know what I want to do, what I must do. It's the only possible way to express what I feel.

I press my lips to his.

He stops moving.

I take a breath of air, afraid I did something wrong, afraid I broke the spell.

But then he responds. Softly at first, hesitant, almost as if he didn't expect me to kiss him back.

I don't think of my father or mother or my sisters and their burdens of pain and grief. My lips burn icy hot, then his frozen tongue tentatively brushes against mine.

My mouth fills with light.
My lungs fill with a mixture
of heat and cold.
I cry out and my hands
grasp his arms.
Everything inside me

     lights up.

We move together,
light and dark,
silver and gold,
starlight and moonlight.
The sensations explode
in sparks that travel

     through me.

I am a golden star—
bright and burning.
I am the star,
   falling,

     burning.

I feel as though
    I will explode
        into a mass
            of starlight.
He will consume me.
And in that moment,
    I don't care
        if he does.

The light goes on and on
until I close my eyes
and see I am part of the sky—
    a diamond placed in the firmament
    to shine bright and full forever.
Everything tingles with a sweet afterburn.
Smoke should be rising from my skin.
I am so warm, my skin glowing.
My stomach is full and burning.
My legs are streaked with trails
            of silver starlight.
He reaches down and takes my hand in his.
    He brings it to his lips.
        Silver tears fall from his eyes.

He starts to shimmer, then in an instant his body is encased in ice-blue flame.

He grows smaller and glows brighter, until his hand leaves mine and the light leaves me, and I see him, streaking across the sky.

I press my hand to my lips, my body still trembling with the memory of him.

I get up and get dressed and shakily make my way back home.

This was no dream.
There are trails of starlight
between my legs.
My stomach aches.
I wonder if there is still
golden light
within me.

Back in bed, I can't sleep. I roam my arms over every part of me he touched and when I press my hand to the window, I see my hand still glows ever so faintly.

I place my hand on my stomach
and there is warmth there,
pulsing bright.
I still see the stars in his eyes.
A universe of stars—
white-hot specks
against a black sky of sensation.
I have merged with a star,
I have become a part of
the firmament.
It sends a new rush
of thrills through me.

I giggle, remembering how good I felt filled with his light, what it felt like to float. To have no cares weighing me down.

If this is the trail I must follow, then I will. Gladly.

Maybe I can gain the power to change what is written in the stars.

I cannot rewrite the past, but perhaps I can find a way to chart our future.

In the morning, I rub my eyes and feel a moment of panic. Was it nothing more than a dream?

I reach down and touch myself and my hand comes back silver.

I close my eyes and my body is white-hot again, reveling in the memory of sensation.

I look up at the sky. The patterns whisper to me more loudly than they ever have before. The pulse of one bright star echoes within me.

Last night, I added my own story to the pages of the sky.

Stanna sits on the edge of my bed. "What do you see up there?" she asks.

I turn to her, careful to hide my hand under the blankets. "I'm not sure you'd understand."

She lifts up the blankets as if she's asking permission to climb under the covers with me. I stiffen, worried she will know that something about me is different. But then I realize that I've done something that my sister has not done. She never got to be with Guvriel because Papa made her wait . . . even when my friends were already getting married.

It's something I might have lorded over her in a different life-time—but that life is gone.

A wave of sadness reaches for my heart, but I push it back. I scoot over to make room.

"Try me," Stanna says. "Explain it."

I look up at the sky and am silent for a few long minutes. Then I smile softly to myself.

"I'll tell you a story," I say.

"Okay," Stanna says with a smile. "Tell me your story."

Once there was a princess who thought she was alone in the world. She had a mother and a father, but they paid her very little attention. She was their only child—the star in their sky, but because she was an only child, she spent a lot of time by herself. So much so that the stars became her only companions. She would go out onto the balcony off her bedroom every night and look up at the sky and make up stories in the shapes she saw.

She would connect the stars, naming each one by pointing at them, and after a while the stars obeyed her. She would touch one and it touched her back—it would shine a little brighter and shake a bit in the firmament that held it.

She moved her bed so that it was under the largest window, and when it was too cold to be outside, she would open the window and stare up at the sky.

There was one star in particular that was her favorite. It didn't burn the brightest, or shine with a clear glow; it was a fickle star—which was why she noticed it. Sometimes it shone bright, sometimes its light was dim, and sometimes it pulsed, lighter, then darker, wavering a bit, and then shining brighter than before.

She thought the star was restless and lonely like she was. Every day, it appeared in a different place in the sky. Still, she knew that it was hers because of the way it shone. She would reach her hand up to the sky as if to touch it—but it never responded to her touch.

Until one day it did.

She didn't know how it happened, or what she did, but then she saw it spark a bit and streak across the sky leaving a silver trail. It blazed golden for an instant before disappearing.

Had she blinked, she would have missed it entirely.

She sat up in bed, distraught. Had the star died? She didn't understand.

She ran to the balcony off her bedroom and searched the sky.

But it was gone.

Quicker than lightning, she sped out of her room, down the large staircase, through the grand hall and outside, across the forest and into the trees in the hope that she might find it.

She didn't know where to run, only that she had to do something— she had to find the star. She worried that if she didn't find it, the star would be lost to her completely.

Something in her heart led her to it.

For years when she'd looked up at the sky, it was always there, watching her, helping her feel less alone in the world. And now it needed her help.

The princess ran and ran as fast as her feet could carry her, and then she came to a clearing in the forest. There was a tree there that looked as if it had been split in two—it was smoldering, not quite on fire, but full of smoke and ash. She was afraid to go near it, but she knew it was where her star had fallen.

She fell to the earth and started to cry. Her tears became tiny diamond stars that littered the ground beneath her feet. She looked up and saw there was a man watching her. He was covered in ash, and at first, she gasped in fear, but then she saw his eyes were wide with wonder, watching her as she had once watched the sky. His hair was nearly white, his skin pale and glowing in the moonlight.

She recognized him. She walked a step, and then another step until she was close enough to see that his skin shone with an unearthly sheen. She reached out her hand and touched his cheek, and saw him tremble at her touch, and she recognized the way he shivered.

"What is your name?" she said.

The star-man opened his mouth, but no words came out.

"Come with me," the princess said, and took his hand, but the star-man wouldn't follow her. He pointed at the sky.

"I don't know how to help you go back," she said. "I'm sorry."

He pointed at her, then at the sky.

"No, I couldn't possibly come with you. I don't know how to fly. And my parents would miss me. Come back with me to the palace!"

But the star-man only put his hands on her face and traced patterns on her cheeks and on her forehead, on her arms and shoulders.

She stood on her tiptoes and pressed her lips to his.

He didn't move at first. But then he kissed her back and she lit up.

When he touched her, it was as though she was touched by the fire of a thousand tiny stars.

The princess began to cry. The star-man touched his fingers to her tears. He held his fingers out to her as if asking: why do you cry?

"I'm sad because I've waited so long to meet you. Because I'm no longer alone in the world."

He leaned over to kiss her again as if to say, "You should be happy," and also, "You will never be alone again."

This time, she put her arms around his neck and kissed him back as though he was the only star left in the sky.

"Come back with me to the palace," she tried again.

He shook his head.

"I'm cold. I must go back," she said. "At least let me bring you clothes and some food. Where will you live? Out here in the forest? You need shelter. I will get myself a coat, and one for you. Wait for me. I will come back."

The star-man walked back over to the tree and curled up inside the bark.

The princess ran back to the palace as fast as her legs could carry her. She crept into her father's room and took some clothes from his wardrobe. She snuck into the kitchen and stole bread and cheese and fruit. She took a pillow from her own bed, and a blanket from the chest. She placed everything in the blanket, then she ran all the way back to the forest. But when she got back to the clearing, the star-man was gone.

She went back home and tried to pretend that nothing had happened, but inside, her heart hurt, and when no one was looking, tears fell from her eyes.

She waited all day until the sun went down, until she could go back to the tree and wait for him again. It was all she lived for. All she wanted in the world.

Something that could be her own.

I'm silent for a few minutes and Stanna lays beside me, listening.

"It's a beautiful story," she says.

"It's not finished yet."

"Why are you telling it to me?"

"Because I needed to tell it to someone."

"Who told it to you?"

"Don't you know?" I tell her. "The most beautiful stories are true."

And then I turn away from her and close my eyes and try to find sleep.

It is customary to blow the shofar from the first of Elul until Erev Rosh Hashana, in memory of the covenant with God and in order to confuse the Sattan, so that he won't know the exact day of Rosh Hashana. Hope is like dust, blown away with the wind; a thin froth driven away by a storm; like smoke dispersed with a tempest. So too is the sound of the shofar.

–The Book of the Solomonars, page 61, verse 2

It is said that high above the town of Curtea de Argeș, a star shot through the sky and landed in the Șinca Veche forest. Where it fell, it formed a cave.

Ivan Simion's youngest daughter, Laptitza, thought that she was the only one to see it fall.

But she was wrong. Basarab's daughter, Theodora, saw it too, and when it fell, she made a wish. And because such is the way with falling stars and dreams, the wish was granted.

Stanna

The strawberry seeds that Anna planted in the forest under the linden tree have more than sprouted, they've taken over. I see Anna starting to come back to herself. Her face is different. The soil is different—it responds to her touch, even though she shrinks from it.

Every day, we go to the woods together—today we gather berries and roots. Mama needs to replenish her medicine stash.

When Anna and Laptitza walk a bit away from me, I turn back and dig up the *tallit*.

I unfold it and it smells like earth. Like moss and soil. It doesn't smell like Guvriel; it never got a chance to smell like him. I wrap myself in the prayer shawl and break down in tears.

I feel him like an echo in my mind—his voice, his soft and silly laughter—but the more I try to remember his face, his smile, his fiery sidelocks . . . the more his image flits away. I want to wrap myself in this shawl and pray and pray and pray until Guvriel comes home to me.

The world is dimmer without him. The longer I wait, the farther I get from him, and the more I start to believe the ugly truth that he may not ever be able to find me—that he may not have survived. It's hard to let go. I don't want to let go. And yet . . .

Anna is trying and she lost more than I did . . .

I keep seeing Guvriel in my nightmares. I see him sometimes as a fox, and other times an owl, but then the owl turns into a helmet, or the fox turns into a horse, and I see Theodor—his long red hair tumbling down. Sometimes he is Guvriel, and his gray-green eyes stare into mine. Sometimes in my dreams I twine my fingers in his hair, and when he turns his face to me I trace his features with my fingers as if I'm trying to understand them. His face is smooth and chiseled at the same time, and that's when I realize it's not Guvriel I'm touching at all and that I don't have dreams anymore. They're all nightmares.

* * * * * *

I pause in the forest and listen, drawing the *tallit* tighter around me. The wind whispers but I don't know what it says. I close my eyes and try to sense everything around me. Guvriel once told me that I was stronger than I thought I was. I try to listen, to understand what I hear. To practice some of the things he taught me. I feel a pulse. Like the throb of another heart. *Guvriel?* My heart calls. I reach out with my senses, searching for him, for the pattering heart of a fox in the underbrush, but then it's gone and I'm alone wrapped in the white shawl.

I open my eyes and I see movement in the trees. Something's here, making its way to me. My heart skips a beat. I take a step back, search the forest floor for a branch I could use to defend myself.

Then Theodor steps into the clearing.

My eyes grow wide. I wonder how long he's been here, watching me wrapped in what must look like a shroud.

"Sir." I bow my head.

"Stanna." He smiles. "Are you alone this time?"

He is giving me a choice. My sisters have wandered far

away from here, but they are still prey in the forest if he is hunting again.

"My sisters are here," I say. "A ways off, looking for berries and bark."

He offers me his hand.

I take it. The fate of my family is at stake.

"What are you doing here if your sisters are elsewhere?" he asks.

I pull the shawl tighter around me. "Just taking in some silence."

"I like silence too," he says. "I never get it though—there's always a guard nearby." He gestures to the left and I see that one of his guards is indeed waiting beyond some trees. "That's a beautiful shawl you're wearing. Very fine craftsmanship."

I feel as if the wool is burning me. "I made it myself."

"Pretty *and* talented? That's quite a combination."

I know my cheeks should flush at his compliment, but I see my sisters coming into view and I panic. What is about to happen has been set in motion. There is nothing I can do to stop it.

"I'll introduce you to my sisters," I say.

He looks at me and cocks his head as if he's considering what I've said. "I would like that very much," he says.

I smile—I can't help myself. It's genuine, and then I feel sad, like I've betrayed Guvriel. What is wrong with me? Am I so faithless? I turn my head away and blush, embarrassed by my own disloyalty. *He promised he would come for me. I said I would wait until the end of time for him.*

I see Anna's head lift like a rabbit on alert. My eyes meet hers and I see the moment when it registers on her face that I'm not alone. She places herself in front of Laptitza.

"Anna, it's okay," I call to her.

"Theodor," I say as they approach us, "this is my sister, Anna, and my other sister, Laptitza, behind her."

"A pleasure to meet you both," he says and reaches out his hand to kiss theirs. "I am Theodor," he says, "son of Basarab the First."

I gasp, but try to hide it with a cough. I knew he was someone important, but it never occurred to me that we'd happened upon the son of the Voivode of Wallachia. I see Anna glance over her shoulder at the guard. I'm sure she must be as anxious as I am. Nothing good will come of this.

"Why don't you join us for a picnic?" Theodor asks me. "I'm here with my men."

"Oh no." Anna looks down. Her cheeks flush and her breath hitches. "We couldn't possibly."

"Of course we can," Laptitza says boldly, surprising us. "We would be delighted." She steps forward.

Anna looks at me, then at Laptitza. I can tell she thinks this is not a good idea. *Do we have a choice?* I try to say back with a look.

We follow Theodor out into the clearing. There are about a dozen men there with their horses. His guard lays out a blanket, and Theodor takes my hand and helps me to sit down. I'm uncomfortable with this casual contact, but I can't say anything. I worry that acting strange about it will only draw more attention to me.

The guard then steps over to Anna and takes off his helmet. He is tall and blond and broad. His smile is wide. He reaches out his hand. "I'm Constantin." He bows before her.

"Anna," she says, and I hear the tremble in her voice.

"It is lovely to meet you, Anna . . . of the Forest." His eyes are serious, but kind.

"Anna Simion."

Even I can see that his eyes carry the light of the skies in them. "Will you do me the honor of eating with me?" he asks her.

Anna must feel as resigned as I do. There's nothing we can do but be kind and gracious. She takes his arm and motions for Laptitza to join them, but Laptitza looks to me.

I'm about to invite her to sit with me when another man, a young dark-haired nobleman, reaches out his arm for her to take. She curtsies, like this is all a game of make-believe, and follows him over to another laid-out blanket.

What could possibly happen? We are outside under the open sky having a picnic in broad daylight. We have nothing to fear. We have nothing to hide.

Anna

10 Sivan 5122

Today we had a picnic in the forest with the prince's hunting party. I sat beside Constantin and he offered me an apple. I think he was trying to flirt with me, but I've forgotten how to behave—how to function in the presence of strangers—how to talk to a man. I know I'll never love anyone the way I loved Jakob, but for the sake of my family, I must attempt to move on.

He cut the apple and, when a slice was about to fall, I tried to catch it, but it dropped. I laughed and my hand brushed his and then I realized it was the first time I'd laughed with anyone but my sisters since Jakob left this world, and it felt like a cold rock turned over in my stomach. My hand fell from his as though he'd burned me.

"Are you okay?" he said.

"Sorry!" I said. "Yes, just clumsy. Here." I picked up the apple. He took it from me and his fingers brushed up against mine again. This time it was deliberate.

I'm not ready for this. Not yet. Maybe not ever. But I wonder if we might actually be free here to be whoever we want to be—to marry whoever we choose. I'm not sure it matters anymore.

And if nothing matters anymore, then maybe the least I can do is sacrifice my happiness for the sake of my family's safety.

By my actions I denied to Stanna what was taken from me. And worse, I intimately know what she was denied.

The weight of it sits inside me like a stone I'll never be able to dislodge.

Perhaps I do have the ability to repent for what I've done.

I looked back at Laptitza and saw her pick up a piece of bread. She paused before it hit her lips. She was about to make a blessing, her lips about to move silently, but then she looked up at me. I shook my head, almost imperceptibly, my pulse rising. And Laptitza nodded back, the slightest of movements.

I watched her take a bite with no blessing as if it was the most natural thing in the world, and the burden of the path we've chosen smothered me like a wet blanket. Suddenly it was hard to breathe. I put my hand to my chest and Constantin looked at me with concern, but I coughed a bit and recovered quickly. It's not the first time she's had to stop herself, but we must break our old habits if we are to move on. And I must find a way out of my grief if I'm to help my sisters.

It all felt so clear to me in that moment—as clear and crisp as the bite of the apple I took. I had the power to save us all.

Constantin offered me a strip of meat. I knew it wasn't kosher, but this wasn't the first time I'd eaten *treif*. I put it in my mouth, unafraid, and chewed. We make choices every minute of every day, but that doesn't mean that we forget the cost of those choices. I hoped that I never stopped remembering what it was like to be a Jew. But I had to make this choice now. I was Anna Simion, not Hannah Solomonar anymore.

"Are you new here?" Constantin asked.

"Yes, very," I said, forcing myself not to think of Jakob. I took another bite of the tough meat. "Our father wanted to seek his fortune in a new land, and when we heard that the Voivode—"

"Theodor's father," Constantin said.

I paused. "Yes," I said, then swallowed hard, remembering the predicament we were in. But what choice do any of us have if we want to survive? Did I have a choice with Jakob? Or was that too fated by the stars?

"When we heard what Theodor's father had done, the battles he'd fought and won, the type of utopia he wants to build in Wallachia, with freedom of faith and equality for all ... we started walking in this direction," I said.

"I'm glad you came," he said.

I thought, *He doesn't know me at all. He couldn't possibly be glad if he knew me.*

"Me too," I whispered.

What choice did we have?

What choice do any of us have?

Laptitza

I help Mama hang the laundry up to dry. When I go back under the cover of night to meet my star-man again, I will take some of the clothes off the line and bring them to him. Just like the girl in my story. Perhaps if I bring him clothes this time, he will agree to put them on, and then he will come with me.

I don't know what Mama and Papa will think of him; he doesn't even speak—at least not in words that they can hear. But maybe I can find a way to convince him to stay.

What would I do if he asked me to join him. Would I go?

What I felt the other night was unlike anything I knew it was possible to feel.

Something tells me that if I had the choice, I don't think I'd be able to resist becoming a part of the dance of the stars in the sky.

Later, I pick some clothes and sneak a pair of Papa's shoes beneath my coat. I tiptoe into the kitchen and take bread and cheese and fruit. I grab a pillow from my bed and a blanket from the chest, and hide it all under my bed until I'm certain everyone is asleep. I place the blanket over my shoulder like a satchel and I creep out. Then I run, as quietly as I can, all the way to the forest.

But when I get there, and I lay the blanket out on the ground, and I take off my clothes and wrap myself in the blanket and reach my hand up to the sky—I wait for hours.

No matter how hard I reach for him—I can see his star in the sky—he doesn't come.

I get dressed and go back home, dragging the blanket behind me. I try to pretend that nothing happened; he must have been busy doing important things that stars do—like shine.

But inside, my heart hurts. My stomach hurts. And the tears that fall from my eyes look like tiny diamond stars.

Neither fire, nor wind, nor the swift air, nor the circle of the
stars, nor the violent water, nor the lights of heaven are the gods
which govern the world. Only the Holy One, Blessed Be He.

–The Book of the Solomonars, page 43, verse 7

Theodora was the firstborn of her family and she felt that
meant that she could decide who and what she wanted to
be. She saw no reason why she couldn't ride and hunt with
men. People liked to call her Princess Theodor, and she
didn't care one bit because she knew, as sure as there were
stars above her head, that she was destined for something
greater than herself. Theodora dreamed of a different
kind of world–like her father. A world where women and
men could act as they wished to, and not as they were
expected to.

What Theodora didn't know was that, as the Black Mist
traveled through the Satu Mare forest all the way to Șinca
Veche, and then down the Arges River that split the city
of Curtea de Argeș in two, that she would fall for Stanna,
hard and fast and besotted completely. Because sometimes,
even in the darkest of times, love blooms.

Stanna

I'm doing everything I can to be a dutiful daughter. I help Mama make bread and I work with Papa out in the fields. Once, I would have given anything to get the attention he gives me now. Everything has changed so quickly.

There is no talk of God or wisdom—no stories shared or lessons learned. He pushes a rusty plow through the earth and I follow him, scattering seeds. It is almost like being a son. It's everything I once wanted—but I never wanted it like this. Instead of formulas to access the divine, the only words he speaks to me relate to crops and temperature, weather and wind—of the mundane kind. He's stripped himself of the things that made him special. We are at the mercy of the elements, not at their command.

My father used to ride a dragon—and this is what he's been reduced to. A laborer in the fields. A horse that pulls a plow.

Maybe if I can find a way to heal him, to bring him back, he can be the one who saves us all. *But he tried that once. He tried and it didn't work*, a voice says.

I shudder, thinking of how disrespectful I once was. Stubborn like earth that refuses the blade of a plow. I didn't want anyone to form me into something I wasn't—and look where that led me.

Why was I so proud? Why did I refuse the hand that only tried to guide me?

"Hold this," Papa says—my new father with his new name who thinks we can outrun our past. I hold the plow up, heavy as it is, so that he can drink water from the jug I carry. The burden of disobedience weighs heavy upon me. It is in these small ways that I'm trying to find my way back.

I remember Guvriel once telling me that the reason we refer to Torah as a yoke comes partly from *Pirkei Avot*—the ethics of our fathers. "Rabbi Nechunia son of Hakanah once said," I hear Guvriel chant it in a sing-song voice in my head, spinning a tale, conjuring wonder, "anyone who accepts upon himself the yoke of Torah removes from himself the yoke of the way of the world." He was explaining how what sometimes feels like a burden can often open up the way to shed the rules and laws of nature. Harnessing yourself to the spiritual world, like an ox pulling a plow, can help you leave the yoke of the physical world behind. My father, the great Reb Isaac, has traded in one kind of yoke for another.

I miss him. It's laughable because once all I wanted was to escape him and his ways that he kept forcing on me. But everything has changed. I have changed. And I would give anything to go back to the way things used to be. I would be kinder to my sisters. I would listen to my father and let him guide me. And most of all, I would be with Guvriel—arguing with him only for the sake of Torah—not for the sake of my own vanity and pride. I see it now. How vain and self-absorbed I was. How stubborn and stiff-necked—*am kshei oref*—like it says in *The Book of Devarim*. I need to find strength now in my stiffness, and a way to save my family and our future generations. But all the rules have changed, and nothing seems to apply the way it used to. The world is both full of possibility and empty of hope.

We meet the hunting party again a few days later. We don't tell our parents about it. It's something that we sisters share—and that feels more important than anything. Mama and Papa go to town: they tell us of Mihai, the kind-hearted blacksmith they meet who helps repair the plow, and Sorina, wife of the baker, Emil, who gives us flour so we can make bread. Papa promises him grain and Mama promises her tinctures of herbs. My parents are imparting everything but their wisdom, and even I know that in our sacred book—in the text that Papa penned with his own hand—it says *"an absence of wisdom paves the way to the land of the dead."* Perhaps we are already there—walking in the land of the dead.

But what else can we do? If we meet Theodor and his men in the forest, we won't be mistaken for prey. And that feels important too. To be seen, somehow.

To remind ourselves that we exist—even though so much has been taken from us.

I'm lost in my thoughts as we set out to meet them. Laptitza is prattling away to Anna about a frog she caught on the banks of the river and how she wants to go back to bathe in its crystal-clear waters and see if she can catch one again. I envy her innocence. But Anna just listens, and promises to take her there later.

The men are already there when we arrive in the clearing. Theodor has eyes only for me, and his gaze makes me uncomfortable. I don't know what I can give him. I left my heart back in Trnava—or maybe it's lost in the woods somewhere, seeking and not finding the fox I once loved. He reaches for my hand. His are soft, uncalloused, and warm. "Come for a ride with me into the forest."

I look back at my sisters. Anna is speaking to Constantin. Laptitza is laughing at something Nikolas said.

"I very much want you to say yes." Theodor pulls my attention back to him and I can see the earnestness in his eyes.

Something in the air is waiting for me to make this choice. I agree, knowing that it will set something else in motion. It's a strange sensation. Fear of the unknown presses against my chest. What does Theodor want from me? What if it's something I can't give? What if Guvriel is still alive and searching for me? What if he finds me, comes all this way only to see me riding a horse with another? I am playing with fire even though there is no flame in sight.

There is nothing new under the sun, I hear the words from *The Book of Kohelet* in my head. *Are we destined to repeat the same mistakes over and over again?* Hannah went with Jakob and look where that led us. But I hear Guvriel quote from *Pirkei Avot* again, every word of his teachings seared into my brain whether I want them there or not: "It is not your duty to complete the work, not up to you to finish it, but neither are you free to avoid it."

There is work to be done here, even though I still don't know the nature of it. I once thought that duty was a burden, but I was wrong. In duty there can also be a world of freedom. A world of love and compassion. I wish he was here to hear me say it. To see the understanding dawn in my eyes. But it's too late. And I won't let opportunity pass me by again. It is not my duty to say no to Theodor. God has brought him to me for a reason. This is a moment I must seize.

I am doing this to keep my sisters safe—to keep my parents in the voivode's good graces. I am trusting God to lead me down a path.

I say yes.

Theodor helps me onto his horse, then straddles it behind me. He reaches his arms around me to take the reins, then gives a shout and we gallop off into the trees. The sun shines down in rays of golden light. We ride in silence and I focus on the sounds of our breaths, the sounds of the horse's breath, the sound its hooves make when they impact the forest floor. I think about how much more ground one can cover on horseback and I wonder how long it will take for us to be able to afford a horse. I could search for Guvriel . . .

"What's his name?" I ask, stroking the horse's mane.

"Torent," Theodor answers. "He's the fastest Hutul in our stables."

"He's beautiful." With Guvriel, conversation was always so easy, but I have nothing in common with Theodor. We lead such different lives.

The branches seem to part as we come to a clearing—one I've never been to before. The horse stops and my heart picks up its pace. I'm alone with a strange man in a forest. I've heard stories of the things that happen to maidens who go off into forests with men. Is that what this is? All I am to him? A peasant girl to warm his bed, to plow with seed?

The tiniest spark ignites within me, like a memory of the old rage which used to make me burn. It wants to melt the ice. *Maybe if I had my serpent it could chase away this man like it once chased away the darkness.* But I squash it down. My fire never led to anything good. I don't deserve to burn with righteous fire when everything I once loved has turned to ash.

He dismounts, takes off his helmet and shakes out his long red hair. I can't breathe. *His hair tumbling down—long and red and silky.* Like the moment in all my dreams just before they turn into nightmares. I turn away from him.

"Stanna, what's the matter? Come." He reaches up his hand to help me dismount.

I have come this far—taken this step—what will happen now feels inevitable. No matter what I do it leads to ruin. I reach for his hand and he helps me down off the horse, which whinnies and tosses its mane; I put my hand out to stroke it.

"He's beautiful," I say, looking at the horse and not at Theodor. Unsure if I want to delay what is about to happen, or if I should turn to him and face the ugly truth.

"Come." He takes my hand and tugs.

I follow. God help me but I follow. What other choice do I have? I could run, but he himself said this horse is the fastest in the land, and I know his guards are not far—and maybe even still hunting these very woods. I am prey either way. Defenseless and . . . I swallow hard and realize, as though a lamp has been lit inside me, that I am not defenseless. I never was. Just too scared and embarrassed to tell Guvriel the truth.

I'm a fiery serpent, I tell myself. *I only need to embrace that and I will never be defenseless again.*

I hear the words of *Perek Shirah* in my head and I understand them for the first time: "*Nachash omer,*" the snake says—"God supports the fallen and straightens the bent." I may be bent and broken, but the Lord our God, the God of Solomon our ancestor, straightens the bent, supports the fallen, and now, in my hour of need, I know He will help me. But only if I help myself.

I turn to Theodor. He can sense the shift in my demeanor. The tiniest hint of a spark burns in my eyes, which sting with tears.

"What's wrong?" Theodor says, touching his fingers to my chin.

"Don't touch me!" I spit, and spin away from him. I feel it— the tiny sputter of flame as it grows bright—in my belly. I close my eyes and revel in the burn as I allow it to engulf me. I will burn down this forest and everything in it if I have to; I will steal his horse and rescue my sisters and we will run again. Maybe if I blaze a trail through the forest, we can find our way back, or discover a new land—or come out changed again, a new type of girl—a woman, or even a beast.

"Stanna." His voice trembles. "You're glowing."

I open my eyes and see him walking towards me. *Why isn't he running away in fear?*

"It's beautiful; you're beautiful," he says.

I look down at myself and I see that I'm covered in flames that look like scales—gold and glowing. My hair has risen around me like a cobra's crown.

Why isn't he scared of me? I'm a serpent. Scaled and hideous. It's the first time I've ever transformed. My breath comes in fast bursts. Every inch of me is alight with flame but I'm not burning. I'm not consumed. I'm pure power and potential. I never knew that it could be like this.

I'm not scaled and hideous. I'm golden.

Theodor doesn't stop. He gets closer and closer. His hands are up in front of him as though he wants to warm himself by my fire, but not get burnt.

"I won't hurt you," he says. "I promise."

"What good is a promissssss?" I hiss, my tongue long and split with flame. "Promisssesss can be broken."

"Hand on my heart," he says, and puts his hand there. "My intention was never to hurt or harm you in any way."

My serpent eyes narrow at him. But he stares back, eyes clear and steady.

I once knew eyes like that, I think.

"Then why have you brought me out here?" My voice is foreign in my ears. I sound possessed, bewitched. I still don't understand why he doesn't cower in fear, why he hasn't run off—or at the very least, tried to stab me with his sword. Then I realize that he can't stab me—I am fire. Fire can't be put out with a blade—only with water.

Water. The words on Guvriel's lips just before we ran, from the *Song of Songs*: "Many waters cannot quench love; rivers cannot sweep it away."

"I swear by the gods that no harm will come to you," he says.

"Why are you not sssscared?" I say, but even I can tell that my fire dims a bit.

"Scared? I'm in awe. You're glorious. Fit to be queen. My father ..." He turns his head. "How can I get you to trust me?" he whispers, more to himself than to me. "May I offer you a drink?"

Water, my mind pulses. I am parched and dry and maybe water will help.

He holds out a wineskin, but I can't grasp it. I close my eyes and take a deep breath and wish for hands. I ask for calm, for ice in my veins. I wiggle my fingers. He puts the skin in my hands. It doesn't sizzle in my grasp or turn to ash. I take a deep breath and open my eyes and see that I'm back to myself again. I take long gulps from the skin, then cough, realizing that it's wine I'm drinking, not water.

"Stanna," he says, "you're safe here. You can trust me."

I'm nervous. I revealed myself—the deepest part of me—to a complete stranger, and not to Guvriel. How could I have done this to him? Maybe if I'd been brave and honest, I could have shown him my true nature and he could have helped me accept it. I could have helped Abba. I could have maybe saved us all. But I was too scared and too self-conscious, too young and stupid to understand. I was afraid of myself. The revelation of what I lost by not being true to myself feels like a heavy burden.

"Can I show you something?" he says. "You've trusted me with your secret; I would like to trust you with mine."

I swallow hard. *There's no going back now.* My heart hurts, but my eyes have been opened, and I can't shut them now that they know what I have the power to become.

"Put your arm out and hold it firmly."

I do as he says. Anything to distract me from my thoughts.

A soft breeze rises through the trees, sending leaves dancing on the air. I blink my eyes against the breeze and Theodor disappears.

I turn around, my arm still held aloft. *Where did he go? Has he left me alone in the woods? But his horse is still here* . . . I blink again and rub my eyes with my free hand.

A large owl with russet-colored feathers swoops into the clearing and lands on my arm. I gasp and nearly let my arm go, startled by the weight of it. Is it . . . ? Could it be . . . ? I narrow my eyes at the bird and it looks at me. I reach my hand up and slowly stroke its feathers, cooing to it softly so as not to startle it.

Its eyes are large and familiar. But none of this is possible. It must all be a dream. Is he . . . ? Is this? But no. It's not possible that one of my father's students has finally found me—here, like this. *Is it?* But where did Theodor go? It takes off from the perch of my arm and circles around the clearing. Then it lands by my feet and when I look up, I see Theodor standing in its place. The owl is gone.

"How?" *I don't understand.*

I thought only my father's disciples could . . .

But this is Theodor, the son of Basarab the Voivode.

There's no way . . .

"There are remnants of the wisdom of the old gods that still walk among us. My father is not Basarab—he was someone else, something else entirely. He was a smoke-walker—perhaps something a bit like you. He converted to Christianity, but he never forgot the old gods. Some say their blood ran in his veins. Few speak of them anymore, but my father was known to take to the skies in various forms. There is much of the world that we don't understand."

"It's incredible," I say. "Are there other forms you can take as well?"

I have seen this among my people, but you are not one of us and that scares me.

He gestures to me. "You're pretty incredible yourself. And yes, actually I can become whatever I desire to be—I only need to wish it, but some forms are more difficult than others.

I have never been a snake," he says, "but perhaps the time has come." He winks.

"I've never done that . . . I didn't know I could . . . " I stop myself from saying anymore.

He comes closer to me. "Stanna," he says. "I see so much sadness in you, but the air around you vibrates with potential. You're like a butterfly about to burst from a cocoon, but you refuse to let go. Why have you closed yourself off so?"

My heart beats fast. The forest branches start to sway and a wind picks up, matching the storm in my heart.

"Are you doing that too?" he asks quietly. Unafraid.

I don't control the weather or the wind. Do I? I close my eyes.

His hand cups my cheek. "Stanna."

A kind of fire grows within me. *He shouldn't be touching me.* I think of Guvriel. The fire singes my insides. I cry out and step away from him.

"What did I do?" he asks, hands held up. The concern in his voice is genuine. But I don't want to be touched. Not by him. Not by anyone.

"I'm sorry," I say, and I turn away from him.

"You are in so much pain," Theodor says. "I wish I could help."

I walk away, embarrassed by my tears, by the way I've behaved. I've endangered my family again. The son of Basarab himself has seen me turn into a serpent. Wallachia is no longer safe for us. We must pack our things and go.

"Stanna!" I hear him rushing through the forest after me. "Stanna, please stop." His hand reaches for my arm, but only brushes me lightly before letting go. "I won't touch you if you don't want to be touched, but please stop. Don't run from me. Tell me what's wrong. Has someone hurt you?"

I stop in my tracks.

Everything in me hurts and there is only one person responsible for my pain—me.

"Talk to me," he pleads.

I sit down on a large tree root and he sits beside me.

"Is it someone . . . ?" he asks tentatively. "Someone you lost? Someone you're still waiting for?"

"Maybe. There is but . . ."

He leans forward. His hair creates a curtain around us. "Stanna," he says. "Look at me. I won't let anyone hurt you."

I give a short, small laugh. "You can't promise that. No one can."

"Well, this is progress," he says. "Laughter is better than tears. I am here to listen if you ever decide to tell the tale."

"I think what I need most now is a friend."

He reaches over for another smaller wineskin on his belt and lifts it up.

"To friendship." He takes a swig, then passes it to me.

I take a sip and it burns a trail through me as it goes down. It isn't wine, but spirit. It feels like the sealing of a pact.

"To friendship," I say, and hand it back to him. "And secrets that need to be kept."

"To secrets, may they ever stay hidden." He takes another swig.

I try to think of something that might distract us from this conversation. I'm not ready to say more, and I'm still reeling from everything that happened. That's when I realize what I want to say.

"There is a story I want to tell you."

"Okay." He smiles encouragingly. "I love a good story."

I take a steadying breath.

* * * * * *

There were once three sisters who lived in a small town. Their father was a scholar—an important man. The oldest sister was beautiful and wise beyond her years; the middle sister was an artist—good with her

*hands but a bit of a firebrand; and the youngest sister liked to gaze
at the stars. She was sweet and innocent. They were all innocent . . .*

I let out a deep shaky breath.

*The older sister fell in love with a prince. She had to wait two years to
marry him. And in the meantime, the middle sister fell in love with a
red-haired student in their town . . . someone with hair like yours . . .*

I pause and look up at Theodor. He stares steadily back at
me, listening to every word. I look back down at my hands
and continue.

*But the middle sister couldn't marry him because she had to wait for
her older sister to marry, as was their custom. And one day, her older
sister did marry, and there was much joy and celebration. The middle
sister knew that her time to be with her love had finally come . . .*
  But then their town was struck with tragedy . . . a great evil . . .

I stop and search for the right words. Theodor puts his hand on
mine and squeezes it.

A black dragon came to the town on the day of the wedding. The older sister's husband was killed and all the villagers fled. And before her family left, the middle sister kissed her beloved. He promised he would follow her, that he would come for her even if he had to search to the ends of the earth to find her, but first he had to battle the dragon and save her grandmother, and his father, and her father's sacred scrolls . . .

As the words leave my mouth, I realize how crazy it all sounds. Clearly there is no way he believes me.

She left a golden trail of tears behind her, hoping he would vanquish the dragon and follow her. She waited hours, then days, then weeks, then months as her family fled through the forest . . .

I stop. I can't go on because I don't know what happens next.

"Did she ever see him again?" Theodor asks after a while.

I look up at him, tears brimming in my eyes.

"The story does not have a happy ending," he says.

"No, I don't think it does."

"None of the good stories do," he says, offering a small, sad smile.

"What if another dragon comes?" I say.

"There will always be dragons. But you're finding your own way to defend yourself."

He places his hand over his heart. "I can feel your pain, right here. It radiates out from your center. You have to find a way to let it go or it will consume you."

I want to laugh. *There is nothing left for it to consume.* But the steady beat of my heart and the remnants of the fire that burned through me and lit up my skin stand as evidence to the contrary.

"All I can do is try to help you heal," he says. "I'm willing to try if you'll let me."

"Okay," I say shakily. "Let's try."

Anna

17 Sivan 5122

"Are you sure it's okay that you're not following them?" I said to Constantin when we met earlier today.

"I promised Theodor I would give him space, but I do have a guard following them at a distance."

"I was actually looking forward to spying on my sister a little bit," I joked, but really I wanted to protect her.

"As entertaining as that might be," he said, "I want to be able to give you my full attention."

My cheeks flushed and I looked away from him. I'm getting good at pretending to flirt. I do feel as though I'm misleading him though. It is not the kind of thing that Papa ever taught me to do—to be false in my dealings with the people around me.

"Can I show you something?" I asked him. Maybe I could try to share something with him that used to matter to me; maybe that would help me feel less duplicitous.

I led him in the direction of the strawberry grove.

"It's beautiful here." He walked in a slow circle, taking in everything around us.

"I can make things grow," I found myself saying to him. "It's

what I love to do, but also what I'm good at. I planted all this."
My arms reached wide as if to take all the grove in my arms.

"You are a bright spark, Anna," he said with quiet confidence,
and closed the distance between us. His eyes were soft and almost
scared. He looked at me like I was precious. Like I was something he was afraid to break. And it struck me in that moment
that the way he looked at me, the quiet confidence in his voice,
was different than the way that Jakob was when he was with me.

Constantin reached his hand out towards me, but I stepped
away. "There are things I need to say."

"Okay," he said, turning his palms up to the sky. "Anything.
Speak and I will listen."

"I want a large family someday. I want my children to be like
olive trees around my table, with long, thick roots that reach into
the ground and are planted firmly. To root myself in a place and
stay there until I get old and can watch them all grow . . . That's
the only thing that's important to me. And my parents are important to me. And my sisters—their safety." I stopped for a minute
and looked at him. His eyes were closed. *This isn't what men like
to talk about, you idiot*, I thought, but if I was to be true to myself,
I had to speak my mind. If I was to deny the very part of me that
was still in so much pain, to move on from the destruction of
everything I cared about, I had conditions.

"Why did you stop?" he said, his eyes open now.

"I'm sorry. I know it's a lot. And probably too soon for me to
have said anything. But I won't have my heart broken again."

"Again? Who has hurt you so? I had my eyes closed because
I was trying to picture it; it sounds like heaven. Like everything
I've ever wanted."

"What?" I said.

"Truly," he said. "Hand on heart—you can ask my men. It's
been a long time since they've seen me show interest in anyone."

"Why?" I backed away from him.

"Don't walk away—please," he said, like he was afraid of startling a fawn. "What is the shape of the future you dream of? Tell me."

"I'll only answer that if you will," I said.

"Children," he said. "Children surrounding my table, like you said. And a beautiful wife always round with my fruit."

My cheeks flushed. My body was betraying me—I felt warm in places where I once thought all was ash. "You're only saying that because I did," I said to him. "How do I know you speak true?"

"There is nothing more beautiful—" His voice cracks. "—than a pregnant woman. The only thing I can imagine being more lovely is if I knew that it was my babe she was carrying." He turned away from me and I thought I saw tears in his eyes.

"Constantin, I'm sorry. What did I say?"

He didn't answer.

I walked over to him and put my hand on his back. "I'm so sorry. I didn't mean to upset you."

"I was in love once," he started, but his voice cracked and he stopped. "I loved her with all of my heart. With everything I had."

I heard the raw edge in his voice and it scared me. I didn't like where this was going. It was a voice that sounded too much like my own, a pain that felt too close to my pain. *No,* I wanted to say, *please no, don't tell me more.*

But I didn't say anything. I waited and listened and kept my hand on his back.

"We were supposed to marry. She was—" He took a deep breath. "Sofia was carrying our child. But I came home one day from having been out fighting for Voivode Basarab only to find everyone in my village slaughtered. My parents, my brothers—" His voice caught. "—and Sofia. A Tatar horde. A senseless raid. And I wasn't there to protect her."

"Constantin, I'm so sorry," I say. "I didn't know."

"It's okay," he said. "Not many do. It's not something I speak about. After it happened, I devoted myself to Theodor and his father Basarab. To the protection of our way of life. To ensure that nothing like that would ever happen to anyone I cared for again. But I'm a coward. Because I never allow myself to care for anyone."

"I . . . I lost someone too," I said, speaking about what had happened for the first time since everything burned.

He turned to face me. "I'm so sorry," he said.

"I saved these seeds from what we ate as we fled through the forest, strawberry seeds," I said softly.

"Why did you flee?" he said, still whispering, still hesitant.

"We fled after . . . " I paused. My throat was tight.

"It's okay," he said. "Let it be."

"No," I said to him. "You deserve to know, and I owe it to his memory to tell the tale. I was married to a man named Jakob. He was heir to the throne, the son of the Duchess of Trnava. We had one night together. And then they ripped him from my arms and burned him at the stake for treason. He was beautiful and brave and I loved him. We waited two years to be together and in one night—" My hands tied themselves into knots. "I'm broken. I'm not whole inside. And I'm not a maiden anymore." I looked up into his eyes and saw that he was crying.

"That someone who's felt the same despair could have managed to light up the forest with strawberries tells me everything I need to know about you. You're stronger than me."

"I don't think anyone is stronger than you," I said.

He placed his large, warm hand on my cheek, and I could feel how rough and calloused it was. "You *are*."

He bent down slowly, his hands light as angel wings upon me, both of us afraid. His lips touched mine lightly; he was being so sweet, so soft . . . I thought of Jakob and the angel—the story Mama told me. I wondered then and I wonder now if all along she'd meant something else entirely. There are two sides to every coin. Where there is darkness, there must be light, or we wouldn't recognize the darkness for what it is. Maybe in my lifetime I was meant to love both a man and an angel.

The body has its hungers and desires, its like and dislikes. My eyes liked what I saw before me, and my body agreed.

I pined for one man for two years and then he was taken from me. Perhaps it's possible to open up one's heart to more than one. The one I lost, and this one, who has lost so much himself. He will never replace what Jakob was to me, but pain is something that we share. It may not be the strongest basis for a relationship, but maybe together we can find a way to grow a family of our own from the ashes of our pasts.

Laptitza

Nikolas stands in awkward silence. There is no food to eat—no natural place for conversation to begin. I feel the ache of the stars in my chest like an ailment. Like I'm only idling my time until they come out again.

Nikolas glances at me, then stares off into the distance. Then stares at some dirt on the toe of his boot.

"Would you like to take a walk down by the river?" he blurts out quickly.

"I'd love that," I say. *It will give me something to do. Something to distract me.*

⋆ ⋆ ⋆ ⋆ ⋆ ⋆ ⋆ ⋆ ⋆ ⋆ ⋆

We walk a short way into the forest and soon we hear the sound of a stream.

"It is beautiful here," I say. "So pristine."

"What do you like to do?" he asks. "I mean, when you're not helping at home. Do you have time for any? Interests, I mean . . ." he stutters, and I can see a spray of pink across his cheeks. "That's probably a silly question." He quickly corrects himself. "You likely don't have time for much of anything else on a farm."

I can't help but smile a little bit. He has a sweet and hesitant way about him. I think, *This is someone I could see wanting to get to know . . . if my soul wasn't pledged to the stars.*

"I like looking at the stars," I quickly say. "I love everything about them and I like to try to read my future in the patterns every night. I like how vast the sky is, and how uncountable the stars feel, how permanent they are—like something you can rely on. Something that will never let you down."

And as I speak it, I realize that I love so much more about the stars than just the fact that he's up there.

"I love looking at the stars too," he says, "but I disagree— stars can fall, and you never know when one will. I think the stars are faithless. But I still love watching them. You should come visit the voivode's palace. We have an astrolabe there that we use to look at the stars from the highest tower of the palace. You can almost touch the sky."

"I would love that," I say. "When can I come?" *I could get even closer to him—to my star.*

"Well, hmmm . . . " I see him hesitate. "I would say that we could go now, except there are no stars in the sky yet. But I sup- pose tonight could work. What time are you free?"

I fidget, my fingers not quite finding a place to rest.

"It will have to be late," I say. "I need to sneak out, or else my parents would never permit it. Is there a way you could meet me? Here? Or halfway? Or send someone to escort me?"

"Of—of course I can! I should have offered! And late tonight is fine—I don't want you to get into trouble. Would—would another night suit better? Another time?"

"Tonight is perfect," I say.

"I will come get you myself," he says. "Where should we meet?"

"I will wait for you at midnight right here, by this river. It's not far from where I live, and I won't run the risk of being seen."

We make our way back to where we started. I'm excited. This

man can take me closer to the stars than I've ever been before. And maybe, just maybe, I will see something there that will give us all hope. Some great secret the sky is waiting to reveal only to me.

*   *   *   *
*   *   *   *   *
*   *   *

I wait for the house to settle, for the stars to fix themselves firmly in the sky, and then I sneak out. When I get to the river, Nikolas is already waiting for me, under the dark cover of tree and sky.

I ride with him all the way to the palace. He ties up his horse himself, and takes me up a back staircase. The stairs go on endlessly. By the time we reach the top, I'm having trouble catching my breath. He opens the door to a moonlit room. There are windows on all sides, and a large metal structure pointing up at the sky.

"Come," Nikolas says, and he leads me over to the device. "Close one eye and look out the other one," he says, as he adjusts what look like gears. "Can you see the stars? They feel as close to you as I am." He sounds as excited to share this with me as I am to be here. It's nice to have someone to talk to. Someone who understands how important the stars are.

I close one eye and squint through the device, and it is as though the door to a new world has been opened. The spaces between the stars and the darkness they contain are visible to me—vivid in a way they've never been before. I hear my father's voice in my head for the first time in a while: "The world is made up of black fire and white fire. The white fire is the holy letters of the Torah but no less important are the dark spaces between them."

I can see all the dark spaces between the stars. I could stay here all night. "For every darkness in the world there is light. But light cannot exist without darkness," I repeat my father's words under my breath.

"That's very true," Nikolas answers, and I remember that he's beside me and that I spoke the words out loud.

"I never want to stop looking," I say.

"I remember feeling that way when my tutor first took me up here. The first time my tutor turned the contraption up to the stars, I couldn't believe my eyes."

My eyes scan the sky through the device and it's only because I'm paying attention that I see it—my star.

It's white and blinding in its fury.

I see it take a dive from the sky

and plummet towards earth.

I know where it's heading—

to the clearing.

To meet me—

but I'm not there.

"I have to go," I say to Nikolas.

"But you just got here," he protests. "Is everything okay? What did you see?"

"I have to go. I have to go. I have to go."

I turn and cross the room. My hands fumble at the bolt on the door.

"I'll come with you," he says. "You can't go out there alone. Please—was it something I said? Something I did?" His eyes are wide with panic.

"It was something I saw. I'm so sorry. I need to get home."

"Okay, I'll come with you," he says. "Maybe I can help."

He can't help. My being with him is what caused the problem to begin with.

How could I have been so stupid?

I accept his help though—anything to get me back to the clearing where my star-man waits for me.

Nothing will ever compare to the way he lit me up that night.

He opened doors for me to an internal sky of sensation—if

I never experience what I felt with him again, I don't think
I'll survive.

★ . ˙ ★ ˙ ★ ★ . ★
★ .   ˙ ★ ˙ ★ . ˙
       .   ★   .

But when we finally get to the clearing, he isn't there. He didn't
wait for me.

But Nikolas waits. He followed me even when my choices
were capricious.

"Can you at least tell me why we raced back here?" he asks.

I must tell him something. I owe him an explanation for my
strange behavior.

"Can I tell you a story?" I ask.

He cocks his head at me. "A story. That's not what I expected.
Okay, you can tell me a story. I like stories," he says. He leans
against the gnarled root of a tree and crosses his legs.

I close my eyes. I look to the inner eye inside me—the one
Papa taught me to draw from when interpreting the skies. I
hear my mother's voice when she told stories—a tune like reading from a scroll. I search for a story that holds a kernel of the
way I feel.

I begin.

★ . ★ ˙ ★ ★ . ★
★ .   ˙ ★ . ˙ . ˙
       .   ★   .

There was once a fox that fell in love with a vineyard.

*Every day he would pass the fence that kept the grapevines secure
from trespassers, and every night he would return and sit and watch
the leaves unfurling in the dew and the grapes starting to burst forth
from tiny white blooms.*

*He longed to wander amid the gnarled roots of the vines and to sip
from the sweet nectar of the blossoming grape clusters, but he knew
that the fence was there for a reason—to keep strangers like him out.*

One day, as he made his way around the fence that surrounded the vineyard, he found a small break in the slats.

He stuck his snout through the hole—he could almost touch the vines. He could smell the sweet juice and felt as though he could taste what it would be like for a grape to burst in his mouth—sour and sweet at the same time.

He decided that nothing would ever taste as good to him as the promise of those juicy bunches, so he refused to eat or drink for three days, and each day that he fasted, he found that he could fit more and more of himself through the hole.

"I only long to taste the bounty," he said to himself, "not to feast or gorge myself upon such beauty—for then I would destroy it, and there would be none left to lust after anymore. I do not seek destruction. I only wish one tiny little taste and I'll be satisfied."

On the third day, the fox was able to squeeze his entire body through the hole.

His eyes nearly filled with tears—he felt as if he had entered a foreign land. The grass was greener, the soil softer—and everything was fragrant and lush. It felt so different here, on the other side of the fence. He wished he could stay in the vineyard forever—far away from his daily cares and the dangers of the woods.

He walked around the vineyard searching for the perfect grape—the one that would satiate his curiosity and quench his thirst with its perfection. When he found it—red and ripe and glowing in the moonlight—the grape found itself into his mouth and his teeth clamped down.

He was hungry. So hungry. For he hadn't eaten in three days. The grape was pure and sweet and tasty—everything he'd dreamed it would be. And before he could stop to think—before he could stop himself—he devoured the whole cluster.

It was so good, so perfect, that it was hard for him to believe he'd actually found the perfect one. Certainly he'd picked the greatest of all the grapes in the vineyard—but to be sure, he tasted another, and *another, and another, and before he knew it he had grown so fat with juice that he couldn't fit back through the hole again.*

"Woe is me!" he cried. "What have I done? Not only have I tasted from that which is forbidden, but I have brought misfortune upon myself. Certainly the owner of the orchard will come upon me in the morning and I will become fox stew."

So the fox began to fast again. He hid amid the thickest of the vines and evaded capture, starving himself and berating himself for his folly, until he was finally able to slip back through the hole.

He ran back into the woods, nearly prancing with joy at the sights and sounds of his beloved forest, and he vowed to never taste from another orchard again.

*   *   *   *   *

I'm silent for a while. Then Nikolas says, "It's a nice story. But I don't think I seek the same things you seek."

"That's okay," I answer.

"I have an idea," he says. "Meet me here again tomorrow night, and I will tell *you* a story."

My heart seizes in my chest. If he meets me here, my star-man will not come . . .

"I don't think I can," I say, "but thank you for offering."

"Can I walk you home?" he asks.

"I know the way. Perhaps we will meet again some time."

"My star tower is yours—say the word and I will bring you there again."

"Thank you." I turn around and walk away.

And all the time I walk, I question if I've made a big mistake.

I can't sort out where I went wrong.

*The Holy One, Blessed Be He sails the eighteen worlds in the
night, and in the last three hours of morning he sails in our
world. Therefore, the early morning is a particularly auspicious
time for prayer. It is a time when the wind fills God's sails.
We may have power over the wind, but no man can possess
her, for in the wind is the spirit of God.*

–The Book of the Solomonars, page 52, verse 6

Sometimes tragedies follow tragedies. Lives and loves play
themselves out across the sky. Day in day out. Year in year
out. And there's nothing that any of us can do to change a
future that's already been set in motion. Sometimes stories
tell themselves and we become but readers–spectators to
the dramas that unfold across the sky.

Stanna

The things I learned from Guvriel are coming back to me—like a fire that's suddenly been given air. The serpent slithers within me, twining itself with my fingers, wrapping itself around my arm, like a fiery little ghost that haunts only me. It's waiting for me to tell it what to do.

But I'm not ready. *The only thing that fire brings is death and destruction*—my mind wars with the little spark that's refusing to go out now that it's been relit. *Burn bright; I am so proud of you,* I hear a voice say. I don't know if it's Guvriel or the voice of my father, or the serpent itself, whispering in my ear, waiting for me to make the first move.

I wish I could ask Anna if this is how she used to feel when she was in command of the garden, or if Papa felt this way when he rode a cloud dragon in the sky. But they've both cut off those parts of their lives completely. And as usual, it's too late for me to join them. All Papa does is work the field and sit by the hearth each evening. He doesn't pray or chant or go out at night to the forest. I haven't seen him utter a prayer in months.

I haven't set fire to anything in so long that I was convinced I'd forgotten how. But the rage has gone out of me. Now the fire burns with something else—the fire of truth. This feels stronger than my rage ever was. I don't need to burn in order to be seen anymore. It's enough that I know the fire's ready and waiting.

Like Rabbi Elazar Ben Azarya who aged seventy years overnight, I've grown up in an instant. The things that used to matter to me aren't important anymore. Guvriel came into my life and taught me that I was so much more than what I thought I was. And now Theodor is asking me, *Who are you, Stanna? Without your family and your past and Guvriel. Who are* you? He's challenging me: *who do you want to be?*

The serpent inside me wants to find out.

* . * . * . * . * . *

I happen upon Theodor a few days later when I'm walking the road to town. I've been searching for someone who might take me on as an apprentice, and I remember meeting Guvriel at the crossroads in what feels like a lifetime ago.

"Stanna," Theodor calls out as he rides closer. His face lights up when I stop and turn.

"Good day. What brings you out here alone?" I say. There is no guard beside him.

"Can we ride? I came to see you."

"I . . . My family is expecting me. I don't want them to worry."

"What if I give you a ride home? You can let them know you're safe, then come out with me?"

"Okay," I hear myself say.

He dismounts to help me up onto the horse and we set off.

"Wait for me here," I say when we arrive at the front door, and I slide down off the horse.

I wonder if that was the wrong thing to do. The son of the voivode is here at my family's home and I didn't invite him in. Was that rude? It was only ever Anna who sat beside father when he met important people and constituents. I've lost all sense of right and wrong.

"Any luck?" Papa asks as I enter. His head perks up from the wood he's whittling.

"No," I say. "Nothing. Where are Anna and Laptitza?"

"Out in the forest, I think," Mama says. "Was that a horse we heard?"

"Someone passing by," I lie, not wanting to tell them more. "I'll be back soon."

"But you just came back," Mama says, her hands on her needlework.

My parents are acting like they're in some kind of dream. I see it now, as if a veil of darkness has been lifted from my eyes. The air inside our home is so heavy and thick with longing and sorrow that I can barely breathe in here anymore. We haven't started again. We're hiding in plain sight. Without our community, without my father's disciples, without our faith, who are we?

I walk out the front door and no one follows.

Theodor takes me down the road, farther than I've ever gone before. It's thrilling—galloping on a horse at high speed, the air icy and crisp on my face. I can breathe out here, and I realize why my sisters and I keep going to the forest—they feel it too. They may not be able to put a name to it, but their lungs thirst for this fresh air.

He leads the horse off the road and into a different part of the forest. It's denser here, greener. Soon he stops the horse, leaps down, and ties him to a tree, then helps me down.

"How did you manage to get away? By yourself?" I ask him.

The look on his face is grave, serious. His eyes a piercing green. He takes his helmet off and I wait for the cascade of red, but it doesn't come.

"You cut your hair!" I say.

He runs a hand through his shorn locks. "I did, yeah." He looks down at his feet, then back at me. Then he takes a step forward, and another step. My heart beats fast.

He reaches his hands out and takes mine in his. "Thank you for coming out here with me. There's something I need to tell you."

He puts his hands on my cheeks, cradling my face like he's scared he's going to break me. I want to tell him that I'm not ready, that I'm promised to another, but he looks so fragile that I'm stunned into silence.

What has him looking so grave? What does he have to tell me?

My heart races as I stare into his eyes.

He leans in and kisses me.

I freeze in place. My lips don't respond.

Tears smart in my eyes. Maybe this is all he ever wanted from me. I'm not sure if I should be angry or relieved.

Yet—something is clearly troubling him.

He pulls away.

"What's wrong? Why are you are crying?" he says.

"I'm sorry, I . . . "

"No." He turns away from me. "You have nothing to apologize for. I shouldn't have done that. It's just that . . . I was scared that if I didn't try now, I might never get a chance. I've wanted to kiss you since the first time I met you. But clearly that was the wrong thing to do. I'm sorry."

I open my mouth but no words come.

"Stanna, I've been dishonest with you," he continues.

"Dishonest?" A thick flood of ice runs through me.

"I only wanted to . . . " His hands flit, nervous and unsteady. I've never seen him like this before. "I had to try at least once before . . . " He looks away.

"Before what?"

"Can we sit?" he asks.

I nod, still confused by what just happened. It's not like last time—I don't feel the need to blaze at him in anger, and I'm not afraid to be alone with him. I'm worried and curious.

We sit in silence for a while as he runs his hands through his shorn hair.

"Can I tell you a story?" he finally says.

"Yes," I say. At the very least it will give me space to think.

He stares off into the trees and begins.

*   * * * * *
*   *   *   *   *
*

Once there was a man who lived in a land that was not his own. Nobody remembered where he came from, and nobody spoke the language of the country he was from. He arrived in the land, hoping that he would find in it a place where he could feel truly at home. Where he might become the father of a people who could be truly free.

But the land he found was being ruled by another. Soon, he'd grown a following of others like him, and they began to gain a foothold—town by neighboring town.

When the prince of the land heard what was happening, he attacked, certain he would be successful in overthrowing this upstart. But instead, his royal troops were decimated. The man succeeded in making his dream come true. He declared the land independent, with freedom of religion and worship for all. He married a woman not of his faith, for he thought that she believed in his dream. She was already pregnant with the child of the prince. Some say her husband disappeared. Others say he haunts the forest and the land, that he became a beast—a smoke-walker—and that one day he will come back for her and for his child.

When the child was born, it was healthy and beautiful, though the baby's mother was disappointed that she hadn't borne a son. But the new ruler saw it as an omen—a sign from God that his rule was right and true. God had blessed them with a child—it mattered not if it was male or female. He called the baby Theodora and sent out a proclamation that God had blessed the new couple with a daughter.

Soon his wife grew pregnant again. This time she bore her husband a boy. The kingdom rejoiced. The voivode's dynasty was secured.

But the son didn't like doing all the things that the other boys in the palace did. And the voivode's daughter didn't like sitting and sewing with the women. But they were young and the voivode was healthy and the children were both loved and indulged so they did as they pleased.

As the girl child grew older it became clear that she was born to lead, to rule like her father did before her. The voivode saw all of this as proof that he had done right by this child—some men are meant to rule, he'd say, but some women are too.

But his wife did not see things the same way. She wanted her child to marry and unite their kingdom with a neighboring one. The child was distraught, and also deeply unhappy. She didn't know why she couldn't just be herself—whoever it was she wanted to be on any given day. A knight by day and a princess by night. For if she couldn't be true to herself, how could anyone ever be true to her?

* * *

Theodor's voice cracks as he speaks. He takes a deep breath and we sit in silence for a while.

But I want to know the ending. I'm about to speak, when he says, "I'm the daughter in the story, Stanna. My name is Theodora."

My eyes go wide. This was not what I expected.

"You were so brave and honest with me. I needed to tell you the truth. I was scared that if I told you, I might never get a chance to show you how I feel. I'm sorry if I touched you, if I kissed you without your permission, but if I never taste another set of lips again, it was enough to last me a lifetime."

"Theodora?" I say like a question.

"Is it really such a difference? The addition of one little letter . . . "

But my eyes are still trying to re-form this Theodora into the shape of the person I know. The longer I stare at him— her—them, the more I see the same person. Everything merges into one.

I had to turn into a creature of light in order to show Theodor my true form. All Theodora has asked for is the addition of a letter to her name.

"I will burst if you don't say something soon," Theodora whispers.

I look up at her. "Do any of us really know who and what we are?" I say quietly. "I think we are always in the process of becoming."

"It is not an easy path," Theodora says. "Be careful what you say. Don't give me false hope."

"No path is easy," I reply.

I'm shocked, I admit: I didn't even once think that Theodor was something other than what he seemed. But as I look at him . . . her . . . I realize that I don't see her any differently now.

"I'm sorry that I kissed you when you clearly didn't want to be kissed. I've been dishonest with you. I've lied to you and I tried to steal a kiss that was not freely given. I hope you can find it in your heart to forgive me."

"Why did you cut your hair?"

"Because my mother has decided to marry me off. The first of the suitors arrives tomorrow. And if today is to be the last day I can wear armor, I wanted everything about me to express what I feel inside. And anyway—" She grins. "—now it will be harder for Mother to find someone suitable. They'll call me the bald princess."

"I think anyone would be lucky to marry you," I say.

Theodora's face falls. "I don't want to marry a man. I want to lead an army."

"And you still can—" I start to say, but she cuts me off.

"You don't understand our ways," she says. "A palace for me will be no more than a prison. When I met you . . . I saw someone who was different. Someone who might be able to understand that every man or woman in their life plays many parts. You're the first person I've ever felt this way about. But I can't promise you anything. In another kingdom, or another world perhaps, but sadly not in this one . . . "

I think about the promise that was made to me—the promise I once made to someone else. "I couldn't have promised anything to you either—for I am promised by word and in my heart to another."

"Perhaps it's better that way," she says sadly. "My future is not my own."

"None of our futures are," I say, thinking about Guvriel and how I once thought my future was set in stone. "I don't want you to promise me anything. Promises can be broken."

"You're stronger than you think you are, if you're still here beside me after everything I told you."

I stare at her shorn hair—still red and vibrant to the roots. Her delicate yet angular features. Her lips uttering words I never thought I'd hear again.

"I will call you whatever you would like to be called," I say. "Sometimes we all get lost. Sometimes it takes us a while to find yourself again." My heart grows brave. "My name is Sarah," I say.

Anna

24 Sivan 5122

I have so much to write and the candle burns low, but I must get it all down now or I fear I'll forget.

There was a knock at our door around dinner time. Eyes met eyes across the table. Our meal consisted of coarse black bread and cabbage soup—perhaps that detail is unimportant, but it was a normal meal, a quiet one, like all our meals here. Nobody had knocked on our door yet, and I think we rather liked it that way. I still tremble each time we hear a knock, for I instantly remember the knock on my door which changed everything.

I saw the hesitation in Papa's eyes. He looked to me like I was the parent and he the child. It hurt, because I know he wants so badly to be able to open a door and not live in fear for what is on the other side. He wants us all to think we are safe, though he does not believe it himself.

He put a finger to his lips—though he didn't need to: we are already all silent and still. He crept to the door, peeked through a crack in the wood, then opened the door.

I heard a familiar voice.

"Good evening, sir. Apologies for disturbing your evening

meal, but there is a matter I wish to discuss with you. May I come in?"

It was Constantin. My heart beat fast. Why was he here? I wondered if something was wrong. My eyes strayed to the door as I caught the look in Stanna's eyes. *Is everything okay?* she silently said to me. *Why is he here?* Everything about the men we meet out in the fields is a secret. Something we've kept between us.

"Come in, come in," Papa said. "Of course."

But my father was confused and scared.

Constantin held his hat in his hands, his head bowed.

I remembered the way he looked that last time I saw him. Lost. Holding enough sadness in him to flood a field. I couldn't ignore him, couldn't cause him more pain.

I got up from my seat. "Constantin!"

"You know this man?" Papa asked.

Constantin looked up and saw me across the table. His face lit up, almost as if he hadn't been sure he was in the right home till then, as if he was more terrified at the prospect of entering my home than he was at facing hundreds of thousands on the battlefield. It was the face of a man that I thought I could love.

Everything about that moment reminded me of things that I'd blocked out of my mind. I was having trouble breathing.

I don't know if it's my fate to love and lose and love and lose over and over again. And if this is yet another mistake I'm making.

He seems to take courage from the air, as he takes a deep breath and says, "I've come to ask for your daughter's hand in marriage."

My heart fell when it should have felt buoyant. *No*, it said. *Not again. Not this pain.*

Papa furrowed his brow. "Which daughter?"

Constantin laughed. A deep belly laugh. He looked over at me. "You've told him nothing?"

"I'm sorry . . . " My face flushed.

"My apologies," he said to Papa. "But I've come to ask for the hand of Anna, the daughter of . . . "

"Ivan," Papa said.

"Anna the daughter of Ivan and . . . "

"Elena," Mama said.

"Despite the fact that Anna, the daughter of Ivan and Elena, has told you nothing about me." His eyes danced. "I assure you both that my intentions are completely honorable. There is nothing I want more than to take care of your daughter and your family by extension. I swear it on my honor, and on the throne of the Voivode Basarab the First, Lord of Wallachia."

I barely know him, my mind raced. *Everything could still go wrong,* my heart said. *In the past, everything has gone wrong.*

But how well did I know Jakob? How well do we know anyone?

Maybe if I got married, my bad luck will leave my sisters and parents alone. Then they can be truly free of the curse that has bound itself to me.

"Do you know this man?" Papa asked me.

"Yes, Tată," I said, using the local word for "father." "I do."

"Sit. Eat with us," Papa said to Constantin.

While Constantin sat at the table, I watched every move he made. I saw that where his fingers gripped his hat, they trembled. I thought of the things he told me the other day about Sofia, and thought about what it must have cost him to come here, to make himself vulnerable again in that way. He was at our table. His heart out on a plate before us.

I reached to take his hat from his hands and my fingers brushed his. He looked up at me and it was as if the sun had risen on his face. I didn't need a book to tell me it was genuine.

I didn't have it in me to say no. I couldn't crush the look I saw there. I knew then that I wouldn't deny him.

Mama got up to bring a drink and some cups from the kitchen. I saw tears shining in her eyes. I followed her.

"A man only looks at a woman once in her life like that," she whispered to me, and then she winked. "Sometimes twice."

"Mama, he's a *goy* . . . " I say the word so softly it's barely there, but still. A word from another life—from a lifetime ago.

"He's a man," Mama says. "And he loves you."

My eyes smarted with tears as I went back to the table. *I don't deserve this kind of happiness.*

"Constantin, what is your family name?" Papa asked as Mama set another plate of food before him, and a cup which she filled with honey wine.

She looked over at me encouragingly. But my stomach felt like it was on fire.

She poured some wine into my cup, then she poured for herself and for Papa.

"Valeriu, sir. Constantin Valeriu."

"A strong name," Papa said.

Not a Jewish name is clearly what he thought.

"Yes, sir," Constantin said.

"What is it you do?" Papa asked.

"I am commander of the voivode's army," Constantin answered.

"I see," Papa said. I looked at him, hoping to see acceptance. But all I saw was fear.

And then it hit me. My father was never going to approve this match. But he would say yes, because he couldn't say no.

Constantin is not a man that people say no to.

Everything about this meeting suddenly felt wrong. I only wanted to relieve the burden from my parents, not force their hand. How was I so blind?

Nothing has changed about our situation, even though this is Constantin and not Jakob. History will repeat itself. The son of a duchess, the commander of an army . . . I am a curse on this family.

I cried. It was the only possible response. *How could I have been so blind?*

"Anna, is this what you want?" Papa looked at me.

I could tell that Constantin was concerned by my tears.

I looked at my mother, and her face fell.

"Yes. This is what I want. It's what I want with all my heart," I said. "Forgive my tears. From the minute I met Constantin, I knew that we were meant for one another."

I must face the only future I can see. My heart will fall and fall again. It is the way of things for me.

I tried to empty my head of all the negative thoughts that threatened to destroy this moment which was supposed to be joyful.

"Are you sure?" Papa asked.

"I will wait for you," Constantin said, "if you are not ready."

"I'm ready." I met his gaze steadily.

Perhaps a night with Constantin will help me to erase the only night I ever had with a man who loved me—a man I loved. It is a night I need to stop reliving over and over and over again in my nightmares. Constantin is sweet and kind—perhaps he is my angel in disguise.

I rubbed the goosebumps that dotted my flesh.

"I will take care of your daughter, sir. She will want for nothing," Constantin said. "We will raise fine strong young boys and girls together."

"If this is what my daughter wants, I will not stand in her way. You have my blessing," Papa said.

My mouth opened with shock. I knew he didn't have a choice in that moment, but those words from my father, his approval, meant so much to me.

Constantin reached his hand out for mine. He touched his lips to my palm, then looked over at me. I swallowed hard. He pulled me into an embrace.

"Thank you," he said, "for trusting me. I will take care of you, and your family. I promise. I'm so happy that you'll be mine, *mireasa mea*—my bride."

Constantin wiped the tears from my face with his thumbs. "Don't cry," he said, as he kissed my salty lips.

It may not be what my parents once wished for me, but neither was Jakob.

Yet if it means safety and protection for everyone I love, perhaps it is more than enough.

Laptitza

I go early
the next night
to wait for him.
I bring the clothes
and the blanket,
the food
          and the shoes.
I am determined
to stay all night
if that's what it takes.

Desperate to see him.
Aching at the lack of him.
I open my hand to the sky,
gather light
          in the center
          of my palm.
I send it out,
like I saw
my father do
in the forest.

My light
like a siren song.

I don't wait long.

A long silver arm
reaches down.
A body follows.
He takes
my hand
in his
I pull him
      down
        from the firmament.

"I'm sorry," I say.
"So sorry
I didn't
wait for you."
My lips
shower his face
with hot white kisses.

"I was only trying
to get closer to you.
Kiss.
I am yours now.
Kiss.
Only yours.
Kiss.
Stay with me."

He presses my hand
to his lips.
Knuckles silver
in the light.
I tremble
at his closeness.
I want to feel him
inside me.

He plucks a star
        from the heavens
places it
        in my palm.
It dances
        in a ring of light
                and then turns solid.
He slips
the silver ring
        onto my finger.
We kiss as silver tears
        fall from his eyes.
The ring burns.

My body glows with light
        as he enters me.
The sky bursts
        in constellations
                of sensation.

Back home
in my bed,
I twirl the silver band
around and
        around and
                around again.

"I have married a star,"
I say out loud.
And it sends
a new rush
through me.
What have I done?
I giggle.
I, Levana Solomonar,
　　　　have married a star.

I rub the spot
on my finger
where I know
he placed the ring.
　　　　　　　　But it's gone.

I sit up in bed.
I rub my eyes
in panic.
Was it only a dream?
Where did it go?
But I can still see
the stars
behind my eyes—
white-hot specks
against a black sky
of sensation.

I know it happened.
I can still feel
the gaping echo
of his absence
between my thighs.

I am not
a maiden anymore.
I have married
a man from the sky.

Even if no one else
      can see the ring
      that binds me to him,
      it's there.

He was here,
      inside me.

Some of the most
powerful things
in the world are hidden—

                and secrets
                sometimes begin
                as tiny hope-full stars.

All the rivers run into the sea, yet the sea is not full. So it is
with wisdom. So it is with the endless light of God.

−The Book of the Solomonars,
page 147, verse 4

Once there was a queen named Marghita who always
believed that her daughter would be empress. When it
seemed like her daughter's life would go a different route,
the queen became bitter with envy and she called on the
only power she still was able to control: a smoke-walker.
The spirit of the Black Dragon.

Stanna

The morning before Anna's wedding, we all wake up early. There's much to do to prepare. Bread to bake and food to make, a floral wreath to weave for her veil.

"Stanna!" Mama cries as she opens the front door. "There's something here for you."

I find her standing by the door, startled by a package that's been left there with my name on it.

"What is it?" she asks. "Who's it from?"

I shrug, which does nothing to allay Mama's fears. *We haven't been here long enough for misfortune to follow us*, I can almost hear her say. There is only one person the package is likely to be from, but I won't speak her name to my mother, who knows nothing of our trips to the forest. She thinks Anna met Constantin by chance in the field. There is no truth between us anymore—it pains me, but I am not the same person, and neither is she, and there are things about who I am becoming that I'm not ready to reveal to my parents yet.

I open the gift. (For that's what it is, I'm sure of it.) *A wedding gift?* The linen that it's wrapped in is finer that anything we own; I see Mama eying it. Inside, there is a note, and folded fabric. I put the note aside.

"Who's it from?" Mama asks again, but I don't answer.

I lift the fabric up and see it is a dress the color of dusk embroidered with silver vines that look like branches and lily-of-the-valley flowers.

"For you," Mama reads, and I try to snatch the note back from here, but she continues. "My *lăcrimioare*." She turns it over. "That's all it says. It must be for Anna, from Constantin. Anna!" she calls.

I've never held a dress so fine before.

"No," I say. "It's not for Anna. It's for me."

"From whom? How?"

"From someone who knew I needed something to wear to the wedding," I say. "Mama, don't worry. All will be well, I promise. This land is bringing us back to ourselves. Isn't that reason enough to rejoice?" I kiss her cheek and take the dress to the room I share with my sisters. I lay it out on my bed and run my hands over the flowers. But this kind of finery feels like something too good to be true.

* * * * * * * * * * *

Theodora stands beside Constantin that night at the wedding. It is strange to see her in a dress. She's commander of the voivode's army—she should be standing by Constantin's side dressed in full military garb. Instead, she is wearing a dress that looks like silver and starlight. Like tears.

The ceremony takes place inside the church that abuts the Basarab stronghold. I have never been inside a church before. My heart beats to the rhythm of the songs the crowd sings—all foreign—and I mumble my lips to make it look like I know the words and the tune. My eyes seek my parents' faces, but they have eyes only for Anna. Laptitza gazes up at the arches above. Does no one else find this strange? Once, my father would have forbidden us to enter such a structure, and now we stand here, family of the bride, and I'm about to watch my father give his daughter's hand in marriage to a Christian. "How the mighty have fallen," I hear the words of King David in *The Book of Samuel*.

No part of the ceremony is recognizable to me, but Anna seems to know what to do. Just when I thought that my sister and I had become closer than ever, we are drifting apart again. This is not the sister I once knew.

After the ceremony, we go out to the square in front of the church and everyone is smiling and laughing, congratulating the happy couple. Theodora finds me in the crowd and her hand closes over mine. She squeezes so tight I wince in pain.

We are invited to the wedding feast held in the court itself, and all the guests make their way inside the high walls.

"My mother wants to marry me off to the governor of Lovech, Ivan Alexander," Theodora whispers into my hair. "She says that dark winds are rising from the south and she fears it is time to form an alliance before the winds of war reach here. Some say he will be the next ruler of Bulgaria. My stepfather has agreed."

"What? No," I whisper back. "That can't be possible . . . "

"The decision is made; nobody consulted me. I must go. I'll see you inside." She walks away to join her mother and stepfather, who accompany Constantin and Anna at the front of the procession.

My heart feels like it stops beating completely. I want to move, but my feet are rooted in place. I opened myself up to Theodora. I showed her the truest part of myself. And now she's leaving me. Just like Guvriel—she's too good to be true.

Anna

15 Tammuz I 5122

Constantin's chest rises and falls in the bed beside me, but I'm awake, my mind racing, my body humming with a glow I haven't felt in months—a glow I never got to feel because it too quickly turned to fear.

Everything about this man is different than Jakob. Everything about the wedding was too. He wore a white wool tunic embroidered in black and red leaves and flowers, and my bridal veil nearly fell to the floor. It was embroidered with strawberry blossoms—a gift from him before the ceremony.

The village priest joined my hand with Constantin's, but only after I converted in the church. I didn't tell my parents about that ceremony. I know what God I believe in—our *Elohim*, it matters not to me what name He goes by.

My parents held tall white candles in their hands and stood off to the side of the altar. Everything was decorated with sprigs of flowers. The priest placed golden crowns on our heads. Stanna and Laptitza handed out white flowers to all the guests—a custom from his town, Constantin told me. I went along with everything. I cared nothing for the ceremony. What mattered was that soon my family would be safe.

I could tell that my parents were uncomfortable, but they put on a good show. They must have taken comfort in the traditions that were similar to before: the candles they held as they walked me down the flower-strewn aisle. The *hora* dances before the ceremony—so very similar to the way we would have danced at a Jewish wedding that it was almost easy to forget it was a priest, not a rabbi (not my father) who officiated.

The wedding was a joyous affair. Except for the priest's blessings, everything was accompanied by raucous music, and Constantin's men were so happy for him. After the last blessing, our family and close friends danced around us. Constantin and I kissed, and everyone threw white flowers into the air.

Everyone cried. Mama. Even Papa. New traditions replaced old ones.

Constantin picked a flower off my veil and tucked it behind my ear. He kissed my cheek and whispered something in my ear that I didn't quite hear, but it made my face flush.

The villagers danced, forming a circle around us. Mama danced with Papa. Laptitza danced with Nikolas. Stanna danced with Theodora. Everyone was happy. When the wedding feast began, I lifted a white cloth off a loaf of ring-shaped bread on the table. *Almost like we used to cover* challah, I thought. *Almost.* A woman broke off a piece and gave it to me. "It's a symbol of fertility," she said as I fed it to Constantin.

"My blushing bride!" Constantin waggled his eyebrows at me, then he leaned over and we kissed. Those that saw let out a cheer.

★ ★ ★ ★ ★

After, he led me to the farmhouse that he'd built with his own hands. He carried me inside, his lips locked to mine.

We made love and he was achingly slow and tender. Both of us cautious, both of us scared, but trying to move beyond pain, beyond fear.

"I'm so happy," he said afterward, tears glittering in his eyes, "and I'm so sad that I'm happy."

"Are you worried that we'll always be comparing?" I said, my head on the same pillow as we stared up at the ceiling as though we could see what was written in the stars beyond it.

"No," he said. "Never comparing—layering a new experience over the rawness of the old one." He took my hand in his and kissed it. "I always wanted to find someone who would be kind and gentle with my heart."

I looked over at him. "Those are the words that I'm supposed to say," I said, marveling at the feelings contained in this bear of a man.

I should have been happy. But I couldn't sleep. I lay in bed shivering. I'd been to two weddings in the space of a year—both my own.

I won't breathe or sleep until morning comes and there's no knock at the door. So I sit and write. If Constantin knew, he'd have stayed awake with me, but I didn't tell him.

This vigil is something I must see through alone.

Laptitza

When most of the dancing
     has died down,
I wander away from the revelry.
     I sit alone in the town square
on an overturned barrel.
     I watch the sky
and absently rub my ring finger.
     I don't like the dark clouds I see.

"Mind if I join you?"
     "Oh!" I jump to standing;
     it's Nikolas.
"Sorry, I didn't mean to startle you,"
     "No, no, that's okay.
     I just needed some air."
"Did everything work itself out the other night?"
     "Oh, oh yes, thank you"
     I say, when I remember
     how I fled.
"You really do prefer

the company of the stars."
He nods at the sky.
  My cheeks flush when I think
  of the company I've been keeping.
"I understand," he says.
"I too prefer
the solitude of night.
I don't like crowds."
  "That must be difficult
  in the palace," I say.
"Indeed," he agrees.
"May I sit?" he gestures
to the barrel.
  I move over
  to make room for him.

  When I look at the sky,
  he looks at me,
  then up at the sky.
"It is said that every soul
is a candle
that lights the heavens."
  "I didn't know that," I say,
  "but I believe it."
"May I tell you
a story this time?"
  "Yes," I say,
  but I don't look at him.
  I'm afraid I'll miss
  something important.

He rubs his hands
on his pants and takes

a deep breath.
"Okay," he says,
and leans back,
resting on his elbows
to better see the sky.

There was once an emperor and an empress and more than anything they wanted to be blessed with a child.

They tried everything they could, but still the empress did not get pregnant. They asked a wise man, but he said their wish would only bring them sorrow. They asked a philosopher, but he said the answer they were looking for was written in the stars—so they asked a witch to read the stars and find out if they would have children.

The witch said they would only have one child and he would be handsome, but they wouldn't be able to keep him for long.

Well, they thought that was better than having nothing, so they asked the witch for an herb that would make their wish come true.

The emperor and the empress brewed themselves tea from the herbs and soon enough the empress was pregnant. They'd never known such happiness.

But on the night the empress went into labor, she saw a star fall out of the heavens. Just before it disappeared from the sky, the star split in two, and at that moment she was struck with a pain so strong she screamed out in a shout heard throughout the kingdom.

She gave birth to two healthy children—a boy and a girl. The emperor and empress were overjoyed. They had been prepared for a son, but this was beyond their wildest dreams.

"You will be the sun and moon in my sky," the empress said, beaming with pride.

The emperor said to one of the babies, "I will give you my kingdom and a princess for your wife."

And to the other he said, "I will give you youth without age and life without death."

But the babies looked exactly alike to him, and he didn't know that he'd mixed the blessings up.

When the children were grown, they came to their father and asked that he honor his promises.

The princess asked for her kingdom and a princess for a wife, and the prince asked for youth without age and life without death.

The king laughed. "Certainly you say this in jest," he said. "Clearly you've made a mistake."

The brother and sister looked at each other and shook their heads.

"We've made no mistake, and now you must honor your promises, or we will be forced to leave the palace and wander the world until we find what was promised to us."

The emperor didn't know what to do, but the empress laughed at him.

"Certainly our daughter was mistaken—she does not want a wife; she wants a husband. And he will inherit her kingdom. All we must do is find her someone suitable—we will unite our empire with theirs."

The emperor thought his wife made a lot of sense, so that is what he set out to do.

But when it was time to introduce his daughter to her intended, she burst into tears and ran out of the palace. The emperor merely thought she was overcome with emotion, but in truth, the princess ran and ran, and she didn't stop.

In fear that they might never see their daughter again, they asked their son if he would go out after her. He said he would, but only if the emperor gave him what he promised him—youth without age and life without death.

The emperor laughed and said, "Of course, but first you must find your sister."

And so the prince set out. He traveled the world, but he never found his sister, until finally he made it back home, and as he arrived, he fell off his horse and crumbled into dust.

The emperor and empress were beside themselves with grief. They cried upon his ashes and tore at their clothes.

"If only I had given him youth without age and life without death,"the emperor wailed. The dirt mingled with his tears and began to form itself into a mass of dust and air. It glowed and swirled until it formed itself into a fiery mass of silver fire, and then it took flight and launched itself into the heavens.

It is said that when that star reached the sky, it split and formed the constellation of the twins, and thus achieved what it had been promised—youth without age and life without death.

But the princess still searches for her beloved, she still seeks a kingdom, and on certain nights you can see her crossing the sky, looking for the lost princess that was promised to her.

Nikolas looks over at me and sees the tears that brim in my eyes. "I'm sorry. I didn't mean to upset you," he says.

"It's a beautiful story," I say. "I don't know what I'm supposed to do next."

"What do you want to do next?" he asks me, as though I have all the choices in the world.

As though any of us do.

"We never know which story is meant to be ours," I say.

"No, we don't," he replies. "But you see, I think they got the story wrong."

"Wrong?" I turn to face him.

"I think it's a story about a princess who rides to the ends of the earth because she wants to be free from what other people think she is."

"I like that," I say. "I think that stories change every time we tell them because we are always changing, like the stars."

I like speaking to Nikolas, I realize. He grounds me.

"What makes you so sad tonight?" he says.
"I think I'm pregnant," I say.
"Oh," he says. "I . . . uh . . . I didn't know."
"Nobody knows," I say.

"A man fell from the sky.
He came to me in my dreams,
and then my dreams became real.
But now he's disappeared.
I've gone out to the woods every night.
That's why I ran from you.
I thought I saw him.
I needed to tell him.
He gave me a ring.
I promised myself to him.
But he's gone now,
I'm sorry I'm telling you this,
but I'm falling apart."

"Laptitza . . . " he says,
placing a hand on my arm.
        I turn to him.
        "Please don't tell.
        Please don't tell anyone," I beg.
"I would never tell. I swear it."

He takes my hand in his and holds it firmly.
"I have a secret too," he says. "And I would never want
anyone to share it without my consent." He stares up at the sky.
"Maybe . . . we can help each other?"
I put a hand on my stomach. "How?"
"Marry me."
"What?" I stand up. "No. I am promised to another."

I turn from him and start to move away.

"I have a ring," I say. "I am faithful."

"Wait, please!" He reaches out. "Just . . . please, listen. Let me say this. And if you still wish to walk away, then so be it."

I stop and wait.

"I . . ." He takes a deep breath. "I cannot succeed my father if I do not have a wife. If you agree to marry me, I will claim your child as my own. I will provide for you. Nobody will ever have to know that the child isn't mine. I can help you. It can be a kind of partnership. You can keep seeing him, this star-man of yours, but this way . . . I can have a child. You will be safe, and my mother and father will be happy."

"What if my star comes back?" I say.

"What if he doesn't?" he says.

"I can't betray him."

"The way I see it, he's betrayed you. But I'll build you a balcony off your bedroom and place the astrolabe there. You can go out every night and wait for him. You may share a bed with him if he comes. Who knows? Maybe I'll find what I'm looking for if I start searching for a star. We can keep each other's secrets. And if he doesn't come back, at least you and your unborn child will be safe from harm."

I stare at the stars for a very long time.

They don't stare back.

I reach my hand out.

This time, a hand reaches back.

It is warm, not cold.

It grips my hand firmly.

"Okay," I say. "I will marry you."

I lace my fingers with his.

We stay that way for a long time, both looking for lost and wandering stars.

Wisdom is the bursting forth, the shining of light in the world. It is the only force in the world that can defeat the darkness of ignorance.

–The Book of the Solomonars, page 93, verse 1

★ ★ ★ ★ ★

Darkness once again swept in like a fog. Evil, once unleashed, needs very little encouragement to spread. Like a spark that falls in a dry forest, it is destined to burn hard, and fast, and destroy those that get caught in its furnace.

Stanna

The next month, I barely see Theodora at all. Preparations are being made for her wedding, which will take place in Bulgaria. I find myself wandering the forest alone at night looking for owls. I don't look for foxes anymore. Half a year has passed since we fled Trnava. Since I saw Guvriel last. I'm lost. Set adrift. An island alone in the middle of a sea so vast, no one will ever cross it—not Guvriel, not Theodora.

My life had once been simple. I knew who I was, where I came from, and what would likely be my future. I don't understand why I once bucked and battled against that with all of my might. And now, stripped of all that once defined us, everything's more complicated. Meeting Theodora changed me, and I don't regret that for an instant. But now I have nothing. Not the old world, or the new.

That's what you get when a snake loves a fox, I hear a voice say in my mind. *No good can ever come of that . . . A snake needs to marry another snake. Fire seeks fire, like calls to like. Sssslide along the foressst floor and ssslide up the barksss of treesss—that issss where you will find yoursssself* . . . But I'm tired and it's late, and I've been wandering the forest for hours. I no longer know if these are my thoughts, or someone else's. They feel dark and syrupy in my ears. Seductive.

I miss Guvriel like a physical ache in my chest, and now I miss Theodora too. A pang of jealously stabs me in the gut so hard, I bend over. Anna found herself a happy ending. I hate my sister. I hate her so much in this minute. She always gets first pick. Always. Why not me?

The spark inside me is alive again, and growing, but this one has no control; this is the type of fire that I know can end forests in an instant.

I take deep breaths and watch them come out hot like smoke. I wander deeper and deeper into the woods. The damp musk of it calms what's brewing within me. Perhaps if I wander deep enough into the forest, I will emerge changed again. Into some other creature. Someone who doesn't burn like I do. Something that doesn't feel pain.

I see a dart of red in the trees.

No. It can't be. Not after all this time. Not after what I've been through. Would he even recognize the person I've become? I'm not sweet and innocent anymore like I once was.

"Guvriel?" I call out. "Is that you?"

I see a bushy tail and follow it. *Anything is possible*, I think—a woman dressed as a man, a person who becomes an owl—or a snake, a Jew who enters a church and marries a non-Jew. Maybe this is Guvriel finally coming to claim me. Or maybe this fox lives in a den and will lead me to him. If not to him, then maybe to another life.

Everything you need is already in your grasp, I hear Guvriel say.

"But it isn't!" I scream to the sky. "I don't even know where to begin!"

There is only the echo of my own voice on the wind. Nobody answers.

I follow the fox. I'm chasing it now. I can't tell if the fox is leading me somewhere or if it's running away from me. After a while, I cannot run anymore. I lose track of the streak of red in the trees. I'm breathing hard and crying. *Clearly it's just a fox*, I tell myself, *and I'm a silly girl, not worthy of love, who believes in stories that never come true.*

I sit down on a log—cold, despondent and alone. I hear voices. They are sweet and dark and they threaten to drown out all other sounds. Maybe it would be better for everyone if I stayed a snake in the woods and never came back. I could sit here and melt into the floor or craft a nest for myself and become a creature of the forest—snake with no love, no desire.

There is a black mist curling around my ankles. I laugh out loud. If the Black Mist has followed us here, then truly everything is lost. *Maybe I'm the one it wants, the one it wanted all alone.* It looks soft . . . inviting . . . Maybe I could lie down and it could cover me like a blanket . . .

The fox appears again, a streak of red in the moonlight. I sit still, hoping that if I don't startle it, it will come to me. If only I had something to feed it. A way to lure it to me. But I already know that I don't. I'm not enough. Not even for a fox.

The fox dances closer to me, darting in and out of the trees, until it starts to circle the place where I sit. The Black Mist rises higher. I wait for the fox. I reach out my hand—the fox bites me.

I cry out in pain and clutch my bleeding hand to my chest. I get up and try to run away, but I'm tired and it's late and I trip and fall. I try to get up again, but I twist my ankle. I'm now scared of the fox, that it will come back, that it will bite me again. I try to get up, try to drag myself somewhere safe, but my arm hurts and my legs ache. I collapse to the forest floor into a blanket of mist. Alone and utterly bereft.

I curl into a ball and allow the dark to take my pain away.

I hear someone knocking at a door, but I am too tired to get up and answer it. My limbs weigh a hundred pounds.

I try to open my eyes, but everything is dark. I'm moving. My head bumps against what feels like a hard wooden log beside me. It hurts. My hand hurts. My ankle hurts. I'm being jostled side to side. The ground is moving. Then I'm lifted and carried. I'm dizzy, so dizzy.

I hear a voice. "Who is it?" The sound is muffled, like from behind a door.

"Constantin, it's Theodora, let me in."

The door opens, light floods my vision even through my closed lids. Footsteps. Then softness. Something I sink into . . . A bed. I try to open my eyes—everything is hazy. I see someone with long red hair and a kind face. Theodora? No. She cut her hair. Guvriel? My heart beats fast . . . I want to ask the person why they're crying but I can't hold up my head. My eyes close again.

"I found her in the woods," I hear someone say. "Her hand is bleeding."

"I'm a healer," another familiar voice says. "At least . . . I used to be. Constantin, boil some hot water."

"My horse is outside; I'll tie it up and be right back."

"What do you need? Bandages? A poultice?" a voice asks.

"No, just some hot water, and . . . if you'll allow me to work alone."

My eyes open. Hannah. It's Hannah! But then I realize that if she's here . . . it isn't Guvriel at all. My eyes fill with tears. Hannah's hands shake as she touches me.

Someone is beside me, stroking my hair. I turn my head. Not Guvriel . . . Theodora.

She gets down on her knees beside me. "I heard you, my *lăcrimioare*," she whispers to me. "My true father walks on clouds of smoke that can take on any form. He is dead but his spirit lives. He told me the forest echoed with your sorrow. I'm so sorry, *draga mea*. I thought it would be best if I left you alone. If I left you to heal, to forget. I only wanted to be your friend ... but even that I couldn't do. I know I said I can't promise you anything, but I will promise you now—I will never betray you or leave you again."

I try to reach my hand up to touch her cheek but I'm too weak.

"You need to get better first. I found you curled up in a coil, like a beautiful snake ... and you'd been bitten by some creature. You must live or I will never forgive myself. We still have so many things to do together—" Theodora brings my hand to her lips and places a kiss in my palm. I turn my head away. I don't want her to see my tears.

"Please, I must do this alone," Hannah says.

Theodora gets up. "I'll be waiting. Let me know if there's anything you need."

There is pressure on my chest. A hand on my arm.

"*El na refah na lah, El na refah na lah,*" like a chant. "*Please, Lord, please heal her.*"

A soothing feeling runs through me, spreading from my hand up to my shoulder.

At first, the cold made me sleepy, but now I'm lulled by this calm warmth. I feel a hand on my head, the way my mother would stroke my hair when I was little. It's been so long since anyone has taken care of me. I try to snuggle my head closer, to take the comfort she offers. If I should die, I think, this is a good way to go.

I hear her singing—"*Én Istenem, Jó Istenem—my God, my good God ...*"—and I let the words and melody wash over me. "*Should the sun rise again, we can kiss again in the morning.*" My shoulders shake and the tears come. As though my insides have begun to thaw. She keeps singing the song, humming the melody as if it could turn back time and take me to a place before all we lost.

The calm gets warmer and warmer, and soon it's not a soothing lull anymore. The pain is back. It's in my lungs. I gasp and open my eyes.

I'm not in my mother's lap; I'm in a bed in my newly married sister's house. It is Anna's voice I hear. And Theodora is standing over me.

Maybe this is a place between life and death, I think. My heart beats impossibly fast. It thunders in my ears. I hear Theodora's voice, feel her hand on my head. "Sleep," she says. "Sleep and I will tell you a story."

Radu Negru was my father. In his time, he was known as the Black Dragon. People say he was descended from a caste of Dacian priests—smoke-walkers, people called them, with powers pulled from the soil of this land—from the very forest where we first met—the Satu Mare. There is a pulse, a current that runs through a people—it comes from the land in which they are born. Not everyone can see it or feel it, but Radu Negru could, and that was how he formed Wallachia and her people. He forged them from the mist that rises from the earth upon which they were born. He did what he had to do to protect the people he loved and the faith he followed, and he created a refuge for them—a land where they could be free.

He and his people were followers of the new faith, but he himself never let go of the traditions of the old gods.

Soon his wife was pregnant, and she begged him to construct the most beautiful monastery in the country for her, in honor of the birth of her child.

Radu Negru wasn't a man who denied his wife anything, so he hired the most talented mason he could find, a man named Manole, and told him to gather as many men as he needed.

Manole only hired nine men to help him. Radu Negru couldn't understand how the mason would be able to build such a monastery with only the help of nine men, but he trusted in powers higher than himself, and construction began.

Except, every day the walls of the monastery would grow, and every night, the walls would crumble. In the meantime, Radu Negru's wife's stomach grew and grew, and he was mad that his wife's stomach was growing at a faster pace than the monastery, so he threatened to kill the mason and his workers if they couldn't find a way to get the walls to stand in time for his child's birth and baptism.

The mason told him that he had a dream where an angel came to him and said that in order for the monastery to stand for as long as the king would rule, he had to entomb within its walls a person beloved by Radu Negru.

Radu Negru was distraught. The only person he loved with all his soul was his pregnant wife. He figured, at least this way he could ensure that his child would be born and die in holiness and purity. And his wife would be immortalized.

The next day, Radu Negru saw his wife out for a stroll on her way to check on the progress of the monastery. He prayed for a rainstorm to start so that she might turn back, but her love for him was stronger than a rainstorm, and she kept walking despite the downpour. He prayed that a fox should cross her path and scare her away, but when the fox appeared she bent down and offered it some grapes from her pocket. The fox stopped to eat, and Radu Negru's wife kept walking. He prayed again that a star might fall from the heavens, an omen of death, and sure enough, a star fell, but she merely walked around it, thinking it an omen of good fortune, and laughed at the scorch-marks it left in the earth.

When she finally arrived, Manole and his workers were waiting for her. They asked her if she would play a game, that they wished to measure the size of her stomach to match the spire to the width of the Holy Mother when she was pregnant. They needed to build walls around her body in order to ensure the spire was of the proper width *and size. She gladly accepted, flattered that she was being compared to the Holy Mother, and certain this would mean the monastery would be blessed by God.*

However, as the walls went up, she began to panic. She started to cry and scream in wails that pierced the heavens. But Radu Negru knew that in order for the walls of the monastery to stand, he had to keep his promise. When it was done, he was wracked with grief, for he realized there would be no baptism. Without his wife, the monastery felt empty and cold.

He asked the builders if they thought they could ever construct an edifice more beautiful. They answered that they certainly could. Fearing that they might create a bigger and more intricate structure for someone else, Radu Negru asked them to meet him on the roof of the monastery for a festive ceremony to celebrate their accomplishment. There, he gave them each a gift—a set of wooden wings. He told them that if they could fly off the roof, he would reward them handsomely. One by one, they fell to the ground and perished until Manole was the last man left.

"What will you do now?" he asked Radu Negru. "For if I perish, as all my workers did before me, you will be entirely alone."

Radu Negru answered, "I will not be alone, for I will fly away after you on wings of smoke, thereby ending my reign. I will be with my beloved, and the walls will come crumbling down."

Manole jumped and where he fell, a well of clear water sprang up. Radu Negru grew wings of smoke and those that saw him said he looked like a black dragon in the sky.

The next morning, the walls of the monastery split open, and out walked his wife, still pregnant with their child.

Some say you can sometimes see him, a black smoke dragon circling the spire of the keep. Others say they've seen him as a smoky-gray owl; still others say a raven, dark and black and fierce. Some say that he is not the man he used to be. That he is dark and twisted now—a black dragon of smoke and mist that haunts the skies above

Wallachia and its surrounding lands, bringing pestilence and plague and spreading hatred.

Legend says that anyone who drinks from the well of Manole will have eternal life. But others say that those who've tried to drink from it have turned into smoke creatures that haunt the night. It is said no birds go near the water for fear of its black depths, and that the keepers of the monastery have placed a large rock over the spring so that no one might be tempted by it.

It is said that for his sacrifice, Radu Negru's wife and child were granted eternal life, and that one day he will return, the raven king, the Black Dragon, a smoke-walker like the old gods, and that when he does, he will reign eternally.

*   ★ . ★ ★ . ★*
★ . ★   ★ . ★
★   ★

"I used to wish for that, as a child," Theodora says. "For his return. But I've seen the things my father does and I know better now. It was not me who called him. Not me who called the mist and brought the darkness to our streets. I don't know why he's back, but I suspect it's something my mother is planning."

Her fingers thread through my hair.

"Basarab trained me to be swift on a horse and good with an arrow. I am not my father. I will not allow his legacy to become my own. Everything I learned about my powers has come from deep inside me. I had to teach myself to groom smoke into form. You can do the same. Smoke and fire are two sides of the same coin—light and dark."

She is silent for a while, humming to herself. "I was scared, *draga mea*; I'd never opened myself up like that for anyone and I only did so because you were so brave—you are my shining star, my inspiration. If you, who's been through so much, could be brave enough to show your true form—golden scales and all—I knew I had to try.

"I don't know if you can hear me, but just being by your side calms me in a way that nothing else ever has. Will you come to Bulgaria with me? I thought you would be better off without me—but I was wrong. I don't know what the future holds, and I know it's not the life you may have wanted, but it's what I can offer. Will you come with me?"

But before I can answer, I hear the sound of hooves outside the door. My heart beats fast. Theodora sees me tense up. Horses never mean anything good . . .

"My men have come," she says. "I sent for them. They brought a carriage. Can I move her?" she asks my sister. "I will take her back to the palace with me. I depart soon for Bulgaria and there are many things still to get ready."

Theodora looks back at me. "Will you join me, *draga mea?*" there is a world of fear in her eyes. She's making herself vulnerable again before me, and I don't have the heart to say no. My heart tells me that this is the future God is setting out for me—two roads—both safe and dangerous in equal measure.

"Is this what you want, Sarahleh?" my sister whispers. In an instant, she looks like Hannah again—young and studious yet full of quiet passion.

"Yes," I say to Theodora. "Yes, I will come on this journey with you."

Theodora turns to Anna. "Thank you for saving her."

"Take care of my sister."

"I promise." She carries me out to the carriage. "I will never leave you," she whispers into my hair. "I will take care of you. You will remain forever by my side."

"Don't make promises you can't keep," I whisper, but I don't know if my lips succeed in forming words that she can hear.

Laptitza

I go to the clearing
      to wait for him.
I wait all night
      until I am frozen
      and still alone.
I wait again the next night.
      And the next night.
      And the next night again.
But he doesn't return.

Anna

1 Av 5122

After Theodora and Stanna took off in the carriage on their way back to the palace this morning, I turned to Constantin. "I'm worried. How will I tell my parents? What will become of my sister?"

"I know Theodora. She will do everything in her power to take care of the people she loves. It's what made us all trust her with our lives and follow her into battle. She is more than what she seems."

"But my sister . . . She was in love before. He was supposed to follow us . . . " I shook my head. "She's been through a lot . . . "

"Shhh . . . " he said. "Come here, *draga mea*. Let's not speak of this right now. I wish to show you exactly how much I love you."

"Because you finally have me all to yourself again?" I teased him.

"Because I would like to see how your healing hands work on me . . . " he said with a smirk.

"Oh, poor baby, does it hurt you somewhere?" I cooed.

"I ache for you," he said. "You will have to use your hands to find out where . . . "

"Well, you will have to wait. I must prepare dinner." I turned away from him.

"The only thing I am waiting for is to see you grow plump and round with my seed, because that is the only future I care about. Mine and yours, and this table someday full of strong young men and women who will put down roots here," he said, and started kissing the back of my neck.

"There will be no future if you do not find time to come home from the palace and plow your fields. It's nearly time to plant the wheat."

"There's only one field I intend to plow tonight." He spun me around and kissed me, gently at first, then with more passion. He lifted me up and I wrapped my legs around him. He lowered me onto the table and reached his hands under my skirts, stroking my legs, reaching up to part my thighs. I gasped as he stroked exactly in the places where I ached for him the most.

I sat up and placed my hands on his chest. "So where does it hurt?" I purred.

He unlaced his pants. "I will show you," he said, and in an instant was inside me. All thoughts of sisters and foxes were lost in the crescendo of sounds that we made. I was close, so close, and then I was lost in the moment beyond all thought that brought us both over the edge. I'd never known that coupling could be like that. And I was suddenly sad that it had taken me so long to find out.

Constantin's seed will take root tonight. I can feel it. He woke something up inside me that was buried by ash but is now remembering how to grow.

By morning, a small plant will grow in the crack between two beams of wood under the table, a sapling that matches the one he planted in my belly. I can feel it underneath my feet. It will grow in the center of this room—a linden tree—and no matter how many times I will try to cut it back, it will just keep growing.

Beware the Black Dragon that haunts the skies. Thy sons and daughters the very teeth of venomous dragons overcame, for thy mercy was ever by them and healed them.

–The Book of the Solomonars, page 96, verse 4

Once there was a star that fell from the sky.
Once there was a girl who loved him.
But one day the star disappeared,
and a dragon took to the skies in its place.

Laptitza

Nikolas brings me
to the palace
to prepare
for the wedding.
Everything happens
so quickly.
Our engagement
is a surprise
To everyone:
My parents,
      still reeling from Stanna
      having moved into the palace.
The voivode
      and Marghita are furious.
Everyone had been so focused
      on Theodora's engagement
      to Ivan Alexander
      that nobody noticed
      a young boy
      and a young girl
      sketching their future
      between the stars.

I go about my days despondent.
I watch the sky each night,
but there's no sign of him.
When it rains,
I stand by the windows
                           and watch.
When it snows
I go out onto the balcony
                           and wait.
I am cold
                  all the time.

I wear the white fur
that Nikolas gifted me
and watch as the skies
as flakes of snow
fall on my cloak.
When will he
                  come for me?

Some nights
Nikolas joins me.
Other nights
he watches me
as I watch the sky.
If he sees a star fall,
                  he wishes on it.
And I don't know
if he's praying for me
                  or for himself.

The night before the wedding
I go to the linden tree

at the heart of the wood.
Nikolas comes with me.
We walk hand in hand.
He wants me to be sure;
he wants me to be safe.
"Tell me about him," he says.
     "He is bright.
     The brightest star
     in the sky."
"Here, we believe," he says,
"that every star
in the sky
is a soul."

     "What happens
     when one of them
     falls?" I ask him.

"What happens?" He laughs.
"They die."

     "You're wrong.
     When a man falls
     from the sky,
     that's when his future
     begins to unfold."

Nikolas furrows his brow.
"My mother
always told me
that a falling star
is a portent of . . . "
     "Of what?"

"Nothing.
I'm sure
it's nonsense."
          "Tell me."
He opens
his mouth
and then closes it.
"It's not important."
          We watch
                    and wait
                              for hours.

This time,
while I wait,
palm outstretched
to the sky—
Nickolas reaches up
and makes a wish:
          If her true love could fall
          from the sky like that,
          maybe mine could too.

I insist on a midnight ceremony—
when the stars will be brightest
and the moon can bear
luminous witness.

I walk around him seven times,
call it a peasant custom
from our old town.
By the time I start making
my slow circles around him,

I am not thinking
of the stars at all.
I am watching my mother,
wide-eyed with wonder
at the beauty of the dress I wear,
the white fur on my shoulders.
My father looks lost, bewildered,
like he's hearing a melody
he remembers
from another time.
Pondering how
he could have lost
so much,
so quickly.

But I can't allow myself
to think such thoughts
on my wedding day.
I concentrate on removing
the barriers between us
with each circle I make,
so we can be together
with only truth between us.

I finish my last circle around him,
look up at the sky one last time.
Nikolas puts his arm around me.

With this ring, I am wed.

Stanna

The night in the woods stays with me like a black fog in my brain. I walk and sleep and eat, but the place where the fox bit me still burns and there's a kind of fever—a panicked burning in my chest. I barely get through Laptitza's wedding. She looks dazzling in a white dress that sparkles with silver beads and thread, and she wears the fur of a large white wolf around her shoulders. I didn't make a veil for her. There is pressure on my chest, as though I bound it with fabric, and there's also a voice in my head that repeats itself over and over again: *Not for you. Never for you. No one will marry you.*

The parting with my parents is difficult.

"I'm so proud of you. You found your own way, my child. My little spark. And you found yourself such promising employment. A future as a lady of a great court," Mama says, tears in her eyes, which spark tears in mine. I turn to my father, but his expression is inscrutable. He hugs me and says into my ear, "Esther did not reveal her people, or her nation," quoting from *The Book of Esther*. I look up into his eyes, hoping to see a spark of light back in them—a spark of the Torah he used to learn and speak all day and night, but his eyes are stones.

I put my arms around him again, but my face falls behind his back because I know, with bitterness that still resides deep in my heart, that these are not the words he would say to me if I was a boy—his son, his heir—he would not be so cavalier about seeing me go. This is not the warning he would give me. The roads that I travel seem to begin and end at crossroads, and over and over again, I make the wrong choice.

The day after Laptitza's wedding, we leave for Bulgaria. The journey takes nearly a week, and I don't remember much of it, only that I watch endless acres of forest go by and muse about how in the space of less than a year I have found myself traveling again. This time by horse and fine carriage.

My hand heals and the fog doesn't cloud my head like it once did, but I still feel weak. My insides burn and ache but there is no fire. My flame feels utterly spent.

Theodora chooses to spend most of her time riding so that I might convalesce inside. I slip from sleep to wakefulness and back, opening my eyes each time in a panic that I'm lost and forgotten again.

Finally, I fall into a sleep that feels like a nightmare. I remember sharp pain, then I'm alone and drifting in an icy river. But I know I'm warm, and the bed I sleep in is comfortable, with lavish blankets and sheets, softer than anything I've ever felt before. I've had this dream before. I've woken up startled and screaming with no one beside me.

For a moment, I think that I'm a ghost and this is heaven—that I've passed on to the world to come. I remember hearing my father talk about this world—a place of endless light where there are seven palaces—each one housing different aspects of creation. I wonder which palace we are in.

I hear a voice and open my eyes. Theodora.

"I can see all your thoughts," Theodora says.

I swallow hard. "Are you dead too?"

"Dead?" Theodora laughs. "No, not dead, very much alive. Though I suppose this is a kind of heaven, being beside you. We've set up camp for the night."

"I think I dreamed of him again. Guvriel."

"I've heard you say his name in your dreams," she says.

"I don't think I will ever be able to forget him, but I want to try."

"I don't expect you to forget him."

She puts her arms around me and covers us both with blankets. Through the window of the carriage as we journeyed, all we saw were endless forests covered in snow. I see the same landscape now through a sliver in the tent flap. It matches the way I feel inside. *He won't ever find me now.* The words creep like frost across my heart.

"Tomorrow we will reach Lovech, the home of Ivan Alexander," Theodora says. "I will present you as my handmaiden, my closest confidante who will remain by my side at all times." She threads her fingers through mine. "Let there always be truth between us."

I chose her. I chose this rather than stay back in Curtea. But as we ride farther and farther away from any hope that Guvriel might keep his promise, I'm not sure it's what I want at all. At some point, I thought I wanted to wrap myself in a prayer shawl like my father's students and spend the rest of my life devoted to study and prayer.

Except that path was never open to me.

"In a way," I say cryptically, "I think that you and I are very much alike."

"Oh yes?" Theodora grins and turns to her side. "How's that?"

"Once, I wanted to be a boy more than anything."

"Really?" She cocks her head.

"Yes, but I don't want that anymore. When you have no one to teach you, you must find a way to teach yourself. But it's not easy," I say.

"No one said it was," she replies.

"I have to figure out who I am without him, and who I am with you. What kind of power I want to have. It's all very confusing with no scrolls to read or anyone to guide me."

"I cannot help you find those things, *draga mea*, but I can share my journey with you."

"I'd like that," I say. "I'm trying to look towards the future."

I remember the story Theodora told me about smoke-walkers and her father, the great Black Dragon of Wallachia. It's clear that what I know about Theodora only scratches the surface of who she is and what she can do. Yet she knows nothing about me. I promised her there would be truth between us, but I can't even begin to explain the world I come from to her. When I was with Guvriel, I knew who he was and what he believed. Where he came from, who his parents were, and their grandparents before them, all the way back to King Solomon himself, and from there back to Mount Sinai where all Jewish souls once stood. It is an unbroken chain of tradition that my family is now actively engaged in breaking.

How do I explain to her how what we once believed governed every minute detail of every aspect of our lives—from what we ate to how we farmed, how we treated our neighbors, how we worshiped God—and the specialness that was my family—my father, our direct connection to the divine via His servant, the great King Solomon himself. The things my father and my sisters could do, the way we once looked at the world. The books upon books that we studied. The scrolls we read from and memorized. The Talmudic debates and the Mishnaic formulas for life as we knew it. How much respect I had for it all despite how much of it was barred from me because of my sex. And the persecution of our people for our belief in our faith—our survival in exile from our Holy Land and how we are fleeing, always fleeing from one Black Mist to another.

It is why we only marry Jews. Who else could possibly understand what we've been through? Is this really the life I want? Or perhaps, like back in Trnava—the life I want is not one I get to choose. Maybe life is a result of what happens to me, not what I'm able to change in the world.

Once, I had simple dreams. I wanted to learn everything I could about myself and my abilities, and on the way I found love in the form of Guvriel who could give that to me—that and so much more. He was smart and playful, a boy on his way to becoming a man and, most importantly, he was everything my father wasn't. I had a future. It was planned out and it was good.

I see his face before me now clearly—it doesn't merge with Theodora's anymore. He looks as he did the first time I really saw him. His mischievous smile, the dimple on his left cheek, his long glorious red sidelocks that swung in perfect curls as he tossed his head in laughter, the way he twirled them absentmindedly when he was thinking, or walking me to town on the way to Mária's house. The last time I saw him he was serious. Frightened. We all were, but in that moment, he was a Solomonar like my father, destined to lead. Our union felt right, blessed by the stars under which we first met and the forest that kept our secrets . . . and now I've lost all of that. How do I explain it all to her? How do I even begin?

"I've lost you," she says.

"What?" I shake my head. "Sorry."

A cloud darkens Theodora's face, blocking out all of her light.

"Nobody should be bound to a life they don't want." She turns away from me. "I wanted you to be free to marry who you please, to live a normal life . . . That was why I tried to stay away from you. I cannot help what I am, the things I desire. But you can be free."

"I will never be free." I chose this. My soul chose this. There are no wrong choices. Perhaps everything *is* both a curse and a blessing. Yet it's still the choice I'd make again. *Justice, justice you shall pursue*, it says in *The Book of Devarim*. But it is truth I want, just like Theodora.

"I know what you're thinking, 'Why did I make this choice?' 'What have I gotten myself into?'"

"My thoughts might wander, but that doesn't mean that I'm not confident in my choice."

She turns back to me. "When I nearly lost you, I felt for a moment what you must feel all the time. Such emptiness I didn't think anything could ever fill it. I don't ever want to feel that pain again. But you are not well. You are not thriving. And I can't help but blame myself. If you wish to leave—I won't keep you."

It's as though a crack has formed in Theodora's armor, and I realize something—she may be wearing a dress, but it's still armor. And now, I'm the cause of the crack in its veneer.

"My body is weak," I say, "but it's not my body which suffers. I don't think I ever properly mourned Guvriel—not only him, but the loss of everything he represented—my home, my religion, our way of life. I need to tell you more, but I'm tired." My hands have turned to ice, as though my body is finally allowing itself to feel the grief that's been sitting like a rock at the very center of me.

"So warm yourself by my fire," Theodora says.

But I need to speak about Guvriel; I need to get this out. And not just in my sleep. *Tell his story*, a voice says.

"You don't look well." Theodora puts her hand on my forehead. "Maybe you should rest . . . "

"No." I take a deep breath. "I want to tell you about him."

She lays her head on my chest. "Then I will listen," she says.

I take a deep breath.

There was once a red-haired boy who fell in love with the daughter of a scholar. Her father was a leader in his community, known for having special powers that came from the great King Solomon himself. He was revered and cherished by Jews and non-Jews alike. Able to read the position of the stars in the sky to predict the future. He spoke to animals in their language, saw things through their eyes, could change his form to theirs. He knew the property of every plant and herb, and could call on the rain and the clouds and command them to take form. He rode a white dragon made of cloud—a serpent with wings and a long tail and the head of a horse and the mane of a lion, its breath so cold it froze the water in the clouds. He and his wife had three girls and each one was gifted with their father's abilities.

But the middle child felt dwarfed by the perfect, easy way her older sister had with plants and her ability to heal others, and she grew jealous of the way her younger sister was always looking at the stars, making predictions and gaining all of their father's love and attention.

She met a boy in the woods one night in the form of a fox, and he taught her truths about herself and the things she could do. It was the first time she felt seen as worthy, valuable, talented.

The red-haired boy was attracted to her intensity, to the spark of fire within her. He asked her to marry him. Her father approved of the match, but not the timing. He hoped that marriage would cure her of her strange behavior, the tendency she had to set things on fire, but his eldest daughter wasn't married yet. And so, the couple had to wait.

They were engaged, though they could not yet marry.

The girl's mother apprenticed her to a weaver in town, something to keep her hands occupied, but her longing for her fiancé only grew. She began to fear that she would never marry. That she would never be anything other than the middle sister shadowed by the wondrous things the others in her family could do. She dreamed that someday people would flock to her. That they would call her the Holy Maiden.

That dozens would turn up to hear her pray and speak words of Torah on Shabbat afternoons. They would beg her to bless them. But it was all just a dream that would never be.

Soon her sister married.

But then tragedy struck.

Her sister's husband was killed. Their family had to flee. The girl was torn from her fiancé's arms before she ever got a chance to be with him. He swore he'd come for her. But he never did. And all her dreams were shattered.

She vowed never to marry if she couldn't be with him.

Some say that you can see her still, wrapped in a prayer shawl, swaying to words that only she can hear. When the winds pick up and start to howl at the window, some say that mournful sound is her, forever mourning the loss of her true love.

"But that doesn't have to be your story," Theodora says, tucking a lock of my hair behind my ear. "You may not be able to change how it begins, but you can change how it ends."

I stare into her eyes. "I think I'd like to try," I say.

Anna

14 Nisan 5123

With both of my sisters gone, things have settled into a routine.

I am mistress of my own house now, my own farm. We are close enough to my parents that I'm able to visit once or twice a week, but far enough away that I feel free in a way I've never felt before. There are no eyes watching me. No community judging every move I make.

The days are long and hard, but fulfilling. The land is rich and green. I've started clearing room for a garden outside. Each day I do a little more. My hands are slowly remembering the things they used to do, awakening together with the soil as it thaws from the long winter. Ground aching, beneath the snow, for release.

Tonight would have been the holiday of Passover. We would have been preparing all day in the kitchen, chopping and baking, setting the table. Instead, I gathered bitter herbs from the fields and placed them in our stew.

For the first time in a long time, I wanted to remember.

I didn't speak of it to Constantin, but as we ate supper, I recited the verses we would have said. *In every generation a person must see himself as if he himself left Egypt.* The words have never felt so true. Have we reached the Holy Land? Or is Curtea yet another encampment in the desert? I told Constantin that all I want is to put down roots somewhere, but what he doesn't know is that my people are cursed to always wander.

I know I'm violating the laws tonight, writing these words down. On holidays we don't write or light fires or do any kind of creative work, and yet here I am. But this is the first time in months that I've cared, and that feels like something too. Something worth remembering.

Constantin and I have spent every night together since the night Stanna left. He hasn't been called to duty yet; he was denied the request he made to go with Theodora as her private guard. I had mixed feelings at the time. On the one hand, I wanted him to protect my sister. On the other, I didn't want to be alone. In the end, it wasn't his choice to make. Basarab ordered him to stay here. It means we are getting to know one another, sharing secrets and pleasures. It means that he's safe.

I bake him corn bread dotted with strawberries—echoing the words I once said in the forest in a kind of forced jest—*If I were ever to marry again, I would bake my husband strawberry bread every day . . . to keep his lips and cheeks pink and his heart red and full so he could stay young and brave and mine forever.*

At night, I watch the rise and fall of his chest as he sleeps, I trace his lips with my tongue. I am safe and we are healthy. *Let him be young and brave and mine forever*, I pray. I feel my belly swell each day. I have everything I could possibly want. Yet the shell of my heart is dry, brittle and empty. I cannot light a fire without remembering; I keep letting the hearth grow cold.

We are all bound with one chain of darkness.

–The Book of the Solomonars, page 78, verse 3

★ ★ ★ ★ ★ ★ ★ ★ ★ ★ ★

Evil comes in many forms and fires start in many ways. And sometimes life doesn't play out the way that we expect it to. In times like these, we have to make a choice. In the end, we do what we must to survive, even if we don't understand the choices we make. There are many different kinds of resistance. Sometimes resistance means letting go.

Stanna

The first few weeks in Lovech are a blur. When we arrive, we're met by servants who cart trunks of clothes and belongings upstairs. Ivan Alexander is out hunting. I think Theodora expected him to be waiting for her—to ride out and meet our carriage—but perhaps it's better this way. We get a chance to settle in first.

We are shown to drafty rooms where a fire has been lit in the hearth but hasn't quite warmed the rooms yet. Theodora announces that I will share her room, and no one else. I spend most of the day attending to Theodora together with the servants. I stand by as they bathe her, arrange her hair, dress her, and prepare her to meet her intended.

The wedding is to take place in a few days. Basarab and Marghita will be in attendance, along with Nikolas and Laptitza, Constantin and Anna. I've never stayed in a room this lavish. I've never seen so many servants. I wonder if this is what Hannah felt when she went with Jakob to attend to the duchess. And then I feel guilty for not asking her more about what it was like. Perhaps I could have prepared myself better. I must force myself not to stare doe-eyed in shock at all the finery around me.

A knock sounds on the door to Theodora's chamber.

"Prince Ivan Alexander wishes to meet you," one of the guards says.

Theodora says, "Yes, I am ready."

"You too," he says, looking in my direction.

I look behind me, but there's no one there.

"Me?" I say.

"Yes, you too. The prince wishes to meet every member of his household."

My eyes meet Theodora's. She nods.

When we enter the chamber of Ivan Alexander, he is seated at a desk. I follow what Theodora does, except I bow my head and curtsy when I stand before the prince. "My lord," she says. "It is an honor to finally meet you."

"My lord," I say.

"Well met, my future bride. I trust the journey wasn't too long or difficult?"

"It was uneventful," Theodora says.

"You are Stanna?" He turns to me.

"I am, your grace," I say.

"Step out of the shadows and let me see your face," he says.

I step forward and look up.

"This is your handmaiden?" he says to Theodora.

"Yes, she is my trusted confidante," she replies.

"I've been told that you've requested that she always be by your side—do you not trust the security in the palace?"

"I am but lonely, your grace, and Stanna reminds me of home. She keeps me entertained."

He looks at me with newfound interest. "Very well. Perhaps Stanna might find time to entertain me as well," he chuckles, which turns into a deep belly laugh that sends chills down my spine.

I see that he is handsome, but there is an edge to him. Sharp like the blade of a knife. I'd grown so used to hating him—hating that he was taking Theodora away—forcing her into a marriage she doesn't want, that I saw his face in my mind as old, gnarly and wrinkled. I couldn't imagine him otherwise. But his hair is dark and thick, his forehead broad, his face long and lean. He has a mustache and a short beard, his cheekbones prominent, his eyes brown and warm but striking in their depth. He doesn't miss a thing. He sees all of my thoughts. I am clearly a curiosity. Something he wants to understand. Who am I and why am I here? I keep asking myself the same questions.

"I heard you made a miraculous recovery," he says to me.

"Your future bride nursed me back to health," I reply.

"I did not know she was skilled in the healing arts," he says, looking at Theodora with appraisal.

"Neither did I, your grace," I mumble.

"No need for titles between us." He flaps his hands at me. "I want my wife to feel comfortable here, and if a trusted maid from home is what she needs—then so be it. I wanted to meet the one who has found so much favor in her eyes."

I bow my head. "Thank you, sir."

"That is all; you may go. I will see you," he says to Theodora, "two days from now. At the altar. Do not be late and do not disappoint me." He says with a straight face and then he laughs again. "But of course, I am merely jesting. I look forward to the consummation of our nuptials, my lady." He takes Theodora's hand in his and kisses it, then looks up. Theodora's gaze is steady.

"Will that be all?" she says.

"Yes, future wife, that is all."

Theodora turns to go, but when I go to follow her, as she walks out of the room and out of earshot, I hear him say, "*Tya e krasiva tazi*, eh?" to the guards in the room with him. He laughs that deep belly laugh again. I don't understand what he said.

"Stanna!" he calls to me as I'm about to walk out of his chamber.

I turn back to face him.

"It doesn't hurt that you are easy on the eyes, eh?"

"My first duty is to Theodora, your grace," I say softly.

"Of course, and I'm glad to hear it. Go back to fussing over my bride. We will meet again." He shoos me out of the room with a motion of his hands.

"Thank you for welcoming me into your household." I bow my head again.

His eyes pin me where I stand and my heart speeds up. In an instant, his face changes. His mouth splits into a wide grin, but it has an edge to it like everything about him. "You are most welcome."

I blush, but I don't know why. I worry that I made a mistake, that I addressed him incorrectly. I don't understand all the words he's said, and I'm confused by the way he looks at me so intensely. I'm afraid of him. Of his power. Of what he could do to me and my family if he ever found out that I'm a Jew. What he could do to Theodora should he ever find out how she feels about me—how we feel about each other. I swallow hard.

"I will see you at the ceremony," he says.

I have overstayed my welcome. I need to leave now. But why aren't my feet obeying? "Yes, of course, my apologies." I bow again and a guard appears by my side to usher me out of the room.

"You have nothing to apologize for, *krasota*," I hear him say as I walk out.

Something about the way he says it sends ice down my spine.

Everything about that was strange. Every day there are new rules for me to follow. New things I must learn about court etiquette. *How will I ever be able to pull this off?* I wish Hannah was by my side. I could ask her what it was like with Jakob, if she felt the way I do now. But I know I'd be too afraid to ask questions that remind her of all that she lost.

"What did he want?" Theodora says. I nearly run into her, lost as I am in my thoughts as I walk fast to catch up with her.

"To say that he's happy I'm here to take care of you," I lie. He barely said anything to me. It was more about what was left unsaid.

The next day goes by in a blur. Guests arrive, preparations are made, and the next thing I know Theodora is dressed for the wedding, a crown of gold and coins sitting beside her.

"Come," she says. "I wish for you to crown me."

I lift up the large headdress. It is woven with fresh flowers, and the golden coins on it jingle as I place it on Theodora's head. Our eyes meet. There are tears in her eyes. Something about this moment feels final. As though I am dressing her to meet her doom.

I reach to secure the crown behind her head, and she rests her head on my arm for a moment and closes her eyes.

"All will be well," I say. But something in my heart is full of foreboding and I can't help but notice that my fingers tremble as I affix the crown securely to Theodora's head.

Why do I feel like everything is about to change again?

She takes my hands in hers and slips an emerald ring onto my finger. "Can you hold that for me during the ceremony?" she says. "Don't take it off." And I see in her eyes the words she doesn't say. *I am giving you a ring.*

I hold Theodora's clammy hand all the way to the chapel. At the doors, we are met by Basarab and Marghita, and by Nikolas and Laptitza. Constantin trails Basarab—his own personal guard. My eyes search the crowd for Anna, and then finds her: with her hair covered, she almost looks like she comes from another lifetime—one in which none of this was possible. Marghita takes Theodora's hand from mine and kisses her cheek. "You look beautiful, *fiica mea.*"

I see Theodora's shoulders tense up. She looks straight ahead.

Regal and strong, ready to meet her destiny, though she'd prefer to be on a horse, galloping towards a battlefield or heaving with the thrill of the hunt, not here, in a chapel, being forced into an alliance she never desired.

Laptitza stands beside me and takes my hand. It is the second time that we have been to church. The wrongness of it seeps deep into my bones. I rub the emerald ring with my thumb.

I watch Theodora make her way down the aisle between Basarab and Marghita. Ivan Alexander stands at the front of the room, awaiting his bride. He grins at Theodora, and I can't help but have hope that this will all work out. But then, the more I watch, I grow suddenly uncomfortable. My eyes dart from Theodora to Ivan Alexander. I try to deny it, but I can't—his eyes are not on Theodora at all. His eyes are on me. I turn my head slightly, to make sure, but again there is no one behind me. Ivan Alexander smiles wider and winks. My veins turn to ice. *Surely that was just a twitch of his eye.* I look down at my hand, which holds Laptitza's hand, and turn the emerald ring around so that the stone faces my palm. I close my hand around the stone and squeeze it so tight it digs into my skin.

I find myself wanting to say a prayer I once knew, words I would have once said during the wedding ceremony—an auspicious time to pray for the couple, but also for yourself. I mouth the words as everyone around me starts to sing. The smell of incense is thick in the air. I've never felt so fully out of place as I do in this moment. *Bless this couple, Lord, and may they be worthy to live in love and find joy in each other.* I say it even though my heart cracks. *May this be a house full of God's blessing, a house full of holiness, a loyal house built on truth.* But the words feel hollow, as though they don't belong in this place with its crosses and high ceilings.

I only look up when I hear the priest begin to chant and the guests fall silent. Theodora is now beside Ivan Alexander, and he's looking at the priest, who is about to join Theodora's hand with his.

I can't shake off the chill I feel.

I wait for Theodora all night. I don't sleep. I wait and watch the stars outside the window. When the door opens, I cross the room, but I see her eyes are red and raw. "I only want to sleep," she says. I see the set of her jaw.

I send all the servants out of the room. "My lady wishes to sleep." I close the door behind them, and bolt it shut.

I help Theodora into bed. I draw the blankets up and lean down to press a kiss to her cheek, but she flinches and moves her head away.

Tears fill my eyes. I watch her for a while. She does not sleep. Her body shakes with silent sobs. I want to wrap my arms around her, to comfort and take care of her like she took care of me. But sometimes the best thing to do is to leave someone be. What I want and what she needs right now are two very different things.

Soon I see the rise and fall of her chest.

I unbolt the door to ask the guards to order some tea and broth to the room, but when I open the door, no one is there. I don't want to leave Theodora, but I am tired and hungry and if she wakes, she might be too. I decided to leave her room and find a set of guards.

"Why are you not guarding the princess's chambers?" I say, when I finally run into them.

"We were not ordered to do so," they reply.

"I order you to guard her chamber until I return. Do not allow anyone in besides me."

I'm making my way down to the kitchens when I bump into

Ivan Alexander. I keep my eyes cast down. I am full of rage for Theodora. She's never been anything other than strong, full of grace and charm, intelligent, witty and proud. The Theodora I left sleeping is broken.

"Your grace." I try to shoulder my way past him, but he reaches out and takes my arm.

"You do not stop to greet me?" he says.

I can smell the spirits on his breath. "My apologies." I bow. "I was merely rushing to get the princess some tea."

"Princess," Ivan Alexander spits. "That is no princess."

I shut my eyes. This is not what anyone should feel or say on their wedding night.

"Oh, don't worry, I knew what I was getting into," he slurs his words. "I'd heard rumors here and there . . . This is a political alliance, nothing more. Follow me."

"Your grace?" I say.

"You heard me."

My heart is beating so fast. Why did I leave Theodora's side? Why?

Ivan Alexander leads me into his room. I stand silently as he shuts and bolts the door behind us. He paces around me in a circle, smiling slyly. "I have a proposition for you."

My blood runs cold.

"I'd heard that she was unconventional—dressing up in battle armor to go out hunting with Basarab's guards. But I also knew her father, the Black Dragon. And I knew that his wife Marghita would want nothing less for their child than to rule over both Romania and Bulgaria. It was a power grab, no more than that. I am under no illusions. Marghita is a cunning woman. Perhaps her daughter is too. What I didn't know was the way that Theodora would look at you."

He pulls out a knife and holds the blade up in front of me.

I hold back a gasp and start to shake.

"I will keep your secrets if you help me keep mine," he says, spinning the blade before my eyes. "I need a future for my kingdom. Do whatever you wish in the privacy of the princess's chambers. But you—*mi krasota*..." He stands in front of me and puts his hand on my chin. He forces me to look into his eyes. My teeth chatter. My eyes burn with unshed tears.

"You will come to me each day and I will plant the seeds of my empire in your womb," he says. "It is a real woman I want warming my bed, not someone with a penchant for shorn hair and dress-up clothes. And you, my dear—" He cups my breast in his hand and feels it as if he's feeling ripe fruit. "—yes, you'll do just fine. You will come entertain me when you are not entertaining my farce of a wife."

He leans forwards and I cringe at the stench on his breath. He plants a rough kiss on my lips. Then he pulls his head away and licks his lips, his hand still fondling my breast. His eyes are glazed over with liquor and desire. He presses himself closer to me, then he takes my hand and places it on his cock. I can't stop shaking. "Theodora will claim your babes as her own and I won't ever have to spend another night with that dry cunt." He grins. "But yours, I can tell, is nice and juicy, eh? This way, everyone wins."

I shudder in horror, swallowing hard.

"You will not tell Theodora that you visit me," he continues pressing himself against my hand. "Only you and I will be aware of this arrangement."

He sheathes the knife and I gulp in a breath of relief, trying to let it out slowly. I'm doing this for Theodora, I think, as I clutch the emerald ring in my fist so tight it cuts me.

"What do you say, my little red fox?" he says, stroking my fiery hair.

I wish I could burn him with it. I wish I could set the castle on fire right now. But I can't. In my moment of need, I cannot become the thing I need to protect me. Because I must protect

Theodora. The word "fox" on his lips is like a blow. I nod shakily, my face streaked with tears. I was meant to marry a fox. Now I've become one.

Perhaps it is for this moment that you have reached the kingdom: I hear the words of *The Book of Esther* in my head.

I can be brave like she was. She did what she had to do for her people, and her children sat on a throne.

I can protect myself, my family, Theodora, my future generations. Through me, the Solomonar line can live on. It's not something that I ever thought was important to me. But now it feels like something I can do. And in the walls of this palace, as the children of the prince and someday king, I know they will.

I won't make another mistake. I will do whatever it takes to protect the ones I love. Even this.

"It's rather biblical, wouldn't you say?" Ivan Alexander continues, freezing me in place again. "You are, after all, a handmaiden? Isn't that what they call it?" He leans forward and whispers in my ear. "I certainly hope that you are a maiden." I close my eyes and nod.

"Oh good," he says. "We begin now."

★ ⸱ ★ ★ ★ ★ ★
★ ⸱ ⸱ ⸱ ★ ★ ⸱

In Theodora's bedroom later, sitting beside her, I try not to cry. I don't want to wake her. I'll have to put on a brave face. I must do everything in my power to make sure that Theodora never finds out. But soon she wakes and looks at me and I can see in her eyes that she knows something's happened.

"He's been with you," she says, voice hoarse.

I stiffen. I cannot tell her. I swore an oath. My sins stack themselves one upon the other.

"What do you mean?" I say.

"I can smell him on you."

"What?" I get up from the bed and start to back away.

"Don't try to deny it."

"I had no choice." I don't want there to ever be dishonesty between us. It's the only thing I can think to say that isn't a lie.

"Did he hurt you?"

"Not with the knife," I whisper.

Theodora reaches for me. "I should never have brought you here with me."

I wrap my arms around my body and close my eyes. "It was the only way to keep you safe."

I hear the rustle of the sheets, then Theodora's presence beside me. She hugs me. I move to shrug her off, but she won't let me.

"This is my fault," she says. "I am so sorry."

I sniffle and take a deep breath. "I would do it a hundred times. A thousand times if I could. If that is the price I must pay for your safety—and mine—then so be it."

"He forced you. He hurt you." Fire blazes in Theodora's eyes.

"He hurt you," I say.

"I married him. It's different."

"It's not different. Nobody should ever treat anyone that way."

"We can leave here; I can take you back home to Wallachia."

"And then what? Bulgaria and Wallachia will no longer be allies? No. It could lead to war . . . People would die. If he can use me, he won't kill me. And he won't kill you. Let's not speak of this anymore."

"I will confront him. I will tell him . . . I can stop this—"

"Don't tell him anything. He may not be able to hurt you, but I am completely dispensable. Let's go to bed. Please."

"You are not dispensable to me," she says.

"I have a question for you. If you can transform into a bird, why didn't you fly away?"

"You're serious?" she says. "I should be asking you the same question."

"I had no choice," I say.

"And you think I did?" she says. "You decide who you allow to have power over you." She tilts her chin up to the ceiling, defiant again.

I laugh, bitterly. "Theodora, you are of royal blood. You matter. I am nothing in this world. I am expendable, worthless. I don't have choices."

"I choose you," she says, placing a hand on my cheek. "I see only you."

"And I choose you," I say back to her. "I chose this life. And if that means I must choose Ivan Alexander too, then so be it."

The lies are bitter on my tongue.

Anna

21 Iyar 5123

Laptitza went into labor tonight. The months after Theodora's wedding have been good to us. Our summer fields yielded bounty as my body grew round and ripe with a baby of our own.

It's an unusually warm night tonight. Nothing about it made me suspect that things would end as they did, I saw no portent of evil in the sky, felt no wrongness in the soil—sometimes that's how the *mazikim* get in—when you least expect it, but I am getting ahead of myself. A maid from the palace knocked at my front door, frantic, out of breath, and told me Laptitza had asked for me.

I didn't hesitate. I packed up a satchel, like the one I once took with me to Jakob's home all those years ago, and I followed her to the palace.

Marghita was in the chamber with us, along with a midwife and some servants. Laptitza cried for Nikolas all night, but he'd been gone a week already. He is away. Basarab is away. Constantin is away. They are off fighting a battle near Velbazhd. It is because of Theodora's marriage to Ivan Alexander that they are there. They are supporting the Emperor Michael, ruler of

Bulgaria, in retaking the north-western and south-western lands from the Serbian King Stefan.

Perhaps things might have happened differently had one of them been home.

In the labor room, I kept wishing there was more I could do to relieve Laptitza's pain, but I was afraid to lay my hands on her. I couldn't cross Marghita or the midwife, who had their own ways of doing things, and I was wary of being accused of witchcraft. I knew that I couldn't reveal too much of what I can do. But when the midwife wanted to give Laptitza a draught to help ease the labor pangs, I asked if I could give it to her. I sniffed its contents as I leaned over, placing a wet cloth on Laptitza's forehead. I smelled hemlock. A ribbon of ice flowed through my veins as I watched a tendril of Black Mist creep out of the jar. I left my trembling hand on Laptitza's forehead to try and take away some of her pain. It gave me a minute to think. Someone wished my sister ill. I quickly dropped the bottle.

"Oh no!" I said. "I'm so clumsy! I'm just so worried about her that my hands shook and it slipped," I lied. "I'm terribly sorry."

"Open the windows please!" Laptitza screamed.

Marghita said, "She's clearly out of her mind with pain. Who knows what kind of humors and demons might fly inside and seek to harm her and the child?"

Laptitza looked at me, her eyes pleading. "Open. The. Windows." She gritted her teeth as another contraction washed over her, causing her to grip my hand so hard I felt as though my bones would crack. I waited until she breathed freely again, and then I went over to the windows.

"What are you doing?" Marghita said.

"If my sister wants fresh air, I will not deny her." *When a woman was about to give birth, we would open the ark where the Torahs are kept in the synagogue—it was a segulah—a kind of charm to help open the door to a woman's womb.* "Where I come from, it's an old folk custom to open windows and doors while a woman is in labor."

"It is a demon who is putting these ideas in her head," Marghita said. "Trying to get in. Don't listen to her."

I ignored Marghita and opened the windows, one by one. Cold air filled the room and Marghita and the midwife crossed themselves and shivered.

"This is unhealthy," the midwife said. "She will catch a chill."

The sky was full of stars, bright and gleaming against the dark night. The moon filled the room with light.

"The door ... to the ... balcony ..." Laptitza whispered to me between breaths, between pangs.

My father used to give the honor of opening the holy ark in synagogue to men whose wives were about the give birth. *Let this be a* segulah *for my sister*, I prayed. As I opened the door to the balcony, Laptitza let out a primal scream and her son entered the world.

I was the only one who saw the flash of light in the sky in that moment.

Laptitza panted, the baby cried, and before the midwife could get the baby out of the way, my sister started screaming again.

"It's a boy." The midwife handed the baby to Marghita. Then she looked back at my sister and her face paled. "There is a second one ..." she whispered.

Marghita and the midwife clamored at me to close the doors and windows, but I refused, and I'm not ashamed to say it. They were too busy with the birth of the second baby to force me. My sister knew what she needed, and my father's wisdom saved her.

Laptitza bellowed again and a second baby came crying its way into our world.

Twins. Two baby boys.

The room was quiet; only the babies whimpered. I looked from the midwife and Marghita to the babies and I saw why.

Each of the babies had a shining golden star on their forehead. Marghita crossed herself.

The midwife's hands were shaking.

Laptitza closed her eyes.

I closed the doors and windows.

Marghita whispered, "These are not my son's children. They are marked by her sin. They carry the mark of the devil. These children are cursed!" Then she looked at me, hatred in her eyes. "This is your fault. You should not have opened the door for the devil. He wanted in; she knew it—" She pointed at my sister. "—and you conspired with her. You let him in!"

She handed the babies to the midwife and sent everyone out of the chamber, even me. I feared for my sister's life. For my life.

I hid in the stairwell until I heard all the footsteps subside. I heard the door open, and Marghita said, "It is customary to bury the afterbirth sheets. I will do it myself to ensure that no evil eye will come upon the babies and their mother."

I followed her and hid behind the door to the kitchen as she went outside. She put down the sheets, which looked heavier to me than they should. Then I saw the bundle at her feet move. I put my hand to my mouth to stifle the sounds I wanted to make. I didn't let any demons in when I opened the windows—she was already in the room. Marghita took out a shovel and began to dig.

Tears streamed down my face.

She dropped the bundle into the hole and covered the wriggling sheets with earth, then she wiped her hands on her skirts, crossed herself, and went back inside. She didn't notice me, hiding behind the door. As soon as she was gone, I went outside. I dug with my hands, dirt filling my fingernails, I'd have dug with my face, with my teeth and my lips if I thought it would help. My tears wet the earth. I felt the earth begin to soften, and it parted for me. I saw white; I felt warmth; I pulled the bundles up out of the earth and clutched them to my chest.

I looked up at the castle windows, but I didn't see anyone looking out. The windows were all closed. The lights out. My hands were shaking so much I could barely use my fingers.

I unwrapped the sheets as carefully as I could and started to cry again with relief when I saw the babies still alive and breathing. The stars on their foreheads shone bright—and I rushed to cover them up again. I strapped the babies to my body with the sheets, creating two slings to press them to my chest, then I drew a circle around me, remembering the story my father told me about Honi HaMeagel. I stepped inside the circle and planted my feet in the earth—not praying for rain this time, but for mercy.

> *"In the name of Hannah Bat Isaac,*
> *daughter of Solomon,*
> Hashem, *Lord of Israel,*
> *I beseech you to aid me,*
> *in this, my time of need.*
> *Is man like a tree of the field,*
> *that he should go into siege before you?"*

My father's words came back to me.

> *"You shall build fortifications*
> *against the city that makes war with you,*
> *until its submission."*

Slowly it turned into a kind of lullaby.

> *"Is man like a tree of the field,*
> *tall as a sycamore,*
> *strong as an oak?"*

I looked down at the babies, cradled at my breast.

"Hăita liuliu, go to sleep,
When you get up, you'll be bigger."

Where could I hide them? What kind of life could I offer them? Had I saved them from one kind of death only to deliver them to another?

"Hăita liuliu," I sang.
"Hear O Israel, God of Abraham,
protect these babies.
Please let them grow bigger,
tall as an aspen tree,
strong as a cedar . . .
In the name of Hannah Bat Isaac,
Hăita liuliu,
Hăita liuliu . . ."

The melody breathed through me.

"Hăita liuliu,
That which is planted in good soil
by many waters,
may it bring forth branches,
may it bear fruit.
Hăita liuliu—
answer me God,
answer me."

I claimed my name and birthright. I never thought it would be me taking my father's place, naming his name as my pedigree to anyone but a future husband. But the world I thought I once knew has been turned entirely upside down and so I did the only thing I could. I gave myself a chance to grow. As I chanted, I felt the energy I once knew so well weaving itself between the words—like a stream that comes from rain, growing in strength, traveling from my mouth down through my body. Like sap travels through a tree, I felt power wash through me. My feet rooted themselves in the ground, and I felt the once-familiar tickle of plants reaching out to curl themselves around my feet.

I closed my eyes and placed my hands on the heads of the babies. And I blessed them.

> *May God bless you and keep you.*
> *May the Lord shine His light upon you.*
> *May He be gracious and merciful*
> *May He lift his face to yours*
> *and give you peace.*

I pulled my feet out of the earth as two tendrils of green began to rise from the soil—one for each soul Marghita tried to plant.

I will show her, I thought, *what happens when you plant a Jew.*

One day, a forest will grow there. One day, there will be nothing left of the castle but ruin.

But my sister's children will live on.

Then I ran as fast as I could towards the forest with the babies cradled in my arms.

It grows late and I must sleep. I will finish my story tomorrow.

Laptitza

Nikolas comes into the room.
      I sit up in bed.
      "The babies! Where are they?"
"Shhh, Laptitza . . ." he croons.
"You must rest."
      But I don't want consolation.
      I want my children.
      "I still hear them crying," I say.
      "Can't you hear them?"
He smooths my hair out of my eyes.
"I don't hear anything," he says.
"Mother says that they were stillborn—
that they didn't even cry."

      I rock my head from side to side.
      "They cried. My babies cried.
      They haven't stopped crying . . ."
      My eyes stare straight through him.
      Maybe I can see past him,
      through the walls of the palace,
      to where my babies cry.

"I don't think Mother's lying," he says.
"I just returned from battle
and I need to sleep."
          "My babies don't sleep,"
          I scream at him. "They cry!
          They want their mother."
He glances at the door,
then puts his hand on mine.
"Mother says the babies
were marked by the devil.
They died before they had
a chance to live, my sweet."

          "No. You're wrong," I say.
          "They were the most
          beautiful babies.
          Boys with golden stars.
          They shone with light."
Please listen to me.
I'm begging him.
Tears wet my cheeks.
          "They live. They cry
          all day and night.
          Why doesn't anybody
          hear them?"

Nikolas sighs.
"I'm going to bathe
and change out of these clothes,
and get a good night's sleep.
I think that you should too."

I grab his shoulders.
"How can I sleep—
(My voice cracks)
"—when my babies cry?"

He removes my hands
from his coat.
"I don't know, Laptitza.
I only know that I have to."

He walks out of the room
and leaves me alone.

My babies are alone.
Who will listen to me?

Wisdom is more beautiful than the sun, and above all the order of stars. It is the force that nourishes the world.

–The Book of the Solomonars, page 31, verse 9

Perhaps the greatest of all human abilities is the power of resilience. Babies survive. They bloom where they're planted. The Black Mist was pushed out of the forest. But by the next morning, tendrils of it crept through cracks between window and pane, between door and frame, and all the way into the palace.

Sometimes, even if you think you've kept your windows closed, all it takes is the tiniest crack of a door, an imperfection in the window frame for the mist to find its way in. Sometimes the evil is already inside, ready and waiting. The mist only needs to find one person willing to allow black thoughts to take root. Someone intent on watering those thoughts so that they might grow.

Hannah

22 Iyar 5123

I hid the babies in a cave in the forest last night, not far from the linden tree where we once buried the relics of our past.

They will die if I leave them there—their cries may have already attracted wolves or foxes, or worse—men. But I had no choice. Last night, I had to choose one grave over another. Too many farmhands here could send word back to the palace. And my parents' home will be the first place they look. With the stars on their foreheads so bright, there's no way anyone can hide them.

This morning I will bring them milk. I will say that I'm going to pick mushrooms in the forest. It's not a good plan, but I don't have another one.

Last night, I decided to cover the entrance to the cave with branches and brush. I was about to go out and scavenge for things, but then I stopped. I felt power thrumming from the earth. I reached out and touched one of the closest trees. It wrapped a branch around my wrist, anchoring me to it.

At first, I pulled away. I was scared that the forest wanted to claim me, to chain me to it. But then I inched closer to the tree again, pressed my hand to its bark, and waited for a response. A vine reached out and wrapped itself around my other wrist too.

I kicked off my shoes and drew a circle around me. I dug my bare feet into the soil and felt a rush of warmth. The roots wrapped themselves around my toes. I held my breath, then I shoved the only thing that came to mind at the tree—a door.

"*Ptach li sha'arei tzedek,*" I said—*open the gates of mercy for me.* I also needed a cradle.

"*Betzel knafeikhah tastireini*"—*hide me in the shadow of your wings.*

The roots left my feet and wrists. They inched their way over to the mouth of the cave. Branches followed, and I watched leaves sprout, green and fragrant, covering the entrance to the cave. I saw other tendrils reaching under the door, making their way into the cave.

For a moment, I was scared. What if they were wrapping themselves around Laptitza's babies—strangling them, claiming them as part of the forest? I gently lifted my feet out of the soil and pushed the branches back. Inside I saw a cradle, made of roots and branches, with soft moss as a mattress and a blanket of ferns and leaves. The babies slept, content and swaddled in the arms of the sheltering tree.

I went outside and put my shoes back on. I felt drained. Exhausted beyond measure, I closed the door to the cave and made my way home.

Stanna

Months go by. I think about my sisters constantly. I wonder how my parents fare. I am alone, isolated. I never appreciated them in my lifetime, I realize that now. Here, there is no one to guide me.

Theodora comes back from Ivan Alexander's rooms one night, where they now sit civilly and discuss affairs of state and military strategy.

She and I don't speak of what happens when I go to him, or that the swell of my belly means that something—someone has already begun to grow inside me—a child I know will change everything. Again.

She reaches her hand out for mine and says, "Come with me."

"Where?"

"Trust me," she says.

And I do. Just as I know she trusts me—though sometimes there is not complete truth between us. Our world has changed around us and we are changing with it. Our choices are not our own, even if we want them to be.

She leads me to the window and opens the shutters to the night air. She steps closer to me.

"Take off your clothes," she says.

"What?"

"Do you trust me?"

I nod.

She takes off her clothes. I stare at her, bathed in moonlight. She is radiant. All hard and soft edges at the same time. Her hair is still short and spiky, slowly growing back, perhaps only to be cut again.

"Why?" I press, all my old fears crowding inside me, clamoring to be heard. *What if she leaves you? What if she hurts you? What if you end up alone and lost in the woods again? What if she becomes just another fox you never see again?*

"There is something I want you to see," she says.

"It's cold outside."

"I would never harm you."

Her words still strike fear within me, because I know how quickly everything I have could be taken away from me again.

I hear Esther's words in my head, "*Ka'asher avadeti, avadeti* whatever I lose, I lose—if I perish, I perish." So be it. This is my destiny and I must embrace whatever comes. I hear my mother's voice, her story—Esther who is my mother, my star. Esther who hid herself in the king's palace. Esther who hid her face behind her veil and did what she had to do to save her people.

I pull my nightdress over my head and let it fall to the floor.

Theodora stands on the window ledge and reaches her hand out for mine.

"What are you doing?"

"Trust me." Theodora says again, but this time her words feel like they hold weight. Like my response enters me into some kind of bargain, and there will be no going back after this.

I shut my eyes. "Okay," I say.

We stand on the window ledge. Our breath is frosty in the night air.

"Close your eyes," she says.

I close them.

"It's time for you to fly," Theodora says as she steps off the ledge, my hand still in hers. We start to fall, and I open my mouth to scream, but then there is a crack in the air, like the breaking of a barrier, the skip of a heartbeat. Fire churns within me and spreads to my arms and lengthens them, to my toes and curls them, sleek feathers rise up from my skin, my body slick with scales, and in an instant, we are flying. Everything around me changes—the air, my skin, my perception of depth and space. I feel smaller, lighter, I look around. It is undeniable that . . . I am not the creature I once was. I look down, expecting to see a snake, but I am not a snake anymore. I am more like a bird. A kind of dragon. *A teli*, I hear a voice say. I look for Theodora and I see an owl flying beside me.

But I am not an owl. I am golden. Scaled and feathered. With wings that work and sing as they slice through the air. *I was never a snake. I realize that now. I was something else entirely.*

I hear the words I once said to Guvriel in my head.

What if I'm a creature that hasn't been discovered yet?

"Everything has been discovered in God's eyes, for He created every living thing."

"Maybe I'm a song that no one has heard yet."

"Maybe you are," he says.

My heart stops in my chest. *Maybe I am.*

I seek my arm, but it doesn't work like it used to—it's webbed and feathered and impossibly large—it scoops the air like a sail. I look to my feet and see claws—my heart is in my throat and I tumble in the air.

The owl swoops beneath me as if to make sure that I don't fall. But I am large enough to crush it. Large enough to devour it whole.

It is thrilling and terrifying at the same time. I am me but not me. Not a snake. I was never a snake. I was a dragon who hadn't found her wings yet.

Like my father—but not like him. I am my own creature. A dragon of fire and air, not cloud.

My heart is beating so much faster than it usually does, and the air, which should be cold, feels good as it whizzes through what must be feathers. We swoop over countryside and Theodora hoots amid the high branches of the trees.

We see a stream that starts in a valley between two high hills and she dives for it, coming to stop on its banks.

I follow her lead.

I wish to hunt. She looks at me, and I can tell what she says. But I'm afraid to open my mouth. We have beaks, not mouths. I don't know if they work in the same way.

I arch my neck up to the sky and wish my father was with me. I wish I'd listened to him. I wish I'd learned everything I could while I had the chance. A stiff-necked girl he once called me, who refused the yoke he placed on me, but he was only trying to show me the way. I wonder if he knew all along that this is what I am. I wish I knew how to ask him.

Theodora's beak touches mine. Her eyes are wet and shining. She swoops up into the sky, crossing the light of the moon. My own eyes fill with tears. It starts to snow.

Theodora swoops down. But I see pride there, not sadness. She's proud of me. Of what I've done. What I've become. She's saying, *trust me, let yourself feel, let yourself go, let yourself free. I knew you could do it.* I open my mouth—there are so many questions I want to ask, but she huffs out a gulp which meets the gust of air that I let out—frost-tinged—and it is like a kiss, the way our breaths dance in the air. I take a deep breath of our twinned breath and realize that she breathes knowledge into my bones. She's showing me the way.

My body starts changing again. My joints feel like they are popping. I hear a crooning— not the sound of an owl, but something more wild and free. The air around us shifts. My heart beats out a different rhythm and I look over at Theodora. Fur covers her body now, not feathers. Where her small beak was there is now a long snout, and cunning, ice-blue eyes with pointy ears that crown the top of her head. I look down and see that I have paws too—but they are a fiery red-orange. I look down at the stream. She is a great white wolf—as white as the snow that still coats the ground. But I am a fox. I jump into the air in what is more like a pounce. I did it! And the one person I want to show myself to isn't with me.

She stares at me, her eyes wide.

I don't understand what is happening, what has happened. I have so many questions.

Why am I a fox and she a wolf? What about our inner natures made this happen? Does Guvriel's heart now beat in me? Will I ever stop pining for him? Nothing makes sense except that I've never felt as whole and free as I do now. I feel at home in my bones—in these fox bones and dragon bones that are mine and not mine. *Teli*. Only me. *I can be whatever I want to be.*

You are more powerful than any of us, Guvriel once said. And this is the first time that I think he may be right. It may be true.

We hunt, rooting out rabbits from the cover of tree limbs. There's blood in my mouth and flesh in my teeth. Once satiated, we frolic on the banks of the river for hours, then dash into the forest.

I never got to experience this with Guvriel. He never got to teach me. He knew I could do this all along, but it's Theodora who dragged it out of me—who found a way to finally make it happen.

Soon the sun begins to rise. Night is ending. A light snow starts to fall again. We race back to the castle. It is farther than I remember, but we are sleek and fast, and the distance we flew before is quickly covered by our speedy limbs. Snowflakes shine on Theodora's fur like tiny points of light, and the closer we get back to the palace, the harder the snow starts to fall.

Theodora stops and puts her paw over mine. Her wolf eyes glow gold. She huffs out a breath that is more like a bark—a howl. I close my fox eyes. I feel my body shrink into itself and I shiver, as feathers replace fur and wings replace paws and I am sleek and scaled again. And so is she. Dark to my light. Black to my gold. But she isn't an owl this time. She's a black dragon. And she is glorious. We take to the sky together and fly in a straight line back to our room. We step onto the ledge, and before I can leap down onto the floor, my hand is entwined with Theodora's again and we are naked and human and staring at each other, some snowflakes still visible in her hair and mine. Breathless and smiling, flushed from the exertion, but we are happy. So happy.

I open my mouth to ask how she did it, wanting to understand, but her mouth leans in for mine and there are no more barriers between us.

Theodora slides her arms around me, her hands in my hair, my hands on her body. Our limbs entwined. Dragon, owl, fox, wolf. Feathers and scales and fur and skin.

She pulls away from my lips, breathless, and says, "You called the snow."

I shake my head. "Only God can control the weather."

"You are more than you think you are," she says, tracing a finger across my hairline and down my cheek.

"I have lost everything that I once was," I say, shaking my head. "But you're showing me the way back."

"Come, there is still time before morning," she says, and pulls me after her to bed.

* ★ ★ ★ ★ ★
★ ★ ★ ★ ★ ★

We lie in each other's arms and Theodora lazily draws circles on my shoulder, then down my chest, ending at my breast. I shiver.

She leans over and kisses my cheek. "I love you in all of your forms. A love like ours comes once in a lifetime."

Tears wet my face. Is she right? Or do I contain enough love for many lives, many forms.

My heart is a country riddled with borders, with room for many kinds of light. Many kinds of love.

"Can I ask you something?" I say, tracing patterns of my own onto her skin.

She quivers, then grins. "Anything."

"If you can change yourself into different forms, why can't you turn yourself into a man? Wolf to owl to dragon and back again—why not woman to man?"

"It doesn't work that way."

"Why not? I don't understand."

"I can only be what I am—nothing more. When I am an owl, I am still me, when I am a wolf, I am still me. A dragon—still me. When I am Theodora, or Theodor, I am still me. That doesn't change. People will always put you in a box when they see one form or another. But you see and accept everything that I am—that is why when I'm with you, I can be whatever I wish to be. You see all of me. Others only see what they want to see."

"I still don't understand. Does that mean that when anybody other than me sees you as a wolf, they don't see a wolf?"

"No. They see a wolf."

"Then why can't they look upon you and see a man?"

"Because their eyes don't let them. Because people are so blinded by what they think I should be that they can't see me as anything else. I don't want to be a man; I just want to be me. Theodora and sometimes Theodor, in pants and sometimes in a dress. Sometimes a wolf and sometimes an owl—and only a dragon when I need to be. When I am with you, the masks fall away."

Tears wet my eyes again. *On Purim, we used to wear masks. The men and the women. It was the one day a year that we could be whatever and whoever we wanted to be. So many masks.*

"Come," Theodora says, rising out of bed.

"What? Why?"

"I need to show you something." She takes my hand and tugs me out of bed.

"I'm tired and it's almost morning. Can't we just rest here together?"

"Only for a moment   we won't leave the room this time, I promise ... "

She leads me over to the window and opens the shutters. "Look," she says.

I see that it's raining now—the sun is rising, but there are clouds on the horizon.

"You did that," she says.

I roll my eyes at her. "Can we go back to bed now?" I turn away. "It's just rain."

"No, Sarah, look," she says, using my real name, as she turns my face to look back out at the sky. She reaches over and wipes away my tears and, as she does, I see the sun finally rise and the clouds drift away.

"My father was the Black Dragon," Theodora says. "People saw him as a great leader, a man who made the first steps to declare Wallachia's independence from Hungary. He spread the word of Christ, but he was fiercely devoted to the old gods.

"The Dacians say that one of their Gods, Zalmoxe, turned a man into a wolf to protect his people from invaders. They called them the Daoi—People of the Wolves. My father's banner was a wolf with a wide mouth—they said that when the wind whistled through its mouth it sounded like the howl of a wolf, calling his people to battle. But there was another figure on his banner—a Black Dragon. The flag bearer who carried the wolf wore a helmet in the shape of a wolf's snout, and his armor was made of scales that moved.

"The serpent is sacred to our people too—winged serpents covered in holy fire. When I met you . . . " She pauses to stroke my cheek, then closes the window, and I don't know if it's frigid inside or not because my blood runs cold at her words.

"When I first saw you in the clearing, bright and shining, a fiery serpent, I thought perhaps that you were one of his creatures, a long-lost sister, perhaps. But you are not his creature. And I knew then that I had to understand you—who you were and where you came from. Perhaps the same root lies at the heart of every culture and civilization . . . " She pauses again.

"But tonight is the night of St. Andrew, the first night of the Dacian new year. On this night, the heavens open. The seen and unseen, light and darkness meet, and time renews itself. What's inside is outside. I wanted to know if the power of tonight would help you discover the source of who you truly are.

"My father didn't get to finish his work. There was a dark side to him—he tried to entomb his own wife and unborn child in the walls of a monastery in the belief that it would keep the walls from crumbling. Some say that as a punishment for his crimes he turned into the dragon that haunts the skies today. But you're different. You're a creature of light.

"The people here, they light candles in their windows tonight to fend off the evil spirits of the undead. They bake pumpkin pies and corn bread. Tonight is the night when the transparency of the borders between the worlds is lessened and revealed. Secrets are unraveled. Forecasts are made for next year. If it is clear and warm tonight, it will be a mild winter. If it is cold, it will be a hard winter. But you . . . you break all the rules. What are you, Sarah? I love you with everything I am, but I need to know."

Teli, I hear the voice inside my head again. The inner voice I'd been searching for since I met Guvriel that first night in the forest. But the one thing my father told me—the only thing: *Esther did not reveal her people, or her nation*—and I'm being asked to betray that now. I feel trapped. Caught in this cage of a palace. Theodora brought me back to myself; but it is not her palace that has caged me now. Not her seed in my belly.

"Some say that when a storm comes," Theodora continues, "it is the Black Dragon who brings it. It is said that there are red haired mountain men who know secrets of the heavens, that they control a white dragon—their cloud riders call the dragon to them and they fight the Black Dragon in the skies. Mother tells me that Father fought one—that they were out to restore balance, to ensure that the mad king's emotions didn't control our skies and the future of our crops. And in the end, the great white wolf and all his followers retreated to the sacred mountains to nurse their wounds. But you are not made of cloud. You are pure fire and air. Are you of that stock?"

"I wonder," I say, "if every nation has its dragons." My mother taught me that there are an infinite number of ways to tell the same story. She was always telling stories, and I don't think I understood her power, which was a quiet strength but no less important than my father's. Which is true? Which is fantasy? We see what we want to see. That is what I can give her.

"We fled our homes in fear and left our past behind us. But I know my father tried to defeat the Black Mist that infected our town and the hearts of the people in it."

These are the words I can give her.

"But my father was defeated. The Black Dragon won that day. Or so he believed. I know one thing to be true—a dragon of light is always at war with a dragon of darkness—without darkness, we would be blinded by the light, without light we would live in darkness. We need both to survive." As I speak the words, it is my father's voice I hear.

"Both sides need each other to survive," Theodora repeats softly.

"There is no good and evil, no light and dark, no man or woman. Every one of us contains multitudes," I say. "Every one of us contains a spark of God."

Theodora takes something out of her pocket. It is a silver ring carved with vines.

"This is for you," she says, and closes my fist around it. "No matter what happens, keep the ring, always. I will always be with you, *draga mea*."

My mouth pulls into a frown. "What do you mean? Where are you going?"

She opens my hand, takes the ring, and places it on my finger. It joins the emerald ring that I still haven't taken off.

"Now, you will always be mine," she says.

But as I stroke the ring with my thumb, I question if I want to be owned by anyone.

The dragon inside me speaks up for the first time. And it says that it wants its wings to beat free.

Laptitza

I pray in the words I used to know
The words that used to be a comfort to me
> *Praise* Hashem *from the heavens*
> *Praise Him, all His angels*

The words I used to use the bless the moon
To call on the stars in the sky
> *Praise Him, sun and moon*
> *Praise Him, all bright stars*

I beg the heavens
Listen to me
> *As I dance toward you*

Hear my cry
> *Though I cannot touch you*

I hear babies crying.
> *The voice of my beloved came suddenly*

"Where are they?"
I call out, but no one comes.
I get up out of bed,
> *leaping over mountains*
> *skipping over hills*

trailing sheets behind me.

> *He was standing behind the wall*

I walk the four corners of my room.

> *Observing through the windows*

"Where are my babies?" I cry out,

but there is no one here.

> *Peering through the lattices*

"Nikolas?"

> *A song of ascents*

No answer.

> *I raise my eyes to the mountains*

I go out onto the balcony.

> *From whence will come my help?*

I'm not dressed for winter.

> *My help is from* Hashem
> *maker of heaven and earth*

Someone came before

and helped me change

out of my nightshift

and into a gown,

> *He will not allow your foot to falter*

she brushed my hair

and tried to wash my face,

> *Your Guardian will not slumber*

but she didn't know where my babies were.

> *Behold! He neither slumbers nor sleeps!*

I held her arms and begged her

to bring my babies to me—

> Hashem *is my Guardian*

she ran out of my room, crying.

> Hashem *is the shade*

I think I hurt her,
   At my right hand.
but I must know
where my babies are.

My breasts are swollen.
They're leaking milk,
   By day the sun will not harm me
   Nor the moon by night.
still no one brings
my babies to me.
I look up at the sky,
   Hashem *will protect me*
   from all evil
   He will guard my soul.
but where the stars
used to be
I see only leaves.
Two aspen trees
have sprouted overnight
and the wind in their leaves
   Who is this
sounds only like the cries
   Who rises
of my babies.
   From the desert
My sons.
   Clinging
Where are they?
   To her beloved.
I go back inside
and draw the cold black drapes.

He didn't come for me.

I put my faith in the heavens;
I swore I'd never marry anyone
but I did.

And now I'm alone.
Even the heavens
have betrayed me.

I no longer want
to see the sky.

Who will bring my babies to me?
I feel empty, where only yesterday
I was full.
I knew in my heart
that he would come for me
But now I feel
I don't know anything at all.

I want to bar myself,
from the light
of the midnight stars.
I have no one else
to turn to.
Perhaps if I step out
onto the balcony

                                        and fall,
                                        a star will catch me.

And let us all say, Amen.

Light and darkness are the same.

–The Book of the Solomonars, page 15, verse 2

Some evil is so unspeakable that the only way we can fight it is by telling a story. Over and over again, until history stops repeating itself.

Laptitza

I am still out on the balcony,
but before I can take another step,
I hear something behind me.
I turn to look . . .
The voivode's guards
have come for me.
Their hands are on my arms.
Something covers my mouth.
I try to cry out, to scream,
to wrestle my way free
but their grip is too strong.
Why are they here?
Didn't we only just sit down
for a picnic together?
They wrench my arms
behind my back and tie
my wrists together.
I don't understand
what's happening.
Why?

I turn my head
from side to side
frantically, trying
to breathe, trying
to see who is behind me.
Is it Constantin?
Please, you know me!
I want to say.
But then I see
Marghita
behind them.
A small, sad grin
of triumph
on her lips.
There is cloth
in my mouth.
My eyes
fill with tears.
Marghita watches
as the guards
pull me down
the hallway,
      out of my room,
               and down the stairs.
She doesn't follow.

They cover my head
with a sack that smells like hay.
Only pinpricks of light get in.
They shove me into a carriage.
I hear horses; the carriage starts to move.
First we bump over dirt and rocks,
then the road grows smoother.

It is not a long ride.
They don't need to go far
to dispose of me.

They open the doors
and heave me outside.
I can feel the light
of the moon
and the stars
through the bag
over my head.
We are outside.
   My feet touch earth.
     I am barefoot.
I hear shovels, digging.
The sound of steel
hitting earth.
Again
   and again
      and again.
I can't stop shivering.
They shove me
    and I fall.
For an instant,
     I think I will land
     and break my neck
     and it will all be
     blessedly over.
But my feet
touch earth again
and my arms feel soil.
I struggle to undo
the bindings

at my wrists.
There is earth
all around me.
I can smell it.
The roots of plants
tickle my nose.
Is it a bug?
The smell
of freshly turned soil
floods my senses.
And then the shovels
                        of earth
                                    begin to fall.

I try to move,
            but there is nowhere to go.
I try to cry out,
            but cloth still gags me.
I can't breathe.
            My eyes fill with tears.
I see stars.
            There is nothing
            I can do
            to stop them.

No one comes
to my rescue.
The stars see everything—
and they do nothing.

The earth rises
with every shovel-full.
It is up to my neck now.

There is no room to move.
My head is still above earth.
When I hear a horse.

        A carriage.

               Footsteps.
The hood over my head—removed.

I blink up
at the light
of the stars.
So bright.
Why do
none of them
save me?
My vision adjusts
and I see only Marghita.
She spits in my face.
"A Jewish demoness—
a *striga* that's
what you are.
You seduced my son
and found your way
into his bed
even though you knew
you carried the spawn
of a different man—
a demon,

      just like you."

She bends down
and I think
that she will

      strike me.

I close my eyes
and wait for
      the blow.
Instead, there's a cool blade
at my throat.
So that's it, I think.
She will slit my throat.

But she doesn't.

She cuts off my hair.

Long copper strands fall
around my head.
I feel the metal
pressed to my skull
and then the *skritch*
of the blade.
She nicks my skull
in so many places,
I see rivers of blood
in front of my eyes.
I don't have hands
that I can use
to wipe the blood away.

The guards fill
the burlap sack
with my hair.
"Burn it,"
she tells them.
"Thou shalt not suffer
a witch to live!"

She kneels down
before me
and takes the cloth
out of my mouth.
Help! I cry out,
as loud as I can,
      as loud as my lungs,
            which are pressed in by earth
                  will allow.

But then
she is shoving something
in my mouth.
I taste dirt.
My body wants
my hands to fight—
to struggle.
But I cannot
feel them
anymore.
           Sh'ma Yisrael!

I choke and gag
and try to dislodge
the dirt
from my mouth,
           Adonai Eloheinu!

but she only shoves
more in.
           Adonai Echad.

So much earth.
My mouth feels
as though it will burst.
My jaw aches.

I start to choke.
Earth at the back
of my mouth.
I can't swallow

         it

             down.

I can still breathe
through my nose,
but just barely.

Marghita gets up.
She wipes her hands
on her gown.
Then she takes
something out of a sack
and I hear the sound
of salt spilling.
A ring of salt
around my head.
Everything blurs.
My eyes water.
I try to breathe,
to keep a clear path
down my throat
for air.
But there are
black shadows
in the corners
of my eyes.
I am too scared
to move my lips.

I am Levana bat Yitzchak,

I say in my heart,

> *daughter of Esther and Isaac*
> *Oh Lord our God*
> *who I know I've forsaken.*
> *Please . . . save me . . .*

Marghita spits.
She curses at me.
"Stay here
 until she stops
 breathing,"
she tells the guards.
I hear a horse,
galloping away.
Then all is quiet
and still.
I try to look up
to the heavens.

> *Ezri me'im* Hashem—
> *My help comes from the Lord*
> *oseh shamayim va'aretz—*
> *who made heaven and earth.*

It hurts my neck,
but if I am to die,
I wish to die
with the stars
in my eyes.

It is the wrong choice.
 The angle only sends
 the earth in deeper.
I struggle and gasp;
I can't breathe;

there is nowhere for
the air to go.

The black velvet I see
is like a night
with no stars.

Hannah

23 Iyar 5123

I woke before dawn again today and made my way through the
forest to the cave. I thought that I was only going to check on the
babies—my nephews—but something had been set into motion
last night that would change our future forever.

I found the babies sleeping peacefully. They must have woken
up, then cried themselves back to sleep again, poor things, but
they are safe, and alive. The forest is caring for them, and that
is all that matters. I changed their soiled clothing and fed them
milk. I know this is not a permanent solution: they need mother's
milk—they need a mother. Soon they fell back asleep, stomachs
full and content . . . for now.

I didn't want to leave them. I cradled one to my chest, and
then the other. What will become of them? Who will take care
of them? I cried and my tears wet their little faces.

When I stopped crying, I put them down and watched the rise
and fall of their chests. Something felt wrong. Something in the
earth. There is a rumbling beneath the earth, a trembling in each
branch and leaf. I felt it then, a disturbance, an unease. The roots
of the trees are unhappy.

I kissed the boys on their foreheads and my eyes filled with tears again.

I will be back again, little ones.

Hăita liuliu, sleep softly.

Hăita liuliu. Hăitu lulu.

I cut through the forest and made my way to the town square. The sense of unease I felt grew. The trees vibrated with something I can only now describe as sorrow. The closer I got, the worse it felt, the trees both getting in my way and urging me on. I walked fast, then ran faster, and faster. The trees whispered in my ears. Something was very, very wrong.

When I got to the center of the town square, the crows were already circling. I saw my little sister and dropped to the ground, hand over my mouth, stifling my scream. "No . . ." I whispered, hoarse. *Her hair . . . her beautiful hair*, I remember thinking, with no rational reason why I thought that when faced with the horror of her death. I fell to the ground and dug my fingers into her mouth, trying to pry out the earth, but it was no use. My little sister was cold and dark. No longer bright. No longer breathing. No breath left in her. No air.

I couldn't breathe. I felt like the air was choking me. As if I'd swallowed earth. And that was when I noticed it—the Black Mist like a carpet, blanketing the floor. Smothering everything.

Levana. My baby sister. My little light. Once I held her like I hold her babies now. My body heaved. It tried to empty me of everything within me. But the life within me held fast.

How can anything matter now that she's gone? I have known too much of loss and not enough love. We all have.

And now there are two motherless boys in the world. Boys who will never know the light that used to shine in her eyes. The soft sound of her voice when she sang our prayers. The way she looked up at the sky and believed, with all her heart, in the power of the stars to save us all.

She was wrong. No angel came. Not to save Jakob, or Guvriel, or her babies, or her soul now.

Leaving our faith behind wasn't enough. Constantin wasn't enough. Nikolas wasn't enough. Even the stars, that shone so bright for her, left her alone and scared in the end.

I don't know how to live in a world without her.

I can't stop my body from shaking, the sobs from finding their way out of my mouth.

I try to breathe, but it's so hard. Was this what it was like for her in her last minutes?

Did she know that no one would save her?

We can only save ourselves, I heard my mother's voice and I knew that I had to go to her. To tell her and Abba what happened here.

Why did I leave her? I could have tried to save her ... but I chose her boys instead.

It is a choice I will have to live with for the rest of my life.

One day, her children can read these words. One day, they'll read how brave she was until the very end.

The sun was rising. I felt its warmth on my face. I didn't want its light or its comfort, but its dawning rays broke through the haze of my sorrow and knew I had to act quickly.

I stood up and took off my shoes. I planted my feet in the earth by her head. My toes curled into the soil and I closed my eyes. Tears poured down my cheeks. I sought her soul. I reached out with my senses and looked for it amid the thick black mist, and then I felt it. A bright spark trapped inside the husk of her body. I tugged, but it didn't budge. I tried to entice it, but it paid me no heed. It wouldn't leave my sister's body even in death.

And then I realized why. I remembered. A *tahara* wasn't done. This wasn't a proper Jewish burial. But I didn't have the time or the strength to dig her out.

My tears continued to fall. I felt the seed of a tree take root, and as I struggled to free her soul, a sapling sprouted. It was not something I asked for. Not something I called into being, but still it came and I sang to it, one of the songs that Levana used to sing . . .

> *May the angel who redeems me from harm*
> *bless the children and call them by My name*
> *and by the names of my forefathers, and may they*
> *multiply like fish in the midst of the earth.*

Its roots surrounded my sister's head, cocooning her body, wrapping around her until she was planted, firmly rooted like I wanted to be, pulled down into the earth and buried within it.

The tree's limbs already reached for the sky like she did.

I whispered softly, begging the ground for the release of my sister's soul.

I gave you life, I said, *now give me this light.*

I felt a small glow sputter and stop, then sputter again and begin to shine. It traveled from the belly of the earth through the roots of the tree and up a branch, until one silver star sprouted from the top of the tree. It shimmered in the near-dawn of sky.

It detached itself from the top of the tree and took flight, spiraling upwards. It rose, faster and faster, until I could no longer see it. I only saw the shimmer it left behind.

This was not the way my sister's story was supposed to end, but her soul is free now. It was the best I could do. The only thing.

She is with her beloved in the sky.

And then I heard her voice on the wind. *"Every star in the sky is a soul. When someone dies, a star falls. It is our job to put the stars back in the sky. Rekindle the light."*

I've always wondered, with so much death in the world, how there were still so many stars.

Now I know that there is more than one way to make a

star. When I get home, I will light a candle and place it on the windowsill.

Perhaps from up there she will see it. Perhaps she can already see her little boys, that they are safe for now, and sleeping.

She is the angel who will watch over us all.

When I looked up at the tree, it was covered in star-shaped leaves.

I saw an owl swoop down, then land on the branches of the tree.

"It is a tree of life, for those who take hold of it," I said out loud, remembering the verse from synagogue, from when we returned the Torah scrolls to their ark.

Then, like I used to do in synagogue when I was a little girl and the *gabbai* raised the Torah scroll so that all could see it, I kissed my fingers, then pressed my palm up to the sky.

$$\star \quad \star \quad \star \quad \star \quad \star \quad \star \quad \star \quad \star \quad \star \quad \star \quad \star$$

I turned in the direction of my parents' home. I had to go tell them that their daughter was gone. I must help them tear *kri'ah*, we must all sit *shiva*. We may have left our religion behind us, but the seven days of Jewish mourning will begin with or without us. Some traditions are as immutable as the stars.

I will mourn Levana in the traditional way. I will sit *shiva* for seven days.

And then I will tell her story.

Stanna

I can no longer deny what is growing within me. Ivan Alexander sends us to a monastery so that Theodora might come back, bearing my baby in her arms and ensuring Ivan Alexander's succession.

But Theodora knows what happens to women who are sent to monasteries, and though I crave the solitude and peace the place affords us—and the relief I get from Ivan's attention—she can't find peace. She paces the halls restlessly, claiming she hears voices in the walls and the wails of babies at night.

"But we are alone here together, *iubirea mea*," I try. "Ivan Alexander can no longer bother us."

"Ivan Alexander will no longer bother you," she bites back at me. "That's all you care about."

Days turn to weeks and she is not thriving. There is no horse she can ride here, no escape. The eyes of the clergy are upon us constantly. We have privacy in our chambers, but no peace.

"Take to the skies," I say to her one night. "Fly through the forest and all around the monastery and you will see that there is nothing and no one to fear."

Theodora takes off that night under the cover of darkness. She soars for hours in the sky and comes back. Her cheeks are flushed and ruddy, her eyes bright in a way I haven't seen in a long time.

"There," I say. "That was all you needed. Some fresh air. A way to be free."

"This place is a cage," she says, out of breath. "Nothing more than a prison."

I hear in her words the way I felt about Ivan Alexander's castle.

"He will order all the doors and windows closed," she says, eyes crazed. "He will bury us here, entombed with the bones of all those buried in the crypt."

"What I see as a sanctuary you see as a tomb," I say.

We go to bed that night, but neither of us sleep for a long time. When I finally do fall asleep, I have a dream.

Once there was a girl whose first love was lost to her, so she fell in love with a dragon.

But the dragon was captured by an evil prince, and she did the only thing she could think to do.

If you love something, her heart told her, you set it free.

And so she did.

Even though she knew it meant that she might never see the dragon again.

She crawled back into the dragon's cage and waited for the evil prince to find her. She didn't care what happened to her. She only cared that her true love was free and happy.

Her love became a wolf—a great white wolf that rode through the skies on a cloud. Others say her love became an owl—swooping in the light cast by the moon. Still others say her love became a black dragon who visits the earth on occasion in the form of a black mist—and sometimes on the tail of a star.

She never stopped looking out her window, waiting for her love.

Sometimes, when she saw a falling star, she would kiss her fingers, then press her hand up to the sky.

⁎

When I wake up the next morning, I'm alone and the window is open.

⁎

I have lost so much, but I press my hand to the swell of my belly and feel the burst of life growing within me.

This is finally something that feels like it's all mine. Something nobody can take from me. I will do whatever it is I need to do to protect it.

I call the clergy to my bedroom and ask what I must do to prepare myself to be baptized.

If one dragon is the same as any other, a wolf the same as any fox, perhaps all faiths are the same in God's eyes. I will be a dragon of light in the darkness. A black mist won't defeat my family, my children, or my people ever again.

I tell Prince Ivan Alexander when he visits that Theodora ran away.

I don't know if he will marry me, but if I can take Theodora's place at his side, then my child's future will be secure. In my child, there is a holy spark of God. There are many different ways to calm a storm, I think, and one way is to put yourself at the very center of it.

My mother once told me the story of Esther—who sacrificed her life so that her son, Darius the Second might sit on a throne. Darius who went on to rebuild the holy temple in Jerusalem, and Esther, who wove the tapestries for the holy ark and sanctuary.

To ensure a future for my sons and daughters, I will put them on the throne.

I've changed before, and I will change again. I will take on a different name—Sarah Theodora. I will become something else entirely.

Not a Jew, but a survivor.

*   *   *   *   *
*   *   *   *   *   *
*

I once made you a promise, I say to Theodora in my mind, thinking back to that day in the wood when my sisters and I tried to be carefree and happy. And for the first time, I hear my own voice, echoing back at me:

If I were to be chosen by one of those fine strapping young lads . . . I would weave him a shirt out of the branches of this tree and it would wrap itself around him and fit him perfectly, and keep him from drowning and protect him from fire, and leave him unscathed when he fights dragons and other kinds of beasts. And then he could live forever.

*   *   *   *   *
*   *   *   *   *   *
*

I rummage through my trunk until I find it. Guvriel's *tallit*.

I open the window shutters and stare out at the sky and make a wish: "Please come back to me . . . even if only for one night."

But I know that promises can be broken.

I'm about to close the window when an owl lands on the ledge and turns itself into Theodora.

There are tears in her eyes.

"I'm sorry," she says. "I didn't mean to leave for so long. There is something I must tell you."

"Come inside. It's good to see you," I say. As I reach out to embrace her, I press the *tallit* into her hands. "When you put this on, it will turn into the finest armor anyone has ever seen—it will shine silver in the moonlight and gold during the day. It is intri-cately stitched with all the creatures of the forest—owl, serpent, wolf and fox—they will protect you. It will keep you safe from fire; when you go through water you will not get wet." I take a deep breath. "I love you enough to set you free."

She opens and closes her mouth but no sound comes out. She clutches the shawl to her chest and starts to cry.

"Your sister . . . " she says, shaking her head as if she's trying to dislodge the words. "Your sister is dead."

Do not fear the darkness when it comes. There is a lamp of darkness that lights the heavens, but out of the hidden, the mystery of the infinite, a line of light embedded within the ring can emerge.

—The Book of the Solomonars,
page 45, verses 4–5

* * * * * * *

There was once a noblewoman who buried two babies because she didn't like the look of the golden stars on their foreheads.

In that place, deep inside the earth, where the babies cried and their tears fell, the Holy One, Blessed Be He made two aspen trees grow. The trees grew tall and lush, until their branches reached the high window of the woman who buried them. Their leaves flowered with leaves that looked like golden stars.

As the wind rustled through the trees at her window, she heard words like "murderer," and "baby killer," stories about her—both true and untrue. At night, all she could hear was the sound of two babies crying.

The sounds were unbearable—deafening.

One day, while her husband and son were out in the

fields, she ordered that the trees be cut down and made into beds for herself and her husband.

When her husband returned home, he said to his wife, "What did you do? Those trees provided shade and such lovely dappled light through the window of our bedroom."

The noblewoman replied, "Their bark was such a pretty color that I had them made into beds for us. I thought it would be a nice surprise. We can plant other trees in their place."

But that night, when she went to sleep in her new wooden bed, she dreamed of leaves and vines and babies tangled in trees. The whispering was louder than before, and the babies cried in her ears. She woke in the middle of the night, screaming, because she was certain that branches and vines had grown from the beds and trapped her. But when her husband pulled off the covers, there was nothing there.

The next day, she ordered her servants to burn the beds and replace them with other identical beds made from different wood.

As the fire raged, two golden sparks jumped out of the flames and landed in a nearby river. The sparks swam along the river and were swallowed by two golden fish. The fish fell down a waterfall and were borne along the rapids until they reached a cave. In the cave were two boys with golden stars on their foreheads. The boys caught the fish and ate them, then they dove into the water and swam…

Hannah

24 Iyar 5123

I wake while it's still dark. I'm staying in my parents' house now. Constantin is still away. He knows nothing of what has befallen us.

Soon my parents will be waking up to sit *shiva*. Soon, ten men will assemble here for morning prayers. I knocked on all the doors in Curtea's Jewish quarter. I gathered the men myself. There is not a soul in this town who doesn't know now that the blood of Solomon runs in our veins. It means we are not safe here anymore.

When Abba heard about Levana's death, he didn't cry. He got up out of his chair by the fire and left the house. Eema and I looked at each other, but we let him go, a few hours later, he came back. He tore the fabric above his heart, then helped us do the same, then he said *kaddish*, the first Hebrew words I'd heard my father speak since we fled Trnava. And only after that, did he allow himself to sit on the floor and cry.

I didn't tell them about the babies. Lord forgive me, but they would have wanted to see them, and I fear I would have condemned them and us to certain death. There is only so much the heart can bear.

Soon, I will tell them. Soon, I will need to sit *shiva* with them. But for now, I must go to the forest.

25 Iyar 5123

So much has happened in a day. Yesterday we sat and cried. Today, when I got to the cave to check on the babies, the wood and vines and ivy parted for me. I rushed inside . . . and saw that the babies weren't there. I panicked—heart pattering inside my chest like a frightened rabbit. Where did they go? How did I fail them? I had hoped that if I could hide them until they grew, I might find a way to save them. To take them away from here. Did someone find them? Someone . . . or something? A bear? A wolf? A man? I walked farther back into the cave . . . and then I saw their swaddling cloths, discarded on the banks of an underground stream. *No—no no no*, my mind raced, my hands shook with fear. I dove into the water.

I knew what I would find. Two bodies dead and swollen at the bottom of the river.

Someone must have followed me. Someone must have found them.

I remember thinking, *At least I can give them a Jewish burial. I will not fail them in the way I failed their mother—my sister.*

I searched the water in vain. I waded through the stream which turned into a river. Shivering, I dove down and let the river carry me out of the cave. I came out the other side, and still, there was no sign of them. I followed the river, my eyes scanning its banks, all the way to the palace.

I knew I was too late. I knew that someone had found them. Perhaps Marghita herself. There was no blood, no sign of struggle. It would have been so easy to drown them. My mind raced. *Why did I not protect them better? Why did I not take them with me? I thought I could save them—but I realize now that I can't save anyone. Not even myself.*

I no longer know what drips down my face—river water or tears.

I saw a fisherman from the palace kitchens on the banks of the river. He caught two golden fish in his net. I watched as he drew the bag up into his boat, then he docked near the palace and hauled out his catch.

I wanted to ask him if he'd seen them, if he saw someone drowning two babies in the river, but there is nothing I can say that won't implicate me. As far as anyone knows, Laptitza's babies were stillborn.

I turned around to go home. *I failed to save her life, I failed to give her a proper burial, and now I'd failed not one, but two of her sons. There is no redemption for me.*

I hung my head as I walked away, distraught and alone. Gutted like those fish were about to be. All the wisdom that my father had imparted to me—all the words he'd written down—all the wisdom of Solomon was not enough to save her, to save any of us.

I walked slowly, silently, lost in my own grief, trying to figure out how I would tell my parents, that I'd failed us all. I'd prevented them from meeting their grandchildren—how could I do such a thing? *There is no redemption for me.*

But then I heard shrieks from the palace. Something compelled me to turn around. To run back. I raced into the kitchen and saw two boys, naked as the day they were born, golden stars on their foreheads shining bright. They stood dripping water by the hearth. I blinked my eyes, scarcely believing what I saw. How could they have grown so quickly? The cook and her assistants were screaming, the fisherman held up a gutting knife, the cook brandished a cleaver.

"Wait!" I said. "Stop!"

"Who are you? Get out of here!" they spat at me.

I felt my toes aching to dig into soil, but there was no earth here. I had to find strength in a different way.

"I am the wife of Constantin Valeriu, commander of the voivode's army. You will tell me what happened here," I said in a voice of command.

"I caught two plump golden fish in the river," the fisherman said. "I thought they'd make a nice supper for the voivode and his wife. I brought them in here and showed 'em to the cook, and she told me to gut 'em. I took out my knife, but as soon as it touched one of their bellies, the fish started to grow, they were shaking and shimmering, golden light was streamin' out of 'em . . . "

"It's true," one of the kitchen maids chimed in. "We all saw it."

"Them fishes were flapping around, and I called for the cook, but as soon as she got over here, she saw, clear as day, that they weren't fish anymore. They grew legs, then arms . . . then they turned into these boys."

"Is there a room I can take them to?" I asked.

"They are devil-spawn," the cook said. "I won't have you bringing them into the palace."

"Well then," I said, my voice growing with a warmth that felt like power. "I'm glad you're not the one in charge."

This was my chance to make things right and I was going to take it.

"Do I need to repeat myself? I am Anna, wife of Constantin, commander in chief of the voivode's army," I said, "and you will do as I command. Now, will one of you please show me to a room?"

At first, none of them responded. They all looked at each other in fear. But then one of the maids curtsied to me and said, "Follow me."

I bent down and looked the boys in the eyes. "I am your aunt, your mother's sister. I am here to protect you. Please come with me."

I placed one hand on each of their backs and urged them forward.

The maid led us into a room which must have been her own chamber. "What is your name?" I said.

"Alina," she replied.

"Alina, thank you," I said. "Can you find them some clothes and hats for their heads? You will be amply compensated. I swear it."

She raced from the room.

I sat on the floor and cried, for I was still in mourning for my sister and could not sit on a bed or a chair. I looked up at the boys and saw that they were watching me. "Do you understand the words I say?" I asked.

They didn't say anything. I couldn't understand how they had grown so quickly, but then I remembered the circle I drew—the words I said when I took them from their untimely grave.

Please let them grow bigger,

tall as an aspen tree,

strong as a cedar . . .

But how?

Alina came back with the clothes. Once they were dressed, I asked her to get one of the voivode's guards.

When I heard a knock at the door, I had a moment of panic. *Maybe the cook sent word and the guards have come for me . . . like they must have come for my sister,* but I prayed that my status as Constantin's wife would protect me—even though nothing else had. When I opened the door I saw them, standing at attention. Waiting for my instruction.

"I request an audience with the Voivode Basarab and his son Nikolas. My husband, Constantin, is still garrisoned with the troops, otherwise he would escort me himself."

"Yes, my lady," one of them responded. "Come with us."

I admit my heart still beat too fast for its own good. I feared

I had made yet another mistake, that they were marching us to certain death—to doom.

But they delivered us to the voivode's audience chamber. "Will you stay?" I asked them.

"We would do anything for Constantin's wife," the first one said. The second guard grunted in agreement.

I turned to face the Voivode Basarab, but Marghita said, "What is the meaning of this?"

I ignored her. I turned to Basarab and Nikolas.

I was sick of hiding. I opened my mouth to tell them the truth—how Marghita schemed and tried to murder these boys— mere babies—Nikolas's rightful heirs, how she murdered my sister in cold blood. But then one of the boys stepped forward.

"We are twin brothers," he said. "Two shoots from one stem, which has been broken. Half lies in the ground and half sits at the head of this table. We were born here in this palace, though half of us now lives in the sky. We have heard our mother singing in the wind, our mother's voice in the branches, our mother's tears wet the earth like rain. Her crying wakes us in the night with the song of our people. This was supposed to be our home. We were supposed to be protected here."

"Now we wish to tell you a story," the other brother said.

"*There was once a man who wished to rule over the free state of Wallachia and he took a woman named Marghita as his wife . . .*" Three cushions spilled out from under Marghita's seat and she slipped and fell off her chair. The boys removed their hats and showed the golden stars on their foreheads.

"It is hatred that caused our suffering. We are children of Solomon, blessed by the God of light. We may look five years in age, but we are twelve in understanding, twenty-four in strength, and thirty-six in wisdom."

I could only watch, wide-eyed, mouth gaping open at this miracle that God had wrought for us.

The Voivode Basarab was the first one to recover. We were all under their spell. "I formed Wallachia as a free and independent state for all people," he said. "All are welcome here. How can this have happened under my own roof?" His eyes pinned Marghita where she stood.

She opened her mouth, then closed it. Then she said, "I'm sorry, my lord. I only saw their deformity—a clear mark of the devil—a mark of that whore's sin. I didn't want to cause my dear son such grief. To see the monsters she had borne—to bring a curse under our roof."

"A curse!" Basarab laughed. "These boys are a blessing. A wonder—"

"Where is Laptitza?" Nikolas asked, interrupting his father calmly.

"She ran away from the palace in the dead of night," Marghita said quickly. "I tried to stop her."

I spoke up. "No." I said. *I won't let this happen.* "Permission to speak, your grace?"

"Granted," the voivode said.

"My sister Laptitza is dead. She was buried in the town square by order of your queen. An aspen tree grows there now, with golden stars for leaves, one that I planted to grow over her grave. But it was Marghita who put her there."

"You lie!" Marghita lunged for me, but the voivode, with a gesture, ordered his guards to seize her.

"A grave injustice has transpired here," he said. Then he turned to Marghita. "You will live out the rest of your days in the Manole Monastery where you belong."

"No, my lord, please no," Marghita wailed, "I was only trying to protect you, and Theodora, and my son . . . " She cried and begged for mercy, but Basarab and Nikolas were deaf to her pleas as the guards dragged her away.

"I would be honored to raise you as my own," Nikolas told the boys, tears in his eyes. "I promised your mother . . . "

But the boys looked to me, then back to Nikolas, and one of them said, "We have heard there is a cave within a mountain. A cave under a lake. It is called Balea. There are others there like us—waiting for us. There is a man there, his red hair blazes with light. He has started an academy—a scholomance, he calls it. A place where we can study and practice our faith without fear" He turned to me and said, "We would like you to take us there."

The other boy turned to Nikolas and said, "We ask that you provide us with as many horses as we need to make the journey and a promise to protect that mountain range. To close access to it each winter when we might practice our faith in freedom."

"I cannot convince you to stay?" Nikolas said. "I would raise you, care for you. It's what your mother would have wanted."

"We belong with our people," one of the boys said.

"Our stars burn too bright for this world," the other boy answered.

"You may take as many horses from our stables as you need," the Voivode Basarab replied.

The candle flickers. The hour grows late and soon I will be in darkness. I must get a few hours of sleep before tomorrow. Today was a long day and tomorrow will be longer. I need my strength for the days to come. I will finish the story tomorrow.

Levana

The palace guards
take Marghita
from the palace.
I watch it happen
from the sky.
I float closer to earth
than any star
has ever dared.
I follow the carriage
that takes Marghita away.
Nobody notices me.
Now that I am a star,
bright as all the heavens,
no one notices me at all.

Once I burned bright,
once I wanted
the attention.
Now I'm just part
of the firmament.
Marghita stands

on the roof
of the bell tower.
The Black Mist
swirls around her.
Tears wet her face,
but I don't care.
She deserves this.

"I only ever wanted
to feel like a star."
She looks up at the sky.
Does she see me?
"I wanted
to burn brightly,
to know I had
a permanent place
in the firmament
of history."
Does she hear me?
"I have failed you, Radu."
She isn't speaking
to me at all.
She is looking for him,
the Black Dragon.
She waits and waits,
but he doesn't come.

Sarah-Theodora

There is no *shiva* for me to attend for my sister. No way for me to send word to my parents without revealing my faith and my people. I must stay and bloom where I've been planted.

My parents will never see or hear from me again.

But I know there is a star that shines high above us. A star, like Esther, who watches over us all.

It is enough.

When Ivan Alexander goes to war, let it be said that sometimes there is a dragon, a serpent of fire, that takes to the skies to ensure his victory.

Balaur, they call it, but I know the truth.

It is a future for myself and my children.

Something written in the stars a long time ago.

A dragon that once lit up the sky and a girl who tried to understand what she saw.

A story that you can tell now, to your children.

Remember me.

Levana

I watch as Marghita climbs up
onto the ledge of the bell tower.
I watch as I see her decide.
I stepped onto a ledge once too.
I wanted to feel
what it was like to fall,
the rush of light,
the slow burn of it,
the last flare of flame
before all goes black
to hang suspended in air,
like a star.
But I never got
to make that choice.
Maybe had I stood there,
I would have chosen differently.
But she took that choice
away from me
She took away
my chance
to be a mother—

to raise my sons.
She snuffed out my light
and now, all I can do is burn.
There is no mercy for her.

My beloved
pines for me—
The Song of Songs
is Solomon's
but this song
is my own.
I pay him no attention
I was lovesick
I shine my own light
And now I am sick of love
Two pieces of me—
two boys
carry a sliver of light
inside them
a piece of my heart
down on earth.
My beloved spoke,
he said unto me:
Rise up, my love,
my fair one,
and come away.
Arise my fair one,
and come away.
Come away.
I answered his call.
By night
on my bed
I sought him

whom my soul loveth;
I sought him,
but I found him not.
But foxes
spoil vineyards
with their greed.
My beloved came
into my garden,
He ate precious fruit.
I opened to my beloved;
but my beloved turned away.
I sought him,
but I found him not.
His head was gold
His eyes like doves
His body polished ivory
Yet my beloved
was no more
than any other.
Awaken not,
nor stir up love,
until it please.
There is dread
in the night
For love
is strong as death.
And jealousy is cruel
as the grave.

Marghita steps off
the roof
and lets go,
and I fall with her.

My starlight traces the line
of her dark descent.

Change comes slowly
or all at once.
Like a spark of light
in a dark sky.
Sometimes it hides
behind a cloud.
Sometimes it falls
and burns.
Sometimes it sits
beside a throne
and waits
for the future to unfold.
My light will guide
the way for others.
I will be there,
shining in the midnight sky
a bright guide.

Hannah

26 Iyar 5123

Abba helped the boys say *kaddish* for their mother this morning.

When all the men left, Eema took the boys to the kitchen to feed them.

They have named themselves. They tell us to call them Hillel and Shabtai.

And I hear my sister's voice in my head, *I will name one for the star of morning and the other for the star of light.*

And I think that if Levana was still with us, she would approve.

I can't help but think that my father finally has the sons he's always wished for. What might have happened had he wished for the daughters he got instead?

But life has a way of surprising us all, I suppose. And even though some destinies are written in the stars, or rooted in the ground—it doesn't mean we don't get a chance on this earth to try and change them.

If our God can move heaven and earth and we are but vessels of his light, there is no end to what we might become—if we allow ourselves the freedom.

"Can I tell you a story?" I hear Eema say to them now in the kitchen. I can see them smiling up at her like we once did.

"*There was a time when everyone knew about the town of Trnava,*" she begins. "*Once, it was a bustling market town that sat at the crossroads between the kingdom of Poland and the rest of Bohemia. Once, the king of Hungary, Charles the First, visited the town and conducted important negotiations there.*" This one is a story that I've never heard. "*But there are stories you don't know. Stories the residents of the town like to keep secret . . .*" she continues, but I stop listening.

I have begun to write my own story in these pages. The story that I will tell my children.

About a girl who fell in love with a star

About a girl whose heart was made of fire

About a girl who found a way to plant herself in the earth and grow

27 Iyar 5123

Constantin came home last night. There was a knock at the door, and I answered.

"I came as soon as I heard," he said, and he wrapped me in his arms. I took comfort in his strength, in the smell of him, in how solid he felt in my arms, but I knew that I couldn't hold on. So much in our world had changed so quickly. My heart had been broken and broken and broken again. I was prepared to let go.

I stepped away and looked into his eyes.

"There is so much to tell . . . " I swallowed hard, not sure how to continue.

"I've heard most of it. Nikolas briefed me," he said.

"I . . . We have to go. We can't stay here. I have to get my family to safety," I whisper. I don't know how to say the words.

They feel like betrayal. *What about the roots around our table?* My heart aches.

"I'm coming with you," he said. I stared at him. I couldn't understand the look on his face. Didn't he know that I'd deceived him? That I'd claimed to be something I'm not? "Nikolas has appointed me as his twin sons' private guard."

"He has?" My eyes grew wide.

"He has," he said and leaned in to kiss me.

"Then it's time for us to go," I said.

We leave now for the mountains. The horses await us outside. *Blessed be the true judge.*

Sarah-Theodora

I van Alexander divorced his first wife Theodora and sent her to a monastery.

I know the truth, and now you know it too.

He never saw Theodora again. She was replaced by the emperor's consort—a woman named Sarah-Theodora who they say was of Jewish descent.

She became empress of all of Bulgaria.

Together they had five children: Kera-Tamara, Kera-Maria, Ivan Shishman, Ivan Asen, Desislava, and Vasilisa.

After Ivan Alexander's death, Sarah-Theodora did not retire to a monastery. She spent the rest of her life surrounded by her children and grandchildren who went on to rule all of Romania, Bulgaria, and Wallachia.

They say her daughter Vasilisa liked to wear armor. She rode a gray horse named Torent and was sometimes seen riding what can only be described as a cloud dragon in the sky.

There is a single pillar extending from heaven to earth . . .
When there are righteous people in the world, it becomes strong,
and when there are not, it becomes weak. It supports the
entire world, as it is written "tzadik yesod olam." If it becomes
weak, then the world cannot endure. Therefore, even if there is
only one righteous person in the world, it is he who supports
the world.

–The Book of the Solomonars,
page 212, verses 6–8

My mother was a storyteller. She wove stories with her words
into great tapestries that played themselves across the sky and
entertained us endlessly. It wasn't until I was older, a married
woman myself, when I learned that her stories had power.
That, in telling them, she was making them come true. They
say these things run in families. The same powers manifest
themselves over and over again. I've done what I can. I've told
the stories the best way I know how. But if I learned one thing
from my mother, it's that sometimes stories have a way of
telling themselves. Forgive me. I did the best I could. I will tell
one last story.

Esther Solomonar

There was once a woman who lived in the mountains. It was said that she had red hair and that she controlled the rain, the wind, the hail, the snow. She knew the nature of the trees, the wild beasts and fish, the birds in the sky. She controlled the planets and the constellations, the purpose of the sky and everything in it. She could heal the sick and curse the healthy for she knew every medicine and potion.

Some say she was born of a people who came to Wallachia from the mountains, from the kingdom of Khazaria. Others say that she came from Magyar, because her people were persecuted there. Still others say she became what she was out of great need—a need to protect her nation, a need to save her family.

It is said that when such a child is born—with red hair and a mark like a star on their foreheads—it is an omen. They will be taken by the Solomonars and raised in a mountain cave for seven years, in a place they call a scholomance, where they avoid the sun and study a sacred book of spells. Only then can they emerge and join the Order of the Solomonars.

It is said that the Solomonars can ride cloud dragons in the sky and control the air. Sometimes they are men, sometimes they are women, sometimes they are something in between. They perform rituals to call the rain and light candles to banish the darkness and call down their dragons from heaven. It is said that some of them are ancient beings—dragons called *teli* that live among us.

They live in forests and hunt with iron axes, sticks that kill snakes, and bridles made from birchbark with which they ride their dragons which are sometimes called *balauri* and other times called *zmeu* and still other times they are called by their real names—their hidden names—and that is when they are called nothing at all—only hope.

They always carry their book of wisdom with them—strapped to their hearts but also memorized fully in their minds. For they claim that wisdom is the best way to fight darkness.

They can speak to animals and take on their form. Some say that they ride with the *moroi* in night hunts, and others say that they are part *moroi*, and still others say that when the weather fights with itself you can see a white dragon chasing a black dragon across the skies.

There are still peasants alive today who claim to have seen them—boys with golden stars on their foreheads, golden dragons with wings and scales, and a red-haired mountain woman who cares for them along with a wizard-like old man who rides a cloud dragon in the sky. There is a saying in Romania, "If you see a fox, it is an omen. It means there are wolves nearby." When people see the red-haired woman, they say she always carries a basket of strawberries.

Author's note

The Light of the Midnight Stars started as all good stories do, with only a kernel of an idea. My father always told me tales about how his mother, who was from Romania, used to light Shabbat candles on Friday night in a closet. By the time I came around, the candles had migrated toa the center of the table, and my grandmother's dementia had taken over. She no longer remembered why she did so.

Growing up, I most commonly associated stories of women lighting Shabbat candles in a closet with the Spanish and Portuguese conversos who kept their Jewish identity and customs hidden because of the Spanish Inquisition. Were there Spanish and Portuguese Jews in Romania? Was that a part of my heritage? I needed to know. But the tangled paths my research took came up with no conclusive answers and kept leading me back to Hungary. Why would my grandmother light candles in a closet if that was where her family originally came from?

What I discovered along the way was that the Spanish and Portuguese Jews were not the only Jews who lit candles in closets. Throughout history there have been Jews who have had to hide their faith and its various practices because of persecution. This happened in places such as Russia, Ukraine, Poland, Romania, Italy, Morocco, Spain, Portugal, India, Mexico, New Mexico, Bolivia, Costa Rica, Peru, Colombia, Ethiopia, and more.

My quest for the truth of my grandmother's heritage kept pointing me in the direction of what was then the Kingdom of Hungary, where sources and research seem to indicate she may have come from, and where Jews were once forced to wear a red cloth in public as a sign of their faith long before World War II—all the way back as far as the thirteenth century. During the Black Death, they were expelled from the kingdom, readmitted, then expelled again a second time. Many of these Jews ended up in Wallachia and other parts of Romania. Bessarabia, a name commonly used to describe the area and often associated with the Pale of Settlement, is said to have taken its name from Basarab the First—the ruler of Wallachia mentioned in this book.

Basarab himself is a figure of legend—he may or may not have been Radu Negru himself, and his wife was Marghita who, legend has it, was the wife of Radu Negru first. Basarab himself may have been Turkic in origin, and some legends even say that he may have been a Khazar, or a mountain Jew who came to the region of Romania seeking religious freedom. What we do know is that Basarab had a daughter named Theodora who married Ivan Alexander of Bulgaria and that at some point Ivan Alexander abandoned her and married a converted Jew named Sarah-Theodora.

What I ended up with was part hypothesis, part fairy tale and no conclusive answers, but I found myself in the midst of a fascinating forest of history. As I walked through the winding pathways of the history of the Jews in medieval Hungary, Romania, Bulgaria and what is today Slovakia, I encountered the mythology and folklore of the region. I delved into local fairy tales along the way, and into the rich heritage of Hassidic tales from the region.

The Light of the Midnight Stars is also fairy tale retelling of the Romanian tale "Boys with Golden Stars" from Andrew Lang's *Violet Fairy Book*, in which three sisters each make a bid to marry the son of the emperor by promising something fantastical. It is the youngest sister who says that if she marries the prince she will give birth to twin boys with golden stars on their foreheads. Golden stars, something Jews were once made to wear in shame, always made me feel like this story was part of my story.

But this fairy tale doesn't have a happy ending. There are dark forces at work in the shape of the prince's evil stepmother as she takes the babies away and tries to kill them and their mother.

How could I not be moved by the idea of children born with golden stars on their foreheads? The six pointed "Magen David" has long been associated with Judaism, long before Jews were made to wear them as badges during the Holocaust. Some say the star first appeared on the shield of King David himself. It was a natural match—the idea that even if you try to hide your Judaism in a closet, our faith has a way of reappearing, perhaps in the shape of a shining golden star on a baby's forehead.

This novel is also a retelling of the Romanian poem *Luceafărul* by Mihai Eminescu—a narrative poem based on Romanian folklore about a princess who falls in love with a star. Eminescu based this story on the Romanian folk-myth of the *Zburător*—a dragon-like spirit with a wolf-like head and a tail of fire that makes love to maidens in their beds at night and causes them to roam the streets at night and refuse to eat for lack of him; a kind of incubus. I've also always wanted to write a Jewish dragon story. And in my research I discovered the *teli*—a serpent-like holy Jewish dragon, also a constellation, said to be part human, part angel. I knew that these dragons had to find a way into my book.

Along the way I also discovered another Romanian legend— the story of the Solomonars, red-haired mountain men who could control the weather and who rode cloud dragons in the skies.

Sadly, they were also often portrayed as caricatures of Jews and part of the anti-Semitic myth that Jews can control the weather.

Who were these mountain Jews and was there any truth to these tales? What if Jews could fly cloud dragons? What if we could trace our lineage and a magical heritage back to King Solomon himself who was said to work miracles, speak to animals, control the weather, make things grow and control the heavens—including the stars?

And that was when I stumbled upon the Hassidic story about Rabbi Isaac Tyrnau (also known as Trnava—a Slovakian town, which, when under Hungarian rule, was called Nagyszombat) and the story of his daughter who fell in love with a prince who converted to Judaism and married her, only to be burnt at the stake as a traitor to the throne, and as a result, all of the Jews were expelled from Trnava. Granted, this story is said to have taken place in the fifteenth century, but this is a fantasy novel, and I'd found the story I wanted to tell.

Rabbi Isaac Tyrnau lived in the late fourteenth and early fifteenth century. He wrote a book called the *Sefer HaMinhagim—Book of Customs*—in reaction to the deaths of so many community leaders during the Black Death and the need he saw for a unification of local customs. My *Book of the Solomonars* combines translations of this actual work with snippets of other Kabbalistic concepts and Hassidic texts.

My "Black Mist" is a combination of the Black Plague/Black Death and biblical leprosy, and a metaphor for anti-Semitism. The Black Plague was often blamed on the Jews throughout Europe and resulted in many pogroms and violent attacks against them.

I've taken liberties with the exact locations of the forests mentioned in the book, and their magical properties—it's hard to know what the landscape was really like in the mid-1400s, where one forest ended and another began. But there is a haunted forest in Romania called the Hoia Baciu, and a mystical temple cave in the Șinca Veche forest. There is a Jewish Hassidic sect today who call themselves "Satmar" after the city of Satu Mare where their rabbi, Joel Teitelbaum, came from. There is a forest near that town bearing the same name. There is a lake in the mountains not too far from Curtea de Argeș that is only open in the summer months. It is called Lake Balea, and in Curtea de Argeș itself, you can still see the ruins of Basarab's castle. The names of the gates of the city of Trnava are all real and taken from ancient maps, along with the names of the Královský and Šenkvický forests. Anything that goes against the historical record is a deliberate choice. This is a fairy tale, but one steeped in the history and geography of a people and a place—as most fairy tales are.

Along the way, I read many tales about foxes—it is said that the Talmudic Rabbi Meir (who lived in the first century CE) told three hundred fox tales that were known for three generations after his death. There are also many Romanian fox tales. The prayers that Guvriel teaches Sarah are part of the *Perek Shirah* (literally *Chapter of Song*) which dates back to the tenth century if not earlier and is a compilation of various Talmudic, Midrashic and biblical texts about creation and the "songs" of all the animals. It is said that if you recite the *Perek Shirah* for forty days straight, a miracle will happen.

It wasn't too far a leap to take it to the place of being a kind of manual for meditation and transformation. The *Tikkun Chatzot* is a custom that I associate with Rabbi Nachman of Bretslav who came many years after the story I tell in these pages, but the concept of getting up at midnight to recite prayers and psalms to God dates back to the time of King David.

The story of the master builder Manole and the monastery he commissions (in which he entombs his wife) dates back to the time of Radu Negru, though the story is a myth.

I didn't set out to write a historical novel, though much of this book is based on real historical events. I know the dates and places don't always line up. I haven't even been able to scratch the surface of all the references, ideas, myths and stories I mention in the book. If you think something in here is a reference to something else, it very well might be. This is a fantasy novel, and much license was taken in order to weave all these various legends, myths, tales and historical events together into the story I wanted to tell. It is a story entirely my own, but based on an incredible history of stories and storytellers that have come before me.

I never figured out where my grandmother actually came from or why she lit candles in a closet—but perhaps the story I was able to tell as a result is more important than the truth. My grandmother was a great storyteller, and my father is a storyteller too. Perhaps the passing on of that tradition—the way that we tell stories in order to make sense of our past, present, and future—is more important than where and how we light our candles. Only that we must keep lighting them.

Glossary

Hebrew

Adar—Jewish month generally in the spring
Adon Olam—Master of the Universe
Adonai—God (the Lord)
Adonai Echad—God (the Lord) is one
Adonai Eloheinu—God (the Lord) is our God
am kshei oref—a stiff-necked people
Amidah—means "standing" but refers to the silent standing
  prayer said by Jews three times per day
ani maamin—I believe
aravot—willow leaves/branches traditionally used on the fall/
  harvest holiday of Sukkot.
aron kodesh—holy ark
ashmurot—might watch
avodah—work
Av—fifth month of the Jewish calendar (summer)

baruch—blessed
bat kol—divine echo

bat mitzvah—a Jewish coming-of-age ritual for girls at
    age twelve
beit knesset—synagogue
betzel knafeikhah tastireini—hide me in the shadow of
    your wings
Bnei Yisrael—Children of Israel
Borei Olam—Creator of the World
brucha haba'ah—blessed is the one arriving (welcome) (female
    conjugation)

challah/challot—braided bread
cherem—excommunication
Cheshvan—eighth month of the Jewish calendar (fall)

Devarim—Deuteronomy

El Givat Ha'Levonah—to the hill of frankincense
El na refah na lah—please, God, please heal her
Elul—sixth month of the Jewish calendar (end of summer)
Elohim—God
erev (as in *Erev Rosh Hashana*)—the eve of/evening
esh—fire
etrog—citron traditionally used on the fall/harvest
    holiday of Sukkot
etz chaim—tree of life
ezri me'im Hashem—my help comes from the Lord

gabbai—beadle or sexton, someone who helps run
    synagogue services
galuy—revealed
Gehennom—Hell
goy—non-Jew

hachnassat orchim—hospitality (literally: the bringing in
    of guests)
hadassim—myrtle branches traditionally used on the fall/
    harvest holiday of Sukkot
Hanukkah—Jewish winter holiday where an eight-branched
    candelabra is lit to commemorate the rededication of the
    Second Temple in Jerusalem after the Maccabean revolt
harei at mekudeshet li kadat Moshe ve'Yisrael—behold, you are
    sanctified to me, according to the laws of Moses and Israel
    (traditional Jewish marriage declaration)
Hassidim—pious Jews (*hassid* literally means "a kind person")
Havdallah—Jewish ceremony marking the end of the Sabbath
heh—fifth letter of the Hebrew alphabet
huppah—wedding canopy

ish—man
isha—woman
Iyar—second month of the Jewish calendar (in the spring)

ka'asher avadeti, avadeti—if I perish, I perish
Kaddish—Jewish prayer said by those mourning for the dead
kehilla—community
ketubah—wedding contract
kiddush levana—the blessing of the new moon
Kislev—ninth month of the Jewish calendar (dead of winter)
kivshan ha'esh—fiery furnace
Kohelet—Ecclesiastes
kri'ah—rending one's garment; a mourning practice

Libavtani, achoti kallah—you have ravished me, my darling bride
lulav—palm frond traditionally used on the fall/harvest
    holiday of Sukkot

maariv—evening prayer

mazal—luck or constellation

mazal tov—congratulations! (or: good luck!)

mazalot—constellations

mazikim—harmful spirits

Megillat Eichah—*The Book of Lamentations*

me'il—(literally: jacket) in later times known as a mantle; the
     outer covering of a Torah scroll, often richly embroidered

menorah—seven-branched candelabra

mezuzah—parchment attached to the doorpost of a Jewish home

midrash—a commentary on the Bible

minyan—prayer quorum of ten men

mishkan—tabernacle

Mishna—first written collection of oral Jewish law
     and tradition

mitpahat—(literally: scarf) a cloth used to wrap up a
     Torah scroll

mitzvot—commandments

Moed Kattan—a tractate of the Talmud that discusses the laws
     of the intermediate days of Passover and Sukkot

nachash omer—the snake says

nahar di nur—river of fire

nekevah tesovev gever—and woman/female will
     encircle man/male

ner tamid—eternal flame

niggun—melody

Nisan—first month of the Jewish calendar (the start of spring)

nozel—liquid

ohr eyn sof—infinite light

oseh shamayim va'aretz—who made heaven and earth

parochet—curtain that covers the holy ark

pasuk—verse/sentence in the bible

Perek Shirah—(literally: a chapter of song) ancient Jewish prayer that contains the prayers/verses of eighty-four elements in nature

Pirkei Avot—*Ethics of the Fathers*

Psachim—tractate of Talmud that deals with Passover

ptach li sha'arei tzedek—open the gates of justice for me

Rosh Hashana—Jewish New Year holiday

Sattan—the evil inclination of Satan

Seder—(literally: order) the ritual meal at the start of Passover

sefarim—holy books

Sefer Torah—handwritten copy of the Bible (the Old Testament) written on parchment

segulah—a charm or ritual of protection, as an adjective it can mean chosen/select

selichot—communal prayers for forgiveness said during the Jewish High Holiday season

Sh'ma—(literally: listen/hear) shorthand for the prayer said twice daily affirming the oneness of God

Shabbat—the Jewish Sabbath which begins Friday at sundown and ends twenty-five hours later on Saturday night, one hour after sundown

Shabbat shalom—a sabbath of peace (a sabbath greeting, like saying hello)

shacharit—morning prayer

Shechina—(literally: dwelling or settling) the divine presence of God in the world (feminine)

shehiyah—staying/presence

Sh'ma Yisrael—Hear O Israel

Shevat—eleventh month of the Jewish calendar (in the winter)

shirah—(literally: song, but can also be poem/poetry) prayers of praise

shiva—seven-day Jewish mourning period

shofar—ram's horn, generally blown on Rosh Hashana

shuckling—technically a Yiddish word, but the concept—movement of the body via prayer—is a Jewish one and a very old one at that

siddur—prayer book

Simchat Torah—Jewish holiday that celebrates the end of the cycle of the reading of the bible/Torah each year

Sivan—third month of the Jewish calendar (end of spring)

Sukkot—feast of the tabernacles, a Jewish harvest festival, generally celebrated at the start of fall

tallit—prayer shawl

talmid/talmidim—student/s

Talmud—central text of Jewish (rabbinic) law

tamid—forever/eternal

Tammuz—fourth month of the Jewish calendar (in the summer)

tahara—preparation of the body for a Jewish burial

tehillim—psalms

teli—constellation/heavenly serpent

Tevet—tenth month of the Jewish calendar (in the winter)

tikkun—correction, also a type of prayer

tikkun chatzot—midnight prayer

Tisha B'Av—national day of mourning the holy temple

Tishrei—seventh month of the Jewish calendar (start of fall)

Torah—the bible (Old Testament)

treif—not kosher

Tu B'Av—Jewish holiday of love

Tu Bishvat—Jewish New Year for the trees

tzaddikim—righteous men

tzadik yesod olam—a verse from Proverbs which means that the
    righteous person is the foundation of the world
tzedakah—charity

yeshiva—(literally: seated) house of study
yichud—(literally: unification) prohibition against a man and
    a woman being alone in a room together (when a bride and
    groom get married, in an Orthodox wedding, they often go
    to a *"yichud"* room where they get to be alone together after
    the ceremony for the first time)
Yom Kippur—the Jewish day of atonement, holiest day of the
    Jewish year
yud—tenth letter of the Hebrew alphabet

Hungarian

Én Istenem—my God
Judengasse (German origins)—Jewish quarter
Nagmama—Grandmother
sziporka—spark/sparkle

Romanian

balaur/balauri—dragon/dragons
draga mea—my darling
fiica mea—my daughter
hăita liuliu—lullaby
hora—traditional Romanian folk dance
iubirea mea—my love
lăcrimioare—tear
mireasa mea—my bride
moroi—poltergeist/vampire/ghost in Romanian folklore
striga—a woman cursed and turned into a monster

zmeu—fantastic creature that appears in the sky and spits fire
    and seduces young girls

Bulgarian

krasota/mi krasota—beauty/my beauty
tya e krasiva tazi—she is beautiful this one

Acknowledgments

Every book has its own path. It's what I tell people in my other job as a literary agent. This one's path was long and winding. And I did eventually come out the other end. There were times that I never thought this book would see the light of day, when, like Levana, I thought there were no stars in the sky to guide me.

But there were stars. And they were there for me all along. This book owes a lot to a lot of people. You are each part of the stars in my midnight sky.

To Brent Taylor, agent extraordinaire and friend, one of the brightest lights. Thank you for always believing in me, even when I don't always believe in myself.

To Nivia Evans, editor and friend, who guided me on this difficult journey—always keeping a light on in the window and waiting for me to find my way. This book is what it is today because of your direction and patience.

To Anna Jackson, my UK editor, and Joanna Kramer, copy-editor extraordinaire. Just like no cake is complete without frosting (in my humble opinion!) you helped me put the finishing touches on this book. I didn't know that the book wasn't quite done until you read it, but now it's done because of your sharp insight and advice.

To Lauren Panepinto and Tran Nguyen—I cannot imagine a more breathtaking cover and interior. Thank you for bringing my book, my words, and my world to life.

To Angela Mann and Nazia Khatun, star publicists, and Paola Crespo, Laura Fitzgerald, and Madeleine Hall in Marketing, and everyone else at the Orbit US and UK teams who helped bring this book to fruition.

To the Highlights Foundation (George Brown, Alison Green Myers, Jo Lloyd, Amanda Richards and everyone else on the team!) who provided me with a space to write and rewrite this book (more than once . . .)—the paths I walked in the forests on your campus, in the snow, showed me and my book how to come out the other side changed for the better. There is no more wonderful place for nurturing words and imagination.

To my beta readers, friends, and advisors. Some of you read different drafts of this book along the way, others provided research advice and Halachic guidance, others supported me with copious amounts of coffee, alcohol, shoulders to cry on and so much more. I am so lucky to have you shining bright beside me. (In no particular order:) Shira and Yoni Buzelan, Karen Xerri, Karen and Mike Feuer, Rav Gedalia Meyer, Sarah and Doron Spielman, Chana and Josh Even Chen, Rachael Romero, Becca Podos, Amber McBride, Jillian Boehme, and so many more.

To my Deborah Harris Agency family: Deborah Harris, George Eltman, Hadar Makov, Efrat Lev, Geula Geurts, Jessica Kasmer-Jacobs, Shira Ben-Choreen Schneck, Ran Keisar, Ilana Kurshan, Ines Austern—thank you for being there through every trial and tribulation.

To my grandmother, Nettie Bunder z"l, who lit the candles that sent me down the rabbit hole that became this book. We may never know exactly why you lit Shabbat candles in a closet, but I hope I told a story that will make you and our ancestors proud.

To my father, Miles Bunder, for always telling stories—some of which have become books. Like this one.

To my mother, Alida Bunder, for always listening to my stories and for reading Andrew Lang's fairy tales to me as a child.

To both my parents for always believing in me. I would not be the writer I am today without you. Thank you for listening, for always being there for me and my family.

To Jonathan for supporting me through everything. You, more than anyone, know what a struggle this book was—but you never lost faith in me. You always listened to my stories and my tears. Even when I interrupted you multiple times a day while you were working to read you a passage from one text or another. Even when most of the childcare fell on you because I was too lost in a forest of words to find my way out. You were always waiting for me on the other side.

To my children: Nachliel, Avtalyon, Lehava, Shaanan, Nehorai (and Pablo) for living in my world and understanding that it is sometimes a strange place. I hope to always fill your lives with stories and good things to eat—even if the house isn't always as clean as you might like it to be, and I'm not always as available as you wish I was. You are all the stars in my sky and you will shine one day long after I am gone. Tell my stories.

To my ancestors and the holy men and women who came before me (both known and unknown)—I hope I've done you proud. Any errors or omissions are my own.